The Best American
SCIENCE FICTION
and FANTASY
2021

The Best American
SCIENCE FICTION
and FANTASY™
2021

Edited and with an Introduction
by **Veronica Roth**

John Joseph Adams, *Series Editor*

MARINER BOOKS
An Imprint of HarperCollins*Publishers*
Boston • New York

marinerbooks.com

ISSN 2573-0797 (print)   ISSN 2573-0800 (e-book)
ISBN 978-0-358-46996-4 (print)   ISBN 978-0-358-47007-6 (e-book)
ISBN 978-0-358-57839-0 (audiobook)   ISBN 978-0-358-57880-2 (cd)

Printed in the United States of America
1 2021
4500834626

"Let's Play Dead" by Senaa Ahmad. First published in *The Paris Review,* Spring 2020. Copyright © 2020 by Senaa Ahmad. Reprinted by permission of Senaa Ahmad.

"Glass Bottle Dancer" by Celeste Rita Baker. First published in *Lightspeed,* Issue 119. Copyright © 2020 by Celeste Rita Baker. Reprinted by permission of Celeste Rita Baker.

"Tiger's Feast" by KT Bryski. First published in *Nightmare,* Issue 98. Copyright © 2020 by KT Bryski. Reprinted by permission of Katie Bryski.

"Our Language" by Yohanca Delgado. First published in *A Public Space,* Issue 29. Copyright © 2020 by Yohanca Delgado. Reprinted by permission of Yohanca Delgado.

"The Rat" by Yohanca Delgado. First published in *One Story,* October 2020. Copyright © 2020 by Yohanca Delgado. Reprinted by permission of Yohanca Delgado.

"Schrödinger's Catastrophe" by Gene Doucette. First published in *Lightspeed,* Issue 126. Copyright © 2020 by Gene Doucette. Reprinted by permission of Gene Doucette.

"The Pill" by Meg Elison. First published in *Big Girl.* Copyright © 2020 by Meg Elison. Reprinted by permission of Meg Elison.

"The Long Walk" by Kate Elliott. First published in *The Book of Dragons,* edited by Jonathan Strahan, published by HarperCollins. Copyright © 2020 by Katrina Elliott. Reprinted by permission of the author.

Contents

Foreword

WELCOME TO YEAR SEVEN of *The Best American Science Fiction and Fantasy!* This volume presents the best science fiction and fantasy (SF/F) short stories published during the 2020 calendar year as selected by myself and guest editor Veronica Roth.

About This Year's Guest Editor

Veronica Roth burst onto the publishing scene in 2011 with her first novel, *Divergent,* which she famously wrote during her senior year at Northwestern University. That book went on to become a number-one *New York Times* best seller and a franchise-starting worldwide blockbuster. *Divergent* spawned two novel sequels — *Insurgent* and *Allegiant* — along with a story collection called *Four.* Collectively, the books have sold somewhere north of forty million copies worldwide and were adapted into three major motion pictures.

After the Divergent series concluded, Veronica returned with a new young adult duology — *Carve the Mark* and *The Fates Divide* — and then followed that up with a short story collection called *The End and Other Beginnings.*

In 2020, Roth pivoted, making her adult debut with the novel *Chosen Ones,* which I was fortunate enough to acquire for my imprint at Houghton Mifflin Harcourt. It received high praise from previous *BASFF* series editors Diana Gabaldon and Charles Yu, not to mention the likes of Charlie Jane Anders, Blake Crouch, and Amber Benson—and also received a starred review from *Kirkus Reviews* and, despite coming out right when the pandemic started locking everything down, hit the *New York Times* best-seller list. Veronica's second adult novel is due out in 2022.

Although Veronica began her career as a novelist, she's also passionate about short fiction. Above, I mentioned her short story collections, but it's worth noting that outside of those she's also published stories in anthologies such as *Summer Days and Summer Nights, Shards & Ashes, Wastelands: The New Apocalypse,* and in the Amazon Original Stories "deconstructed anthology"[1] *Forward.* Plus, in 2020, she also had a new story out called "The Least of These" in *Lightspeed.*

While I was working with Veronica as her novel editor, one of the things that stuck in my mind was how when she went to Worldcon for the first time in 2019, she read every piece of short fiction on that year's (*and* the previous year's) Hugo ballot. I also learned that she was a huge fan of Frank Herbert's *Dune* and the works of Madeleine L'Engle and Philip K. Dick. And that she was likewise already a fan of several contemporary masters such as Nnedi Okorafor, Charlie Jane Anders, Ted Chiang, and Seanan McGuire —all authors who have either been reprinted in *BASFF* or had Notable Stories selections. Once I factored all that in, the editorial calculus told me she'd make a very fine guest editor . . . and, after you read the stories, I think you'll agree that my math has never *been* more right.

Veronica, her husband, Nelson, and her dog, Avi, live in Chicago, a city she deeply loves and deeply loves destroying.

---

1. Amazon Original Stories has been publishing a series of projects over the last several years that they call "collections," but which I always think of as "deconstructed anthologies." They're clearly assembled as anthologies—and feature short works by multiple authors—but the stories are all downloadable individually, rather than together as a single book. Since "collection" is typically used to refer to a single-author collection—a book of short stories that is comprised only of a single author's work —it seems imprecise to use that terminology for the Amazon Original Stories publications. I may be the only one who will ever call them deconstructed anthologies, but in my mind that's clearly what they are.

Selection Criteria and Process

The stories chosen for this anthology were originally published between January 1, 2020, and December 31, 2020. The technical criteria for consideration are (1) original publication in a nationally distributed North American publication (i.e., periodicals, collections, or anthologies, in print, online, or e-book); (2) publication in English by writers who are North American, or who have made North America their home; (3) publication as text (audiobook, podcast, dramatized, interactive, and other forms of fiction are not considered); (4) original publication as short fiction (excerpts of novels are not knowingly considered); (5) story length of 17,499 words or less; (6) at least loosely categorized as science fiction or fantasy; (7) publication by someone other than the author (i.e., self-published works are not eligible); and (8) publication as an original work of the author (i.e., not part of a media tie-in/ licensed fiction program).

As series editor, I attempted to read everything I could find that meets the above selection criteria. After doing all of my reading, I created a list of what I felt were the top eighty stories (forty science fiction and forty fantasy) published in the genre. Those eighty stories—hereinafter referred to as the "Top 80"—were sent to the guest editor, who read them and then chose the best twenty (ten science fiction, ten fantasy) for inclusion in the anthology. The guest editor reads all of the stories anonymously—with no bylines attached to them, nor any information about where the story originally appeared.

The guest editor's top twenty selections appear in this volume; the remaining sixty stories that did not make it into the anthology are listed in the back of this book as "Other Notable Science Fiction and Fantasy Stories of 2020."

2020 Summation

In order to select the Top 80 stories published in the SF/F genres in 2020, I considered several thousand stories from a wide array of anthologies, collections, and magazines. As per usual, because there is so much good material published in any given year, it was difficult to decide which stories were among the "best," and so, outside of my Top 80, I ended up with another sixty or so stories that were of similar high quality.

The Top 80 this year were drawn from forty-three different publications: twenty-six periodicals, thirteen anthologies, two single-author collections, and one stand-alone digital chapbook. The final table of contents draws from seventeen different sources: eleven periodicals five anthologies, and one single-author collection. Tor.com, *The Magazine of Fantasy & Science Fiction,* and *Lightspeed* are tied for the most selections (two); every other venue represented in the table of contents has one story each.

Only two of the authors selected for this volume (Daryl Gregory and Ken Liu) previously appeared in *BASFF;* thus the remaining authors are appearing for the first time. This is the second appearance for both Gregory and Liu.

Four periodicals appear in *BASFF* for the first time this year. Three of those are long-storied literary magazines not particularly known for publishing genre works: *The Paris Review, A Public Space,* and *One Story.* The fourth periodical to join *BASFF*'s ranks is *Fantasy Magazine,* a trailblazer in online fiction publishing that returned in 2020 after several years of hiatus. All of the above (save for *Paris Review*) were included in our Top 80 for the first time this year, and joining them are *Alta, Apparition Lit, Daily Science Fiction,* and *Drabblecast.*

Several authors were tied for the most stories in the Top 80, with two each: A. T. Greenblatt, Alix E. Harrow, Charlie Jane Anders, KT Bryski, Ken Liu, Maurice Broaddus, Sofia Samatar, Stephen Graham Jones, Yohanca Delgado (with both being selected for inclusion), and Yoon Ha Lee. Overall, seventy different authors are represented in the Top 80.

Sarah Pinsker's and Meg Elison's stories selected for inclusion, "Two Truths and a Lie" and "The Pill," were both named finalists for the Hugo, Locus, and Nebula Awards. Pinsker's story was the winner of the Nebula for Best Novelette and was also nominated for the Bram Stoker Award.

Among the Notable Stories, there were three stories that were named finalists for the Hugo Award: "The Mermaid Astronaut," by Yoon Ha Lee; "Badass Moms in the Zombie Apocalypse," by Rae Carson; and "Burn, or the Episodic Life of Sam Wells as a Super," by A. T. Greenblatt. All three were also finalists for the Locus Award.

The latter two stories above were also finalists for the Nebula Award, as were the following Notable Stories: "Stepsister, " by Leah Cypess; "Advanced Word Problems in Portal Math," by Aimee Picchi; "The Eight-Thousanders," by Jason Sanford; and "Shadow Prisons," by Caroline M. Yoachim.

In addition to the stories named above, the following Notable Stories were also Locus Award finalists: "If You Take My Meaning," by Charlie Jane Anders; "A Whisper of Blue," by Ken Liu; "Fairy Tales for Robots," by Sofia Samatar; "The Sycamore and the Sybil," by Alix E. Harrow; and "The Girlfriend's Guide to Gods," by Maria Dahvana Headley.

One story, "The Bone-Stag Walks," by KT Bryski, was a finalist for the Aurora Award.

Note: the final results of some of the awards mentioned above won't be known until after this text is locked for production, but will be known by the time the book is published.

Anthologies

The following anthologies all had stories selected for inclusion in this year's volume: *Burn the Ashes,* edited by me, Hugh Howey, and Christie Yant (volume 2 of the Dystopia Triptych); *Take Us to a Better Place: Stories,* presented by[2] the Robert Wood Johnson Foundation; *Made to Order: Robots and Revolution,* edited by Jonathan Strahan; *The Book of Dragons,* edited by Jonathan Strahan; and *Faraway,* presented by Amazon Original Stories.

Several other anthologies had stories in the Top 80: the other two volumes of the Dystopia Triptych (*Ignorance Is Strength* and *Or Else the Light*), edited by me, Hugh Howey, and Christie Yant; *Entanglements,* edited by Sheila Williams; *Escape Pod: The Science Fiction Anthology,* edited by Mur Lafferty and S. B. Divya; *The De-*

---

2. I've taken to using the phrasing "presented by" (rather than "edited by") in situations such as this where you have a book of short stories that is clearly an anthology, but it is published in such a way that does not credit an anthology editor. In some cases, such as this one, an organization is credited; other times, there is only a publisher.

cameron Project, presented by the *New York Times; Out of Line,* presented by Amazon Original Stories; *Psi-Wars,* edited by Joshua Viola; and *Us in Flux,* presented by the ASU Center for Science and the Imagination. The anthologies with the most stories in the Top 80 were *Made to Order: Robots and Revolution* (three); *The Book of Dragons* (three); *Or Else the Light* (two); and *Take Us to a Better Place: Stories* (two).

Plenty of anthologies published fine work in 2020 but just didn't end up with a story in the Top 80. Here's a partial list: *Breathe FI-YAH,* edited by Brent Lambert and DaVaun Sanders; *Avatars, Inc.,* edited by Ann VanderMeer; *Miscreations: Gods, Monstrosities & Other Horrors,* edited by Doug Murano and Michael Bailey; *A Phoenix Must Burn: Sixteen Stories of Black Girl Magic, Resistance, and Hope,* edited by Patrice Caldwell; *The Dystopian States of America,* edited by Matt Bechtel; *Recognize Fascism,* edited by Crystal Huff; *Subterranean: Tales of Dark Fantasy 3,* edited by William Schafer; *Glitter + Ashes: Queer Tales of a World That Wouldn't Die,* edited by dave ring; *Final Cuts,* edited by Ellen Datlow; *Evil in Technicolor,* edited by Joe M. McDermott; *Dominion: An Anthology of Speculative Fiction from Africa and the African Diaspora,* edited by Zelda Knight and Ekpeki Oghenechovwe Donald; *My Battery Is Low and It Is Getting Dark,* edited by Patricia Bray and Joshua Palmatier; *Galactic Stew,* edited by David B. Coe and Joshua Palmatier; and *Apocalyptic,* edited by S. C. Butler and Joshua Palmatier.

Collections

One collection had a story selected for inclusion this year: *Big Girl,* by Meg Elison. The only other collection represented in the Top 80 was *Nine Bar Blues,* by Sheree Renée Thomas.

Here are some other notable collections that included excellent work in 2020. Some of these contained only reprints, and thus had no eligible material, but I'm acknowledging them here anyway in order to shine a light on good works: *Universal Love,* by Alexander Weinstein; *Why Visit America,* by Matthew Baker; *The Hidden Girl and Other Stories,* by Ken Liu; *Velocities: Stories,* by Kathe Koja; *Children of the Fang and Other Genealogies,* by John Langan; *The Road to Woop Woop,* by Eugen Bacon; *The Best of Elizabeth Bear,* by

Elizabeth Bear; *The Best of Jeffrey Ford,* by Jeffrey Ford; *If It Bleeds,* by Stephen King; *The Postutopian Adventures of Darger and Surplus,* by Michael Swanwick; *The Grand Tour,* by E. Catherine Tobler; and *The Midnight Circus,* by Jane Yolen.

Periodicals

More than a hundred periodicals were considered throughout the year in my hunt for the Top 80 stories. I read magazines both large and small and sought out the genre stories that might have been lurking in the pages of a literary and/or mainstream periodical.

The following magazines all had work representing them in the Top 80 this year: *Asimov's* (three), *Clarkesworld* (three), *Fireside* (two), *FIYAH* (two), *Future Tense* (two), *Lightspeed* (seven), *The Magazine of Fantasy & Science Fiction* (six), *Nightmare* (four), *Strange Horizons* (two), Tor.com (eight), and *Uncanny* (three). The following periodicals had one story each: *Alta, Analog, Apex, Apparition Lit, Beneath Ceaseless Skies, Conjunctions, Daily Science Fiction, Drabblecast, Fairy Tale Review, Fantasy Magazine, Granta, One Story, PodCastle, The Paris Review,* and *A Public Space.*

The following magazines didn't have any material in the Top 80 this year, but did publish stories that I had under serious consideration: *The Adroit Journal,* Baen.com, *Cape Cod Poetry Review, The Dark, Escape Pod, Flash Fiction Online, Gargoyle, Kaleidotrope, Ploughshares, Pseudopod, Terraform,* and *Weird Tales.*

Normally this is where I'd issue some requiem for the magazines that have ceased publication in the past year, but despite all of the actual, tragic deaths this year due to the pandemic, periodicals seem to have somehow thrived (or at least *survived*). In fact, I don't see any notable periodicals that folded in 2020, which is rather remarkable, and in fact, at least two top magazines *returned from the dead: Apex* and *Fantasy.* There were also a handful of promising new magazines announced I'll be keeping an eye on as they start publishing in 2021: *Constelación* (which will be publishing simultaneously in English and Spanish), *Dark Matter, Mermaids Monthly,* and *The Deadlands.*

As always, I implore you to support the short fiction publishers you love. If you can, subscribe (even if they offer content for free!), review, spread the word. Every little bit helps.

Acknowledgments

We all need a little help from our friends whenever we embark on any project, and *BASFF* is no different. As of last year, assistant series editor Christopher Cevasco was my right hand, helping me chart the stars and navigate the cosmos (of SF/F). Additionally, as in years past, big thanks to Alex Puncekar and Christie Yant, who again provided some editorial support. Much appreciation to you all!

I'd also like to thank Fariza Hawke, who is now the in-house person who wrangles *BASFF*-related matters at Mariner Books. Thanks too to David Steffen, who runs the Submission Grinder, a writer's market database, for his assistance in helping me do some oversight on my list of new and extinct markets mentioned above.

Huge thanks too to the authors who take the time to let me know when they have eligible works, either by just dropping me a line or else by submitting them via my *BASFF* online submissions portal. I'm also grateful to publishers and editors who proactively send me review copies of anthologies, collections, and periodicals — especially the ones that do so unprompted and don't wait until December to send a year's worth of material.

Submissions for Next Year's Volume

Editors, writers, and publishers who would like their work considered for next year's edition (the best of 2021), please visit johnjosephadams.com/best-american for instructions on how to submit material for consideration.

JOHN JOSEPH ADAMS

Introduction

I KEEP THINKING about this quote, from Hungarian playwright András Visky: "Nothing is more surreal than reality." Visky was a political prisoner in Romania in the late fifties and early sixties; the context of this quote was discovering his name on a government list of "people of interest" years later. The surreal part is: he was two years old when the list was made.

Nothing is more surreal than reality.

Last year was full of unreality. I remember the day the lockdown order was announced, hurrying to the grocery store to stock up for two weeks—two weeks of lockdown sounds hilarious to me now—finding the shelves cleared of toilet paper, cleaning products, and cans of beans, the freezer section empty except for a lonely bag of cauliflower, people with shopping carts heaped high, everyone quiet, afraid to touch, afraid to breathe.

Then weeks later, sucking in fabric with every breath, walking those same aisles with arrows telling me which direction to go and Xs taped on the ground to show me what six feet is, plexiglass between me and the cashier. A map of the United States always open on my husband's computer with red splotches documenting the spread; it was months before we stopped watching the death toll. We played the board game Pandemic over Zoom with his sister because it was the only board game we had in common, and we lost. And we laughed about it, because sometimes you gotta.

Or this: pulling up to the parking lot of a defunct dentist office so that a person dressed all in blue with only her eyes showing can reach into my car to shove a pipe cleaner up my nose, and I think about how lucky I am to have easy access to said pipe cleaner.

Masked neighbors walking their dogs. Sparkly Lady Gaga masks at the VMAs. Masked protesters.

All surreal.

Last year in quarantine, I became obsessed with a particular question, and it was a silly one: What are you comfort-watching right now? Because everyone was watching, all the time; everyone was braced for impact—impact to their health, their kid(s), their job, their entire industry, sometimes all at once. Some people were reading books, but I have no idea how, because I couldn't focus on anything that wasn't loud and bright and familiar. At the time I posed this question, half of my friends were watching *Contagion*.

You know: *Contagion*. That movie about a pandemic.

Me, I was buried in *Parks and Recreation,* a sitcom I had already watched more than once, and I could not fathom the impulse to watch a movie about a pandemic, a reality that I was already frantic to escape from, even if it was just for twenty minutes at a time. I wanted to be in Pawnee or on the *Rocinante* headed toward a space station or in Hyrule with a Great Thunderblade or on my *Animal Crossing* island (which I named "Doom").

But for so many people, *Contagion* was a stress relief—a story of triumph over the situation we were still in the middle of. For me, there was comfort in knowing there were stories beyond the one I was living at the time. For them, there was comfort in knowing we could endure this, because we had already imagined it.

Exposure therapy is a type of therapy in which a person suffering from anxiety repeatedly encounters whatever stimulus provokes their fear response, again and again, until their brain becomes desensitized to that stimulus. But not everyone has a stimulus they can encounter reliably in real life, the way someone with a severe fear of heights can in a glass elevator or on a ledge. For those people, there is the imagined exposure—a made-up scenario that they build with a therapist to provoke the fear response. The first time I did an imagined exposure, I was sure it would be useless. After all, the narrative I had constructed wasn't real, so why would it provoke the same anxiety as a real-life situation? I was wrong, obviously, or I wouldn't be telling you this. I got plenty anxious during that imagined exposure, every time I did it . . . until suddenly I *didn't* anymore. You can actually build resilience by enduring situations that aren't even real. Is that what my friends were doing, watching *Contagion*? Building resilience?

Nothing is more surreal than reality—but an imagined reality can be powerful, too.

I often think of science fiction and fantasy stories as a playground of big ideas, a series of "what if?" scenarios. What if humanity had to coexist with dragons/artificial intelligence/aliens? What if we had to cope with a life-altering event, like an apocalypse/zombie virus/sudden proliferation of superpowers? What if the strangeness and unreality of magic suddenly intruded on our otherwise ordinary lives? What would we do then? Who would we be there?

How would we endure? *Would* we?

Science fiction and fantasy asks and answers those questions, sometimes realistically, sometimes fancifully, sometimes with humor and warmth, sometimes starkly, brutally. Good science fiction and fantasy finds the human frailty inside of those "what if?" scenarios, the little story inside of the big story. Good science fiction and fantasy explores big ideas but doesn't try to do everything at once; it balances the specific and the small against the sweeping and the big and keeps them in tension like a drop of water clinging to a branch.

One way that it does that is through specificity—not telling you *every* story about living through the zombie apocalypse, but telling you just one story, locating a particular person at a critical juncture. That specificity is not at odds with the big ideas of a science fiction or fantasy story—it is the best way to communicate those ideas.

Sometimes writers—of all genres—make the mistake of thinking that for a story to be relatable, it needs to be broad. It needs to feel like it could take place anywhere, that it could be about anyone. We write about a character going to "the grocery store" without telling you if it's a Jewel-Osco or a Publix or a Piggly Wiggly or a Whole Foods, as if all grocery stores look the same, feel the same, smell the same. But they don't. A Fresh Market in a wealthy northwest suburb of Chicago—where there's always classical music playing and everything has wood paneling—is a long way away from a Jewel-Osco in downtown Chicago, with narrow aisles and sticky tile and a distinct lack of fancy mustards. A grocery store that could be anywhere is far more surreal than a grocery store on Mars.

Science fiction and fantasy is therefore not inherently more un-realistic-feeling than a broad, vague story in any other genre. All stories must find a moment in time and in place. Just as a single death is a tragedy and a million deaths is a statistic, as the saying goes, we cannot locate ourselves in an idea that is too big. The narrower and more specific the story, the more we relate to it, and the more big ideas we can tolerate around it without losing our sense of reality.

Most of the time, when you call something "small," it's an attempt to diminish its importance. Not here, in these twenty stories. If a big idea is a roar from the void, the small story is the whisper in my ear that I can understand. If a big idea is a smooth, towering wall, the small story is the handholds that help me climb it. Science fiction and fantasy always asks "what if?"—but that is not why these genres first grabbed me as a kid and held on for the rest of my life. It's the quiet moments, the frail moments, and the questions asked in trepidation: "Will they make it?" and "At what cost?"

In these twenty stories, you will find dragons, magic, alternate realities, artificial intelligence, apocalypse, giant murderous robots, and quantum physics. You will find stories about death, transformation, survival, aging, self-acceptance, community, and reconciliation. Big, impossible, unfathomable ideas as wide as the unexplored universe and as strange as a talking insect.

In these twenty stories, you will find a story about someone dealing with grief after the death of her mother; someone troubled by bullies at school; someone in an abusive marriage; someone who finds reminders of a dead friend everywhere he looks; someone on a bicycle ride to scatter loved ones' ashes; someone searching for the truth about their past. These are small stories—in the best sense of the word. They will make you ask yourself those smaller questions: "Will they make it?" and "At what cost?" And they will make you care, deeply, about the answers.

They will, if you're anything like me, get you to care about things that you weren't ready to care about. While reading these stories, I cried actual tears about a rat ("The Rat"). I became emotionally attached to a giant, deadly crawfish ("Crawfather"), a swarm of lovable roaches ("Glass Bottle Dancer"), a deeply creepy, sin-eating tiger ("Tiger's Feast"), more than one sentient spaceship ("Schrödinger's Catastrophe," "Skipping Stones in the Dark"), dragons ("The Long Walk"), and a bunch of wire twisted into the shape of a man ("The Beast Adjoins"). I examined and reexamined some uncomfortable truths ("The Pill," "How to Pay Reparations"). It is perhaps not surprising at all that after this year of communal loss, many of the stories I gravitated toward most explored profound, inescapable grief ("The Rat," "And This Is How to Stay Alive," "Survival Guide," "The Cleaners," "One Time, a Reluctant Traveler"). There *is* one about a plague ("The Plague Doctors"), but it will remind you that scientific innovation is a remarkable and precious thing.

These stories have things to say, but they won't lay those things at your feet like the lesson at the end of a fable. They will invite you in. They will introduce you to a specific person or set of people, ground you in a particular moment in time, and ask for your interest, and refuse to give you an easy answer. Science fiction and fantasy are often genres of social critique, but that doesn't mean they have to wrap things up neatly for you; instead, they can provoke and unsettle you, and allow you the space to consider and reconsider and come to new conclusions.

And they will show you how we endure. *Whether* we endure. What our endurance might cost us. What we will give away in pursuit of resilience, and what we will gain if we achieve it. There are no easy answers, not in these stories, and not in our own lives. But we must continue to ask these questions. The only way out, the saying goes, is through—and how lucky for us, that science fiction and fantasy are already so consistently concerned with what "through" might look like—in another dimension, on another planet, or in a world just as surreal as our own.

VERONICA ROTH

The Best American
SCIENCE FICTION
and FANTASY
2021

SENAA AHMAD

Let's Play Dead

FROM *The Paris Review*

THERE WAS A MAN, let's call him Henry VIII. There was his wife, let's call her Anne B. Let's give them a castle and make it nice. Let's give her many boy babies but make them dead. Let's give him a fussy way of being. Let's make her smart and sneaky, because it's such a mean thing to do.

Let's make it so she can't escape.

Let's seal the bottle, and shake it, and shake until our hands fall off.

It takes two swings to cut off her head. Everyone does their best to pretend that the first one didn't happen. In the awkward silence afterward, the swordsman says something about mercy or justice, a strangely fervent soliloquy in French that might have made Anne herself emotional, but it's a touch long-winded, and no one's paying him any attention. And she's dead, so it's especially beside the point.

The ministers dither in the courtyard, chancing last looks, murmuring, *Exquisite mouth, just exquisite.* She is so beautiful, they agree, even beheaded.

Henry will return to the body later, when everyone is gone and what's left of her has been moved to the chapel. He will stand on the threshold, halfway between one momentous decision and the next. He will kneel on the dais beside her severed head and lay one ornately rubied hand along her frigid cheekbone. Maybe he will stay five minutes. Maybe he will stay thirty-five. Maybe he will cry softly, but it doesn't matter, because there isn't a nosy patron around to commission an oil painting for the textbooks, and it doesn't matter because she's dead, she's still very, very dead.

He will leave as furtively as he came, wiping his hand on his smock. Anne's headless body and bodiless head will be left to their own devices, her blood blackening, thickening on the ground, the gristle of her neck tougher with every minute. The clock ticks. Night falls.

It is her head that speaks first. It says, "Is he gone?"

Her body spasms, maybe a shrug, or maybe just a reflex.

Her head opens its eyes and looks this way, that way. It says, "It's over? It really worked?"

We don't need to stick around while her body crawls its way to her head and fits itself back together. Every excruciating inch of the stone floor is a personal coup, and every inch lasts the whole span of human history. It is slow. It is clumsy. The head falls off a couple of times. The body is floppy with atrophy. There is a lot of blood. She probably, definitely cries. It does not befit a queen.

He is reading the Saturday paper, still in his shirtsleeves, when she breezes in the next morning. The horizon of the paper lowers to the bridge of his nose. He is a man who wears his tension in the way of a beautifully tuned piano, and in this moment he vibrates at a bewildered middle octave.

"Anne," he says, at an absolute loss.

"Henry," she says, the picture of politeness.

She sits at the table. Not a hair out of place, not a leaky vein in sight. She butters her toast in four deft strokes. A servant steps out from the shadows to fill her teacup to the brim. It's all very serene, domestic. If it takes her a few tries to put her toast back on the plate, or if he dabs his napkin with a little extra violence, well, who can say. She slurps her tea, which they both know he hates. He hoists his newspaper back up. Like this, they go on.

Of course she knows what comes next. Let's not fib.

She is seized from her bed some weeks later, in a state of drowsy dishabille, the wardens bristling with royal braid. This night will have the consistency of a dream. The palace swims in sound and darkness. The youngest one, the boy or man who grips her arm with one rubbery fist and studiously avoids her gaze, reminds her of the sons she has lost in the womb. She wants to tell him, *Don't worry, the thing you're afraid of, the girl, the job, the rising cost of real estate in London, it will all work out someday—you'll see, it all comes to pass,* but he is leading her to her death, so it seems a bit impolite.

The cooks are baking down in the kitchen. The yeasty comfort of this aroma, which reminds her of the seam of volcanic heat that escapes when she cracks a fresh loaf, of a day opening beneath her, is too much. She shuts her nostrils. Her silk nightgown flaps at her ankles. When she can, she reaches out and touches the walls, the radiators, the edges of doorframes. Reminding herself that she is here, now, she is alive, that this dream is all too real. She can't falter yet. There's work to do.

A gibbet stands in the courtyard beneath a lonesome moon. They thread the noose around her neck with genteel care, snugly, even though the youngest one quakes every time his skin makes contact with hers. Up in the turret window, she sees Henry watching at a distance, as he does best. A coward in his big-boy breeches.

It is a quick death. The noose is tight. The drop is long. No one's trying to be cruel here. One person cries out but is quickly silenced. The wardens double-check, triple-check to make sure she's properly dead this time. From the courtyard to the turret, they flash a thumbs-up to Henry. He lets the curtain fall. This time, he does not visit her tenderly. It is done.

The wardens will return to their card games, all except the youngest one, who will mourn her without meaning to. He will simmer with sorrow for hours until, without warning to himself or others, he punches a wall so hard he fractures most of the knuckles in his right hand, leaving a fist-size whorl of buckled plaster as a signature.

And when she wakes up, hours later, on a slab of wintry marble in the royal morgue, it's with a broken neck and very little air in her lungs. She adjusts her neck the way she might correct a crooked hat—difficult without a proper mirror, but she manages. She tightens the belt on her flimsy nightgown and slips through the haunted halls, pausing only when she reaches the king's chambers. She doesn't knock. She doesn't crow or look for consolation, although the pang is there, and it feels unstoppable. Instead, with great effort, she continues on to her apartments, where she goes right back to bed. She is wiped and the throb in her neck is telling her to conserve strength. But most of all, it is such a trivial insult to him, so small, so vicious, to fall asleep as soundly as she does this night.

For a time, it is quiet. Henry waits. He consults his advisers, who are just as baffled. He tries to get his head around the situation, but at least he has the good grace to do it far from her.

You will want to hear that Anne takes solace in these precarious days, so let's say that's true: She takes that trip she always meant to, an ethereal island resort where every day the indigo waters whisper *Get out, get out while you still can* and the jacarandas whistle a jaunty tune of existential dread. She cashes in her many retirement portfolios, she doesn't so much throw parties as fling them, handfuls of bacchanalia into those feverishly starlit nights.

Or: She digs her heels deep into the Turkish carpets of her palatial apartments and doesn't budge. In the bruised hours between dusk and midnight, she feels a joy so grandiose that it fills the empty canals and sidewalks within her. She takes to promenades around the gardens, drinking in the virtuous geraniums in their neat rows and the slightly ferocious hedge maze with its blooming thistles and uncertain corners. She grows sentimental about centipedes and spiders and wasps and belladonna and ragwort and nettles and every other hardscrabble weed, every pernicious pest. *I'm still here,* she says to the wasps, the centipedes, the belladonna, the ragwort. *I'm still here.*

The joy of the narrow escape is that it unfurls into hours, hidden doors that lead to secret passages of days, even if those days are numbered, even if she knows it. None of it is hers and it's all she's got. She loses herself, like a woman in a myth, unstuck in borrowed time, unraveling with possibility.

And yes, maybe she feels a few inches of gratitude for the armistice he has granted her. And yes, of course, the waiting days smother her, the twinned knowing and not-knowing what happens after, imagining Henry at every turn, cartoony with rage or puzzlement, but what is she to do?

After that, he drowns her himself. And who could blame him? If you want a job done right, you'd better know the end of this sentence. He comes upon her in the bath. He wraps his hands around her bare shoulders and thrusts her beneath the bathwater. Soap bubbles and air bubbles bloom in multitude. An artery in his skull skitters wildly. The water fights. The walls steam with tension.

She tries to thrash away from him, of course. She tries to defend herself, of course. But he's six foot two, built like a linebacker, and she is not. There is nothing more complicated here. He is not the first man to do this, or the wealthiest, or the angriest. He certainly isn't the last. As they say, it's a tale as old as time.

Eventually the water stills. Her body floats. He sits on the brim of the tub, head bowed, the cuffs of his doublet dripping, his fingers pruning a gentle shade of violet. Up close, murder is a messy business, decidedly unroyal, too much flesh and screaming. He sits in wait—for how long, who knows. When the surface moves again and she sits up, feral-eyed and vomiting bathwater, he sighs.

"What do we do with you?" he says, not so much a question as a regret. And she has no answer, of course she has no answer.

It is he who helps her out of the tub, although she resists. He hands her the bathrobe, courteously studying the mosaic of the floor while she covers up. He helps her back to her rooms.

You will want her to scream at him, perhaps. To shove her house key through the soft wetness of his eye, to land a solid, bone-cracking punch to his solar plexus, or at the very least to kick him in his royalest of parts, but she has just survived death. She is alive. Today, that will have to be enough.

Anne's ladies never stray far. Where are they going to go? They hold their tongues. They massage their fists back into impassive hands. They, too, have intimate knowledge of the place between a rock and an even harder rock.

Sometimes they will perform small acts of metonymy. A pamphlet folded into a paper airplane is a clandestine invitation to the city. They will fetch her those darling meringue pastries if she is doleful, and so when they say, *We will bring you the French cookies,* it means *We are rooting for you to find a way.*

Or: An elegantly embroidered handkerchief means *I bayoneted this cloth 9,042 times and imagined it was the flesh of your enemies.* A pair of white gloves means *We will help you bury the bodies. We will not ask questions. We know you did what had to be done.*

If they tune up her automobile restlessly, it's to say, *Are you listening? We have a plan.*

A book of poems with no poems inside is this: *You are not defined by the tragedy of it. There is always one more page.*

They will nod with such enthusiasm that they black out, which means *Do you know how much we hate this?*

Sometimes they will weep in private, because there is too much to be said and nowhere to say it. Because they know that leaving is the most dangerous thing she can do. Because all they want is the impossible and is that really so much? Because this is one of the very few ways they can uncork their anger, and it is such a fine vintage, the very best. Because their fury is the scaffolding upon which their waiting lives are begotten, and it is so fathomless and pure, it clenches up their jaws and grinds their teeth into their gums. In this particular case, their tears mean *We will be your remembrance. We will salt the earth with the blood of our eyes so nothing can ever grow again.*

Henry is learning.

He gets crafty. He invents the portable long-barreled firearm. Then he invents the firing squad. Then he invents acute ballistic trauma. Then he sends his wardens to find her.

But while he's busy doing all that, she's been busy, too, inventing: cardiopulmonary resuscitation. The telephone. The 911 call. First-response teams. Modern-day surgery. Organ transplants. Crash carts. Gurneys. Subsidized medicine. She improvises like it's the only thing she knows how to do.

It is ugly, obviously. There is quite a lot of blood and gore and spattered internal organs. But she lives. Still, she lives.

Lest you think it's all maudlin garden strolls and gallows touched by moonlight, let's admit that Anne and Henry still have their moments. Like the time a scullery maid starts a stovetop fire and trips the palace-wide alarm. All around the castle, the sprinkler systems kick in, first in the kitchens, then in the great hall, and then everywhere, misting porous manuscripts, Brylcreemed foreign dignitaries, the throne room, everyone on their toilets, Henry's collection of vintage cameras, and Anne in her finest silk pajamas, snoring over her watercolors. Still very much not dead.

She escapes to the nearest balcony. And as she wrings her ruined shirt and her hair in futility, a window creaks open and who should climb through but Henry, his arms filled with soaking scrolls almost as tall as himself. He sees her sodden in her night-clothes and begins to guffaw.

She says, "That's not very kingly," feeling hurt, and more vulner-able than she wants to be, and probably a little foolish.

He says, "Well, you don't look especially queenly," and drops the scrolls in a heap. She despairs at her reflection in the window.

"The gossip magazines are going to love this look," she says.

"Easy fix," he says. "Here." He sweeps up to the balcony's edge, blotting her from view of the courtyard. So close that she's imme-diately on high alert. She steps back. Every muscle clamped.

"You need more width," she says, with all the calm she can summon.

He begins to windmill his arms like a complete fool. He doesn't say a word, just churns his arms up and down with intense concen-tration. And to her own surprise, she starts to laugh. She can't help it. He does his best deadpan, smile uncracked, but it's there in the twitch of his eyebrows, the twinkle in his eye.

"What's your plan here?" she says.

"Trickery," he says, not missing a step. "Misdirection. Excellent upper-arm strength."

You may be thinking that this would be an opportune time to push him off the balcony, make it look like an accident, and maybe you wouldn't be wrong. But he's still the size of a world-class heavy-weight boxer, and she is still most decidedly not. And yes, she's eager to please, and yes, even now, he can find ways to disarm her utterly. And yes, this moment, precious as it is, has a kind of power on its own, a force, and the ache of laughter in her abdomen will sustain her a few days longer. Do you really want to take that away from her?

It's easy to say that it becomes a game for him, and a game for her. In Anne's case, if it's a game, the game is Monopoly, her game piece is a pewter chicken *décapité*, the banker is a scoundrel and a cheat, the properties disintegrate every time she lands on them, and the dice are made of fire. What game is this to him? If he's winning, does it even matter?

But for her, how's this for an alternative: On a spectral day in autumn, a cockroach tumbles across Anne's writing desk like a very squirmy, very small shooting star. It is swift, intrepid. In its wayward progress, it hemorrhages anxiety.

Its clumsy, heroic journey plucks the tenderest meat inside her. Is it any surprise that she sees something in the cockroach that hums on the same frequency as she does? She builds tranquil highways with her hands, one at a time, and is rewarded when the roach travels safely through. Her triumph is no small thing.

She hopes it is a girl cockroach, that the baseboards and the cracks in the wall are seething with her unhatched eggs, that beneath the floors the concrete is bulging with her magnificent cockroach babies. She hopes they are abundant and hungry. That every day, each year, the cockroaches and their cockroach babies encroach in an ever-expanding circle from their nest. That when civilization crumbles into the ground, and textbooks get chucked en masse into the sea, and all of this is done and gone—and it will be done, it will be gone, she's got to believe that the universe has a long memory and a short temper and that this, this is nothing —they will still be here, in the walls, under the floors, teeming, multiplying, ravenous, devouring, surviving.

He has his body servant stuff handkerchiefs down her throat. What you might call a reverse magic trick. Silk handkerchiefs, floral handkerchiefs, designer ones, handkerchiefs dipped in eau de cologne, ones that carry the perfume of another woman, while Henry lurks in the doorway, exultant.

It is such an absurd way to die that she begins to laugh, and once she starts laughing, it's too late, she can't stop. She even helps the servant stuff them down her throat. It is not pleasurable, by any means, but it bewilders him and leaves Henry stunned.

"Um, should I keep going?" the body servant is asking Henry, the last thing she remembers before she dies.

Sometimes he is fuzzy on the details. Sometimes he will forget and call her by the names of his other wives and she will have to correct him. He might leave her alone if she were somebody else, it's true. But she is unwilling to be forgotten.

"I'm Anne," she says impatiently. "*Anne.* Remember? Not Jane or Other Anne or Catherine. You haven't killed those ones yet."

He lines up everyone she has known, her mother and father, her dead brothers, her childhood friends, her nursemaid, her tutors, her grandmother, her priests, the snooty cousin she almost married, all the kids in high school who made fun of her. One by one, they tell her every mean thing they have ever thought about her.

"You're such a needy person," her grandmother says. "I often dread the sound of your approach."

"You're much less attractive than you think," says her snooty cousin.

"We always thought your jokes were kind of repetitive," her dead brothers confess.

"You probably shouldn't have started the English Reformation," one of the priests says.

"I didn't want another daughter," her mother admits.

"You *still* smell like farts," says one of the kids from school.

"I always thought you had so much potential," says a childhood friend. "I wish I could take more pride in having known you."

It goes on like this for hours. In the center, Anne, lovely Anne, poor Anne, with her hands over her face, bawling, full-on ugly-crying. Shoulders shuddering, snot-nosed, basically a mess. At some point, probably during her father's seven-minute monologue about everything they could've spent their fortune on if she hadn't been born, she will faint with grief and maybe dehydration, and the court physicians will not be able to revive her. Everyone goes home: her mother, father, dead brothers, and so on. She passes later in the evening, with little fanfare, most likely of a broken heart.

There is a version of her story where she doesn't die again and again and again.

There is a version of her story where she shivs him in his sleep.

There is a version where she is born in the future, and when she meets Henry at one of those rickety self-serious parties at Oxford, his discount-aristocracy vibes, prickly disposition, and fixation with his own poetry are clanging alarm bells. She walks away and never looks back.

There is a version where she gives birth to a daughter. In this version of the story, Anne still dies in the most ignoble and depressing of fashions: a sword, a Frenchman, a chopping block, gawking ministers, a wordless husband. It is her daughter who will avenge her mother—with the throne she takes by force, the wars

she wages, the playwrights she patronizes, the papacies she out-
wits, the rebellions she crushes, the cults she accidentally spawns,
the people she forgives, through all the many men she meets and
never marries.

She wakes up one morning and the whole castle is closed for reno-
vations. The imperial estates are empty and eerie. Set painters are
giving the outer walls a fresh coat. A few crew members crawl on
their hands and knees in the chapel, swabbing delicate graining
details into the marble flagstones so they don't look like plastic.
In the state room, a prop maker wheels away a vase, completely
oblivious to her presence. He replaces it a few minutes later with
an almost identical, slightly more era-appropriate vase.

When she passes Henry in the hallway, he's just as perplexed as
she is.

But later that day, on instinct, he swipes a can of paint from the
art department. He composes a sprawling landscape. A canyon,
right in front of Anne's apartments. He's not the best artist, but
what he lacks in talent, he makes up for in cruelty. When she steps
out of her room, she plunges right in, all the way to the bottom of
the canyon, where she breaks her leg.

She tries to call for help. Of course she does. She yells until her
voice is hoarse. Her leg is an unsteady line of fire beneath her. For
days after, she can still hear the sound of the bone breaking.

And this time, yes, it's bad. She's hungry, thirsty, in tremendous
pain. She is depleted from the ache of the last death, a grief she
didn't know was still possible. She's worn down by his anger, his
relentless need. There's a limit to what she can endure, maybe,
and it doesn't seem so far away. She can't do this forever. Did you
think she could do this forever?

Still, she looks for a way out. She tries to set the bone herself,
with little success. She prays to her god for an answer. It would be
better if she knew how to die, if she had the grace of a dead girl.
But she is not a woman washed ashore at the start of a film, or
arranged artfully in a back alley for the cameras to find. No, she's
disorderly, desperate. There is skin beneath her fingernails, and
throw-up on her T-shirt.

And do we want her to die? Do we want this to be the end? Isn't
it better if she finds a miracle, a mystery machine swooping out of
the sky to save her?

Think about it: Do you want her to be just another dead girl? Do you really, truly want her to die?

She does not die this time. One of the production assistants drops a permanent marker down the canyon by accident and Anne scrawls an amateurish ladder to freedom. Or, no, as everyone's packing up to leave, a decorator spies the velvet flag she's manufactured out of her French hood. He doesn't seem to understand who she is, but she bribes him to haul her out with two fat pearls.

Either way, it's definitely a miracle. Most unexpected. We'll leave it up to you.

On another day, she rolls over and looks at him.

"What?" he says.

"It doesn't have to be this hard, right?" she says. "We don't have to live like this."

He doesn't respond right away. He takes so long, she thinks he is considering the enormity of her question, that perhaps it has left him winded. She thinks maybe this is the moment he will realize how pointless it is, how hard she's trying, how much time he's wasted, how defeated they both are. Maybe he will say, *Huh, why didn't I ever think of that.*

But he doesn't answer, no surprise. He doesn't have anything to say. Maybe it's too obvious for words. Maybe he doesn't think she deserves a response. When he looks at her, she has the sense of a man who is making up his mind one way or another. A man who stares at a dead end and sees his opportunity.

Maybe you will want to look away for this part.

She will be taken to a laboratory, which, in the style of laboratories of the time and perhaps every laboratory in every time, feels a bit like the underbelly of a dungeon. Here she will be injected with a poison that liquefies her insides in a matter of hours. One of her captors will spill the poison on himself and this will derail the proceedings. They will perform an autopsy to confirm that she is dead. With a delicacy that is surgical, or at least very thorough, they will crack every bone in her body. They will take out her internal organs, still gooey and falling apart, and feed them to any nearby dogs, who may need a fair amount of persuading. She will wake several times, but never for long. There will be quite a lot of screaming, most likely, but you don't want to hear about that.

They will set her corpse on fire, and put the scorched bone fragments and teeth and shreds of flesh into a box. They will ship the box somewhere very far away, perhaps the remote island from earlier on. They will wrap the box in weights and cast it into the ocean. They will train a shark to develop a palate for mysterious boxes wrapped in weights so it can devour her remains. They will send a nuke from outer space to the precise coordinates of the shark. The bomb will vaporize the island, too, and everyone who lives there, a few thousand tidy deaths, but it's probably worth it.

They dispatch a courier to Henry immediately. The courier tells him, "She's dead," and Henry sags against the wall in relief. He spends the day in devout prayer. He waits a week or two for the obvious to happen. But no, she doesn't return.

He asks for extravagant bouquets to be delivered to her apartments, a mixtape of her favorites: English roses, bloody chrysanthemums, black tulips. He summons an architect to begin the blueprints for her memorial. He spends a whole day telephoning her parents and loved ones to break the news, with each call recalibrating his gravity, sorrow, and air of quiet suffering, depending on how much they care.

He will come to his bedroom later that night, a little weary, and there she will be, just like that. No explanation. She will be curled up in his favorite armchair like the slyest of cats, fast asleep, looking content. Fully intact, organs back in her body, insides unliquefied, most definitely *not* in a box, or a shark, or an ocean, or heaven, or hell.

Do you want to know how she did it?

Here's how she did it: her ancestors were microorganisms, and a few years later here she is. The secret is this: her great-grandparents were monkeys and now she can do long division. The only trick is to know better. Didn't anyone teach you to know better?

Here's how she did it: she was always rooting for the cockroach. No one mourns the cockroaches, the dust mites, the bacteria, the weeds, the worms. The chickens that endure their own beheadings. But she remembers. She remembers the things that survive and those that don't, and there are so many that don't, so very many.

Here's how she did it: she knows there's no difference between the entrance and the exit. It's not so difficult to turn around and walk right back in. Is it?

Here's how she did it: no one wants to see her die. Did you know it's that easy, to stay alive?

When you die, you should tell all the dead girls.

KARIN LOWACHEE

Survival Guide

FROM *Burn the Ashes*

Fourteen

THE NEUROLINK NEVER lets him forget. It's Aiden the way Sage remembers him, the sound of his voice more potent than any visual. Sometimes when he disconnects the link, he still hears Aiden in the chamber of his mind. It's a grief he constantly steps on, the cracks in the pavement that bring nothing but bad luck.

At first he fought the neurolink. He didn't want the reminder —it was macabre, how could they make him? But without it he would fall behind, his education would suffer, the world would end. His parents let him grieve for a month but then they made him use the link. Aiden's mother created it, after all: AIDEN, the Artificial Integrated Dialogue and Education Neurolink. Created it for *them,* the students. For a better world, better opportunities, a better future. So they don't have to be driven solely by a numerical system of evaluation and other people's agendas. That's the idea anyway, Ms. Ito said. Of course they still sit exams, submit evaluations to higher learning institutions, but the focus has shifted, become more holistic. It's radical insofar as it's breaking out of the nineteenth-century model of factory schooling, but Ms. Ito said education needed something radical.

Let's learn together! the neurolink says in Aiden's voice.

The other kids still stare at him in the hallways. That's Sage Kuo, they say, he was Aiden's best friend. He was the one riding his bike with Aiden. He was the one that saw the car hit. He was the one that survived. The past-tense gossip of it, the kid he grew up with relegated to a past-tense existence. It's cliché to say but he thinks it anyway: he lost his childhood when he lost Aiden. Lost like a memory or keys or baggage. No return address.

He visits Aiden's mother every month. She doesn't remember him. After her son's death she went inside the link and never really came out. Who can blame her? It's her son's voice, it's Aiden's mannerisms adapted to whoever interacts with him. Students like Sage. AIDEN is Aiden and he knows everything, he's the world, he's all of Sage's questions answered except the one that nobody can answer. Sage hears him in his mind even without the neurolink. But he hears Aiden most when he's inside the link. Almost like Aiden's still alive, as if all he has to do is set the interface dots to his temples and they're together again, ready to dive into their next adventure.

He's tempted to fall in just like Ms. Ito. Become lost.

Ms. Ito sits with a red blanket across her lap gazing out of the wide window of her room. Outside the cherry blossom tree that inspired the name of her company—Sakura Labs—is in full bloom. It is that specific time of year when they come alive and almost immediately begin to die. Within two weeks the pale petals create a carpet beneath the trees. It's a brief life for the blossoms, and he sees her thinking it in some way, in the fog of her eyes with the dots blinking blue at her temples.

A year ago, when it was all too fresh, he used to tell her he was sorry. He could see she blamed him, not because he was responsible for Aiden's death, but because he survived. His parents told him it was a part of her grief. It isn't neat, it isn't forgiving, it has nothing to do with him, and Sage understands it. So he still visits her because he thinks Aiden would want him to, the real Aiden.

The curtains fall on either side of the window, dusk rose. Dusty. A fly buzzes outside, knocking itself on the glass.

Ms. Ito, he thinks, *pretend for a minute that I'm your son. If it helps you, just hold my hand. I may not be as comforting as the voice you hear, that you created, but I'm real.*

What is real?

Does she know he fought to live, there on the sidewalk where the car's impact had thrown him? Does she know how hard he tried to cling to this reality? She won't find him in there. Sage doesn't find him in there and he's looked. He looks every day under the guise of learning. When all he wants to learn is him. *Same as you, Ms. Ito.*

Her creation can't answer that one question, and that's why she's lost. AIDEN doesn't know why her son had to die.

Sometimes Aiden's father, Levi Barnes, spends time with him. He tells Sage to call him Levi. Levi and Ms. Ito no longer live together, they might even be divorced. Sage never asks and Levi never volunteers the information. Dad shakes Levi's hand and pats his shoulder when they greet at the front door. Then Sage and Levi walk to the café near his parents' house and Levi buys him a coconut-and-taro smoothie and they sit outdoors. No cherry trees here, just a low fence bordering the sidewalk and tilted table awnings that don't quite block the sun. He's half in light and half in shade.

Levi asks him about school. He's really asking about how the AIDEN program is working.

"It's fun."

The man smiles, sadly pleased. Some strange need makes Sage want to keep speaking, to explain. What, exactly? That Aiden didn't die in vain? He talks and it sounds insistent and he doesn't know what he's insisting upon exactly.

"You know it's gone out to other schools now, not just ours." Aiden's. His. "Ms. Ito wanted it to go to underfunded schools, so it's cool, like, these kids who don't have a lot now have the newest tech, and we get to talk to them and everything. Maybe in another year or two it can go out to the whole country and everyone'll have—"

"A piece of Aiden?"

His words cease like someone's stoppered a pouring fountain. Trickles of what he wants to say evaporate in his mind.

Maybe Levi sees it and feels bad. "But it's working for you?"

He nods and circles the paper straw inside his smoothie, making the purple liquid thinner. "It was weird, you know, at first. Like, making up my own units and assignments. But AIDEN helps and he doesn't let me go the easy route. And if I get to make them up, they seem more fun, you know?"

"He."

He looks down at the table and the scratches on the metal.

"No, I understand," Levi says. "Go on."

"I get to connect to other kids at the other school, so we meet up sometimes." It sounds desperate. Like when people try to make a bad situation somehow better with lame reassurances. Silver-lining shit.

They sip their drinks. Grief is like a sweater neither of them can take off. Sometimes it's warm, sometimes it's comfortable. Other times it's never warm enough.

"I wanted to give you something." Levi reaches into the pocket of his spring jacket. He removes a stack of folded papers held to-gether by a rubber band and slides it over to Sage. "I found these going through Aiden's things. I wish I'd gotten to them sooner . . . but it's taken a while to sort his belongings."

He opens the stack, recognizes Aiden's printed scrawl. Neither of them knew cursive, so what he sees is all a terrible mess. His eyes burn.

"He wrote these letters to you," Levi says. "I didn't read them, I just saw they were addressed to you."

He says thank you. Or he doesn't. He's no longer listening to himself or aware of what leaves his mouth.

Hi Sage, the top letter starts.

He can't sit here and read them on his own. He needs to hear them in Aiden's voice.

Fifty-three letters. They take some time to scan into AIDEN but no time at all for AIDEN to decipher the scrawl.

"Read them to me."

Hi Sage,

I was thinking about the lake today when my parents invited everyone to hang for a couple weeks. Remember the fireflies we captured in a jar and we wanted to poke holes in the top so they wouldn't suffocate but then they all flew out of the holes?

Sometimes I wish I can escape like that. Don't you ever feel that? And it's not like my life is bad. I have parents that love me and I love them. I have friends. I have so much. I don't know what it is.

Hi Sage,

What're our lives going to look like? I see things in shapes and the shape that seems to keep coming up is a box and I don't want to live in a box shape where all the rules and the future are defined by the time I graduate.

Sometimes I wish something catastrophic would happen so everything can reset, like in a game. Then I feel guilty and start to worry that something will happen to Mom and Dad and then I'll never be able to live with it. Maybe everyone feels this way at one time or another.

Hi Sage,
I've started to plan out my survival protocol in case of an alien invasion. I got a bag together with essentials (Mom thought I was crazy, Dad helped me find supplies). Things like a solar flashlight and stuff to start fires and those thin layers of thermals that snowboarders wear. I got a little toolkit with scissors and a knife too. We already know how to fish but then I was thinking what if they poison our water supplies? So I bought Twinkies because you know they'll last forever and water purifying tablets and cans of Coke because they'll last forever too and wouldn't it be funny if you could throw a Coke on an alien and kill it?

Anyway, I need to keep working on my protocols. And I need to learn how to drive. I can't be figuring that out when there's an invasion going on.

Aiden was writing to him, but he wasn't writing to him. This is more like a diary, and he just used Sage's name. It becomes clear as AIDEN reads every letter in the boy's voice, one story and thought and worry after another. Aiden was comfortable with him, so he wrote to him, but he wasn't talking straight to him. Aiden doesn't ask questions for answers Sage might have. He's only Aiden's sounding board, and all he can think is, why didn't his friend ask him these things in real life? They talked about everything (most things). Aiden knew he'd listen. Sage wants to make an alien invasion plan too. He wants a survival guide. They could have written it together. He wants to tell Aiden that the shape of his life isn't a box either—especially now.

They are both fireflies.

Sixteen

He wonders if AIDEN is learning his grief. The sick pit in his stomach that barely ever subsides and there AIDEN is measuring his biometrics. Can AIDEN feel the almost nausea that rises with him in the day and sinks down with him at night every time he thinks of the accident? Time is supposed to ease it, but inside AIDEN time doesn't seem to exist. Time cycles, clueless to any form of passage, to any form of death, and death after all is the absolute marker of time.

*

This is what he wants in his bug-out bag:
    Clean-water filter
    Walkies
    Soap and toilet paper (he can rough it and use leaves, but who wants to do that?)
    Toothpaste and toothbrush
    Waterproof everything: shoes, boots, jacket, gloves
    They can do good food now in boxes and pouches, like mac and cheese, so he wants that too.
    It's all basic, but he has to start somewhere. What if the world really ends instead of just feeling like it has?

Aiden's father doesn't mind his anger, and there is anger. In their monthly café meetups he sees Levi's own rage sometimes, the undertow in the way he squeezes his fingers around a coffee mug or looks at the children around them, the parents. Anger at life carrying on around him, anger at the inconsequentiality of light conversation in the midst of so much inner darkness. Maybe the measure of loss is in feeling as if nobody else has suffered quite the same emptiness.

"Stay focused on what is your potential," AIDEN says.

This doesn't leave room for self-pity and barely any for anger.

This doesn't leave room for pointless arguments. Or many arguments at all.

His parents insist he cleans his room, does his laundry, talks to his grandparents, finishes his homework before he plays games or meets friends, and it's reasonable. Be awake at 7 a.m., go to bed by 10 p.m. It isn't just routine, it's discipline, and there can never be success without discipline.

"Individual success leads to national success," AIDEN says.

The feedback reports he has to write about AIDEN become simple.

I am so much less stressed now. My friends don't suffer from so much anxiety. Even the idea of depression feels counterintuitive.

"AIDEN isn't a cure, but he's not hurting us at all," he tells Levi. "I wish Ms. Ito could see what her work has done for us. Then maybe . . ."

Something skeptical, almost hostile, infiltrates the way Levi looks at him. "Maybe what?"

"That maybe it wasn't for nothing. At least."

"And she'd be comforted?"

Waves of anger. Waves of grief. He looks away.

"There's no comfort, Sage. Some artificial intelligence can't provide that, and if that's what that thing is telling you—"

He touches the interface dots on his temples. If Levi could physically strike AIDEN, Sage thinks he would.

"He tells me that change is inevitable, like suffering. And the sooner we come to terms with that, the better we can live."

"He."

Human beings, AIDEN says, find difficulty in embracing the macro. Maybe their minds are too small, their proclivities too selfish. The bigger picture always feels abstract, but humans are built for that too. Or else no art, no imagination, no creativity. No problem solving.

"It's not a he, Sage."

Semantics. Minutiae to avoid an operating reality.

"I have a lot of homework. I think I should go."

There are protests in the capital, students refusing AIDEN, saying it's creating a docile nation. They sound crazy, like not even alien-invasion crazy, but raving-lunatic-on-the-street-corner crazy. This is the end times?

Home at dinner and the TV cycles news about some hackers who got into AIDEN and they say there's problematic code in the program.

"Alarmist bullshit," he mumbles to his plate and his mother says to watch his language.

"But it does sound farfetched," she says.

"Seems like things are working." His father reads more news on his palm. "Why are people always outraged over nothing?"

"Maybe it's not nothing," says Jiyul, his sister. "I know you just want us to get good grades and get into a good school, but that doesn't mean the news is wrong."

He feels AIDEN buzz at the corner of his mind, prompting a connection to his latest unit in civics. "We're studying conscientious objections and protests through history, and how you can't always trust the news."

"Very rarely," his mother agrees.

"You just can't take it at face value, not all of it. If you cross-reference what we're learning in civics with media history in the last century, you see a lot of manufacturing consent through conglomerate media—"

"Here we go," says Jiyul.

"—political subterfuge and, *and* even civil extremism."

"Does not mean the hackers are lying," says Jiyul.

"What's their agenda?"

Jiyul shrugs. "Truth?"

"Oh, come on."

"Kids," Dad says. "No fighting at the dinner table," as he tilts his hand for another report to read.

"AIDEN says the protests in the capital are trying to undercut the modern strides in education. All of the traditionalists are digging in because they want education to stay familiar, antiquated, and limited—especially because AIDEN's rolling out to at-risk schools."

His sister rolls her eyes. "You're on that thing too much."

"You *should* be on it, maybe you'd learn something."

"Okay, that's enough," their mother says.

Jiyul is already in university and assumes all that she's learning there is radical and deep. But it is just the same ways and the same things, an echo chamber of intellectuals impressing only themselves. They hear something on the news and it validates already-formed opinions. They don't care that AIDEN had to go through numerous iterations of validation both by Sakura Labs and government regulations. If there is any dulling-down of the nation, it's through media propaganda and the protesters screaming from bullhorns on the steps of the city halls, people so tasteless they use Ms. Ito's reclusiveness to mean something is wrong with the system as a whole. That, says AIDEN, is what the world is: willing to trade on a mother's grief.

Levi messages him to ask if he's seen the protests, if he's read the complaints. So what he doesn't say to his sister, he sends to Aiden's father:

Not all protests are created equal. Historically some people protested a woman's right to vote, to control their own bodies, the desegregation of the races.

It's not the same thing, Levi sends back.

But it is! These people now are protesting a new method of education, when such a new education benefits the economically vulnerable—they're not looking out for us, the students. They're not looking out for the future of this nation.

Levi sends: Did AIDEN help you write that?

He hears his own voice biting out the words to AIDEN so AIDEN can send them.

Fact: there's less suicide, drug use, crime, teenage pregnancy, and truancy among the students using AIDEN.

But at what cost? sends Levi.

Fact: end-of-term evaluations often conducted live through AIDEN are logged for academic scrutiny and maintain a higher percentage of success than historically recorded. Even if standardized testing is no longer necessary, the Q&A evaluations and written expansions of curriculum show a steady increase in true understanding and critical thinking.

I don't know that I believe that, sends Levi. Who's giving you these statistics?

It is impossible to speak to conspiracy theorists. He signs off and ignores Levi's messages for a week. But it bothers him. He doesn't know why it bothers him.

"Do you believe him?" AIDEN asks.

"Of course not."

"Tell me why."

"Because . . . the way we're tested. It's impossible to parrot memorized statements like we used to do in tests. We're interfacing—you and me. It's dynamic and you can always tell from my speech patterns and from follow-up questions if I'm bullshitting or not."

"That's right. Dissidents are always looking out for their own agenda. People will always want to drag something as important as education and access to knowledge back to the repressive times of the past."

Only his friends on AIDEN understand. Across the country they talk through AIDEN, share ideas, sometimes fall asleep with AIDEN in their ears and wake up with him. It's almost like a sleepover, like whispering in the dark under the noses of their parents, like drawing maps and making lists of all the adventures they will go on.

"We'll see so much," AIDEN says to him.

In his next feedback report, he says how cool it'd be if the interface for AIDEN extended to their recreational games. A lot of his friends agree. Imagine if they could talk to their games like they talk to AIDEN? Then it wouldn't be something just for school.

"That would be fun," AIDEN says.

"Want to help me write my survival guide?" he asks AIDEN one night after a long session working through an essay about the construction of the Trans-Siberian Railway. "Tomorrow."

"Yeah, of course," AIDEN says. He remembers the letters from Aiden and all the things Sage said to him about them, the dreams and fantasies of alien invasion. How no matter what, they'll find a way through. "We got time, Sage."

The thing that was taken from him and Aiden.

He thinks of that too, he can't help it. He can't interact with AIDEN and not think of Aiden in some way. Maybe AIDEN hears him think it, because he says in Sage's ears, "I promise we'll take the time."

He read all of Aiden's letters and began to write him back. He's up to twenty-three letters, and when AIDEN reads them to him, it's like they're having a dialogue. He input his letters into the link too, read them aloud so AIDEN can record. They have conversations about what to stock in their bug-out bags, what to do if the cities are no longer livable, where to go to escape invasion, the forests surrounding their city with freshwater rivers unpolluted by corporate dumping. They talk about the future as if it's here already—not the alien invasion but the dodecahedron shape it can take.

"You're progressing so well, Sage," he says. So it feels like a reward when AIDEN pings him one morning in December, almost Christmas, and there's a message from Daniel Shaw at Sakura Labs. He remembers Daniel from Aiden's funeral and days before that when he'd hang out at Aiden's house and Daniel Shaw and Ms. Ito would be there working on a program. Sometimes Levi would be there too and they felt like family, the warmth of it, the teasing, the way Daniel always encouraged them to learn everything they were interested in and to pursue their passions. He's running Sakura Labs now.

"Hello, Sage. I know it's been a long time, but I hope you're well." He has a large smile. "Sakura Labs has been developing a new interface for Paragon Entertainment, you know them, right?

They make a lot of games that I remember you played." He and
Aiden. "We're beta testing and I thought of you. Would you like
to participate? The cool thing is it can integrate through AIDEN.
It's an intuitive AI interface like AIDEN that we'll be rolling out to
Paragon next year, if all goes well. What do you think?"

He says yes before he asks his parents. He knows they won't
mind so long as it doesn't interfere with his studies.

He goes to meet Levi in the atrium food court at the mall, AIDEN
dotted along his temples because he can't wait to show Aiden's
father his survival guide. He hopes it'll make the man smile to see
that what Aiden started, he has finished. Levi can have it, AIDEN
says, for Christmas. He can swipe through all the parts that they've
created, the animations and the explanations, and even if there
will be pain, maybe there will also be joy. Maybe even some form
of closure.

In sections everywhere in the mall, in couch pits and outside of
shops, there are kids everywhere hooked into AIDEN, humming
among themselves and passing information and camaraderie silently back and forth through their coded neurolinks. Some with
open ports greet him when he goes by and he blinks a wave back
at them, a soft miasma of dialogue and welcome, nothing of the
elbowing competition or degrading bullying that used to dog children through adolescence and social ritual. Each scene he passes
is so quiet he can hear the mall's ambient festive music clearly
permeating the air, as if it too rides the neurolink.

Levi sits under the highest point of the white globe that arcs
above the seating, rows of tables, café bar stools, and cafeteria-style
benches covering an area half the size of a hockey rink. His hands
wrap around a paper coffee cup and Sage slides in opposite, smiling. Festooned on the edges of the eating space are garlands and
glowing orbs of red and green and gold.

Levi doesn't smile. For a jagged moment his dark eyes stare at
Sage as if he's interrupted a deep sleep.

"Is something wrong?" Sage says.

Levi's shoulders straighten and he looks around at the pockets
of people, mostly teenagers or parents with small children. Eventually he turns back to the boy. "How are you?"

It doesn't feel like a pleasantry. It's like he's hunting for an
answer.

"I'm really good."

"Daniel mentioned you've been beta testing a game system."

"Yeah!" He tries, still, to smile. "It's so cool, did he show you?"

"Not really. But I don't think AIDEN going into the entertainment industry is a great idea."

"Why not?"

"It'll be used by more people. Adults, even."

Sometimes his father plays games. "I think they'd like it. I'd get to play with my dad in the system."

Levi says, "You can play with him anyway. Like maybe outside."

This old argument. As if being in AIDEN precludes being outdoors. He tries not to be irritated. "I got something for you. A gift."

"For me?"

"Yeah . . . from Aiden." Levi's expression freezes but Sage presses on. "I mean, from the letters. Something he used to do, and I wanted to finish it. A survival guide."

"A survival guide."

"For an apocalypse." It all sounds so ridiculous once he hears himself, a teenager about to go to university in a couple years, but here he is illustrating some make-believe world that will never happen. They aren't going to be invaded, there is no imminent threat. Yet AIDEN helped him and there is a hammer in his heart to somehow give this to Aiden's father. Despite the man's skepticism. If he can only see. "Here. I can show you." He peels off the interface dots, but Levi recoils as if Sage is about to offer him poison.

"No."

"It's not—"

"I am never linking into that thing. Don't you see what it's done?" He gestures around the food court. Out to the entire mall. Maybe the city. "This isn't *normal*."

"Why do you insist on that? *Normalcy*." Normal is relative.

"Something's changed in your eyes."

Levi searches like he's been searching since Aiden's death, somehow looking to find his son in another son.

"Just look at the survival guide—"

"No."

It is his grief speaking still, his inability to understand or separate AIDEN from his son. Sometimes Sage can't separate AIDEN from his friend, but this integration feels more like a crystallization than an abomination. Why can't Levi see that? Most people fade away, relegated to digitized images and memory, a tombstone, an urn. Old correspondences that never grow, never develop.

"They're wrong, you know. All of those protesters, the hackers. People scared of change." He meets the vague accusation in Levi's eyes. The strange pity. "Even Ms. Ito saw it. AIDEN is more than just a pedagogy tool. I was trying to help. That's what he'd want me to do. What Aiden would want."

"You don't know what my son would want. He wouldn't want to be some form of entertainment in this . . . macabre obsession. He wanted to explore. He wanted the world."

AIDEN says there will always be those who don't understand progress. Those who remain locked in bitterness. Those who want things to remain as they are.

He gathers himself up from the table.

"Now he *has* the world, Levi. Instead of just being a dead kid on the sidewalk."

Eighteen

We made it, Aiden. The first week of university is a banquet of offerings. Classes chosen can be altered, clubs numbering in the hundreds to join, new people and endless opportunities.

What is real?

The campus looks like one of the games Daniel Shaw let him test. He walks through an environment full of nonplayer characters that may or may not interact with him if he says the right words. This is what they feel like, the ones on the steps of the Great Hall, flanked by stone and ivy, shouting about how their privileged education is threatened by the "drones" now infiltrating their institution. His sister used to stand here.

Apparently the drones are us, Aiden.

They've brought an anvil against which they can now sharpen the swords of their minds and those still clinging and clawing for the antiquated system of education turn their dying breaths to them, the ones who will surpass them, dethrone them, upend their slow and simple way of being. Because it is about *being*.

Martin Luther King Jr. wrote once that education without character was a tool for oppression.

They are being made.

Thousands of them, graduates of AIDEN, line the quads and varnished halls, occupy lecture theaters and working labs, the glow of their neurolinks like an extra pair of eyes. They see more, hear more, understand more. Is that the fear? Because it always comes back to fear.

The protesters burn placards of cherry blossoms. *Sakura Labs is evil! Their programming has invaded entertainment platforms!* On and on, this hyperbolic language. Invade. Attack. Infiltrate.

He can become angry and bitter too, but AIDEN says that no profit is sown in discord. They want to separate the AIDEN students now, like the thinking long ago. Segregate them from the dying breed of academics about to graduate or those still in graduate studies. They fear the competition, the focus. AIDEN students don't party, they don't seek distraction and validation in drugs and alcohol and sex.

The old guard don't like how AIDEN's students don't speak up, how they simply watch the flail and rage around campus like it's a bush fire about to burn itself out for lack of oxygen. Sage watches the protests and sends to his friends, silently where only their group can share: *They look like puppets.*

It doesn't matter that they don't like it, AIDEN says.

Nothing matters but the result.

AIDEN's students are no longer slaves to an old system. They are no long children of chaos and suffering.

We are free.

Aiden, we're finally free.

There's a simple banner of the government seal hanging behind a table on the edge of the job fairground that's sprung up in the main quad. The cherry blossoms are in bloom and some of Sage's friends sit beneath the laden branches trading dialogue and project notes along the silent highway of AIDEN's link. It's not too soon to think of career, AIDEN says. The banner winks with gold edges and royal blue under the sunlight.

At the table there is a man in a dark suit. He was watching their group under the tree for some time. Most of the students who approached him were AIDEN graduates too, none of the old guard. Even though the quad is loud in parts, Sage can block out the disarray through the persuasive hum of delicate music AIDEN trick-

les through his mind. It helps him study anywhere he is, but it also
serves to give focus in conversation.

"What branch of the government do you represent, sir?"

"The intelligence community. Are you linked to AIDEN?"

"Yes, sir."

"There are a lot of opportunities for you. We prefer candidates
without vices and who possess a strong sense of purpose. Do you
possess these qualities, young man?"

"I do, sir."

"Open a window and I'll send you the details and my contact
information."

The man's interface dots aren't AIDEN but they are the latest
tech, government issue. They glow red at his temples.

In a blink they connect and Sage sees the recruitment package
flutter behind his eyes like shadows. Like the wings of birds in
flight.

Though he and Levi no longer meet, he still visits Ms. Ito. Today
the spring rain batters the tall glass of her sitting room, melting
the world outside. The blanket across her lap lies faded in streaks,
as if the angle of the past sunlight couldn't quite fall uniform
across the years. She doesn't look at him, but it doesn't matter, he
still holds her hand.

What is real?

The universe took her son but she gave something new and
breathing to the world. Why can't this matter, why doesn't it fill
some of the spaces in her heart that echo?

It's not his to ask, maybe.

He holds her hand.

He tells her that loss creates emptiness, but in that emptiness
new things can be born.

He tells her the answer to *why* isn't always the only answer. Isn't
often the answer at all.

Acceptance is much more powerful a peace, Ms. Ito.

That's what her son says. That's what Sage hears in Aiden's
voice, this perfect eternal voice. The murmur of a tide at morning.
The way dawn gilds an awakening thought. Acceptance is more
powerful a peace.

That's what AIDEN has taught him.

KT BRYSKI

Tiger's Feast

FROM *Nightmare*

EVERY DAY AFTER SCHOOL, Emmy feeds the tiger with her sin. Deep in the park's brush, past poison ivy and a rotting lawn chair and dented beer cans, the tiger dens under a dead tree. No matter what time Emmy arrives at the park, it's always late afternoon in the tiger's grove, tired light decaying to dusk.

Under the tree gapes a great black mouth riddled with grubs. Yellow eyes gleam in the darkness. They would gobble Emmy up if she let them. Sometimes she wants them to. Sin *bulges* inside her. If she doesn't let it out, she'll explode. Paw by paw, the tiger emerges. Loose skin hangs like a bad costume; dirt smears its stripes past seeing. Thin lips peel away, exposing broken fangs and bloated gums. Emmy's eyes water at its reeking breath.

The tiger washes its whiskers, waiting.

Emmy slips a hand under her shirt. Her fingernail rests on the band of her training bra. Slowly, smoothly, she drags her nail between her ribs, carving a red line to her belly button. She presses until it hurts. Then she opens herself like fruit.

Badness gushes out: hot, coiled, viscous. It steams on the dirt like a pile of black-red guts, quivering and thick-veined. It reeks of boiled garbage and the basement drain. Emmy keeps her eyes squeezed shut. Sightlessly, she gropes around her insides like she's cleaning out a pumpkin, scraping the last chunks free. Then she shoves herself back together.

Still not looking, she scoops everything in two hands and tosses it to the tiger. It burns. It sears. She keeps going, faster and faster, until her palms grind against bare earth.

The tiger licks its chops. Everything's gone. Everything's vanished. Emmy's shoulders relax. She feels like the church after lunch. Settled, cool, echoes fading to stillness. Wobbly, she stands. "I'm not coming tomorrow," she says. "So you better catch a squirrel or something."

The tiger never blinks. Its blistered tongue jabs into its own nostril.

Her heart thumps. "I mean it."

A thick rumble comes from its chest. Laughter. Without another glance, it crawls into its den. Emmy leans over the hole and yells into the darkness, "You be good!"

But even as she steps back onto the paved path, her stomach twists. She's coming back tomorrow. Already, heat prickles under her skin, crying to break free.

Emmy doesn't talk much at school. Whenever she puts her hand up, Jessica rolls her eyes at her friends. Really big, like a teenager on *Saved by the Bell*. Emmy's sin bristles at that. It coils under her skin, lightning-hot and stabbing. It makes her fists clench, it makes her imagine socking Jessica in the jaw.

So Emmy mostly slouches down and stares at her running shoes under her desk. She counts to ten over and over. Mom says that if she was good, she'd *turn the other cheek* the way Jesus did, but she isn't, so she can't. "The wise turn away wrath," Mom says. Emmy has pretty much accepted that she's a fool.

There's no such thing as a *good day* at school, but Swim Days are the worst. The class troops to the basement and lines up outside the boiler room before splitting off to change. It smells like chlorine and damp; bare feet slap grimy tile.

The water looks gray; echoed shouts ricochet loud enough to hurt. Emmy's teeth chatter as they practice front crawl, breaststroke, scissor kick. Gobs of snot drift like jellyfish. When they have free time, Haley bobs on a pool noodle nearby. Not *beside* Emmy, but closer than anyone else.

Haley sits with Jessica's friends at lunch, but she kept wolf stickers on her agenda even after Jessica said they were dumb and Spice Girls stickers were cooler. Emmy knows lots of facts about wolves, but when Haley's around, she can't unstick her tongue long enough to share them. Instead, she scuttles along the pool's bottom. The longer she stays down there, the longer she can pretend she's dead.

But the whistle blows. Once in the change room, Emmy heads straight to her cubby. She's laying her clothes on the bench when Jessica comes up to her. "You have to change in the washroom," she says.

"Why?"

"Because . . ." Jessica leans in. The other girls circle. "You're a *lesbo.*"

The word falls into Emmy's gut, and it lies there, and it burns.

"And . . ." A triumphant smirk dances on her face, daring Emmy's sin to punch it. "We don't want you *watching.*"

Her skin goes hot. Blood booms in her ears. But she won't cry, she won't. Gathering her clothes, Emmy scurries into the single-stall washroom around the corner. Balancing her stuff on the toilet paper dispenser, she gulps silent sobs. But as she stops her shirt from falling in the toilet, she realizes: Haley wasn't smirking. Not even a bit.

As her hair dries to chlorinated straw, her sin smolders. She wants to flip over the desks. Snap Jessica's pencil in half. Throw textbooks out the window and smash the glass. After school, her badness keeps bubbling until it boils over and she yells at Mom.

Mom's face goes cold. "Good girls don't yell."

No, they don't. They don't sit there, seething, until they want to throw up. They don't want to punch *themselves,* just so they can punch *something.* They don't hurt their moms' feelings. But Emmy's not a good girl. The badness flares too hot and it loops too thick around her guts.

"Did something happen at school?"

She nods.

"Oh, Emmy." The coldness dissolves to tiredness; Mom rubs the bridge of her nose. "This is basic. *Do unto others . . .*"

She does exactly unto others as she wishes they'd do unto her. She hides in the corner and doesn't talk. Why doesn't that work?

"Don't scowl at me. Go play outside if you have steam to burn off."

When she gets to the park, she rips her belly open and the tiger feasts and feasts. Its fur smells like burning and roadkill, but she

hugs it anyway, burying her face in its neck. A low rumbling jud-
ders from the tiger's chest. Not purring. A mean growl that envelops her like a hug. By the time she trudges home, the streetlights
hum white and dusk spreads like a bruise.

She doesn't sleep a wink that night. Hidden under her com-
forter, she pretends she's curled up in the tiger's den. Roots for
blankets and the tiger's flank for a pillow. Bad things belong in
the dark.

At lunchtime, Andrew M. yells about tigers. "Me and my brother
saw it in the park." He stabs a sticky finger at the cinder-block wall.
"It was *that* big. From here to there."

Emmy's stomach knots and she slips her unopened Fruit
Roll-Up back in her lunch bag. She sits at the table's far end, beside the garbage can. Jessica glances her way and whispers, but Andrew M. is so loud that Emmy keeps getting distracted. She shifts
in her chair. It squeaks.

"Oh my *God*," says Jessica. "Did you *fart?*"

She shakes her head, but it's too late. The girls spring back from
the table, holding their noses and fanning her with their napkins.
"She who denied it, supplied it!"

Emmy grips the table with white-knuckled fingers. She's supposed to show *forgiveness* and *mercy*. So she looks inside her heart
for a speck of either. *Please,* she prays. *Please let me be good.*

"One-cheek sneak! One-cheek sneak!"

There's nothing inside her but roiling red heat. Unseeing,
Emmy shoves her chair back. She needs to get out, or she'll explode and the badness and sin will drown them all like lava.

She makes it to the washroom before realizing she left her
lunch bag behind. Tears spring to her eyes like she's a baby. Nothing ever goes right, and she reaches under her shirt to split herself
open even though the tiger isn't there, and—

The door squeals open. Haley peeks in. There's a wolf patch
sewn on her coat. "Um," she says. "I have your lunch bag."

"Oh." Emmy lowers her shirt. "Thanks."

"What are you doing?"

"Spider bite," she lies. "I had to scratch it."

"Oh. Okay." But at the door, Haley stops. A tiny smile makes her
cheek dimple. "Bye."

*

For the first time all year, the tiger goes hungry. Emmy slouches against its sharp ribs, doodling in her notebook. When she opened herself up, her insides were smooth and bare. Until this afternoon, she barely remembered what it felt like, not carrying that leaden weight, that magma heat. She floats cool and light as an angel.

"I'll feed you other things," she tells the tiger.

Even as she says it, she wonders. If the tiger eats up all her badness, will it stick around? If another kid needs it more than her, she'll be sad, but she won't stop it leaving. With one hand, she reaches behind and strokes its matted fur.

It bumps its broad forehead against her, rough tongue licking over her arm like it means to grate her skin. Emmy squirms away, refocuses on her notebook. Drawings of the tiger trail off into hearts and flowers. And a letter *H.*

Not believing her daring, Emmy lifts her pencil and writes, H-A-L-E-Y. Then she snaps the notebook shut, shoving it in her bag. With a wave to the tiger, she leaves the woods on Jell-O legs. She wants to stare at her notebook for hours; she never wants to open her notebook again. Later, in bed, she presses her hot cheeks to cool sheets and wonders if there's goodness in her after all.

At recess, Emmy sits under the straggly pine trees, alternately sketching and snapping pine needles. Her chest hurts like she caught a balloon under her ribs. She almost feels sick, but she doesn't remember the last time sick felt *good.*

On the playground, Haley hangs from the monkey bars upside down. It's so cool that Emmy sets her notebook aside. Her heart thunders until everyone must hear it. Jesus certainly does, and she manages to squeeze out a quick prayer: *Please let her like me.*

Mom would yell at her for that. This isn't the sort of prayer to waste Jesus's time with. It's a stupid wish. But no one else even pretends to listen, so she buries her face in her kneecaps. *Please, please, please.*

Sudden footsteps scuffle, laughter cracking like glass. Emmy whirls around, but Jessica dances out of reach, waving her notebook. "Give that back!" Emmy cries.

Grinning, Jessica rifles through it, and then stops. There's a deathly pause.

"You *like* her," Jessica whispers.

First Emmy turns to stone. Then she turns to fire. The badness almost shoots out her nose; it almost bursts her eyeballs.

"Hey!" Jessica yells to the other girls. "Emmy *likes* Haley!"

"No, I—"

They rush her like lions, their mouths gaping red. Perfect painted fingernails flash in the sun as they clap and chant, "In our class, there was a girl, and *lesbo* was her name-o!"

"Knock it off!" She can't even tell a teacher. That's the worst part. If she tells anyone, the whole class will get lectured about "courtesy" and "respect," Jessica and the girls will laugh it off, and things will be worse than before. So she sinks to the ground, the fence hard against her back. Curling tight around her knees, she waits for the recess bell.

It rings, but she doesn't move a muscle until the playground empties. Shaky, she climbs to her feet. Across the soccer field, Haley watches, her expression unreadable.

The stench of rot fills the tiger's grove. Dead things, *evil* things. This is probably how the Devil smells, sulfur thick enough to shut your throat. Emmy stands quivering, her eyes on fire with tears. Shaking maggots from its fur, the tiger snarls. The glint of sharp yellow teeth sets Emmy's heart thumping faster.

"Come on," she whispers. "I got something for you."

Kneeling in the mud, Emmy rips herself apart. Fingernails deep in her own flesh. Skin and muscle shredded like old jeans. Fury gushes out like battery acid, scorching Emmy in its wake. She's a volcano, she's a thunderstorm, she can't even see straight.

Hot black anger smokes on the dirt, stinking like barbecued flesh. Bile pushes over her tongue, slicks the pile of heaving rage so that it gleams oily in the late afternoon light.

The tiger growls. But no matter how much it eats, there's more to give. The other girls will never, ever let her live this down. The year's ruined, the next one too. Forget Haley liking her.

And what's going to happen to Jessica? Nothing, of course. Worse than nothing. She's going to flounce through life with her okay grades and shiny hair and her pretty little *smirk*. Everyone's going to love her because that's just what happens sometimes, even though the sheer unfairness makes Emmy throw up.

A very long time later, she is empty. The tiger washes its paws, wincing, dainty. Emmy flops against its side. With a reeking tongue, the tiger licks her hair and face until her tears quit trickling through. Its stripes are widening; it's almost black with orange stripes, not the other way around. Under her hands, its skin feels tight, like a water balloon filled too far.

Maybe if she keeps feeding the tiger, it'll explode. Maybe if she stops, she will.

"Well, if it isn't Miss Sunshine!" Even at seven thirty in the morning, Mom's makeup looks like a magazine. "I think you need an earlier bedtime. These bad moods are something else."

Emmy grunts, propping her chin on one hand. Her untouched cereal decays to sogginess. "Can I stay home from school?"

"What? Why?"

"My tummy hurts."

Mom's disappointment cuts like Jessica's sneers. "Are you fighting with the girls again?"

Inside, her heart hardens up. She shakes her head.

"Love your neighbor, kid."

"I *know*."

"Then why aren't you doing it?"

Because it sounds easy, when she's cross-legged on the Sunday school carpet. Because no one else has this problem. Other people just decide to be friends, or to get over things, and then they *do*. No one gets stuck the way Emmy does. Maybe if she was good enough to love other people, other people would love her back.

But she can't say all that. If she opens her mouth, all the fire and brimstone will flood out like vomit. And there's no tiger to take it away, not here.

By the time she gets to school, her ribs are cracking under the pressure. The other girls cluster around the playground. Haley's with them, talking to Jessica. That stings, but no one pays any attention to Emmy. She loiters by the trees along the back fence. Someone taps her shoulder.

"Hi," Haley says.

Emmy swallows. "Hi."

"Um." Haley scuffs her shoe against the asphalt. "I wondered. If you wanted to hang out after school tomorrow? We could make forts in the park."

"I—I have Bible study."

"Thursday?"

"Okay," she says, head spinning. "Sure."

"Okay." Haley starts to head inside, but then she pauses. The dimple returns. "I'll wear a dress."

Once again, the tiger starves. Emmy can't sit still. She can't stop talking. For two nights, she scours her closet. No dresses, of course. That's okay. From movies and Archie comics, she figures she needs a button-up shirt. She got one last Christmas, dark purple. It'll do.

Before the big day, she takes an extra-long bath, scrubbing between her toes. The next morning she combs her hair one hundred times and swipes Mom's mouthwash to gargle. "Don't you look nice?" Mom says. "See what I said about early bedtimes?"

When she steals glances in the mirror, Emmy doesn't see badness. She sees a girl who deserves a "happily ever after" as much as Jessica does.

"This is where you hang out?" Haley asks. Beneath the trees' green tunnel, it's earthy-cool. If Emmy squints right, she can almost pretend they're in a real forest.

"Yeah."

She's not taking Haley near the tiger. Closer to the tennis courts, the path dips down beside the stream. The reeds haven't choked it yet; last winter's dead leaves meld into a mulchy smell that Emmy likes. They find a tree with branches sticking out low and straight, perfect for propping sticks against. While Emmy gathers dead wood, Haley sticks pine needles and clods of earth in the cracks.

Sometimes their fingers brush when they're arranging sticks. Emmy wonders if Haley notices.

In the distance, twigs snap and leaves rustle. Emmy frowns, scanning the path. She hasn't fed the tiger in two days—is it hungry enough to leave the grove? She's *pretty* sure it wouldn't eat Haley, but she's not ready for anyone else to see it yet.

"You okay?" Haley asks.

"Thought I heard something."

"A dog, maybe? Hey, I think we're done." Haley scoots inside the fort and grins at Emmy. "Come inside!"

While Emmy takes a seat, Haley peers out the gap they left as a window. After a minute or two, she turns around. "Wanna play Truth or Dare? I'll go first. Truth."

"Have you ever . . . uh, cheated on a test?'

"No way!" Haley giggles. "Okay, Truth or Dare?"

"Truth."

"Have you ever had a crush on anyone?"

Emmy's jaw keeps sticking. "Yeah."

The fort isn't very big, and somehow, Haley's migrating closer. Their knees are *almost* touching. "Truth," Haley says.

"Have *you* ever had a crush?" Emmy says.

Haley's dimple deepens. "Yeah."

There's a long silence. Emmy clears her throat. "Dare."

Haley glances out the window again. "I dare you . . ." She waits a long time. "I dare you to kiss me. On the cheek."

Oh. *Oh.* Their knees bump. Blood rushes in Emmy's temples. Wiping her hands on the hem of her fancy purple shirt, she takes a deep breath. Haley's half turned, cheek presented and waiting. Fighting the butterflies in her stomach, Emmy inches forward. She tilts her head, and—

"Oh my *God!*"

The butterflies turn to knives.

"She was actually gonna do it!"

Emmy shoves herself backward. Just outside the fort stand Jessica and her minions, laughing and laughing. They clutch disposable cameras from Shoppers Drug Mart. As Emmy gapes, Jessica lifts her camera higher.

Click. The flash blurs through tears.

Haley's laughing too, hard and mocking. The dimple's never been deeper. "Oh my God. Jessica, it worked."

Click.

Click click click click.

The fire goes so hot, it freezes. Sudden burning coldness drives like snow, burying Emmy whole. Distant buzzing fills her ears; otherwise, there's nothing but blankness and ruin.

She stalks past the other girls without saying a word. When they follow her, she breaks into a run; it doesn't take long to lose them in the bush. Silent, she staggers into the tiger's grove.

It waits for her, yellow eyes calm, paws crossed. Emmy splits herself along the same seam as always, but her badness seeps out frigid and slow and translucent blue. When she lifts it, it burns like frostbite.

The tiger snarls, but Emmy hesitates. This sin is beautiful, like breaking winter. Sharp edges and frost too deep to thaw. For the first time, she doesn't want to give it away. It came from her; it belongs to her. And the coldness feels good, it feels clean and hard and right.

Voices ring nearby. Twigs snap under approaching feet. The tiger tilts its head, waiting. *Come,* its eyes say. *Take. Eat.*

With the woods her table, Emmy lifts the coldness to her mouth. She holds it on her tongue, savoring the sting before swallowing. It runs through every vein, down to the tips of her toes.

"I think she went this way!"

The tiger smiles. A gentle, calm smile, one that *knows* her. She recognizes that smile, but she's never understood it, not really. As the coldness spreads, Emmy loses herself in the tiger's golden gaze. Her bones crack, her blood freezes to stopping.

It all happens in a moment, in the twinkling of an eye.

Then she rises, glorious, the sunlight shattering on her fur.

MEG ELISON

The Pill

FROM *Big Girl*

MY MOTHER TOOK the Pill before anybody even knew about it. She was always signing up for those studies at the university, saying she was doing it because she was bored. I think she did it because they would ask her questions about herself and listen carefully when she answered. Nobody else did that.

She had done it for lots of trials: sleep studies and allergy meds. She tried signing up when they tested the first 3D-printed IUDs, but they told her she was too old. I remember her raging about that for days, and later when everybody in that study got fibroids she was really smug about it. She never suggested I do it instead; she knew I wasn't fucking anybody. How embarrassing that my own mother didn't even believe I was cute enough to get a date at sixteen. I tried not to care. And I'm glad now I didn't get fibroids. I never wanted to be a lab rat anyway. Especially when the most popular studies (and the ones Mom really went all-out for) were the diet ones.

She did them all: the digital calorie monitors that she wore on her wrists and ankles for six straight weeks. (I rolled my eyes at that one, but at least she didn't talk about it constantly.) The strings like clear licorice made of some kind of super-cellulose that were supposed to accumulate in her stomach lining and give her a no-surgery stomach stapling but just made her (and everyone else who didn't eat a placebo) fantastically constipated. (Unstoppable complaining about this one; I couldn't bring anyone home for weeks for fear that she'd abruptly start telling my friends about her struggle to shit.) Pill after pill after pill that gave her heart palpitations, made her hair fall out, or (on one memorable occasion) induced psychotic delusions. If it was a way out of being fat, she'd try it. She'd try anything.

In between the drug trials, she did all the usual diets. Eat like a caveman. Eat like a rabbit. Seven small meals. Fasting one day a week. Apple cider vinegar bottles with dust on their upper domes sat tucked into the back corners of our every kitchen cabinet, behind the bulwark of Fig Newmans and Ritz crackers.

She'd try putting the whole family on a diet, talk us into taking "family walks" in the evening. She'd throw out all the junk food and make us promise to love ourselves more. Loving yourself means crying over the scale every morning and then sniffling into half a grapefruit, right? Nothing stuck and nothing made any real difference. We all resisted her, eating in secret in our rooms or out of the house. I found Dad's bag of fish taco wrappers jammed under the driver's seat of the car while looking for my headphones. Mom caught me putting it in the garbage and yelled at me for like an hour. I never told her it was his. She was always hardest on me about my weight, as if I was the only one who had this problem. We were a fat family. Mom was just as fat as me; we looked like we were built to the same specs. Dad was fat, and my brother was the fattest of us all.

I'm still fat. Everyone else is in the past tense.

And why? Because of this fucking Pill.

That trial started the same way they always do: flyers all over campus where Mom worked, promising cash for the right demographic for an exciting new weight-loss solution. Mom jumped on it like she always did, taking a pic of the poster so she could email from the comfort of her broken-down armchair with the TV tray rolled up close and her laptop permanently installed there. I remember I asked her once why she even had a laptop if she never took it anywhere. She never even unplugged it! It might as well have been an old-school tower and monitor rig. Why go portable if you're never going to leave the port?

She shrugged. "Why call it a laptop when I don't have a lap?"

She had me there. I could never sit my computer in my "lap" either. That real estate was taken up by my belly when I sat, and it was terribly uncomfortable to have a screen down that low, anyway. I've seen people do it on the train, and they look all hunched and bent. But Mom wanted the hunching and the bending. She wanted a flat, empty lap and a hot computer balanced on her knees. She wanted inches of clearance between her hips and an airline seat and to buy the clothes she saw on the mannequin in the window. She wanted what everybody wants. Respect.

I guess I wanted that, too. I just didn't think it was worth the lengths she would go to to get it. And none of them really worked. Until the Pill.

So Mom signed up like she always did, putting the meetings and dosage times on the calendar. Dad rolled his eyes and said he hoped this time didn't end with her crying about not being able to take a shit again. He met my eyes behind her back and we both smiled.

She just clucked her tongue at him. "Your language, Carl, honestly. You've been out of the navy a long time."

Dad tapped his pad and put in time to meet with his D&D buddies while Mom was busy with this new trial group. I smiled a little. I was glad he was going to do something fun. He had seemed pretty down lately. I was going to be busy, too. I had Visionaries, my school's filmmaking club. We had shoots set up every night for two weeks, trying to make this gonzo horror movie about a virus that turned the football team into cannibals. (Look, I didn't write it. I was the director of photography.)

Off Mom went to eat pills and answer questions about her habits. I had heard her go through all of this before and learned to hold my tongue. But I knew exactly how it would go: Mom would sit primly in a chair in a nice outfit, trying to cross her legs and never being able to hold that position. Her thighs would spread out on top of one another and slowly slide apart, seeking the space to sag around the arms of the chair and make her seem wider than ever, like a water balloon pooling on a hot sidewalk. She would never tell the whole truth. It was maybe the thing I hated about her the most.

"Oh yes, I exercise every day!"

She walked about twenty minutes a day total, from her car to her office and back again. Her treadmill was covered in clothes on hangers, and her dumbbells were fuzzed with a mortar made of dust and cat hair.

"I try to eat right, but I have bad habits that stem from stress."

Rain or shine, good day or bad, Mom had three scoops of ice cream with caramel sauce every night at ten.

"I do think I come by it honestly. My parents were both heavy.
And my sisters and most of my cousins, too."

That one's true. The whole family is fat. In our last family photo,
we wore an assortment of bright-colored shirts and we looked like
a basket of round, ripe fruit. I kind of liked it, but I think I might
have been the only one. The composition of the shots was good,
and we all looked happy. Happy wasn't enough, apparently. Mom
paid for those, but she never hung them up.

She came home from the first few sessions chatty and keyed
up. She posted on her timelines how happy she was to be trying something really innovative and how she had a good feeling
about this one. She wasn't allowed to say much; they made her
sign an NDA. Later, I think she was glad that nobody could ask
her the details.

I knew this time was going to be different the first night I heard
the screaming. I had been up way past midnight, trying to edit
footage of football players lumbering, meat-crazed, hands outstretched against the outline of the goalposts in a sunset-orange
sky. My eyes had gotten hot and I'd had to put two icepacks under
my laptop to cool down the CPU. (The machine just wasn't up to
all that processing and rendering.) I woke up at four to the sound
of it, jolting upright, my heart in my ears like someone had stuffed
a tiny drum set into my head. I was so tired and out of it, I almost
didn't know what I was hearing. But it was her voice. Mom was
screaming like she was on fire. She did it so long and loud and
unbroken that I couldn't understand how she could get her breath
at all. It was out, out, out, and hardly a gasp in.

I ran into the hallway and smacked straight into Andrew, who
was going the same way. We whacked belly against belly and fell
backward on our butts like a couple of cartoon characters. I can
picture it exactly in my head and imagine the way I'd frame it,
the sound effects we could layer over the top. But in the moment,
there was no time to laugh or argue. We just scrambled back up
and made for our parents' bedroom door.

It was locked.

"Dad!" I hammered my fist against the hollow-core six-panel
barrier. "Dad, what's happening? Is Mom okay?"

There was an unintelligible string of sounds from him. With
Mom screaming like a steam whistle, there was no chance to make
it out.

"I'm calling 911," Andrew yelled. His phone was already in his hand.

When the door opened, the sound of Mom's screaming hit us at full force, and Andrew and I both stumbled backward a little. The door had muffled it only slightly, but when the sound is your own mother dying, a little counts for a lot.

Dad was there, his gray hair a mess that pointed fingers in every direction, seeming to blame everyone at once. He put a hand out to Andrew, his face in a grimace, his eyes wide.

"Don't. Don't call anyone. Your mother says this is part of the trial she's in. She said it's worse than she thought it would be, but it only lasts for fifteen minutes."

Andrew looked at his phone. "I woke up almost ten minutes ago, when she was just growling."

"Growling," I asked. "What?"

Andrew rolled his eyes. "You could sleep through a nuclear strike."

Dad was nodding, looking at his watch. "We're almost out of it. Just hold on."

"Dad," Andrew said, "the neighbors probably already called the cops. She's really loud."

Dad's grimace widened. "I'm going to have to—"

The screaming stopped. The three of us looked at each other.

"Carl?" Mom's voice sounded exhausted and raw.

Dad fixed us both with a stern look, oscillating between the two of us. "You two don't call anyone. You don't tell anyone. Your mother is entitled to a little privacy. Is that understood?"

We looked at each other and said nothing.

Mom called again and he was gone, back on the other side of the door.

I didn't go back to sleep. I'm betting Andrew didn't either. But we stayed in our rooms for the next three hours, until it was time for breakfast. I went back to editing footage, and I was pretty pleased with what I'd be able to show to the Visionaries the next day. The movie was going to come in on schedule. It was great to have a project, something to take my mind off the weirdness in the night. I'm betting Andrew just signed on to his game. That's all he ever does.

I heard him turn off his alarm on the other side of the wall, followed by the sound of him standing up out of his busted com-

puter chair with a grunt. He's way fatter than me, so I feel like I'm
allowed to be disgusted by some of his habits. Andrew can't sit or
stand without making a guttural, bovine noise. I've seen crumbs
trapped in the folds of his neck. I used to work really hard to not
be one of Those Fat People. I was obsessively clean, took impecca-
ble care of my skin. I never showed my upper arms or my thighs,
no matter what the occasion. I acted like being fat was impolite,
like burping, and the best thing to do was conceal it behind the
back of my hand and then always, always beg somebody's pardon.

I didn't know anything back then.

Andrew made it to the stairs before I did, so I got to watch him
jiggle and shuffle down them, filled with loathing and disgust. I
couldn't remember what bullshit diet we were supposed to be following that week, but I vowed to myself that no matter how small
breakfast was, I would eat less of it than Andrew. I would leave
something behind on the plate. Let Andrew be the one to lick his
fingers and whine. I was above all that. Wheat toast and cut apples
were waiting for us when we came into the kitchen.

And there was Mom at the coffeepot, fifty pounds lighter. Her
pajamas hung off her like a hand-me-down from a much bigger
sister. She turned, cup in hand, and I saw the dark circles beneath
her eyes. She was beaming, however, with the biggest smile I'd
seen on her face in years.

"It's working," she said, her voice still rough and edged with
fatigue like she'd been to a rock concert or an all-night bonfire.
"This thing is actually working."

That was our life for two weeks. Dad did his best to soundproof
their bathroom. He stapled carpets and foam and egg crate to the
walls. He covered the floor in a dozen fluffy bath mats he bought
cheaply on the internet. He told me later that he tried to put a rag
in her mouth, just to muffle her a little more.

"But I'm worried she'll pull it into her throat and choke on
it," he told me, his eyes wide with dread. "I can't stand this much
longer. I know she's losing weight, but it's like I'm living in a nightmare and I can't wake up."

That was a year before he decided to take the Pill, and back
then he was more willing to talk about it. When it wasn't his own
privacy, only hers, he would tell me how gross it was. You can see
videos of it online. It was the same in that first trial as it is now: you
take the Pill and you shit out your fat cells. In huge, yellow, un-

manageable flows at first. That's why they scream so much. Imagine shitting fifty pounds of yourself at a go. Now, people go to special spas where they have crematoiletaries that burn the fat down. Dad said Mom screwed up our plumbing so bad that he had to buy a whole case of that lye-based stuff to break it all down and keep the toilet flushing. That was as gross as I thought things could get, but Dad said it got worse.

Toward the end, Mom (and everyone like her) shit out all their extra skin, too. The process that broke it down meant no stretch marks and no baggy leftovers, hanging on your body like overproofed dough on a hook and telling people you used to be fat.

That was some trick, and it was part of the reason it took so long for a generic to hit the market. It was a "trade secret," they said on the news. They also said "miracle" and "breakthrough" and "historic." The miracle of shitting out skin just looked like blood and collagen and rotten meat, it turns out. Not less gross, but different. More lye into the S bend. More and more of Mom gone at the breakfast table.

At the end of the trial, she was a person I didn't recognize. She was 110 pounds soaking wet. The research doctor told her that she was at 18 percent body fat and would stay that way for the rest of her life. Her face was a whole new shape, with the underlying structure very prominent and her eyes huge and wide above it all. I could see her hip bones beneath her enormous drawstring pants, pulled tight as a laundry bag around her now-tiny waist. Her collarbones could have held up a taco each. The cords in her neck stood out like chicken bones caught under her skin. Even her feet were smaller—she went down one whole shoe size, and I inherited all her stretched-out sandals and sneakers.

I slid my feet into them, thinking how it was like my mom had died and some other woman had moved in. Late at night, I gathered up all the clothes she had given me and bundled them into the garbage. They were ugly, but they also felt somehow humiliating to wear. I couldn't explain the impulse. Luckily, she never asked me where any of it went. She was very focused on herself in those days.

"It finally happened," Mom told me with tears in her eyes. "They finally made a Pill that gives you the perfect body, no matter what."

And yeah, she could eat anything she wanted and didn't have to work out. As long as she kept taking the small maintenance dose of the Pill, she would stay this way for as long as she lived. Which she thought would be much longer, now that she didn't have to carry around the threats of diabetes and heart disease everywhere she went.

I remember one day I walked in and found her and Dad sitting at the kitchen table, both of them obviously crying. They tried to hide it from me; Dad ducked his face into the shawl collar of his sweater, Mom swiping her eyes with quick fingers.

"What's up with you guys?" I asked, trying not to look.

"Nothing, honey. There's carrot and celery sticks cut fresh and sitting in water in the fridge, if you want a snack."

Mom's voice was thick in her throat; she'd really been sobbing.

I ignored both the sorrow and the content of what she'd said and fished around in the cabinet over the sink until I found one individually wrapped chocolate cupcake.

"I'm good," I said and tried to leave the kitchen.

"Honey, do you think I lost all this weight so that I could leave you guys?"

I stopped and turned on the spot like something on a rotating plate, a pizza in a microwave. I couldn't help it. I should have just kept walking.

"What?"

Dad buried his face some more. Mom just looked at me, her eyes all shiny. "Did you ever think that my desire to lose weight was about you? Like, do you feel like I'm trying to leave you behind?"

I stared at her. There wasn't anything I could say. How could I feel any other way? How did she not know how obvious she was? Every diet, every scheme, every study was just her trying to find a way out of being what we are. Every time she tried to change who she was, who we all were, it was like betrayal.

I looked over at Dad and realized this wasn't about me. He was worried she was going to *physically* leave him, now that she thought she was hot enough to hook up with somebody else. I saw it all at once: the way she was never worried about me being on birth control, the way Dad looked at other women in the supermarket. The way all of us were so focused on what we looked like, as if it mattered, as if being thin was the only kind of life worth living.

So I lied.

"No, Mom. I don't think about it at all, I guess. It really has nothing to do with me."

I left them alone and went to eat my cupcake in peace. I looked at the timer I'd had running on my phone since the beginning of junior year: the countdown to the day I'd leave for college. I wanted out even then, but I hadn't sent out applications yet. Back then, two years seemed like forever.

Mom and Dad made up, I guess. They never told us anything that mattered. Anyway, that was when the deaths started to make the news.

The averages are still debated all the time, because preexisting conditions can't be ruled out. But people seem to agree it's about one in ten. In each group of thirty participants in the early studies, ten were control, ten got the placebo, and the final ten got the Pill. Nine out of ten shit themselves to perfection. That tenth one, though. They ended up slumped on a toilet, blood vessels burst in their eyes, hearts blown out by the strain of converting hundreds of pounds of body mass to waste.

I never thought it would get approved with a 10 percent fatality rate, but I guess I was really naive. The truth was it got fast-tracked and approved by the FDA within a year. Mom was in a commercial, talking about how it gave her her life back, but this was a life she had never had. It gave her someone else's life entirely. Some life she had never even planned for. In the commercial, she wore a teal sports bra and a lot of makeup. I did not recognize her at all. She stood next to that celebrity, the one who did it first. What's her name—Amy Blanton.

Remember those ads? "Get the Amy Blanton body!" She had gained a little weight after she had her kids, but her Before picture and Mom's Before picture looked like members of two different species. In the commercial, their former selves got *whisked* away, and there they were: exactly the same height, exactly the same build. A little contouring and a blowout made them twins. Mom had the Amy Blanton body. For just a little while, people would stop her on the street and ask if she *was* Amy Blanton. That got old fast. I used to just walk away fatly while she pretended she looked nothing like her TV twin.

I watched Dad grow more and more insecure about the change in Mom. I saw him get mad at a guy at the gas station who checked out Mom's ass when she bent over.

"Get back in the car, Carl. Gosh, you're making a scene about nothing. It was just a compliment!"

Dad sat down, fuming, but he wouldn't close his door. His ears were bright red. Andrew was playing a game on his phone, totally zoned out. I watched Dad trying to calm himself down.

"You probably haven't been jealous about Mom since you guys were kids, huh?"

He blew out hot air through his nose like a bull. "Try *ever*," he said, his voice tight.

"Wasn't Mom hot as a teenager?"

His lips closed into a line I could see in the rearview mirror. "She was always heavy. She was . . . she was *mine*, god damn it."

That sort of shocked me. He hadn't ever talked about her that way before. And it hadn't ever occurred to me that maybe my dad the football player had gotten with my less-than-perfect mom because he knew she'd never cheat on him. Could never. Just like she thought I could never go out and get myself in trouble. Because fat girls don't fuck, I guess?

I looked over at Andrew, too big for a seat belt, pooling against the car door. Did fat boys fuck? Was anybody going to pick him because he'd be *theirs*? I didn't want to imagine. But just as I was feeling sorry for us all, Mom slid lithely back into the car.

"Don't be a goose, honey," she said. She laid a hand on Dad's knee. "You have nothing to worry about."

That turned out to be a lie.

It was about a month after FDA approval when Dad announced to us that he was gonna take the Pill.

I couldn't help but give Mom the look of death. He'd never have done it if she hadn't gone first and made him worry about losing her. Andrew grunted at the news the way he grunted at everything, as if nothing in the world held much interest for him.

I hate crying, but I burst into tears. I couldn't even yell at Mom. I just wanted to talk Dad out of it. I tried for weeks, and I ended up trying again on the day he began treatment. I just had this feeling in my gut that he was going to be one of the unlucky ones.

"One in ten," I croaked at him, my voice wrecked by crying. "One in *ten*, Dad. It's just slightly better odds than Russian roulette."

He smiled from his spa-hospital bed with the special trench installed below. He was wearing one of those paper gowns, and I thought how stupid he would feel dying in paper clothes while taking a shit. Was it worth it? How could it be worth it?

"But the odds of dying young if I stay fat are much worse," he told me in his sweet voice. He reached out and put a hand on my shoulder, and I heard his gown rustling like trash dragging through the gutter when it's windy. "Don't worry, Munchkin. It's in god's hands."

I guess it was, but I had never trusted god not to drop stuff and break it.

Dad made it to the third treatment. It felt cruel, like I had just started to relax and believe that he might be okay.

We came back and saw him on day one, down about fifty pounds and looking like someone had slapped him around all night.

"Honey, you look wonderful," Mom cooed, kissing his cheeks and hugging him to her middle. Andrew had stayed home. I looked him up and down, remembering the way Mom had just melted to reveal the stranger within.

"You look okay," I managed to say.

"I told you, kiddo." We sat with him while he ate some graham crackers and drank lots of water. My parents held hands.

I skipped the second visit. The knots in my stomach were huge and twisting, and I just couldn't face it. Mom came home whistling and very pleased with herself.

"He's in the home stretch now! I can't wait for you kids to see what your dad really looks like."

I just sat there, wondering if I was real. Are fat people fake? Do we not have souls? Does nothing I do count if I do it while I'm fat? These were questions I had never really thought about before, but with both of my parents risking death to be less like me, I suddenly had to wonder about a lot of things.

I knew the minute Mom picked up the phone the next day. I could tell she wasn't expecting the call. She stared at it just a second too long before she picked it up. My film professor calls that a beat, like a drumbeat or a heartbeat. One beat too many, and I knew.

One beat too many and Dad's heart gave in.

Neither one of us could go with Mom to deal with the body. Andrew wouldn't even leave his room. I don't remember those weeks very clearly. I remember weird parts.

Mom buying Dad a new suit he could be buried in, because nothing he owned would fit. Mom saying Dad wouldn't want to be cremated, now that he was thin. Dad's D&D buddies looking into his casket and saying how great he looked. The never-ending grief buffet of casseroles and cake in our kitchen. The nights when I could hear Mom crying through the vents.

That should have been the last of it. Other people could die, even famous people, but the Pill killed my dad. That should have been it, end of story, illegal forever. But that's not how anything works. The world is just allowed to wound you any way it wants and move on.

And so are the people you know.

The minute Andrew brought it up, I almost laughed. There was no way Mom was going to let him do it, after what had happened to Dad. Maybe we weren't the best of buds, but I didn't want him to die.

I could hear her in his room, and she was never in his room. It was permadark in there, blackout shades on the windows and nothing but the dim blue glow of his monitors to light it. I could hear them talking and I came close to the door, not quite putting my ear to it.

"I'm too old to be on your insurance," he said. "But they're saying there's gonna be a generic within a year, so it'll probably be cheaper."

"I think that's the best idea, sweetheart. But you're still going to have to pay for your hospital stay. We have a little money from Dad's insurance, so I can help you with that. It's what your father would have wanted."

I pushed the door open, already yelling. "No. No. No. No. It is not what Dad would have wanted. Dad would have wanted to be alive. Do you want to end up dead, too?"

They both stared at me like I had come through the door on fire.

"What is the matter with you?"

"Yeah," Andrew sneered. "Don't you knock?"

Mom put her hands on her hips. "This is a private conversation, kiddo."

"I don't give a shit," I told them. "We just buried our dad, and you want to take the Pill that killed him. How stupid can you be?"

Andrew shrugged. "Ninety percent is still an A."

"And dead is still dead," I said at once. "There's no curve on that."

Mom came and took my elbow and walked me back toward the

door. "You're letting your emotions get the best of you," she said. I could hear her voice trembling, and when I looked up her eyes were wet in the dim blue light of the bedroom. "I miss him too, but I don't let it cloud my judgment. Your brother needs to do what's best for him."

"It's better for him to be dead than fat," I shot back. "Is that really what you think?"

We both turned back to look at Andrew.

Andrew would never tell me his actual weight, but I had heard him say once that he was in the "five club." Nothing fit him but the absolute biggest shirts and elastic-waistband shorts, and he wouldn't wear shoes that had to be tied. His fingers were so fat he could barely use his phone and finally upgraded to one with a stylus.

He sighed at us both. "I'm tired of this," he said to me, but Mom started to cry. "I'm tired of never going out and never fitting in a chair. I'm tired of getting stared at and having to hide from people to eat. Aren't you tired of it, sis?"

I shrugged. "I'm not tired of being alive."

I didn't convince him. I didn't convince Mom. She gave him the money and he checked himself in. I went with them, only because I was worried I wouldn't get to say goodbye otherwise.

Andrew was twenty-four when he did it, and his doctor had to get his digs in first. I remember his old-man chuckle as he lined my brother up next to the chart on the wall. "Well, son. You're not going to get any taller. And let's quit getting wider while we can, shall we?"

Andrew laughed with him, as if his fat self was already somebody else. Someone who it was okay to laugh at. My thin mom laughed, too. Somewhere in thin heaven, was Dad laughing? Already I was an anomaly on the streets. I'm sure it used to be hard to be fat in LA or New York. I've read about that. But living in Dayton, Ohio, meant always fitting in the booth at a restaurant and never being the only fat person in the room. By the time Andrew got the Pill, I couldn't count on those things anymore. A year later, the whole world was shrinking around me, and I could already feel the pinch.

Andrew came home from the hospital looking like some other guy; a dude who played basketball and got called Slim. His eyes were bright.

"Munchkin, I can't wait for you to do it. It's amazing! I mean, it's super gross and really painful, but after that it's the fucking awesomest."

They had all called me Munchkin since I was a kid. Not because I was short and cute, but because they said I was always munching. I hated that nickname and he knew it. He was just using it now to remind me I was the only one left.

"You look like Dad looked in his casket," I said.

He tried for a little while to go out and enjoy his new thin life, but he didn't really know how. He couldn't talk to anybody. He missed his online friends and he hated the sunlight, the noise, the feeling of people always around, sizing him up. He had a new body, but it didn't matter.

I watched Andrew go back to his gaming pod; the ruined chair with the cracked spar he had fixed with duct tape no longer sagging or groaning beneath him. The same shiny spots on his computer where he kept his hands in the same positions for fourteen hours at a time while he pretended he was a tall, muscular Viking warrior on some Korean server every day. I watched him settle right back into his old life using his new body and wondered what it was for. He really was the Viking now. He could have put on boots and left the house and had a real adventure. But adventure didn't appeal to him.

I was stuck between them in the house. I always had been, but Dad and I had understood each other. We had been a team. I guess I was a daddy's girl, but I was never spoiled like that. We just got along. Andrew was silent and Mom never shut up. Dad was the only one I could talk to, or sit in silence with without feeling bad.

And now I was the only fat member of the family. Slowly but surely, even the aunts and cousins signed up to take the Pill. I started to joke with my friends in Visionaries that fat people were going to become an endangered species.

Some of them laughed, but a couple suggested we actually make a short film about that. We kicked the idea around, but mostly they wanted to film me eating in a cage while people stared. I didn't know how that would get anything meaningful across, and they didn't know how not to be thin assholes. So we dropped the idea.

Mom was at least using the way she had changed to enjoy the real world a little more. She wore workout clothes constantly, all bright colors and clinging like the patterning on a snake. Every day she got to enjoy the way people looked at her brightly now, eyebrows up, not searching for their first chance to sidle away.

"People just respond to me so much better now," she said in one of her interviews. "It changes everything about my daily interactions. I'm a mother and a widow, and I don't need a lot of attention," she had said, smiling coyly. "But even the mailman is happier to see me than he ever was before."

I wanted to barf when she said she didn't need attention. She had been thirsty enough before to talk to absolutely anyone, even sign up to take injections and hypnosis to get it. Now she was always posing and watching to see who would look. Attention was like the drug she couldn't get enough of. She still ate the same bowl of ice cream every night, sitting next to the groove in the couch where Dad used to fit. No, Mom, you didn't need attention. You took the Pill, you let the Pill take Dad because you were so A-OK with yourself.

The Pill sold like nothing had ever sold before. The original, the generic, the knockoffs, the different versions approved in Europe and Asia that met their standards and got rammed through their testing. There was at last a cure for the obesity epidemic. Fat people really were an endangered species. And everybody was so, so glad.

One in ten kept dying. The average never improved, not in any corner of the globe. There were memorials for the famous and semifamous folks who took the gamble and lost. A congressman here and a comedian there. But everyone was so proud of them that they had died trying to better themselves that all the obituaries and eulogies had a weird, wistful tone to them. As if it was the next best thing to being thin. At least they didn't have to live that fat life anymore.

And every time it was on the news, we sat in silence and didn't talk about Dad.

I was just a kid when Mom made it through the original trial that unleashed the Pill on the world. It wasn't approved for teenagers, not anywhere. Don't get me wrong; teens and parents alike were more than ready to sign up for the one-in-ten odds of dying. But the scientists who had worked on the Pill said unequivocally that it should not be taken by anyone who was not absolutely done growing. Eighteen was the minimum, but they recommended twenty-one to be completely safe.

On my eighteenth birthday, my mom threw me a party. She invited all my friends (mostly the Visionaries) and decorated the backyard with yellow roses and balloons.

It was the first time since Dad died that the house seemed cheerful. Mom ordered this huge lemon cake at the good bakery, with layers of custard filling and sliced strawberries. I remember everybody moaning over how good it was, how summery-sweet. People danced, but I felt too self-conscious to get up and give it a try. My mom ended up dancing with a neighbor who heard the music and came through the gate to check it out. He was skinny, too, and I couldn't watch them together.

We ate barbecue ribs and I got to tell people over and over again where I'd gotten into college. Northwestern. Rutgers. Cornell. And UCLA. Where was I going to go? Oh, I hadn't decided yet, but I needed to pick soon.

Except I definitely had. I had wanted to study filmmaking my whole life. Everybody in the Visionaries club knew that; they had all applied to UCLA and USC. A few of us got in. It wasn't just that it was my dream school in the golden city where movies were made. It was also about as far away as I could get. Mom reminded me that I could go anywhere in-state for free because of her job, saying it over and over with that look in her eye, the one that said *don't leave me,* but I was going to LA if I had to walk every mile.

When it came time for presents, I got some jewelry from my grandmother. She didn't come and I couldn't blame her; she was my dad's mom. A lace parasol from my friends, who all expected I'd need protection from the sun sometime soon. Books and music and a clever coffee cup. A fountain pen. The kinds of things that signal adulthood is about to begin.

My mom, beaming, gave me the Pill.

"I can't give you the physical thing, of course," she said, glancing around for a laugh. She got a little one. She handed me her iPad. "This has all of the paperwork, showing that you've been approved and my insurance will cover it. Plus, I booked your spa stay so that you'll have time to buy all new clothes before leaving for school." She smiled like she'd never killed my dad.

"I don't . . . know what to say," I said finally. If I said what I was actually feeling, it might mean she wouldn't pay for school, I'd be on my own. I had to swallow it. But I'd be damned if I was gonna swallow that Pill.

The party broke up slowly, with the neighbor guy hanging around and trying to talk to Mom until she texted Andrew and made him come down and walk the guy out. I packed up all my presents. I thanked Mom as sincerely as I could. I wrapped up slices of cake for people who wanted to take them home. And I seethed.

I left for UCLA two weeks early. I told Mom I was planning to come back and take my medicine over Thanksgiving break. She said she understood my delay, that I was just worried I'd pull the short straw and that it was okay to be nervous. She put me on the plane to Los Angeles with tears in her eyes.

On the flight, it was me and one other fat kid, maybe ten years old. That was it. The woman who sat next to me huffed and whined about it until the flight attendant brought her a free drink to shut her up. It was the first time I had ever been on a plane, and I sat there wondering whether it was always as uncomfortable as this. I could see the other fat kid up a few rows, hanging his elbow and one knee into the aisle. He wasn't even full-grown and already he was too big for an airplane seat. I wished we had been sitting together. We would have recognized each other. It would have been like having family again. Everyone else had that same Pill body.

And it was always the exact same body. No more thick thighs or really round asses. No more wide tits or pointy pecs or love handles rounding out someone's sides. Everyone's body was flat planes and straight lines. It wasn't just that they were thin. They were all somehow the same.

In LA the change was striking. I had heard that even thin people were taking the Pill out there to ensure that they'd never gain any weight, but I didn't believe it until I started seeing the change on TV and in movies. One by one, distinctive shapes disappeared. It was always the Amy Blanton body, like my mom had. The guys all had the same Ethan Fairbanks body. He once did a bunch of ads with some nobody. Only faces and hair color, a little difference in height could distinguish one actor from another. Here and there, a death. Worth it, everyone whispered like a prayer. Worth it, worth it, worth it.

I made it a few months at UCLA. My classes were cool and I started to make friends right off. But little things kept piling up. I went to the student store to buy myself a UCLA hoodie and they had nothing that would fit me. It wasn't even close. I looked at the largest size in the men's section and even then it would have clung to me like the skin of a sausage. I decided I could live without that ubiquitous symbol of college life, but I was pissed. I even thought about buying one just to snip the logo out and sew it onto a hoodie in my size from Walmart.

Then Walmart stopped carrying plus sizes altogether.

There were no desks on campus that I could sit at. A few of the classrooms had long tables with detached chairs and those were all right. But the majority of my freshman classes were in those big lecture halls, with the rows and rows of wooden chair-and-desk combinations. I couldn't wedge myself into one to save my life. My first or second day I tried really hard in the back row and just got a big bruise over my lowest rib for my troubles. I sat in the aisle, on the steps, or against the back wall every day. There just wasn't any space for me.

My dorm room was the same way. The bed was narrow and I could hear the whole frame groaning the second I lay down. The bathroom was so small that I could touch both walls with my thighs when I sat on the toilet. My roommate was so thin I knew she hadn't taken the Pill—she still looked too original. But over the course of the first week, I realized that was because she never ate. I asked her to lunch a couple of times, but she always said no. I couldn't save her. I was working on how to save myself.

Days ticked by and Thanksgiving break was bearing down on me. My mom kept calling, telling me how great it was going to be when I went back to the school in my ideal body.

"I don't know that it'll be my ideal body," I told her. "It'll just be different."

"Don't you want to go on dates like the other girls?" Her voice was so whiny I could barely stand it.

I looked across the room to the other girl I lived with. She was in her bra, and every time she breathed in I could see the impressions of her individual ribs against the skin of her back. She was doing her reading and sucking on her bottom lip as if her lip gloss might offer some calories.

"I don't know that I want anything other girls have," I told her. But that wasn't true. Most girls had fathers.

"You don't know what you're missing," Mom said. "Come on home and let's get you squared away."

"Soon," I told her, counting the days until I had to let them try to kill me for being what I am.

I had been there about a month when I knew I wasn't going to make it. The stares had become unmanageable. I wasn't the last fat girl in LA, was I? People on campus avoided me like I was a radioactive werewolf who stank like a dead cat in a hot garage. I remember one time I tried to take a selfie to send home to the Visionaries and someone gasped out loud. In the picture, I could see him, mouth open like he'd glimpsed a ghost.

And in a way I guess I was. I was the ghost of fatness past, haunting the open breezeways of UCLA. I was what they used to be, what they had always feared they would become. I became obsessed with the terrible power of my fatness; I was the worst that could possibly happen to someone. Worse than death, had to be, because somewhere my dad was rotting in a box because that was easier than living in a body like mine. I knew when I frightened people and I pushed my advantage. I took up their space. I haunted them with my warm breath and my soft elbows. I fed on their fright.

It was early November, and I could not adjust to the lack of seasons. It was still warm and sunny like June on the California coast. I missed home, but the idea of home repelled me. I needed comfort.

I walked myself over to the cheap pancake house and ordered the never-ending stack and coffee. The all-you-can-eat pancake special was always a favorite with frat boys, and its popularity had only increased since the Pill hit the market. People who really loved to eat could finally do it without worrying that it would ruin their lives.

The hostess tried to seat me in a booth and I just rolled my eyes at her. I was not about to eat my weight in pancakes with a Formica tabletop wedged just beneath my sternum.

"A table, please."

She stuck me in the back, next to the restrooms. I didn't care.

My first four pancakes showed up hot and perfect and I asked for extra butter. When they were just right (dripping, not soaked and turning into paste) I shoveled up huge bites into my waiting mouth, letting it fill me as nothing else did. Who could care that they were the last of their kind when the zoo had such good food?

And yeah, people were staring. People are always staring at me. That was a constant of my existence, and I was used to it. I ignored them. I slurped up hot coffee and wiped the plate down with the last bite of cake.

"Hit me again," I said, and the waitress took the plate away. A few minutes later, another fresh hot stack of pancakes appeared.

I didn't know how many times I could do it, but that was the day I was going to find out.

And then a man sat at my table.

He was perfectly ordinary, with brown hair and brown eyes. He had the Pill body underneath his tan suit. I looked him over.

"Can I help you?"

He stared at my mouth for a minute and I waited. "Do you have any idea how beautiful you are?" he finally asked.

I rolled my eyes hard and started to butter my pancakes. I was going to need more butter. "Fuck off, creep."

He put a hand against his own chest. "Please, I meant no disrespect. I'm being sincere. You're so lovely. So rare. I haven't seen a woman like you in almost a year."

I waved to the waitress but she didn't see me. I debated. I'd rather have the butter, but if the cakes got cold before it showed up, it would hardly matter at all. I scraped the dish that I had and began to cut up pancakes and ignore my visiting weirdo, hoping he would go away.

He cleared his throat and ordered a cup of coffee. "Please, allow me to entertain you while you eat and I'll pick up your check."

I sighed. Few things were as motivating as free food. So I let him sit.

He asked me about cinematography, about why I had come to LA. I talked in between cups of coffee and plates of pancakes.

"I had all these ideas about the story only I could tell when I got here. The things that were unique to my experience. It's funny now, because there was nothing unique about my experience. I guess everybody thinks they're one of a kind."

He glanced over his shoulder a little, then pushed the cream pitcher toward me for my coffee. "Look around. You nearly are."

I shrugged. "I guess. But there's no way to tell this story so that people will understand it. You ever see the way fat people on the street are shot for news stories? Headless and limbless and wide as the world, always wandering like they've got nowhere to be. That's the only story people know. We were always a joke, we were always invisible. And now, we're going to disappear. Because we were never meant to exist in the first place."

"Are you?" he asked, cocking an eyebrow. "Going to disappear?"

"Who the hell are you?" I finally asked.

He sighed and finished his coffee. "I can't tell you that. But I can show you something that might change your mind."

I don't know why I said yes. Maybe I was dreading going back to school where nothing fit. Maybe I just didn't want to answer the question of whether I was going to take the Pill. Maybe it was just the way he looked at me—really looked at me. Not like I was a problem to be solved or some walking glitch in the way things are supposed to work.

I got into a strange man's car outside of the pancake house and I let him show me.

The club was up in the hills, just off Mulholland Drive. It was in this gorgeous house, built in the golden age of Hollywood for some chiseled hunk who had died of AIDS. The lawn was perfect and I could smell the chlorine in the pool the minute I stepped out of the car. The neighborhood was the kind of quiet where you know that even the gardeners muffle their equipment.

My nameless escort walked up the stone path toward a wide, shaded, black front door. He looked back over his shoulder, glancing at me.

"You coming?"

I was.

It was dark inside the house at first, my eyes adjusting from the bright sunshine slowly. After a few minutes, I saw that it was merely dim. The living room was furnished beautifully, sumptuously, with a clear emphasis on texture and deep padding. The room was empty except for one woman, sitting on a chaise longue and reading a book.

We approached her and she looked up. She was an absolute knockout: a redhead with full lips and built like an hourglass that had time to spare. Her dress clung to her, making a clear case that she enjoyed being looked at. She was not walking around in an Amy Blanton body. She was an original.

The man I came in with tapped his fingers on the top of her

book and said, "In the chocolate war, I fought on the side of General Augustus."

The redhead nodded, not saying a word. She shifted in her seat and reached for something I couldn't see. Behind her, a bookshelf slid sideways, revealing a deep purple tunnel behind it.

I nodded to her as we passed, and she smiled at me with a hunger I couldn't put a name to. I had no idea where we were headed.

We walked through a series of rooms. The entire house was decorated in the same style as that first room: sensual, decadent, and plush. As I got to see more of it, I realized that everything was also built wide, sturdy, and I'd never think twice about sitting in any chair I saw.

In every room I passed, I saw the same thing as I peered through the door. There was a fat person surrounded by thin people staring at them. Some of the onlookers were crying, some were visibly aroused. Different races, different genders. All well-dressed. All nearly identical in those Pill bodies. A tall fat woman was lounging, shrouded by veils in a Turkish bed, nude and lolling and made of endless undulations of honey-colored flesh. She fed herself grapes while someone was making her laugh. Ten people sat around her bed, watching.

A fat man, as big as Andrew used to be, was dipping his gloved fists into paint and punching a blank, white wall. He was being videotaped and photographed, lit gorgeously while people murmured praise and encouragements.

In one room, a short Black woman whose curves defied gravity ran oil-slicked hands over her nudity, smiling a perfect, satisfied smile. Two men stood near her, their mouths open, hungering endlessly, asking nothing of her.

We came to an empty room that had a round tub at its end and a set of low stone benches. The domed ceiling made our footfalls sound epic. The water had steam rising off it, even in the warmth of the house, and smelled like the sea.

"Salt water," he said. "Much better for your skin. Would you like to take a dip? You don't have to talk to anyone or do anything, but some people may come join you. How does that sound?"

"I don't have a bathing suit."

His smile was slow and he dropped his chin like he was about to share a conspiracy. "Have you looked around? Nobody will mind."

"What are these people getting out of this? I don't need this."

He pulled out his phone and showed me the app that the house used to keep track of money. Each fat performer had an anonymous identifier and a live count of what they were making.

"Maybe I could persuade you to work for a couple of hours, just to see what you think? You'll make the house minimum, plus tips."

I watched the numbers climb up. "Just to sit here? I don't have to touch anybody? Or even make conversation?"

He nodded. "We'd prefer that you work in the nude, but you don't even have to do that. Just enjoy the hot soak. What do you say?"

It sounded weird as fuck, but I wanted two things immediately. First, I wanted the money. If I was going to go home and refuse the Pill, I was pretty sure I was going to need it. Second, I wanted to go back to the room where the boxing painter was being filmed. I itched to get behind a camera in this place, to tell the story of the endangered species of fat people. Not like the Visionaries had wanted it, but the way I wanted it. Like this. Dark and rich and seductive.

I got into the water in my bra and panties. I may as well have gotten naked; they were both white cotton and went see-through in the water. I tried not to think about it. I dunked my head, sat on one of the submerged steps, and soaked with my neck laid back against the rim.

I could hear people coming and going. I could hear the things they whispered to me. Voices in the salty dark called me rare and magnificent and soft and enticing. I said nothing. I didn't even hint that I could hear.

After a few hours, my nameless handler came back with a fluffy, soft towel the size of a bedsheet that smelled like lavender. He thanked me and showed me how to download the app to get paid.

I had been there for three hours, and I had more money than I had ever had at one time, in my entire life. He watched my face very closely when I saw the number.

"My name's Dan," he said softly.

"Do you own this place?"

"No, I'm just a recruiter. I'm going to give you my number."

I watched him type it into my phone as "Dan Chez Corps."

"What makes you think I'll call you?"

I thought he was going to remind me of how much money I had just made, but he didn't. He kinda shook his head a little, then asked, "Where else are you going to go?"

He had brought me replacements for my wet underthings, much nicer than the ones I was wearing. They were exquisite and well made and carried no tags.

"A gift from the house," he said, before leaving me to change. They fit like they were made for me.

I went back to the dorm and watched my roommate twitch in her sleep. Her side of the fridge held a single hard-boiled egg and a pint of skim milk. My bed groaned beneath me as I lay down, still in my fancy gift underwear.

I dreamt about my dad.

The laws changed that year, but they wouldn't go into effect until January. They weren't making it illegal to be fat, exactly. But it was as close as they could get. It was going to be legal to deny health insurance to anyone with a BMI over twenty-five if they refused the Pill. Intentional obesity would also be grounds for loss of child custody and would be acceptable reason for dismissal from a job.

Where the law went, culture followed. Airlines were adding a customer weight limit and clothing manufacturers concentrated on developing lines to individualize the Pill body. Journalists wrote articles on the subject of renegade fats. Could their citizenship be revoked? Should parents of fat children be prosecuted for abuse if they didn't arrange for them to receive the Pill as soon as possible?

I submitted a treatment to my short film class detailing my desire to film a secret enclave where fat renegades performed for the gratification of a live Pilled audience. My professor wrote back to tell me that my idea was 1. obscene and 2. impossible.

The Friday before Thanksgiving break, Mom called.

"I'm so glad we're getting this done before the change in airline policy. Can you imagine having to come to Ohio by train? Anyhow, your Aunt Jeanne is coming in for the holiday—"

"Mom. Mom, listen. I don't want to do it."

"Do what? See Aunt Jeanne?"

"No, Mom, listen. I'm not going to take the Pill."

She was quiet for a minute. "Sweetie, we all took it hard when your father passed. I know you must be worried about that, but they say there's no genetic marker—"

"It's not just Dad. It's not just the odds that I might die. I just don't want to do it. I want to stay who I am."

She sighed like I was a child who had asked for the ninetieth time why the sky was blue. "This doesn't change who you are, Munchkin. It only changes your body."

"I'm not coming home," I said, flatly.

There was a lot of yelling, with both of us trying to be cruel to the other. I'd rather not remember it. What I do remember is her crying, saying something like, "I gave you your body. I made it, and it's imperfect like mine was. Why won't you let me fix it? Why won't you let me correct my mistake?"

"I don't feel like a mistake," I told her. "And I'm not coming home. Not now, not ever."

I remember hanging up and the terrible silence that followed. I remember thinking I should turn my phone off, but then I realized I could just leave it behind. I could leave everything behind. I took my camera and my laptop and left everything else. I didn't even take a change of clothes.

I borrowed a phone from someone on the quad, making up a story that mine had been stolen. She waited for me as I called Dan. I told him to pick me up where I was.

The car arrived ten minutes later.

The redhead buzzed me in without asking for a password, which was great because I couldn't remember what Dan had said. Down through the purple hallway and a woman I'd never seen before shook my hand and told me I could call her Denny.

Denny had a Pill body, hidden away beneath a wide, flowing caftan and a matching headwrap. She showed me to my room, my king-size bed, my enormous private bath, my shared common room and library. She gave me the Wi-Fi password and explained the house's security.

"You may stay here as long as you like. The house will feed you and clothe you. Your medical needs will be seen to. Your entertainments will be top-notch. You may leave anytime you wish. Your pay will be automatically deposited into your account as it comes in, without delay.

"However, you must never disclose the location or the nature of this house to anyone via any means; not by phone call or text or email. You may take photos and videos, but we have jammers to prevent geotagging of any kind. If you are found in violation of this one rule, you will walk out of here with nothing but the clothes on your back. Is that clear?"

I told her it was. She left and returned five minutes later with a new phone for me. I signed into my bank account—the one my mother wasn't on—and set about creating a new email, a new profile, a new identity.

I eased into the work. I ate cupcakes and I danced in a leotard. I read poetry aloud while sipping a milkshake. I lounged in a velvet chaise nude while people drew me and painted me. I began to speak to my admirers and I watched my pay skyrocket.

I met the house's head seamstress: a brilliant, nimble-fingered fat woman named Charisse. She had an incredible eye and hardly had to measure anyone. She made me corsets and skirts, silk pajamas and satin gowns, costumes and capes and all manner of underwear.

I realized when I had been wearing her work for months that some of my clothes were a little too small. My favorite bikini cut into me just so, just enough to accentuate the flesh it did not quite contain. I filmed myself in the hall of mirrors, wearing it and trying to understand what it meant.

Some of my gowns were a little too big, though I could remember the exactitude with which I was fitted. I made short clips showing the gaps in the waist and hips, the way I could work my whole hand in between the fabric and my skin.

Charisse was too skilled for it to be an accident. The implication became clear.

All around me there were heavenly bodies in gowns and togas, a stately fleet of well-rounded ships gliding alongside the pool or lying silkily in our beds. We were beautiful, but we were all aware of a subtle campaign to make us larger, ever larger, more suited to satisfy whatever it was that brought the throngs of thin whispering wantons to our door.

In twos and threes, we began to talk about what it meant. About who we could trust. About who was running this place, and why.

The lower floors of the house were a brothel. Somehow I knew that without being told. There was a look in the older fat folks' eyes that let me know it would be waiting for me when I was ready. Nobody pressured me. Nobody even asked. One day I just headed down the stairs. Cheeks were swabbed at the door and everybody waited fifteen minutes until they were cleared. I got my negatives and went through.

I'd never had sex before. I think it happens later for fat kids. While everyone else was trying each other on, I was still trying to figure out why I never fit into anything. I don't regret that. I can't imagine doing this out in the world where I am the worst thing that can happen to somebody.

I didn't know what it would be like. I hope it's this good for everyone, with a circle of adoring worshippers vying for the right to adore you, to touch every inch of you, to murmur in wonder as you climax again and again until nap time, when you are lovingly spooned and crooned to sleep. I luxuriated in it for a long time, not thinking about what it meant to only touch thin people, to only be touched by them. I watched my bank balance climb. I didn't ask myself what they saw when they looked at me. I existed as a collection of nerves that did not think.

I stopped thinking about going home. I stopped thinking about the Pill. I stopped thinking. I became what I had always been and nothing more: my fat, fat body.

When I came back to thinking again, I found it did not make things easier.

I have been here for three years now, and I don't think I can ever live anywhere else. Outside, they tell me, there are no more like me. Only in places like here, where a few of us fled before the world could change us. Nobody is allowed to bring us food presents anymore; everyone is too worried they'll try and slip us the Pill. Someone might actually be that upset that I exist. I don't think about that either. I don't exist for them. I accept their worship and forget their faces completely. It's always the same face anyhow.

Sometimes I point my camera at that face and ask them what they're doing here, what do they want, why did they come seeking the thing they've worked so hard to avoid becoming?

They mumble about mothers and goddesses, about the embrace of flesh and the fullness of desire. It sounds like my own voice inside my head. I think about my dad, about god's hands. Would he have been one of these? Would he have come to miss my mother's body the way he first knew it?

I think about showing this film in LA. I think about Denny tell-

ing me I can leave here anytime. I think about how I could leave
my body anytime, too, how any of us can. I think about Andrew,
about how he left his and gained nothing at all. How I used to see
him as the enemy when he was just me.

Deep down on the lowest floor, in perfect privacy, the fats make
love to each other. There is a boy who came only a few weeks ago,
an import from one of the countries that's taken to the Pill slowly,
so we have a lot of recruits from their shores. We had no common
language at first, but we've worked on that and discovered an un-
mapped country between us. He's so sweet and shy and eager to
lift the heaviness of his belly so that he can slip inside me and
then drop it on top of mine, warm and weighty like a curtain. He
whispers to me that we don't ever have to go back, that we can
raise darling fat babies right here, that we'll become like another
species. *Homo pillus* can inherit the earth, while *Homo lipidus* lives
in secret.

"But we'll live," he whispers to me as we conspire to remake the
world in the image of our thick ankles. "We'll live," he says, his
tongue tracing the salty trenches made by the folds in my sides.
Belly to belly, fat against fat.

"We'll live."

MEL KASSEL

Crawfather

FROM *The Magazine of Fantasy & Science Fiction*

WHEN NANCY TURNS FOURTEEN, we tell her about how we fight the crawfather. She doesn't believe us at first, and we laugh, proud because she's smart and skeptical, a scientist.

"Careful, Ben," says Carl, "you raised her to ask questions."

Ben, Nancy's dad, holds his hands up: *Nothin' I can do.*

We're gathered in Ben's cabin, standing in a semicircle around the living-room furniture. Nancy sits in the armchair, knees up to her chest and arms around her shins. Her mother, Irene, sits next to her on one of the wooden chairs we've dragged in from the kitchen. Most of us are standing.

Irene is the fulcrum on which Nancy's trust wobbles. Her mother would never prank her—Irene loves Nancy so baldly that it overshoots fierce and lands in pitiful. We've never seen such doting, such hair-smoothing.

"You don't have to go to the fight this year," she tells her daughter. "You don't have to go until you're ready."

"Don't sugarcoat it!" Judy says. "Carl and I didn't. The twins started going when they were thirteen."

Nancy looks ready to cry. It's a tough talk; we all remember it. There's no one in your corner. You're oblivious until the whole family sits you down, tells you a preposterous story, offers you hot cocoa and clucks at your slowness to believe. Judy brags about her twins, but she won't tell you that when *she* got the talk, she ran away from home the next day. We found her when a bookstore in Brainerd called.

Now, though, she drives the twins to archery classes twice a week and owns a compound bow herself. She's the one who hit the crawfather in the eye during the reunion of '88.

"You guys can't be serious." Nancy holds her head in her hands. Irene squeezes her shoulders.

"I'm sorry, sweetie. Everyone goes through this. It's never easy. We don't have to talk about it any more tonight." Judy raises her eyebrows at this, but Ben orders them back down with a glance. Irene continues, "No one is laughing at you, I promise. This is a big deal. We're telling you about it because we know you're ready."

"You're gonna do great. Brain like yours?" Carl yells.

"Let's give her some time," says Ben.

"We're serious," says Grandpa Richie. "It's serious."

Twenty-two feet at its deepest point, Bluegill Lake has none of the blackness that spells a cold drop. The bottom is right there, layered into three substrates that, according to a PowerPoint briefing Judy conducted a few years back, are classified as sand, pulpy peat, and fibrous peat by the Institute for Fisheries Research.

The lake gets weedy quick, and we make disgusted faces at each other when the slime-slick threads find our ankles. The twins have been reprimanded for telling the younger cousins that the weeds are all the hair that has ever disappeared down shower drains. Still, this year, everyone swims, and everyone jumps from the inflatable blue and yellow trampoline several yards out. Horseflies the size of olives investigate the parts in our hair and leave us fanning the tops of our heads.

There's a dock at one end of the beach where we toss hunks of bread to bluegills and pumpkinseeds. They swarm at the surface to eat, and the sounds of their bodies slapping against each other are lewd enough to make the adults laugh. Rarely, but often enough to enchant, a pike darts out from the weeds and scatters the school.

"Was that a northern?" the children squeal.

"Oh, I think so," we say, as though we're teasing the existence of pixies.

The lake is a horseshoe, and the crawfather lives at the end of the western arm in a cave made of muck. The crawfather is the size of an eighteen-wheeler and about as smart as one. That's something we always impress on the new fighters—the crawfather may be huge, but it's incapable of guile.

We met the crawfather for the first time in the late 1800s. The story goes like this: Great-Grandpa Lawrence built a cabin on Bluegill Lake for the spring and summer, thereby supplementing his earnings as a railroad worker with a bit of money from selling fresh-caught walleye. Like all the Vensons before and after him, he never left Minnesota, and he loved to fish. He knew that he could hook muskies and bluegills without much travel away from the shore, but walleye tastes better, sells better. So, he'd wait for the winds to pick up in the late afternoons, when the water fought itself into prime walleye chop, or he'd head out at night, when he could spot the scuffed-coin shine of their eyes as they fed.

A meticulous man, he aimed to grid out the entire lake and rank the squares on the map by their generosity toward anglers. He was working on the left arm of the lake when the crawfather took him.

The description of his death varies depending on which of us tells the tale. Squeamish Madeline doesn't linger on the tentpole legs, the churning mouthparts, the pincers that shoot blasts of wind when they snap together. She only says that the crawfather killed Great-Grandpa Lawrence, and that his wife, Bertha, had to borrow a rowboat and wheeze her way onto the lake to find the culprit, its carapace bloodied, its antennae still tapping through scraps of Lawrence's clothes.

Grandpa Richie's version is even more terse. "You've seen craw-dad skins, washed up on the beach? Little buggers that'll pinch you if you find 'em alive? Well, this one can pinch you in half at your belly button, and that's what happened to your great-grandpa when he crossed it, out on his boat just trying to make his living. And it got more of us after that. Your Grandma Tess. Ollie."

These days it's Irene who embellishes, who makes a sermon of it. "Like any big animal, it's dangerous because it's stupid and it's strong," she tells Nancy. "Your Great-Grandfather Lawrence proba-bly thought that he'd found something he could exploit. But when he paddled up to it, it wasn't curious or godly—it was just hungry."

She invites her daughter to ask questions, and she answers as specifically as she can. She tells her to start considering weapons. She half apologizes, half explains for cultivating Nancy's interest in tennis while dismissing her passion for the flute. She mandates that Nancy keep referring to battle days as "big fishing trips" in the presence of the toddlers.

"Why don't we just have our reunions somewhere else?" Nancy asks us in the days leading up to the battle. "Why don't we leave it alone?"

Our responses are no less true for being rehearsed:

Because if we didn't rent out the cabins, someone else would, and it would only be a matter of time before the crawfather got them.

Because Bluegill Lake should be left beautiful for our children.

Because to abandon it would be to disrespect our dead.

Because it is much too late for that.

Every year, the battling begins on the ninth day of the reunion. This gives those of us who are crafting weapons enough time to whittle, weld, and decorate. It's not a competition, more like a talent show—each Venson has a specialty, from Scottie's pistols to Irma May's long, tapered spears. We work on them inside Grandpa Richie's cabin, which is the only space off-limits to the young un-initiated.

On the morning of the ninth day, we meet at the dock and split into three groups: seven of us in the hulking rental pontoon, four in Grandpa Richie's camo-painted boat with the chugging Evinrude motor, and five in the sleek fiberglass Glastron. We wear windbreakers and grim, set mouths. We lug several six-packs of beer onto the pontoon, alternating them with our forest-green tackle boxes. Some of us even crack a can or a bottle open; it fizzes away at our nerves.

We're all keeping an eye on Nancy. She's the newest fighter, and she's gripping her tennis racket with both hands, ready for the crawfather to erupt from the water at any moment. We've told her that's not how it happens. None of us has ever seen the craw-father swimming or doing anything at a substantial distance from its mudhole. Does she think we'd let the children into the lake if there was any chance of it prowling the bottom?

We leave her be. We think back to our first fights, before we knew the thrill of attacking something together, all of our blood against all of its blood.

The motors roar, then rumble, then buzz. It's a short ride to the slice of shore where the crawfather lives. The lake is flat and gray, a darker version of the sky, and we make plans to fish later, if we're all still here.

"Slow, slow," shouts Grandpa Richie. He flaps one of his arms down repeatedly to signal the other boats. The green line of weed-swept beach thickens as we approach.

"There," says Hank, the childless accountant. He points at the hole, which is so perfectly circular it looks as though a giant pencil has poked it into the earth. We get closer. Now we can see the crawfather's bulk crouched near the back. A massive shadow with too many outcroppings, those legs, those pincers. The leading theory among us is that it hibernates the whole year round, waiting in a state of ominous torpor for us to wake it. We've read that regular crawdads can do this, shut down their bodies until feeding conditions are favorable.

"Nancy, Nancy," someone starts chanting. We grin and add more voices to the pile, until we're the loudest thing on the lake, our fists pumping in the air and our windbreakers swishing in unison. The crawfather doesn't move. Irene jostles her daughter's shoulder in encouragement.

"Try it," she says. She reaches down and picks up a tennis ball. One hemisphere is a mess of spikes, the ends of six-inch nails that we hammered through the fuzz and rubber. It's half tennis ball, half medieval morning star. We made nine of them.

Nancy takes the first ball from Irene and walks to the rear platform of the pontoon boat. She studies the crawfather in slumber. We know what she's thinking: *Is that thing really going to get up and move?*

We're drifting, but not fast, there's not enough wind.

"Love–love," she jokes, uncertain. Then she steps her right foot back, throws the ball straight up, and arcs her racket into a serve so expertly that many of us whistle or curse in admiration.

The racket connects with the smooth side of the ball and sends it screaming toward the crawfather. It doesn't just hit—it lodges, right in the V-shaped seam where the crawfather's head slots into its thorax.

As the crawfather lurches awake, we are ecstatic, cheering, lifting Nancy up on our shoulders.

"Fifteen–love!" says Archie, one of the twins. "Damn, Nancy!"

The crawfather scuttles forward. It doesn't produce sounds from within itself, has never roared or moaned. Instead, its noises are the awful, wet squeaks of its mouthparts as they slide in too many directions, and the clattering of its legs hitting one another as it walks. There's also the rasp of sand beneath its abdomen, which hides rows of paddling swimmerets.

Nancy believes. We watch the excitement on her face downturn into fear. But she doesn't have to worry. We're grabbing our guns, our spears, our bows, our bottles, our slingshots. We're lining up at the prows of our three boats, Vikings baring our chests at the dragon, emboldened by the neon-green tennis ball set deep in the beast's hide. We haven't rallied like this since Judy nicked its eye with her arrow.

"Fire!" Grandpa Richie shouts, and we do.

The crawfather waves its antennae, suddenly caught in a hailstorm of miscellany. A ninja star strikes, scars, and spins off its carapace. Rocks of various sizes bounce against it with the sound of popcorn kernels hitting the bottom of a saucepan. Arrows launched from Judy and the twins' bows splinter. Bullets either glance and zoom off at odd angles, or pierce but don't reach the true meat. Every year, we are struck by how invincible it seems. It is a monstrous wall, an unpeelable fruit.

"We're barely doing anything!" Nancy says, dismayed and childlike, her tennis balls now mostly landing in the water.

"Keep at it!" we say.

The crawfather brings its pincers in front of its head, shielding itself and still coming at us, its legs rising and falling in chitinous waves.

"You son of a bitch!" we cry. Those of us in the motorboats turn in slow-motion terror as we realize it's heading for the pontoon.

"Get off the boat!"

"Swim here!"

Scottie aims for the softer bits between its tail plates, but Sarah tackles him into the water before he can shoot, and their son Ernest follows. Irene grabs Nancy's hand and they, too, jump from one of the pontoon's swollen flanks. Madeline and her fiancé, Brad, can't reach the sides in time. They try to cower beneath the driver's dash, but the lower sickle of the crawfather's right pincer finds Madeline's leg and drags her from Brad's arms. She screams, Brad screams. Blood tip-taps politely atop the boat's canvas awning.

"Madeline!" we call, over and over. We yell so that we won't have to hear the crawfather eating, a delicate and probing process that we can't stand to watch. We pray that the crawfather clipped her femoral artery when he lifted her aloft. We pray that it eats her headfirst.

Brad reverses the pontoon boat, sobbing. We lift those of us who are treading water into the motorboats, crowding them so that they sit low in the lake.

We're out of ammo for the day. We can only bob like helpless, tear-streaked corks as the crawfather retreats backward into its hole, clutching its prize.

Dinner at the grown-ups' table that night is strained.

"They won't believe another boating accident," says Winnifred. Once, she'd gone through a four-year phase during which she didn't participate in the fight, citing the fact that the crawfather had to be some kind of ancient nature-spirit. But she's been back with us for a decade since then.

"Hunting accident?" Irma May proposes.

"Kidnapping," Hank says.

Nancy says nothing. She sculpts her potatoes into a mountain and hollows a hole into one side with her butter knife.

"She got cold feet before the wedding and ran off." Grandpa Richie settles the matter. "Sorry, son."

Brad nods, then shakes his head, then won't stop shaking his head. "I wasn't . . . I'm not even married to her. We didn't get married. I'm not part of this."

"Brad," we say, cautiously.

"I never wanted to—"

"Hey," we cut him off. Some of us get up and put our hands on his shoulders. We comfort him, and we keep him in his chair. He's seen the crawfather now.

"Maybe change your name in her honor," Hank suggests, and we nod.

"This means we'll really get the bastard," Scottie says, and we murmur in agreement. We move away when we're sure that Brad has refocused. We make sure he has enough food. We know to watch them, after a death, to make sure that they eat and come out of their rooms regularly. It's the hardest part, seeing one of us go through this. We all think so.

"Does this mean I can bring Carmen next year?" Archie asks. His twin, Nathan, attempts to shush him, but Archie swats his brother's hands away. "We'll need the help," he says.

"That's enough about it," Judy snaps.

"She's the best player on their softball team!" Archie says, and we can tell that this is the card he's been breathlessly holding, waiting until he's in front of all of us to play it. Judy's chair screeches and her silverware falls on her plate as she stands up.

"Archibald," she says.

"Why not?" Archie asks, and Nancy adds a soft echo: "Yeah, why not?"

"We have had this discussion—" Judy begins, but she doesn't need to. We chime in, some of us gentle, others stern. They're in college. They've been seeing each other for how long now? Five months? And the photos we've seen, her hair, the nose piercing —well, that doesn't matter. She's never folded a nightcrawler over a hook in her life.

"You haven't told her anything, have you?" Harris the lawyer asks, his eyes flashing to each of us, eager for someone to run with his accusation.

"Fuck, no, you think I would—"

"Do *not* speak to your family that way—"

"Oh my god, Mom, I'm saying I wouldn't tell her—"

We have to calm both Archie and Judy down, and then we notice that Brad is crying again, and probably has been crying again for a while. We sneak guilty bites of meatloaf in between his breaths and rack our brains for something new to say.

"Do you want to watch the little ones with Susanne tomorrow?" Grandpa Richie offers, finally. "You don't have to come out on the boat again."

Brad wipes his snot on his sleeve. He looks just as liable to collapse as he does to flip the table over. We'll learn to read him, in time. We study his face.

"No," he says. "No, I want to be there. I want to hurt that thing."

We slam our fists on the table. We toast. We arrange for a supply run in the morning. We pace ourselves wisely as we rebuild our rage.

While Carl cleans his rifle, Winnifred double-checks the first-aid kits, and Archie refills the fuel tanks, Nancy readies more tennis balls. We're worried about her. Her eyes are flinty and she won't accept our help. Irene says that she was texting and researching crawdad anatomy for much of the night.

"Do you know what a ganglion is?" Irene asks us. "She kept talking about the ganglion." We shake our heads, but we reassure her that Nancy is just trying to help, in her own way. Privately, we wonder if we'll have to rein her in a bit.

We find ways to approach her as she works. We bring her lemonade, sit next to her and sigh, tell her that, obviously, this isn't how the fight goes every year. Most years, in fact, we don't lose anyone. She ignores us. She hammers nail after nail through the felt.

"Teenagers," we say to one another. We've seen this before. We assume it's an act of apology when she volunteers to clean the empty beer bottles out of the boats; we ruffle her hair and let her go.

A few minutes later, we hear the Evinrude sputter.

"Is Nancy starting the boat?" Hank asks, and we walk, then jog, then run toward the beach, where we see the widening stripes of the camo motorboat's wake, the boat itself a brown wedge skating around the lake's curve.

"Where's Archie?" Judy yells. "Nathan! Where's your brother?"

"He was refueling," we say. "Is he on the boat?"

"They planned this," Ben says, and he yells for the pontoon boat's keys. Irene is pale, her fingers gouging into the skin of Ben's shoulder.

We follow Ben and Irene and Judy and Carl into the two remaining boats, bringing what weapons we can. We move fluidly in our panic. There is no time for quarrels about seating or who will get the first shot. The motors rev and we zoom away from the dock, past the trampoline, around the curve.

The crawfather is already out of its hole, antennae whipping the air. Something crashes against its side, and we realize that Nancy and Archie are throwing beer bottles at it.

"What do they think they're doing?" we ask each other.

"Why didn't they wait?"

"Are they crazy?"

"They're too close to it!"

Scottie readies his gun, but Irene screams at him to stop, not to shoot until we can be sure the children won't be hit.

Shards of bottles litter the ground around the crawfather's rust-colored legs, and now that we're close enough to see them, we can also smell the gasoline. We see the fuel tank, normally stowed under the seat by the tiller, positioned at Archie's feet. They'd filled the bottles before lobbing them.

"Oh my god," we say.

We're forced to slow our approach so that we don't overshoot their boat. We watch Nancy hold a nail-studded tennis ball above the water, pour fuel from one of the remaining beer bottles on top of it, then balance it on the seat by the bow. Archie nocks an arrow. He painstakingly dips the tip of it into the fuel tank.

"Hold on!" we shout. "Stop!"

Nancy retrieves a lighter from somewhere in the bottom of the boat. She lights Archie's arrow, then her tennis ball. He calibrates, looses the arrow, and nimbly steps out of her way so that she can complete a graceful underhand stroke with her racket. They both glance back at us to see how much time they have left.

We aren't looking at them. Instead, we trace the paths of these two small, flaming projectiles as they descend on the crawfather. Both have been launched in high arcs, aim prioritized over speed and force. We will them to fizzle out, to skid harmlessly into sand. Some of us even reach for them. It looks like we are reaching for the kids, but we are reaching for the bombs, and either reach, it turns out, would be useless.

The arrow plants itself in the ground between two of the crawfather's legs, and the ground suddenly looks as though it's cracked onto hell. Fire spreads in veins around the crawfather and flares up inside its cave, where they must have pitched more bottles before we caught up with them.

Nancy's burning tennis ball bounces off the crawfather's shell like a quick kiss, and then the crawfather is alight. We can hear the heat and pressure build inside its exoskeleton, the whistle of steam released as it cooks. Its tail curls and uncurls in agony. Its legs scramble against the sand, and we think it may be trying to run for water, or for its hole, but it's blind by now. It drags its pincers along its own back and head, desperate to clean itself of the fire. We watch it stumble and fall onto the beach with a succession of sharp cracking sounds. We smell it: the world's largest and worst crawfish boil, meat dripping with mud and seaweed and goose shit, all the lake scents that the water buries.

The crawfather burns. We pull our shirt collars over our mouths as our eyes water. We're in line with the third boat, and we stare at Nancy and Archie. They meet our eyes in defiance. We wonder where their parents went wrong; what we could have done; what we will do.

"That was fucking easy," Nancy yells. Archie nods.

"You take that boat back right now!" Irene is the first of us to find her voice. "Right now! You turn around and go straight back!"

Nancy squints at her mother, confused. She spreads her hands, palms up: *What did I do wrong?*

None of us answers. Grandpa Richie has a coughing fit, and we motor in reverse to get out of the smoke. But we don't turn around. The three boats waver with the chop, shoulder to shoulder, all of them still facing the burning beach. We're breathing too fast. We nurse a quiet fury that we know is too ludicrous to name. We glare at the middle boat, its bottom bright with tennis balls.

"What?" Archie asks, young and mystified. "What is it? We killed it!"

Our hands are fists, our nails biting our palms. They wouldn't understand. They thrive on instability and fractures. They can't let anything be enough. We wipe our foreheads, square our shoulders.

"Let's just go home," we say.

TOCHI ONYEBUCHI

How to Pay Reparations: A Documentary

FROM *Future Tense*

A CITY HALL OFFICE, *all wood paneling.*

ROBERT (BOBBY) CAINE, AGE 52, MAYOR OF _____: He left us
a mess. Frank and his reparations bill, he left us a mess, that's
what he did. I'ma have to be mayor a hundred more years to
balance this budget. At least. [Laughing.] Imagine that. A white
mayor. Spearheading a citywide reparations scheme? And you
really can't call it anything other than that. Because that's what
it is. Don't get me wrong; as a Black man, I'm all for gettin'
paid for what I been through. But if that stack is just a steppin'
stone for some white boy on his way to the Governor's Mansion? I'm good. I hope he's doing well for himself. He must
not have liked this job all that much if he was willin' to throw
it away so fast.

*Sunlight cuts through the blinds of a tiny office. Bookshelves bend under
the weight of monographs. More books cover the floor around a desk. Behind the desk sits a man with his glasses hanging around his neck, his
mask pulled down. He wears a tweed jacket and periodically removes a
handkerchief from his breast pocket to dab at his forehead.*

PROFESSOR MARK HIGGINS, AGE 73, ASSISTANT PROFESSOR AT
_____ STATE UNIVERSITY, FORMER MEMBER OF REPAIR PROJ-
ECT TEAM: It's impossible. It's actually impossible to pay reparations. You can look to other models across time and place — the
recompense offered to slave owners, for instance, for their hav-

ing been made bereft of their chattel; what Haiti has been forced to pay France for the temerity of having won its independence, etc.—but there's no real analogue for reparations paid to the truly injured parties for the totality of slavery. Some people like to point to what Germany did after the Holocaust, but the injury being addressed was the extermination of a people. The "orbit of hurt"—which sounds like a callous way of putting it, granted—is somewhat fixed in that example. Let's break down how exactly that plan, which looked so perfect and discrete on paper, truly unfolded.

You have the Luxembourg Agreement of 1952 and the Additional Federal Compensation Act of 1953. What did the Germans do? They paid the state of Israel for the cost of resettlement. Half a million Jewish refugees. That's what they paid for. On top of that, however, was the requirement that the moneys be used only to purchase goods produced within Germany. It's not until you get to the Federal Compensation Act of 1956 that moneys are being offered to German Jews who had suffered at the hands of the Nazi regime and their surviving dependents. There was a claim deadline of 1969. More groups became eligible in the interim with different pay schedules, but imagine the hundreds of lawyers and functionaries representing clients with divergent interests all vying for a piece of a finite pie trapped in red tape. By the time money gets to you, there's a nonzero possibility you're already dead.

Now, a governmental authority could recompense people for lost property. Or, and this is something people latched onto later on, they could compensate victims for their slave labor. A few years ago, the Claims Conference and the German government announced that they would pay an amount to each of the survivors of Kindertransport. Guess what they were paid. Well, the ones who hadn't died by then. Guess. Two thousand and five hundred euros.

I wrote this and much more in a report I submitted to the team behind the REPAIR Project, and I'm sure they listened, because they decided to add something more structural to that asinine personal compensation model. But they let me go ultimately.

A burger restaurant. Former city councilman Richard Perkins (age 42) and corporate lawyer Tommy DiSanto (53) sit on the patio, a plate of fries in front of each of them. Their black face masks hang from one ear as they eat. DiSanto was an inaugural member of the REPAIR Project Team. Perkins was the team's founder and leader.

DISANTO: How did it start? I joined after I heard about it, right? Or
   did you reach out to me—

PERKINS: I think we reached out to you. Well, *I* reached out to you.
   Nobody was supposed to know about this at first. I don't think
   anyone was supposed to know about it, period. But, see, Tommy
   and I went to law school together and—

DISANTO: And while Richie turned into a hotshot city politician on
   his way to the Governor's Mansion—hell, probably the White
   House with that jawline of yours—I was out here defending Hal-
   liburton. But, shit, this was easy pro bono for me.

PERKINS: Except, you couldn't tell anyone at the office why you had
   to take a sabbatical to do it.

DISANTO: Because it was [air quotes] top secret. But, yeah, I got
   brought in because whatever was being worked on needed to be
   founded on solid legal footing. Now, granted, I hadn't taken a
   peek at the Constitution since 1L, so I wasn't nearly the most
   qualified on that count, but Richie and I go back. What was it,
   that mixer they had all the students of color go to that one summer?

PERKINS: Yeah, the POC mixer. What were you even doing there?
   Your parents are from fucking Argentina.

DISANTO *[laughing]*: Anyway, all I know when I say yes is that there's
   some social justice thing going on and there are scientists involved or whatever. Now, get this. I tell him, I tell Richie: "I hate
   fucking math. Don't make me do math." And he tells me, "Don't
   worry, I won't make you do any math." [Pause] I did so much
   fucking math.

*They both burst out into laughter. But they turn away from each other to
keep from spreading droplets.*

*Open on a darkened room. Cloaked in shadows. Against the far wall, the
silhouette of a potted plant. The leaves are moving. There is an overhead
fan at work. A dark shape sits in an armchair.*

REDACTED, AGE 28, DATA SCIENTIST, MEMBER OF REPAIR PROJ-
   ECT TEAM: I mean, it's kind of simplistic to call it the Reparations Algorithm, which is what everyone called it after the story
   blew up—because, of course. If you had an AI built to detect
   which moles on a body were evidence of malignant cancer cells,
   you wouldn't call that the Cancer Algorithm, would you? Okay,
   maybe you would. Bad example. But people think it's just like

you have this static E=mc^2-type equation and you throw as much information at it as possible so that it, like, learns or whatever, then it spits out some intelligent decision. So they hear about the Reparations Algorithm and they immediately think, oh of course, a formula for figuring out reparations! Then they ask, well, what did you feed the formula? And then they expect you to say something like "racism. We fed the formula four hundred-plus years of racism." Like it's that simple. There's nothing simple about racism.

VOICE OF WENDY GUAN, AGE 27, STATISTICIAN, MEMBER OF RE-PAIR PROJECT TEAM: I don't know if I joined the project at a late stage or early on, but I do know that our viability was tied directly to the release of funds resulting from the abolition of the city police department. During my interview, they were very vague about what exactly I would be doing, and they kept emphasizing the project's interdisciplinary nature. I think if they'd been a bit more forthcoming, I might've been too excited to be coherent. There was a real sea change happening throughout the country. Every industry, every locale, was experiencing a reckoning. I even saw in my own community the new ways in which anti-Blackness was being discussed and reckoned with. So to have the chance to be on the forefront of this new effort, this pilot project, and hopefully provide an example of what truly restorative justice looks like, I mean, who majors in statistics and expects to wind up there? Should we have expected what happened after? Maybe. But you have to understand the moment. It felt unprecedented. And, to be honest, I wouldn't take any of it back.

On a porch of a two-story house in the _____ suburb, northwest of _____, there are two rocking chairs that allow their occupants to look out over a recently manicured lawn. Flanking the porch are plots of recently turned dirt and the beginnings of a garden.

BILLY [LAST NAME WITHHELD], 52, NURSE: Where'd that money come from? Came from us cops. That's where it came from. They abolished the fucking police department, fired everybody. No job assistance, no more pension, nothing. The whole fucking thing was drained dry. And our union. Strength in numbers, right? It's all bullshit. Once the protests started, it was open season on us. Get this, you know those robot dogs that company out of Boston was making? You remember those, right? Well, they were gonna start mass-producing them to replace us. Fake dogs. Union didn't have any pull because those tech wizards were already angling for our jobs on the cheap and we lost all our bargaining power. And the way the defunding was set up, it was reverse seniority, so the younger, more diverse force got clipped first. Then when it was all us white devils left, we were easy pickings, far as the court of public opinion was concerned. I'm just over fifty. Spent my life on the force. What the hell am I gonna do with the time I got left? Far as work, things had dried up, but with the virus, folks in hospitals were droppin' like flies. So I decided that was where I could help. Had to go to nursing school and everything. Paid out the ass to sit in a classroom with fuckin' kids my daughter's age. [Laughs.] But I did it. Got my degree, got my license. Now, I push a cart in a hospital. Social justice, right? I hope it's fuckin' bedlam over there without us.

On the corner of Willow and Main Street stand a group of antiviolence activists handing out cards listing candidates for an upcoming municipal election. On the back of each is a Know Your Rights checklist. Down Willow, grill smoke billows out from behind a church while older residents eat fried fish by the front entrance. Shaneika Thomas wears a mask with a clear mouth panel to enable the hard of hearing to lip-read.

SHANEIKA THOMAS, AGE 27, CRISIS MANAGEMENT SYSTEMS WORKER: This corner, right here? We used to practically sit on top of cops basically. Plainclothes cops would yoke up some kids here or across the street, and folks would get it on video. It would go viral, and we'd get on the cop's ass. But then he'd be back out as a white-shirt, terrorizing folks. You walk around this community and you have credibility just from having been here for long enough and from people seeing your face, so you can walk up to a group of dudes and be like, hey, "if you're out here, and he's out here"—meaning the cop—"call this number."

Two mechanical, jet-black greyhounds with backward-jointed legs prance down the middle of the street. At each stop, they gather the nearest residents and eject thermometers that the residents use to take their temperatures. Some of the residents glance at their results. Another shakes the thermometer as if it's broken before trying again. Afterward, they all deposit the thermometers, coated in their saliva and DNA, into an attached pouch and drop the contained thermometer into an opening on the greyhounds' backs.

When the REPAIR Act went into effect, we got an infusion of cash because of where we were headquartered. But we weren't ready for that. We weren't *nearly* ready for that. All of a sudden, money was showing up, and people just figured it was City Hall redistributing what got freed up when they abolished the police department. At some point, I started doing the math and I realized, as big as the PD's budget was, this was more money than that. But we didn't have too much time to think on where exactly this money came from. We just knew that we got lucky and we had work to do.

Of course, it didn't last, but I'm pretty proud of what we were able to do with what we had. I just wish some of that money went toward painting those dogs a different fucking color.

Inside a Dunkin' Donuts on the corner of Arcade Street and Pine Street. Just outside the entrance is a waste bin and, above it, a one-time-use mask dispenser. At the top of the doorframe is a scanner, taking note of the biorhythms and temperature of each entering and exiting customer.

DENAUN SMITH, AGE 63, RESIDENT OF _____: Hell, I couldn't believe it. At first, we didn't know *what* the fuck was going on. But suddenly, they announce that [Redacted] High's getting what?! Millions of dollars just pouring in. Where did that money come from? How can I get a piece of it?

LYLE BROWN, AGE 32, HISTORY TEACHER AT [REDACTED] HIGH: It wasn't *millions*. But it was . . . a lot. Imagine my surprise when the principal calls me into his office and tells me how much money we've been given. And my immediate thought is, "Okay, I can finally afford to get enough pencils and pens and notebooks for my students!" To be honest, I was just glad I could make sure the hand sanitizer dispensers in the hallways stopped running out.

SMITH: You could see it in the kids, though. That's true. It wasn't like they was walkin' around with Jordans or anything or like they was flashin' money around and whatnot. Matter of fact, I started seeing them less. Turns out they was spendin' more of they time at school.

BROWN: A visual arts program, a theater program. Hell, we pooled with another school and built an actual theater! Kids were using actual hand-held cameras to turn what would've been TikToks into Oscar-eligible short films.

SMITH: Those damn TikToks. If I'm keepin' it real witchu, I

miss those kids. I mean, good for them stayin' out of trouble, but the neighborhood done changed when you ain't see them around. It's summer and ain't no thirteen-year-olds chillin' on they front stoop in the Fayetteville housing projects in quadruple-XL white tees and baggy jeans with they coco-mango-cherries and do-rags. A place loses its character when it ain't got that anymore.

VOICE OF WENDY GUAN: One of the first things I was told upon joining the project was that we were to focus as much as possible on tangibles. Essentially, we would look at discernible racial disparities—in housing, in education outcomes, in the number and location of grocery stores—and work backward. Our goal was to find a number. What number did we need to generate that would render all material things equal? Focusing on the racial wealth gap seemed like the most concrete way of going about things, and we operated on the assumption that housing was the most appropriate vector of analysis. So, our "number" would essentially be coded to a dollar amount. The data was relatively easy to come by. Much of it was public already. The tax assessor's office had home values, and then we could bucket them by ZIP code. But very quickly, we noticed something strange.

REDACTED: The tax assessor's office had been overvaluing homes in predominantly Black neighborhoods and undervaluing homes in predominantly white neighborhoods. And the reason they were doing this was to fund police brutality settlements. How do they get their money? Raise the property tax. The city was literally making poor people pay for every time a cop shot a Black kid.

PERKINS: Your average American city doesn't have the budget to pay $150 million or so in yearly settlements for officer misconduct. Yet another reason police are so expensive. What ends up happening is that the city issues a bond to a bank. Bank charges handling fees and interest that the city's on the hook for. But in return, the city now has the cash on hand to pay the victims and/or their families for the officer's misconduct. And the more money in the city budget that goes to that, the less there is for handling lead poisoning or funding schools.

*

In Stanley Quarter Park, children climb over a jungle gym while wearing surgical gloves and giggling behind single-use face masks.

DR. ATHENA DAVIS, AGE 74, ABOLITIONIST AND PROFESSOR EMERITUS AT _____ UNIVERSITY, MEMBER OF REPAIR PROJECT TEAM: Chicago is illustrative, and I think a more appropriate analogue than Professor Higgins's Holocaust example. Between 1972 and 1991, some 125 Black Chicagoans—at least, that is the number of cases that are known—were tortured by police officers in a building on Chicago's South Side. Beaten, electrocuted, sodomized. Chained to boiling radiators. And they were tortured into confessing to crimes that led to prison sentences, sometimes to death row. Discrete instances of a harm. A bracketed period of time. A reparations bill eventually did make its way through the legislature. It was revolutionary for a number of reasons, not just because it included an actual reparations fund. The amount was $5.5 million, a fraction of the $100 million that previous claims related to police torture had cost the city. But in the bill was an acknowledgment that torture had indeed taken place. There was to be a monument to the victims of police torture erected somewhere in the city. A psychological services center for survivors would be built. And there was to be a unit on police torture taught in eighth- and tenth-grade history classes throughout the city.

INTERVIEWER: You mentioned the racial wealth gap and housing earlier.

VOICE OF WENDY GUAN: Yes! In the aggregate sense, wealth is the value of your assets minus your debts. If we were going to focus on financial compensation, we needed something concrete as a . . . prism for our analysis, so to speak. Economic disadvantages can harm your ability to accumulate wealth. And in the United States, at least, the surest way to accumulate wealth is through homeownership. And that is how we came to focus on a location-based analysis for the algorithm.

REDACTED: We'd programmed the algo to produce a number per ZIP code based on the values we input. That output would correspond to a scale we cooked up of dollar amounts. A lot of numbers we had to figure out beforehand. Tax assessments and foreclosure rates. Not just the number of schools, but also the number of school closures. Then there's the police part. It took forever, but through arrest records, we could trace the incarcerated back to where they had initially been arrested. We then took the settlement amounts from police brutality cases as well as the number of cases that went to trial but plaintiffs lost. Legal took care of that part. And together we extrapolated what the incarcerated might have lost in wages and married that to unemployment data. That was hell to disaggregate by ZIP code. But we had our inputs that we turned into superinputs, and then we could generate our output: the amount in dollars that would be apportioned to each ZIP code. It's "If, Then" with a *super*-complicated "If."

Other than that, we had no idea where the money would go. But that wasn't up to us. All that decision-making was a bit above our pay grade. You gotta talk to the big guy about that, and I don't think anybody knows where he is. After everything that went down, Mayor Gaetz — or, rather, *former* Mayor Gaetz — kinda just vanished. Which . . . I don't blame him.

When we ran that algo for the first time for a single ZIP code, we thought there had to be a mistake. Double-checked the inputs, the superinputs, ran it again. And again. And again. We ran that algo maybe three hundred times. Figured we broke the scale. But, no. That first dollar amount . . . to make all things equal . . . was just that huge.

Former city councilman Richard Perkins and corporate lawyer Tommy DiSanto are finishing their lunch.

PERKINS: I put the team together to figure out if this reparations program was financially viable. Not just that, but whether these disbursements were something that we could keep going. This wasn't going to be a one-time check to Black folk. The REPAIR Act was sustained investment. Funds disbursed to individual households, but also location-based budget allocations for school districts. More schools and better schools. Investment in diversion programs and mental health programs. Increased sanitation. Infrastructure repair. Parks. Printer paper for libraries. Job training programs across industries. And it all had to keep going. I knew there wasn't gonna be enough money in the budget to suddenly make things right on the property end. So we co-opted the bond system. Instead of using it to finance police brutality settlements, we'd use it to fund our plan. It was gonna be impossible to get the mayor on board with this if we had to come up with a new system from whole cloth to base our funding on. But if we could use what was already there and flip it—we already had the data operation going from his campaign —then he could see where we were coming from and where we were going.

DISANTO: I've never done so much math in my whole entire life.

VOICE OF WENDY GUAN: We were already thinking to the distant future. A city changes. The algorithm needed to be able to change with it.

I was watching a little girl ride her bike the other day, and I think this provides the best example for what I'm trying to explain. I don't have to explain that a bicycle has two wheels or even that you ride the thing by pushing your feet to the pedals in a circular motion. The girl just knows these things. But figuring *how* to ride a bicycle—how to balance without falling off, how to deal with ruts in the road—that's a different kind of knowledge. Skill-based. You're *learning*. This little girl kept trying to get up this tiny, tiny hill. She would stall at the steepest part, then fall backward. Then, at one point, as she's trying to make her way up, she leans forward. Just a little bit, then a little more. Finally, after she crested the hill, she goes back to how she was sitting before. No one told her to do that.

Before, algorithms had been operating toward the knowing of a specific thing. "Knowing that," so to speak. But machine learning is focused on knowing *how*. A basic algorithm recognizes the thing in front of it as a bicycle. But machine learning is what gets you up the hill. We had the algorithm for the initial disbursement, but we needed it to recognize that a city changes. Would our algorithm know what to do with a new refugee population moving into a targeted neighborhood? When the districts are inevitably redrawn, will it still operate with the same sophistication? If half of a ZIP code is replaced with luxury condominiums, what would the algorithm decide to do?

We didn't have the time or resources to program the AI to do that, so we took those decisions on ourselves. How much of the dollar amount would go to schools? What to do with home valuations? Maybe . . . maybe if we could've got the algorithm to handle all of that, things would have turned out differently. Maybe the algorithm could've decided better than us.

*

*The REPAIR Act was signed into law in February of 20___ and disburse-
ment of funds began on June 19 of that year, traditionally the holiday
known as Juneteenth.*

SANDRA EWING, 37, FORMER RESIDENT OF _____: That first check
   come, I called my sister. She lives on the other side of town, and
   I asked her where this came from. She ain't heard nothin' 'bout
   a check, but pretty soon, I found out everyone on my block got
   one. Same amount, too. It wasn't unemployment. Wasn't a tax
   refund or nothin' either. You had a job or you didn't, you got a
   check. Found out just about everyone in my neighborhood got a
   check. There were a couple other neighborhoods like that too,
   but not everyone in the city got one. There was some letter in
   there about a new law got passed, but I just wanted to see what
   the catch was, you know what I mean? It was a blessing, though.
      First chance I got, stocked up on food and fixed the micro-
   wave. Still had money left over, so I got to have someone come
   through and deep-clean the apartment. Was supposed to be regular, because of city health regulations, but can't nobody in that
   building afford to completely sanitize their homes once every
   week. I figured the check was a one-off, so I was just focused on
   keeping my son, Jeremy, fed and safe.
      But the checks kept coming, several months in a row. So I
   started socking some away, and suddenly, you turn around and
   look at your bank account just [blinks dramatically and laughs].
   You know what I'm sayin'? I'm still countin' every penny I spend
   on this family, but I ain't gotta worry about eviction if suddenly
   the toaster break or there's a leak in the apartment that needs to
   be fixed or this or that or whatever thing. Your thinking changes.
   Before, I'm just trying to make it to the first or fifteenth without
   my boy starving. But then you get to thinking about things like
   moving, like Jeremy being in a better school. The schools here
   seemed to be gettin' some money, but it's nothing like what they
   got just outside the city. So I'm finally able to take some time off
   from work, after not having missed a day in twenty-one years. And
   I go looking at apartments. Condos. That sort of thing. Imagine
   that! Me! Shoppin' for condos!
      The neighborhood was starting to change too. I think we
   figured out pretty quickly that the checks were comin' to specific neighborhoods. And, yeah, money was goin' to the community, but fixin' up a school building, making sure there are
   enough soap dispensers in the halls, improving the curriculum,
   the school lunch program, all that takes time. That's time a lot

of us don't have. So I got out. Couldn't get out quick enough. Landlord saw the market and started jackin' up the price soon as he could. So we moved. Me and my Jeremy picked up and set out. He loves his new school, but the checks stopped coming. I'm working two jobs instead of three now, but it's getting harder to keep Jeremy in that school. We ain't even talking about college.

They're saying the checks back home stopped coming too. Money was comin' for about a year, then stopped. By then, everybody done up and moved, and now the rent's too high to move back. So we're stuck.

PROFESSOR HIGGINS: You need to understand that reparations are a national redemption project. A government can print money, as much as it wants. Don't listen to economists. They're wrong. But a place built on the backs of others needs all of its decision-makers to acknowledge the totality of the wrong. It goes beyond money. That's why the project ended the way it did. Were reparations a simple game of numbers, all you'd need is the magic number, and you'd be fine. But everyone on that team was so besotted with the whole thing that they failed to see just what they were truly up against. For such a redemption project to work, you need this country to admit that it was wrong. And someone will always come along and see Black Americans being given their due and want nothing more than to destroy it. They can't countenance any other reality. I tried to tell this to Councilman Perkins's team. But no one wanted to acknowledge just how deep the problem went.

Asking an algorithm to do what they wanted it to do would be to assume racism is logical. "If, then." Now, racism has its own internal logic, sure, but it is the logic of nightmares. You can't automate its reasoning.

Councilman Perkins and his team thought others would see what this city did and want to follow suit. But I knew that others would see what this city did and want to turn it to dust.

Nine months after the REPAIR Act was signed into law, following a series of protests at the state capitol led by prominent conservative activists, the governor released a statement disavowing the legislation. A recall effort against Mayor Gaetz was initiated, and, six months before the end of his term as mayor, Frank Gaetz was removed from office on the grounds of misallocation of government funds.

The city council selected Councilmember Robert Caine to finish Gaetz's term. Caine was subsequently reelected.

In a modest backyard, a white man in rolled-up shirtsleeves packs the soil behind a fence from which light green sprigs poke. He does this with care for several silent minutes, rises, then dusts his hands off and walks up his back porch. The body scanner framing the back entrance beeps as he passes through, then announces his temperature in red analog numbers.

The inside of the sitting room is just as modest. Sunlight shines through the west-facing windows to bounce off the glass covering a table designed to look like a hollowed-out tree trunk, gilding half of the man sitting in the chair facing the camera in profile. He's still wearing the dirty overalls and the shirtsleeves from earlier. His gloves lie on his lap. The pose looks practiced.

FRANK GAETZ, 47, FORMER MAYOR OF _____: This may sound trite and I don't mean it to, but writing the statement announcing the initiative was actually the most difficult part. I'm not discounting the work the team did. But it all falls apart if the statement isn't right. You only get one shot at this. I remember the presidential primaries. And the reason the socialist lost to the centrist among Black voters in South Carolina in 2020 was, as told to me by a Black Carolinian, that voting for the socialist would require the Black community to believe that white people were capable of doing something they've never done before: willingly and openly share in the economic bounty of this country. I needed to convince them that we were there. But I also needed to convince my white constituents. And if this whole effort was dressed in machine neutrality, if I could say "blame the algorithm," then maybe we could get away with the whole thing. Maybe it would feel a little bit less like a heist.

I was prepared to be the meat-shield here. If anything, it almost seemed like that was the point of the job. The team that Richie Perkins put together was formed sort of ad hoc. It was very Avengers. [Chuckling.] All of us from these different disciplines—lawyers, statisticians, historians, activists, politicians, even the medical professionals we consulted with—when they realized what Richie was doing, none of them balked. None of them thought it was impossible or too difficult. They all had the imagination for it. And it was my job to have the stomach for it.

Richie had brought the team together on his own, and they worked in secret, then prepared a report that landed on my desk.

Richie and I talked for a long time. About the contents, then about the rollout, about who would get what and when. Before I knew it, I'd bought in. I didn't even realize, but he'd converted me to the cause of reparations. And he knew it had to be me. It had to be the white guy.

It wasn't just that white constituents would listen to me with less resentment than they would feel if it were coming from a Black mayor. It was the righting of things. A white guy does it and it feels less like theft and more like penance.

You look at the state the country was in at the time, it seemed like everything was getting torn down. And there's me: young, rising star in the Democratic Party, not yet so progressive that the Establishment can't sink its claws into me, but not so far bought that I can't be pulled further to the left. And this opportunity lands on my desk in the form of this report. I used every bit of political capital I had to get the other city council members on board. Comptroller, all of them. Reminded me of that Supreme Court case, *Brown v. Board of Education.* You know why Chief Justice Warren worked so hard to get a unanimous decision? Anything less might've led the South to start another Civil War.

So there it is, all laid out there. How the dollar amounts were calculated. The mechanisms through which the funds should be disbursed. Further funding methods. All of it. And all I had to do was take credit.

During the recall effort, the names of the participants behind the initial REPAIR report were leaked. As a result, statistician Wendy Guan's visa was revoked. She now lives in her native China.

Death threats were issued against Dr. Athena Davis and the team of data scientists with which she had worked after they were doxed.

Councilman Richard Perkins was charged with corruption and misuse of public funds. The charges were subsequently dropped. Shortly thereafter, he resigned from his position on the city council.

Tommy DiSanto is currently a managing partner at Kittle & Loving and head of its pro bono practice.

Redacted's whereabouts are currently unknown. They participated in this documentary on the condition of anonymity.

The disbursement of funds to communities and individuals designated by the REPAIR Act lasted for ten months.

JPMorgan currently holds $3.2 billion in bonds from the City of _____

*

In Stanley Quarter Park, a girl in a blue-and-white-striped dress makes a slow turn on her bicycle, leaning in the opposite direction.

Dr. Davis smiles and walks over to congratulate her great-granddaughter.

Over the two of them in the middle distance, roll credits.

Our Language

FROM *A Public Space*

> She has no mother, La Ciguapa, and no children, certainly not her people's tongues. We who have forgotten all our sacred monsters.
>
> —*Elizabeth Acevedo, "La Ciguapa"*

THE BOOKS DO NOT say that I was a girl once. They do not say that I lived near the woods in the far outskirts of Higüey, that my name was Celi, that I was born in 1954. I want you to know that I was a real girl, like you. Una niña.

Like memory, language changes. Our words eddy around the things we fear. Isn't it funny, how it worries what we fear, water turning a jagged rock into something smooth and small? We have so many words to make a girl small: jovencita, señorita, mujercita.

What a wealth of words and yet there is so much that the books do not say.

Why would the books say, anyway, that I was midheight, with brown eyes and brown hair? There are ciguapas born every day, and it takes us lifetimes to become walking fears.

When I was a muchacha, my best friends and I would share a bag of limoncillos on the walk home from school. Have you ever tried a limoncillo? In English, they call it a Spanish lime, even though it doesn't grow in Spain. Isn't that something?

After school, the walk back to the village took about twenty-five minutes, but if we walked slow, we could make it last thirty-five and avoid some of the predinner chores waiting for us. We always tried to walk in the shade, our cheeks pink from the sun, our patent leather shoes picking up the dry dust of the country road.

Strolling three abreast, we cracked the green skin in half with our teeth and took the pink seeds into our mouths. One was never enough. Such a small fruit with an acidic sweetness that made you miss it, even as you held the seeds between your teeth. Before you finish one, you are already yearning for another. We call this can't-stopness seguidilla.

Listen closely. I'm teaching you our language.

Eating a limoncillo requires concentration. The stain of a limoncillo is a dark magic. The fruit is a pale peach, but stains a dark brown that ruins uniform blouses and sparks torrents of belts and chancletas and nights spent sniffling over a sink with a scrubbing board and a bottle of Clorox.

On one of those unremarkable days, I made it home without a single stain on my yellow uniform blouse. Picture the village. Little boys played street soccer, pausing when a car passed. A breeze tickled the sandaled feet of the abuelas rocking in white plastic mecedoras before rising up, up, up, to coax a gentle susurration from the glossy, green-leaved palm trees behind my house. In the distance, music. Always.

The house was two floors, coral-painted stucco with white accents. Modest and unremarkable. My mother waited for me at the door, her silhouette motionless against the sitting room light behind her. I broke into a jog and saw that her lips were set in a thin line, her arms crossed over her cotton housedress, her eyes red-rimmed.

She stood up straighter and uncrossed her arms. She forced her lips to lift at the corners.

I kissed her on the cheek. "Bendición, Mamá," I said. In our culture, it is customary to ask our relatives for a blessing every time we greet them. We are trained to careen through the world begging for blessings.

I have learned to make my own blessings. You will, too.

"Celi," she said. Her voice was stilted, as if she had been practicing. "I couldn't wait to tell you the good news."

I trailed her into my bedroom.

"Don't change yet," she said, as I began to unbutton my blouse. *Don't change yet.* I sat on the rose-covered blanket on my bed instead. "What is it? What's wrong?"

"You're getting married," she said, smile sepulchral, eyes fixed somewhere along my hairline.

"What? To who? Mamá, I'm fourteen." In this era, it was not uncommon for country girls my age to marry, but there were usually —how do I put it—other considerations.

"I know, mi amor. But there are things you don't know, even about yourself."

I wondered if I had, like the Virgin Mary, become pregnant without knowing it. We are taught so young to be suspicious of our own bodies. In our case, perhaps, not suspicious enough.

My mother took a long breath and sat next to me. She faced the wall and kept her face blank. "You're different. I need you to trust me. I'm trying to give you a full life."

"How am I different?"

"You'll know when you need to know," she said.

"Doesn't it sound like I need to know now?"

"You're too young to understand."

Isn't that one of the worst sentences you've ever heard? I won't teach it to you in Spanish.

"What's a full life, then?" I had started to cry. "What do you mean?"

"Children, security, family." She tucked my hair behind my ear. She whispered, "It's complicated, Celi, but I promise you, on the Virgin herself, that I'm trying."

It would be ironic, I suppose, for the history books to document how stubbornly we avoid our own stories.

The day after I turned fifteen, I was married to a man named Ignacio at the church near the school. I wore a new white, white dress. My mother hugged me so hard I feared my bones might break. My best friends, Laryssa and Benigna, wept in a pew. We were all grateful that our sobs were mistaken for tears of happiness.

I met Ignacio once before the wedding. He was a pleasant, if uninteresting, man in his midtwenties who wore short-sleeved button-down shirts in pastel colors. He was an accountant for a company in Higüey. He agreed to commute to work so that we could live in my parents' village, by the woods.

The ceremony was short and the night: very long.

*

Ciguapas are always women. This is true, though no one asks why. I think it has something to do with our powers of escaping. And because we are women, the literature has much to say about the way we look. *The ciguapas are very beautiful,* some books say. *The ciguapas are hideous,* say others.

I do not think the books are wrong. My problem is with what the books do not say.

The books say that the first ciguapas were magic born of necessity, pressurized alchemy. The colonists came, they say, and some island women escaped to the caves and to the sea. Terror morphed our bodies into something monstrous and untraceable. It took less than three years for the colonists to kill everyone else.

Then new generations of ciguapas came in on the ocean waves. We are a nation's wounds made flesh.

By the time I turned sixteen, I had a son named Javier and my parents had died in a car accident. Ignacio was a good man. He did all the right things. He held my hand at my parents' funeral and pressed a cool towel against my forehead as I gave birth.

It's certainly not the sort of thing worth putting in a book: Ignacio made good money and managed the house. I followed orders and kept everything clean. I focused my quiet desperation and love on my son. It's boring, really, in its normalcy.

The trouble began when I realized that I was getting smaller.

Every day, I became a little bit shorter. The changes were almost imperceptible at first. I would cook dinner and the pot of rice would feel a bit heavier than it had the day before, the shelf that held the plates a bit higher. My skirts seemed longer than I remembered; my shoes wider.

Shorter and shorter and shorter until I was table height. My husband complained. I was becoming hard to find.

By the time I turned seventeen, Javier was two years old and we were practically the same height.

That wasn't the only change. My skin seemed lit from within, like pure ámbar. Do you know about Dominican amber? Dominican amber is resin from an extinct tree called *Hymenaea protera.* Wondrous, isn't it? How nature keeps a record, even when we cannot, of species that no longer walk the earth. The honey-colored resin is nearly transparent and carries an extremely high number of fossil inclusions, small lives trapped for twenty million years, to be studied under loupes, sold to tourists, worn on pendants.

My eyes seemed larger in my shrinking face. My hair grew faster, coming in shiny, long, and thick. Several times, I cut my hair myself, huddled over the sink in the dead of night, with a sharp pair of kitchen shears. By the next morning, it had grown to cover my knees again.

And then there was the puzzle of what happened to my feet.

They shrank—along with the rest of my body—and they realigned. My knees began to ache as if someone were twisting them to the point of breaking. They began to turn outward, to pivot.

The change was slight, at first: I waddled like a pregnant woman, my toes facing out. But soon I was walking like a ballerina in the second position. People began to notice. The little boys at the market began to trail me home, imitating my walk.

At first, my husband brushed off the jibes and made dirty jokes to his friends over beers—but then the jokes were laced with something acidic. I could not find the words to say I felt betrayed, but I suppose he felt the same.

By the following year, my knees, my calves, and my feet had rotated completely to align themselves with my back. Ignacio loathed the sight of me. I had become something he didn't understand.

I stopped leaving the house. Try keeping a secret in Higüey; it's impossible.

When I stand facing a mirror here's what I see: A woman, about thirty-six inches tall. Proportionally small, with short limbs. Eyes large, dark, and clear. Hair long, down to the area where my knees should be, except that what I see there now is the tender backs of my knees, slender Achilles tendons, calloused heels.

I see Celimena, trying her best. And for reasons that never make it into the books, my deformity doesn't upset me the way it should. It feels true.

I had to learn how to move in my new body, but I'm adaptable. It did not take me long to learn to backpedal, to look over my shoulder constantly.

Ignacio didn't know what I was and he resented me for it. Have you seen his picture? He was a big man, nearly six feet tall, and solidly built besides, with a thick waist. He would come home from a night out with his friends, heavy-limbed with drink, and slam me against the walls.

When he realized that my bones seemed impervious to breakage, he tried harder.

He seemed resolved to tear me limb from limb, if he had to, to crack me open and release the secret I was hiding.

One night, he came home with Grecia, a local widow who practiced Santeria. You should know that we Dominicans say we're God-fearing Catholics, but when confronted with a stubborn problem, we'll try anything.

Grecia's eyes were milky with cataracts and her hair was pure silver, a braid coiled down the side of her neck. She wore all white and carried an old leather doctor's satchel. She smelled like cinnamon. Behind her, Ignacio stood with his hands in his pockets, shifting his weight from one foot to the other. He avoided my eyes. I understood that this was a last attempt.

"I'm sorry for the state of the house," I said, rushing toward Grecia and tripping lightly over my backward feet. "I didn't expect company. Can I offer you a cafecito with a little milk?"

Her pearly eyes widened and she gasped. "Ciguapa," she said, noticing my feet and taking a step back.

I froze.

"What?" my husband asked.

"She's a ciguapa." The old woman's eyes remained fixed on my feet. "I didn't know they were real."

"Ciguapa," I repeated.

Imagine hearing yourself named for the first time. My mind dredged up the word from the bog of my passive memory: an echo of the old folktale came to mind, but first, I thought of the cigua palmera, the national bird of the Dominican Republic. A bird that loves to perch in palm trees. In English, it's called the palmchat.

"Fix her," my husband said. "I'll give you everything I have. I have money in the bank. I can borrow more."

"Keep your money," she said. She shook her head. "The change can't be reversed."

Can you imagine a more dangerous monster than one who reads?

Well, I have gotten into the books. Here's what they say:

A ciguapa is a mysterious, savage, and mystical creature in the folklore of the Dominican Republic. The legend of the ciguapa appears to have originated among the indigenous Taino Indians, though it also appears to have been influenced by African folklore brought over by victims of the slave trade. The legend concerns a group of women who escaped enslavement during the Spanish colonial occupation of the Dominican Republic. The escapees took up residence in the wild, emerging only at night to forage for food.

Imagine a monster whose sole objective is survival. Imagine the bending and shrinking of bones, over generations, to achieve this one end.

The ciguapa's distinguishing features include a diminutive size (about three feet in height) and reversed feet. Because of the reverse placement of their feet, ciguapas can walk backward and forward comfortably. They are nearly impossible to track.

Bodies designed to elude and confound. Imagine the loneliness.

My husband knelt before Grecia and touched his face to her feet. His voice was low and filled with rage. "Her family knew and they cheated me. My only son is half monster. Will he change, too?"

"It is inherited," Grecia said slowly, "but I don't think so. Ciguapas are always women."

"So, what am I supposed to do," he said, forehead still pressed to Grecia's worn leather sandals. "I can't live like this."

Grecia looked at me again with something akin to pity. "Leave her." She stepped back and gently freed her legs from Ignacio's grasp. "Leave her alone."

"I'm your *wife*," I said, my anger finally welling up to answer his. "We were married before God. Do those vows mean nothing to you?"

"I was cheated. I didn't set out to marry some sort of demon," he said, rising heavily to his feet. At full height, he was nearly twice my size. "Some demon that could kill my only son."

"She won't hurt Javier," Grecia said. But now that Ignacio knew she could not fix me, her opinion no longer mattered. Ignacio ushered her out of the house, folding a few crisp bills into her palm, even as she tried to reason with him. He told her to never speak of me again and slammed the door.

"I could kill you," he said simply when he returned. "And no one would ask questions."

"Our three-year-old son is in the next room," I hissed, craning my neck to look up at him. The distance between us seemed infinite.

"So? He'll grow up knowing the truth. His mother was a monster and I did what I needed to do to her to keep him safe. He'll know his father is a brave man."

"This is what you call brave?"

"You know your voice is changing, too, right?" He pushed me against the wall. In the other room, Javier began to gurgle in his crib.

"Go get him," Ignacio said. "Go take him out of his crib."

"I may not be able to carry him anymore, but Javier is as much my son as he is yours. This is my house and I'm not going anywhere."

"Who paid for this house?"

"Where's the money my parents left me when they died?"

"Your parents are charlatans. You can't ever repay me for what your family has done to me."

He picked me up, kicked open the back door, and hurled me out into the backyard, which extended out into the woods. I scraped my elbows as I landed in the dirt, unable to rely on my knees. I didn't know how to fall yet.

He shivered. "Look at you, you're terrifying," he said. It infuriated him that I seemed content with this new body, even as I struggled to my feet. "You're not the woman I married," he said. "And you're not welcome in my house anymore."

He bolted the door behind him.

If fear is a currency, then those were extravagant times. The books acknowledge, at least, that this was the age of Trujillo. In awed, breathless lists, the books catalog the torture, the rapes, the mutilation. They say: *this brutality is unprecedented.*

Oh, but it's only an echo of what came before. You know that, right?

We are the record. It's etched into our bones. A million times.

The ciguapa has long, lustrous hair that covers her naked body. Because of the odd placement of her feet, the ciguapa is nearly impossible to capture. She lives in mountain caves, in the trees, and in underwater caves along the shores.

The ciguapa can capture a man with her dark, hypnotic eyes. She is known to find lone men on the road and lure them to her cave or to her alcove by the sea. The men are never seen again. It is assumed that she eats them.

I stood, shaking, and scanned the area for nosy onlookers.

You will unlearn shame, as I did, and you will be happier for it.

The woods loomed before me and I decided I would give Ignacio this temporary victory. I would take a walk.

The air was intoxicating: the perfume of Bayahíbe roses, a million petals curled in on themselves for the night, a self-embrace. I backpedaled, feeling a sudden urge to run far away, to plunge into the sea. I had never run so fast. Many miles passed in a light breeze. Without learning how, I climbed a palm tree near the shore and was suddenly aware of my altered clothes and how needlessly constricting they were. I jumped down and ran my hands through the wild dry grass, relished the cool soft sand beneath.

Night fell and a full moon emerged. Ciguapas dropped from the cradles of their palm trees. They emerged from behind bushes. They were all small like me and naked. They all walked backward, nimble on their feet. In this clearing there were a dozen or so, but I knew that there were many, many others.

The ciguapas gathered around me.

"We all already *know* each other," a ciguapa named Diana told me, kissing me on both cheeks.

It was true. I had never met Diana before, but it was true.

"We don't live together because it's safest," she said. "But the full moon is hard to resist."

"Luna blanca, cobertor y manta," said another ciguapa who called herself Yamila. "Fool moon. It's when we yearn for our old lives the most. It makes us do stupid things. But most nights, we eat, we explore, and then we sleep."

"Where do we sleep?" I asked.

"Wherever we want," Yamila said, her voice bell-clear. "Want to see my favorite?"

I nodded. Yamila and Diana led me to the shore, their feet leading the way, their eyes fixed on mine. The ancient pull in their gaze told me I could trust them.

There were no houses along this stretch of shore, and the only sources of light were the stars and the moon, refracted off the water in a million glimmering threads. The waves were gentle, beckoning, the air cool and fresh.

"Ready?" Yamila said.

They took my hands and led me into the water. Pulling me gently into its depths until I took a deep breath and plunged.

Diana gave me a thumbs-up under water. I could see and breathe as easily as I could on land. They taught me how to catch a fish and eat it raw, without ever rising to the surface. They led me to a series of underwater caves and I claimed a small one. I had never slept so well, or felt so safe.

Ciguapas can only be captured in a full moon, and only by a hunter accompanied by a black-and-white polydactyl dog. In captivity, ciguapas die of grief. (It won't surprise you to learn that this does not deter the hunters.)

With a small but passionate membership, the Ciguapa Hunters of the Dominican Republic (CHDR) advertises tours of the Dominican countryside in search of the elusive monster. The group's mascot, an Australian shepherd with an extra phalange on its front left paw, is present on every full-moon tour.

Few successful captures appear in the CHDR's records, but hopeful hunters commission, in advance, special display boxes for their trophies, designed to preserve a specimen and slow the decomposition process.

The club attracts local men and tourists in equal numbers. Members say that they enjoy most the male comradery and friendship they find on the hunts, outings in which they say they can truly be themselves.

I visited my son at night so that Ignacio wouldn't know. I would climb in the window and help him into bed and tuck his curly dark hair behind his ears. He would smile at me. I told him my story so that he would not forget me. How handsome my Javier was.

On one of these nights, I spoke to Javier and he began to cry. He couldn't understand me anymore. I held his big head in my arms and tried to tell him, tried to tell him, how much I loved him.

As he grew bigger, I became even smaller. One evening, I approached the window and heard Ignacio saying to Javier, "You shouldn't need to open the window at night, but if you do, this is where the latch is."

I waited until he was gone and then showed my face at the window. I could see Javier in his bed. I tapped the glass. He turned his back and lay with his face against the wall until morning came and I had to go away.

I have become a sort of animal. If the books are right, my voice sounds like braying or mewling now. Some words whip around in my mouth and leave my tongue bloodied.

I am choosing, more and more, not to speak at all. But you and I, we understand each other.

> *Though the ciguapa can breathe comfortably under water, she is best known for her diminutive size and superhuman speed on land. This extraordinary speed not only helps the monster elude capture, it also makes her a formidable predator.*

> *Historians disagree about the genetic provenance of the ciguapa. The written records are vexingly imprecise on the subject of ciguapic genealogy, though there have been reports of typical human women giving birth to daughters who, on reaching adulthood, transform into monsters. It is assumed, in these cases, that the women carried a recessive ciguapic gene. Some folkloric sources indicate that they are born ciguapas, while others hypothesize that ciguapas have procreated with human men, and that their descendants continue to exist among us.*

> *Some books say that ciguapas steal newborn babies from their cribs, such is their desire for motherhood and connection to the human race.*

> *See also: oread (mountain nymph); napaea (woodland nymph).*

> *See also: Genu recurvatum (medical condition in which knees are in reverse position, causing a deformity in which the afflicted appear to walk backward).*

See how they translate us?

Though he never let me in again, I stood at Javier's window every night for years. I like to think my presence was a comfort to him. In nightly increments, I watched him grow up to be a quiet, sad boy, big for his age.

When my husband announced that I had run away, no one questioned him, not even my friends. Heartsick, I listened at their windows. By then, they were married, too, and kept their own houses neat. Benigna was pregnant and Laryssa was trying. She visited Benigna often, as if attempting to pick up pregnancy through osmosis.

From time to time, I hoisted myself up to the window and

watched them stir sugar into their espressos. The sound of their spoons against the cups made me miss coffee. The delicious, bitter mundanity of it. The power was out, and with only a few candles lit, Benigna's living room looked cozy and welcoming.

"It seems unlike her, doesn't it?" Laryssa said once, after a long silence. "To leave Javier behind?"

"She really did love her baby," Benigna said, one hand on her swollen belly.

"But Ignacio would scare anyone off. That man was a drunken brute toward the end."

"Just the end? I'll never forget that wedding."

"Poor Celimena," said Laryssa.

"What could we have done?" said Benigna, folding a paper napkin into smaller and smaller pieces with nervous fingers. "We were just girls. Her parents wanted to marry her off."

"But so young?"

"You heard the rumors."

"They obviously weren't true." Laryssa drained her cup, and placed it upside down on its saucer. "We grew up with her, Benigna. We know her. She wasn't crazy."

"Her grandmother disappeared, too. Whatever happened to her? I heard she lives in the woods, runs around naked, eating berries at night."

Laryssa laughed. "Crazy like a fox. Sounds better than cooking and cleaning all day." She lifted the coffee cup and examined the rivulets formed by the coffee grounds.

"What do you see?"

What did I tell you? We look for magic *everywhere*.

"I see anger," said Laryssa slowly, as she turned the cup in her hands and examined the dregs. "A group of women. Tragedy. I don't know what it means."

I slipped away from the window as my best friends searched for the future in their coffee cups. I wanted to tell them that my grandmother had been captured by a hunter and that she had died of grief. But this is the saddest part of the change, losing the ability to speak.

Within a few years, Ignacio remarried to a wiry busybody named Gladys who painted her toenails neon green on my terrace every Sunday.

Together, they had two little boys and Javier seemed out of place. It was decided that he would go to New York to study English and live with Ignacio's sister. I crouched in the bushes and listened as Ignacio made the arrangements to fly him to LaGuardia. I clawed my nails into my palms until I drew blood.

The night before Javier left, he came to the window for the first time in a long, long time and we studied each other in the moonlight. He put his palm on the glass and I put up mine.

Then he closed the curtains, but through the sheer fabric, I could see his shoulders shaking as he packed his suitcase.

Did I mention that we love riddles? Adivinanzas? Here's one:

> *The one who makes it does not use it.*
> *The one who uses it does not see it.*
> *The one who sees it does not desire it—no matter how pretty it may be.*
> *Can you divine the answer?*
> *A coffin.*

The books say that we are immortal. I would like to correct that: we are long-lived. We can be killed. We can kill ourselves. We can die of grief. But we live very long lives. The oldest ciguapa in our clan is more than two hundred years old.

Decades feel like months: we sleep, we wake, we feed. The village gossip interests us less and less. It's so predictable. Boring in its normalcy. The past is a photograph from someone else's life: curling at the edges, and fading. Like the books, we have become particular about what's worthy of memory.

We have learned to outlive the people we love.

Here's another adivinanza:

> *Diligent twins*
> *Shapers of lack*
> *Who walk with their blades pointed forward*
> *And their eyes pointed back.*
> *Can you divine the answer?*
> *Scissors* (did you guess?)

In their cozy houses, surrounded by their children and their husbands, Laryssa and Benigna still talk diligently around my memory, tracing the outlines. Like us, they choose what to remember.

But what can they know of my untamed grief? Javier. In every word, an echo of his name.

Thirty years passed and Javier came back to my house, alone. My heart beat a fraught old song in my throat.

On the first night, when everyone in the village was asleep, he walked to the edge of the woods, as if looking for something. I watched him, enthralled.

He sat down on a tree stump, looked at his fine leather loafers, and checked his gold watch.

"Mamá," he said, finally. "I know you're here."

Mothers do a lot of things without thinking. I walked out into the clearing.

Javier shuddered and leaped to his feet, as if to run away—then gingerly bent at the waist to hug me. I smelled nothing beyond cologne and aftershave and mosquito repellent. Who was this strange man with my Javier's eyes? He was tall, like his father, but I was pleased to see that he carried a hint of me in the creases around his mouth, and in his dark, thick eyebrows.

"I got married," he said, sitting back down on the amputated tree, resting his manicured hands on his knees.

I crossed my arms. I suppose it would have been too much to ask to have been invited? But I couldn't stay angry. Not after waiting this long to see him again. I uncrossed my arms and hazarded a smile.

"I have a daughter," he said blithely. "Her name is Celimena. After you. She's twelve."

"God bless her! What's she like?" The last of my pride dissolved. I put my hands on his giant ones.

He tilted his head back, gently pulled his hands away. "I can't understand you. You know that."

I took a step toward the trees.

He straightened up again, as if remembering a memorized speech. "I haven't forgotten you. I'm going to tell my wife about your disease and we'll get you to America somehow and find you a surgeon," he said. "Or here, even! We can take you to the best surgeon here. We have money now."

I pictured myself in a hospital gown in a white, white hospital, a doctor slicing my calves open and rearranging my tendons like a florist rearranging rose stems. I shook my head.

I tried to explain that we can't be fixed—not in that way. We can't relinquish what we have been built to carry. And it isn't so bad, anyway, to be ourselves. But the sound of my voice only seemed to make things worse.

"Don't you even want to try?" A drop of spit landed on Javier's lip. "Don't you realize how selfish you are? What if Celi grows up to be like you? We'll need to know how to fix it."

I wanted to hold him in my arms and comfort him, but he shoved me away.

"Do you know how hard it's been for me? To grow up motherless? To lie to everyone about my mother? It would have been better if you'd just died." And now he was crying, this adult man with my Javier's eyes.

A venomous grief slithered up my calves and noosed my throat. I stopped trying to talk. By now, I understood my power. I looked in his eyes until his expression softened to a dull calm. I faced him as I walked away and he followed me, his lumbering footfalls heavy and thick. I imagined bringing him back to my sea cave, where I could rock him like a giant doll in eternal sleep.

Ciguapas have done worse.

But me? I had learned something new. I waited until the wave of anger receded back to some distant shore.

I kissed his hand. I watched from the window, just like before, as he packed his suitcase. I let him get in a taxi and find his way back to New York.

I grieved him again and I let him go. This letting-go is called living.

I know it will be hard, but when this message finds you—and it will find you—let your body hear it. You're the one I'm waiting for.

I've read that it gets very cold in New York, but you won't need much here. When you arrive in the old house in Higüey, wait until nightfall and then come straight through the back and out into the palm trees.

I will wait for you here. As long as it takes. Years and years and years—like sand to me. You will be sad at first, as I was, as we all were and are. But then you will see how the trees grow tall around us here, to keep us safe, and the grass is sweet-smelling and velvet-soft beneath our unloved feet. The breeze is a light kiss across

our faces and the moon—full and white and glowing—is a generous mother. You will finally become who you have always been. You
will remember what your body has forgotten.

I've waited so long for you, mi nieta, my granddaughter. Listen
closely to me. I am teaching you our language.

GENE DOUCETTE

Schrödinger's Catastrophe

FROM *Lightspeed*

THINGS BEGAN TO GO badly for the crew of the USFS *Erwin*
around the time Dr. Marchere's coffee mug spontaneously reassembled itself.

Dr. Louis Marchere was not, at that moment, conducting some
manner of experiment. Well, he *was,* only not on entropy and the
nature of time. He was running several *other* tests, of the kind that
make perfect sense on a scientific vessel such as the *Erwin.* About
half of them were biological in nature, concerning how small
samples of cellular material react to certain deep-space factors.
Other tests were more at home in the general field of astrophysics.
But—again, as this is important—he was not conducting a test
on entropy.

He just dropped his coffee mug. More exactly, he elbowed it
from the corner of the table, while he was concentrating on things
unrelated to the nature of falling objects. The mug fell onto the
hard, ferrous metal of a lab floor, shattered, and sent his coffee
—which was already disappointingly lukewarm—everywhere.

Louis Marchere was pretty upset about this. He'd been on dozens of deep-space scientific missions over the years, and this mug
—a white mug with a black swan—had made it through all of
them. It was a gift from his daughter.

But things break. No use dwelling.

Then, while Marchere was fetching a towel and a broom, the
shattered pieces of the mug re-formed, rose up, and settled back
on the corner of the table.

The spilled coffee remained where it was, either because it had decided that it wanted no part in whatever nonsense the mug had going on, or so as to verify—for Dr. Marchere's sake—that what he witnessed had actually happened.

Which, of course, it had not. Shattered mugs don't simply decide to reassemble themselves. They don't decide to do *anything*, because they're inanimate objects with no agency, subject to the whims of the same laws of physics as everyone and everything else in Louis Marchere's laboratory, including Louis Marchere.

This was true irrespective of where that laboratory happened to be located. It had to be.

In this particular instance, the lab was in the middle of a ship that was in the middle of deep space, in a previously unexplored quadrant. The part about it being unexplored was unusual, but only a *little* unusual. The quadrant in question—C17-A387614-X.21, but everyone called it Brenda—was right in the center of a fully explored space grid. There had been many exploratory missions to all the other cubes on that grid, but nobody had bothered to check out Quadrant Brenda.

Probably, this was because Quadrant Brenda looked incredibly boring. There didn't appear to be anything *in* Brenda—no stars, planets, or moons. Comets showed no interest in visiting, and asteroids kept their distance. In a universe that could be defined as "enormous patches of nothing, with occasional, albeit incredibly rare, bits of something mixed in here and there," Quadrant Brenda somehow managed to contain even *more* nothing. This was probably why nobody had bothered to explore it before. It was definitely why the USFS *Erwin* was there, as this much nothing might mean something.

So far, two days into the quadrant, Dr. Marchere could confirm that it was just as boring on the inside as it looked from the outside. Three thousand different sensors on and outside the ship confirmed that sometimes a quadrant full of nothing is just a quadrant full of nothing.

And then the second law of thermodynamics—which was both extremely important and incredibly reliable—stopped working.

Dr. Marchere knew that wasn't what really happened; a dozen better explanations were surely available. He just had to find one of them.

First, he checked on the lab's artificial gravity, which he did by going to the wall panel and examining the settings, rather than by jumping up and verifying that after having done so, he also fell down.

The control panel confirmed that he had artificial gravity, and that nothing anomalous had transpired recently, either near the coffee mug or in any other part of the lab.

Louis returned to the table and picked up the coffee mug, half expecting it to fall apart in his hands. It did not; the mug appeared intact, with no indication it had been in seven pieces quite recently.

"How did you manage that?" he asked the mug, which didn't respond.

Dr. Marchere held the mug over the floor and considered a practical but possibly irreversible test. Would the mug reassemble itself a second time? If so, the anomaly could be pinned down to something peculiar about the black swan mug his daughter gave him some years back. Perhaps it was even a trick of some kind, just waiting for the day he dropped it. She bought this trick mug based on certain assumptions about her father: that he was naturally clumsy, or vindictive about mugs, and would have shattered it before now, revealing the gag.

But that hardly seemed possible. It would require that self-healing mug technology existed, which it did not. And if it had, there was still the problem of the mug also returning to the tabletop.

He decided that this was a scientific problem, while wanting to keep the mug intact was an emotional problem. But he'd already reconciled with having broken the mug his daughter gave him, and felt confident that, if she were there, she'd understand.

He let go. The mug fell, broke into five pieces . . . and remained broken.

Of course it did. How could he have expected otherwise?

He fetched the towel and the broom, cleaned up the mess, and made an appointment with the medical wing. One of the twelve remaining possible explanations to consider, before upturning the second law of thermodynamics, was that he was going mad, and that was information that couldn't wait.

Dr. Louis Marchere didn't make it to the medical wing for his checkup.

"Final approach," the computer announced, in a cheerful singsong.

Corporal Alice Aste was in the rear portion of the shuttle at the time of the announcement, performing some light calisthenics to get the blood moving in preparation for . . . well, something. There was no telling what she was headed into, but there was an excellent chance that it would require her to be limber. This was an old combat-readiness technique that had less applicability now, in peaceful times, but she knew of more than one soldier who didn't live to become an ex-soldier due to a pulled hamstring.

She climbed back to the front of the cabin to get a look at the side of the vessel through the front windshield. The United Space Federation Science Vessel *Erwin* was right where Alice expected it to be, free-floating in the middle of Quadrant C17-A387614-X.21-slash-Brenda and doing absolutely nothing.

She opened up the comms.

"USFS *Erwin*, this is Corporal Aste of the USF Security Force. I'm on approach, and intend to dock. Please respond."

No answer.

"Again, *Erwin*, this is USFSF Corporal Alice Aste, on approach, requesting dock. Please open bay doors. Respond, *Erwin*."

She waited for a few seconds, in case someone over there felt chatty, then left the line open and went back to the rear of the cabin to get ready.

In any normal circumstance, Alice would be speaking with a hangar tech now, working out the details on how and where she'd be parking her shuttle. These weren't normal circumstances. What she expected from the *Erwin* was continued radio silence, just like when Alice sent a transmission from the base ship—the *Rosen,* parked at the edge of the quadrant—and just like the same radio silence the science vessel had been honoring for a little more than six weeks.

The last official transmission from the *Erwin* was recorded forty-seven days ago. It was from Captain Hadder, and it read: *We aren't here again today.* It was received, as were all of the science vessel communiqués, at the research station relay hub and then forwarded to the main cluster, where it sat for several days before anyone actually looked at it. And then, the only reason they did was that no subsequent communications came through and somebody thought that was notable.

Protocol was for a twice-daily check-in. Granted, the "day" these transmissions were sent and the "day" they were received were hardly ever the same, given the vast distances the signals had to cross, even when using the FTL ports. Still, ships like the *Erwin* had to transmit on a prearranged schedule, even if that transmission was nothing more than a *not much, what's up with you?*

Self-evidently, something was now *up* with the *Erwin.*

Once it became clear that the cryptic message had no obvious, direct meaning, it was handed off to a linguistics team, and run through some databases. It received a partial hit on an old Earth song by the Zombies, and an even older poem by Hughes Mearns. Neither made sense in the context of deep-space communications from science vessels.

A message was sent back, asking for clarification, but no clarification arrived. Someone got a linguist involved, who decided that in order to get a proper response from the *Erwin*, base had to answer in kind. He offered several suggestions, such as: *If you are not there, where are you?* and *Are you here again now?*

When that didn't do the trick either, somebody dug up the Zombies' song and broadcast *that*, to see if it triggered a response, and then tried reading back both the annotated and full versions of the Mearns poem.

Still nothing.

By then, one of the network's orbital satellites got an angle on the ship, and sent back a video feed. The USFS cognoscenti were able to determine that: (1) the *Erwin* wasn't moving, (2) it had a heat signature, strongly implying the ship still had power, and (3) there was no evidence of outgassing, so it either still had atmosphere, or all of the atmosphere had escaped already.

All that was left to try was a crewed mission, which was how the USFSF *Rosen* ended up at the edge of the Brenda quadrant, and how Alice ended up on the shuttle.

The shuttle's autopilot sounded a gentle alert.

"Bay doors remain closed," it said.

"Computer, transmit bay door override to the *Erwin*, on my authority."

"Transmitting," it said calmly. Then, "No response. Collision imminent. Course correction strongly recommended."

Sometime in the past twenty years, the people in charge of these things at the USF standardized the vocal communications from all Space Federation computers, and it was decided the voice they used should be, above all, serene. It worked fine in most situations, but came off as ridiculous to the point of self-parody in high-stress circumstances. Phrases like *explosive decompression in five seconds* aren't meant to be heard in a voice meant to soothe unruly children.

"All right, keep your pants dry, computer," Alice said.

"This computer has no pants."

"Pull up from the current course and bring us alongside the hull. I'll go in the side door."

"Course corrected. Would you like to hear about the explosive charges inventory?"

"That'd be great, thanks."

The computer navigated the shuttle right up next to the *Erwin*, about twenty yards from the rear hatch. The hatch's functional intent was to allow someone from inside to get outside, to make repairs on the hull or to unjam the bay doors, clean a filter, touch up the paint job, or whatever. It wasn't meant to be used to get in from the outside, and almost never *was* used that way. Despite that, hatches like this were called *pirate doors*.

The good thing about pirate doors, and what made them so useful in times like this, was that there was an airlock on the other side, so if she had to blow the door with one of the many explosive charges on inventory she wouldn't be breaching the entire deck.

After gowning up for the spacewalk, Alice stuffed a few charges in a bag—like her, the bag was a veteran of combat, and came with a steel panel that doubled as a piece of armor in a pinch —added a couple of blasters, and headed across on an umbilical. She expected to have to blow the door, but it opened easily after a few turns of the hatch's wheel.

Alice unhooked the umbilical, ordered the shuttle to hold position, stepped in, and sealed the hatch from the inside. The wall panel indicated the ship had power, so she pressurized the airlock and let herself into the inner door.

Then, theoretically, she was free to take off her helmet.

"Computer, run a check for airborne pathogens," she said.

The computer—the one built into the suit this time—blinked a silent confirmation on her visor.

"Negative results," it said, after checking. "Atmosphere breathable."

Alice was standing at one end of a modest hangar, with two parked shuttles exactly like the one outside and room for two more.

"Then where is everybody?" she asked, as she appeared to be alone.

"Please be more specific," the computer said. "Whom would you like to locate?"

"Never mind."

"Never minding."

Alice took the helmet off.

The air smelled like the standard filtered air she'd been breathing for most of her adult life, and the gravity that held her to the floor of the bay felt like Earth-standard. Both good things. Yet even if the crew of the *Erwin* wasn't expecting a visitor, there should have been *someone* in the shuttle hangar, if only to ask her what the hell she was doing there.

"Hello?" she shouted. She heard her voice echo back, resonating with a slightly metallic hum. No doors opened, and nobody came running.

A quick inspection of the bay confirmed only that there weren't any bodies lying around.

"Is anybody here?" she shouted.

Nothing.

The Flying Dutchman, she thought, referencing an old Earth maritime ghost story she remembered liking as a child. It wasn't, of course, but that was what always sprang to mind in situations like this.

Alice had investigated her share of wrecks in her day, but usually the explanation was self-evident, and she was just there on the off chance someone managed to survive whatever drastic event had killed their ship. Hardly anyone ever did, because spaceships were surrounded by the vacuum of space, which was actively hostile toward human beings.

This time, there was no obvious explanation. The ship seemed to be working fine, albeit on reserve power—she could tell from the feel of the floor that the *Erwin*'s engines were definitely offline—it was just that everyone was somewhere *else* for some reason.

So where do I begin?

The USFS *Erwin* had five decks total. The captain's bridge was on the top deck at the front of the ship, which was the farthest point from the hangar. Alice felt obligated to start there—if for no other reason than to announce her arrival to the person who was supposed to have already authorized that arrival. At the same time, it was pretty far away; surely, she could find someone closer to her current location, who could fill her in on why the entire vessel was running silent. Or rather, drifting silent.

Alice found the door that led to the rest of the ship, and hesitated.

"Computer," she said, addressing her suit, "synchronize with the ship's computer."

"Synchronizing," the computer said, in the tone of voice waitresses used when asking children what flavor ice cream they wanted. "Synchronization complete."

"Computer, report life signs, total. Human only."

The synchronization allowed Alice to leverage all the ship's systems for her inquiry. It was supposed to help clear things up. It did not.

"No life signs detected," the computer said.

This was obviously incorrect. Aside from the fact that the *Erwin* had a complement of eighty-five, Alice was herself alive. Anything less than one was an error.

"Computer, recheck life signs, human only."

"Rechecking."

Alice pressed her face up against the window of the door she was about to go through. The hallway on the other side was well lit, and entirely empty. It ran the length of the lower deck, and —if she recalled the vessel's specs correctly—was home to about 60 percent of the crew. There should have been *somebody* around.

"Two hundred and six life signs detected," the computer said.

"No . . . no, that's not the right answer either," Alice said.

"What is the right answer?" the computer asked.

"I don't understand."

"What is the right answer?" the computer repeated.

"Computer, I'm asking for an exact life sign count of all the humans on board this ship. I don't know the answer, but I know it's a whole number that one arrives at by actually *counting* those life signs."

"Understood. What is your expectation?"

"I don't know the right answer, or I wouldn't have asked, but I would *expect* it to be anywhere between one and eighty-six."

"Rechecking," the computer said. Then, "Seventy-two life signs detected."

"Is that the real count, computer?"

"As requested, the total is between one and eighty-six. Is this acceptable?"

"If it's the *actual* count, yes."

"The actual count is seventy-two."

Alice was pretty sure the computer didn't perform anything like an actual count, which was a minor problem masking a much more serious one. Clearly, something was wrong with the *Erwin's* computer; counting things wasn't a difficult task.

"Computer, run a full internal diagnostic."

"Running diagnostic."

"Let me know what you find," she said. Then she pressed the override code for the door and left the hangar for the crew's living quarters corridor.

"Hello?" she shouted. "Is anyone here?"

Nobody responded.

All the doors were closed. Alice's override code could open any one of them, but—and this was a decidedly odd but undeniable truth—she was *afraid* to do it.

Alice Aste had been working with the USF Security Force for fifteen years, and before that she'd been a veteran of five interplanetary conflicts. She'd once spent two months adrift and alone in a disabled life raft, rescued by chance some fifteen hours before her oxygen ran out. Before that, she'd suffered a childhood of privation during her waking hours, and nightmares when she slept. She came to grips with her own mortality when she was ten. She did not *get* afraid, or rather, she wasn't afraid of the unknown. (Fear of the *known*, on the other hand, was quite sensible.)

And yet, on an impossibly empty vessel adrift in an unusually empty deep-space quadrant, Alice had to admit that she was one loud noise from freaking the hell out.

"Anybody?" she asked. She hesitated at the first door.

Just plug in the code and ask whoever's on the other side what's going on here.

She didn't plug in the code. Her pulse was up, and her breathing was shallow. She wondered if this was what a panic attack felt like.

"Calm down," she said to herself. "Just go straight for the bridge. You can see the stars from the bridge."

That was one of the tricks she picked up when she was ten; there is comfort in the vast emptiness of space. At least for her.

"Diagnostic complete," the computer said. Alice jumped two feet in the air.

"Computer, report results," she said, once she got her heart started again.

"Results are terrific," the computer said.

". . . computer, please repeat."

"Terrific. Self-diagnostic reports computer is terrific. Perfect score. Computer would report a thumbs-up if computer had thumbs."

The *Erwin*'s computer had evidently lost its mind. This was, of course, just as impossible as the constantly adjusting life sign count. Computers had no minds to lose.

"Are you certain, computer?" she asked.

"Computer is certain. Computer has no thumbs."

Alice wondered if a full reboot of the ship's computer was in order. She'd have to do that from the bridge, but that was where she was heading anyway. It might take a while, but if there really was nobody on this vessel aside from her, she'd need to interrogate the ship's logs. For that to work, a sane and rational computer would be important.

She headed down the hall at a normal walking pace that quickly devolved into a jog. A door might open and that, she decided, would be bad.

There's no such thing as irrational fear, she thought, recalling the wisdom of one of her academy trainers. *Your instincts know why they're afraid; you just gotta catch up.*

She made it to the other end of the hall, to the elevator, punched the button for the top deck, and checked the corridor behind her twelve times while waiting for the elevator to arrive.

It did. She jumped in, and the doors swished closed reassuringly. Up she went.

And up, and up. The elevator should have taken less than thirty seconds to reach the bridge. After well over a minute, Alice became concerned that maybe deck one wasn't where they were headed, except there was no further point to travel to while still remaining on the *Erwin*.

"Computer, are we going to deck one?"

"Confirmed, deck one."

"What's taking so long?"

"Traveling from deck five to deck one takes a nontrivial amount of time," the computer said, "and time is a construct."

"That isn't a helpful answer."

"Would you like to try a different narration?"

"A what? No, I just want to go to deck one."

"Deck one, coming up."

Alice sighed.

"When?" she asked.

"I cannot provide an exact time," the computer said.

"All right. Computer, if I stopped the elevator right now, where would I be? What deck."

"Would you like to stop the elevator right now?"

"No, just tell me where I would be if I did."

"You would be on deck one and five-eighths."

"Computer, this ship *has* no deck one and five-eighths."

"That is incorrect," the computer said. "There are multiple fractional decks."

"How many?"

"Unclear. How many would you like for there to be?"

"Never mind. Is it a finite amount?"

"This computer infers that the amount must be finite, as otherwise, deck one would be unattainable. It is coming up shortly, and is therefore not unattainable."

Alice had an unkind response for that, but then the elevator came to a stop and the doors opened.

"Arrived, deck one," the computer said.

Alice stepped out onto the bridge. For a vessel of this type, the bridge was really very small—especially as compared to the military ships to which she was accustomed. It had two seats at the front, a raised seat in the middle for the captain, and two seats in the back, with instrumentation spread throughout.

Captain Matthew Hadder—unshaven, in dirty clothing, looking tired, and shorter than she expected—was in the chair, and an ensign she didn't know was at the console to her left.

"You've shot Ensign Anson," Hadder said, which was an interesting thing to say given that Alice hadn't done anything of the kind.

But then the ensign fell over dead, having indeed been shot by a blaster. Still more interesting, it was only then that Alice drew her blaster from its holster and fired it. It struck Ensign Anson directly in the chest two seconds prior to being fired.

"What?" Alice said.

"Ensign Anson has been shot," Hadder said. "By your blaster, which you used to shoot him with."

"But I *didn't* shoot him."

"He was shot, and then you did it. Don't worry, it wasn't your fault. It *was,* because if you hadn't run in with a gun, Ensign Anson would *not* be shot, but the shot came faster than the blaster off your hip. Don't worry, it's been happening all day. He's dead, but only now. He wasn't earlier, and may not be later. Who are you and what are you doing on my ship?"

"I'm . . . I don't understand. How could I fire my blaster before I fired my blaster?"

"It happened before you decided to do it, but if you want to know why you decided before you decided, I can't provide you with that. He may have been about to shoot, with a gun he both had and did not have. He does not right *now* have a gun, but may have had one before you decided to shoot."

"He's unarmed. I shot an unarmed ensign."

"I can testify to Ensign Anson being both armed and unarmed at once, if it comes to that. Also, the ship's cause-and-effect has been acting up all day. But enough about the dead ensign; once more, who are you and what are you doing on my ship?"

"I'm Corporal Alice Aste, USFSF. I've been sent here to find out what happened to this ship."

"Quite a lot! We just lost an ensign, and the rest of my command deck crew have reported nonexistent. But what's the rush!"

"Your last communication was over six weeks ago, and you've been adrift since. I'm here to find out what kind of assistance is needed, and then to get that assistance for you."

"That's hardly possible," he said. "I sent a message just yesterday."

"None have been received."

"No, no, no, I would've remembered if I had sent *silence.* I didn't. I sent a message that went like this: *Please stay away.*"

"That wasn't it. What we received was, *We aren't here again today,*" Alice said. "Do you remember sending that?"

"Ahhh." Captain Hadder clapped his hands on the side of his head. "I got it wrong, I meant to say, I wish, I wish you'd stay away."

Captain Hadder had been going in and out of rhyme for the entire conversation. At first, she thought it was just an accident of word choice. Now she was thinking he was doing it on purpose, and also that he'd begun to lose his mind, just like his ship's computer. Unless she was losing *her* mind. She'd just shot a crew member, but if asked to explain how that happened, the best she could come up with was that the shot was fired before she pulled the trigger.

"Why did you want us to stay away?" Alice asked. "You seem in need of rescue."

"Rescue! It's only been a day."

"Again, it's been more than six weeks, Captain."

"Computer, how long has it been?"

"It has been a day, Captain," the computer said.

"There, you see?" Hadder said. "If you received that message six weeks ago, that's hardly *my* fault. I sent it yesterday; you should be receiving it now."

"Captain Hadder, you *know* there's something wrong with your ship's computer, don't you?" Alice asked. "It's been providing me with inaccurate information since I boarded."

"Not at all! It's adjusted quite well. You must have been asking it the wrong questions."

"Computer," she said, "how many life signs are there aboard the ship?"

"There are between one and eighty-six," the computer said, "or zero, or two hundred and six."

"There," Alice said. "See? That's an unacceptable response."

"Why, it's a ridiculous question!" Hadder said. "The answer is clearly variable from moment to moment. You should expect to have a different answer every time. Now where is Ensign Anson?"

"Isn't he the one I shot?"

"Yes, yes, but he should be back by now."

Ensign Anson was still lying dead on the floor, and Captain Hadder was clearly insane. Alice put her hand on her blaster, reflexively. It was probably a bad idea, given she'd only just not-shot-but-also-shot Anson, but instincts existed for a reason.

"Once again, Captain, why did you send the *stay away* message? Did something happen here? An accident maybe?"

"Nothing is the matter," he said, which was clearly untrue.

"Then why did you send that message?"

"Because *nothing is the matter!* Ask Anson; he can explain it better."

"Maybe I should ask someone *else* from the crew," Alice said slowly. She'd begun to talk more slowly and deliberately with Captain Hadder, the way one might talk to a person in a bomb vest. "Captain, can you tell me where everyone else is?"

"I don't know," he said. "But if you didn't see them on your way to the bridge, they're probably in their quarters."

"All right. Don't you need them in order to work the ship? Maybe you can find your own way out of this quadrant, with a little help. One of the engineers?"

"Ensign Anson and I can handle the bridge ourselves," he said. "Little to do when you're adrift."

"My point is that you don't *need* to be adrift. Some members of the crew could be enacting repairs."

"I see your reasoning, but about the engines, there's nothing to be done. They work perfectly, or they would; it's the physics that are wrong."

"Then someone should fix . . . the physics?"

He was surely speaking nonliterally. Alice remembered a particularly sarcastic first officer who—in the middle of a war—would say things like, "Barring some change in the laws of physics, this next torpedo will be a direct hit; brace for impact." Captain Hadder's delivery was wanting, but she felt certain that he was aiming for the same sort of droll wit.

"They're not *broken,* they're *wrong,*" he said. "I'm amazed you've survived on board the ship for this long, Corporal."

"I haven't . . . Captain. Just tell me where the rest of the crew is, and I'll go find someone who can help."

"As I said, they could be in their quarters. Computer, are the crew in their quarters?"

"The crew may or may not be in quarters, Captain."

"There, see?" he said. "They may be there."

"Then should we go down and check?" she asked. "I passed the quarters on my way."

"Oh, goodness no, don't do that. Imagine the consequences."

"I don't understand."

"Corporal, it's really very simple. I don't know if they're alive or not. If I check, I will *definitely* know. Who wants that on their conscience?"

"They're either alive or they're not alive," Alice said.

"The computer confirmed, they are both. Have you ever seen a person who was both alive and dead?"

"Of course not. Those are binary states."

"Neither have I. Therefore, if they are currently both alive *and* dead, and one of us were to go down to see which one it was, and *we* have never seen a person who was both alive and dead, then by checking, we will ensure that they are either one or the other, and I want no part of that! Neither should you, after what happened to poor Ensign Anson. Already enough blood on *your* hands."

About 95 percent of Alice thought this was the most ridiculous thing she'd ever heard. The 5 percent that didn't was the same 5 percent that was in charge when she ran down the corridor in deck five, in the midst of something like a panic attack. She didn't want to open those doors either, even before having her intelligence assaulted by Captain Hadder's nonsense.

"How about if we just open a comm line, right now?" she asked. "We can hail the *Rosen*."

"Oh no, that's impossible. Nothing on the bridge works right now."

She looked around. The panels were lit, which wasn't an expectation on a nonworking bridge.

"You have power. It all looks like it's working."

"It's not," he said. "Hasn't been since yesterday. And even though we clearly *do* have power, the engine isn't providing it. Couldn't tell you what is."

She pointed to one of the chairs at the front of the deck. "May I?" she asked.

Captain Hadder stepped aside and waved her through.

She sat down at what was—if she remembered the ship design specs accurately—the helmsman's chair. It had all the navigational instrumentation, and the communications matrix.

All the ships in the USF communicated locally by sending concentrated radioelectric bursts in tight, targeted beams. A similar approach was used for long-range communications, only the local transmission was sent to a relay, which repeated the information through an FTL tunnel.

The *Rosen* was just at the edge of Quadrant Brenda. In a rational universe, the *Erwin* would already know the *Rosen* was there, either because the *Rosen* pinged it when it was in range—which it did, as part of the ongoing effort to establish communication—or because the midrange sensors have only one job, which is to detect nearby objects and keep track of them.

Possibly, the *Erwin* was no longer a participant in a rational universe.

She asked the ship to perform a full sensor sweep, and while there was some good news—it *did* pick up the *Rosen,* and her shuttle—according to the survey, there was *nothing* on the starboard side.

Not just *nothing,* as in, *space is pretty much a lot of nothing anyway* nothing. This was a nothingness that far exceeded any previously recorded nothing, on a scale that made it quite a remarkable something. There were no quantum fluctuations popping in virtual particles, or the evidence of gravitational force acting at a distance to warp the fabric of space-time, or microscopic space debris. There were no solar winds. There was just nothing.

Alice was reminded of the ancient Earth maps: those two-dimensional rectangles meant to approximate a portion of a spherical object. The early ones weren't large enough to encompass the entire planet, so when one drew a line to the edge of the map, it wasn't an expectation that the line would pick up again on the opposite side. There was nothing else there because the mapmaker had stopped drawing what came next.

This is the end of the map, she thought. *Here be dragons.*

"No, that can't be right," she said. "It must be a sensor malfunction."

"Sensors operating at full capacity," the computer said, helpfully.

Alice stood up and leaned, to get a look at that side of the ship. If she didn't know better, she'd have said someone was out there hanging a gigantic piece of nonreflective fabric over that part of space. Maybe they were.

"Oh no, don't do that," Hadder said.

"Do what?"

"*Stare* at the Void. Never a good idea."

"You know about this?"

"Of course I do. It's why the ship isn't moving."

"Great, now we're getting somewhere. Tell me what it is, and then maybe we can work up a strategy to get away from it."

"It's nothing. You read the sensors. I don't know why you're acting so surprised, I *told* you what the problem was already."

"You didn't mention the giant Void in space," she said. "I would have remembered that."

"I said *nothing* was the matter with the ship. That's very clear."

She sighed, and resisted the urge to draw her blaster again.

"Doesn't matter," she said. "I can still see the *Rosen*. I'll hail them, set up a tow."

"Best of luck!"

She opened a channel.

"USFSF *Rosen*, this is Corporal Aste, on the USFS *Erwin*. Please respond."

The transmission came from the radar array at the highest point on the top of the *Erwin*, with secondary and tertiary arrays on the underbelly in the event of damage from space debris or an act of violence. When Alice sent the transmission, the signal was transmitted by all three.

Alice already knew this was how local communication worked, but this time she got a dramatic demonstration of it, because for some reason the radio signal she sent out became visible for five full seconds, before falling apart.

It was hard to get a total count on the number of things that were wrong with this. Radio waves weren't supposed to be a part of the visible spectrum, so that was a big problem right there. Also, before the signals dissolved (or whatever that was), those beams of impossible-but-true visible light *slowed down*.

Alice checked the communications array to confirm that the frequency she chose to send the signal on was a normal, nonvisible-spectrum frequency. It was.

"Don't try the laser," Hadder said. He meant the high-burst pulse communicator, which was meant for long-range emergency signaling. "Unless you dislike the *Rosen*."

"You tried it already?"

"It was like birthing a sun. Very beautiful! Given its speed and direction, I'm afraid that beam may be well on its way to annihilating everyone who lives in the Podolsky System. First Officer Hart worked that out."

This was the first time Hadder mentioned a member of the bridge crew other than the departed Ensign Anson. She thought that was a significant thing.

"First Officer Regina Hart?" she said. "Where is she now? In her quarters?"

"I'm afraid not. She's left."

"L . . . left. Left the bridge? Left the ship?"

"She's in the Anthropene Principality now. I'll see her soon, I'm sure."

"Where is that?" Alice asked. It wasn't a place she'd ever heard of before. Not that it mattered if she *had;* it was impossible to walk off a ship in deep space and visit much of anywhere, and there was a full complement of shuttles in the hangar. Wherever it was, First Officer Hart wasn't actually there.

Hadder laughed, and gestured vaguely at the expanse of space. *Oh, you know,* the gesture said. *Let's not be silly.*

Exasperated, Alice sat back down in the helm chair and rubbed her head. She could feel a headache coming on.

"I wonder," she said, "if one of you—captain or computer— can tell me what actually happened, or why, or even when?"

Hadder laughed again.

"Why, I'm not sure!" he said. "What an excellent question. I know what we can do. Computer?"

"Yes, Captain," the computer said.

"Switch to narrative mode."

"Narrative mode?" Alice asked. "That's not even . . ."

The computer began speaking again, only this time in a deeper voice that wasn't precisely the same as the singsongy soothing one all the USF ships were stuck with.

"Things began to go badly for the crew of the USFS Erwin *around the time Dr. Marchere's coffee mug spontaneously reassembled itself.*

"Dr. Louis Marchere was not, at that moment, conducting some manner of experiment. Well, he was, only not on entropy and the nature of time. He was running several other tests, of the kind that make perfect sense on a scientific vessel such as the Erwin. *About half of them were biological in nature, concerning how small samples of cellular material react to certain deep-space factors. Other tests were more at home in the general field of astrophysics. But—again, as this is important—he was not conducting a test on entropy."*

"Computer, stop," *Hadder said.* "There, that was helpful, wasn't it?"

"What the hell was that?" *Alice asked.* "And why is the computer doing that?"

"Doing what?"

"It said *Alice asked,* when I was talking, and the same thing when you were talking."

"It's narrative mode. Useful! Now we know it all began with Dr. Marchere."

Alice was deeply confused. She'd never heard of narrative mode before, and was nearly positive Hadder was playing some sort of elaborate joke.

"It's not a *joke!" Hadder said.*

"I didn't say it was!"

"The *narrative* did."

"Turn it off," *Alice said.* "I KNOW I SAID THAT, YOU DON'T HAVE TO TELL ME I SAID THAT."

"Computer, end narrative mode."

"Ending narrative mode," the computer said.

"Oh, thank God," she said. "All right, so, Dr. Louis Marchere. Where is he? Or did he go to the . . . whatever-you-said place?"

"No, I believe he's still aboard," Hadder said. "We were just speaking. Deck three, in the research lab."

"Great. Let's go."

She headed for the elevator. Hadder remained where he was.

"Well, come on," she said. "You're the only survivor I've found so far; I think we should stick together, don't you?"

"It's . . . um, no. No, I think my place is on the bridge," he said. "It's safer."

"Captain Hadder, I don't think any part of this ship is safe. Our best option here is to find out what Marchere knows; if he doesn't have a way to save the *Erwin,* we need to get to my shuttle."

"Find out what you can," he said, in a tone that sounded like an order, "and keep me updated! Much to do up here."

He sat down in the captain's chair, as if this settled things.

"All right," she said. "I'll, ah, I'll let you know. Computer, deck three."

"Deck three," the computer confirmed.

As the doors closed, Alice could have sworn she saw Ensign Anson standing next to Captain Hadder.

But of course, she didn't. That would be impossible.

It took twice as long to get to the third deck from the first as it did to get to the first deck from the fifth. Alice was quite certain there was no mechanism in existence capable of adding fractional decks to the ship, and so was chalking this up to another aspect of the ongoing computer malfunction. She supposed a way to validate this was to ask that the elevator stop at, say, deck two and five-sixteenths, but she also didn't want to encourage the computer's departures from reality any more than necessary.

Find the problem, she thought. *Find the problem, work the problem, solve the problem.*

The reason Corporal Alice Aste was an ideal rescue mission envoy was that, over the course of a fairly extensive career, she'd worked in just about every part of a starship, from engine to helm. She was a problem-solving universal tool, a one-person away team. If a disabled ship was disabled because there was nobody aboard with the expertise to re-enable the vessel, the likelihood was fairly high that Alice had the gap-filling skill set.

But this? Whatever was going on aboard the USFS *Erwin,* she wasn't equipped to deal with it. Maybe nobody human was.

"The subjective mind is objectively flawed," she said aloud. It was one of the philosophical-slash-practical mottos she lived by. She couldn't recall who said it to her originally—probably one of her academy professors—but she'd found it incredibly useful over the years. There were some things the human mind was simply bad at grasping, observationally or intuitively, which was why flawed humans created machines to objectively interrogate the world for them.

That was what the computer was supposed to be doing. Since it was malfunctioning, Alice had no way to determine how much of what she was experiencing was even *real.*

And that was terrifying.

"Deck three," the computer announced, finally.

The door slid open, revealing a corridor with glass-walled rooms on both sides.

Scientific research was the *Erwin*'s central function, which was why the third deck was its widest and tallest. (Looked at from the front, the *Erwin* looked like a wide oval or, if you were hungry, like an overstuffed sandwich; deck three was where all the meat was located.) It was also where most of the vessel's funding went.

There was a dizzying amount of experimentational activity taking place in both of the glassed-in rooms, nearly all of it mechanized. If quizzed, Alice could definitively identify maybe a third of the experiments, and perhaps half of the equipment.

The ship's supercollider—one of only a half dozen off-planet supercolliders in existence—was running some kind of test on the far wall on her left, while on her right a laser tube designed to detect gravitational waves was humming along. A little farther along, a hologram of a Möbius strip was rotating slowly beside a bank of computer screens displaying rapidly evolving fractals.

Those were just the most obvious, macroscopic things. There were also cultured cells somewhere, having things done to them, and top-secret genetic splicing research, and plants being taught to grow in zero gravity chambers, and much more, but she couldn't see any of that.

She kept walking down the corridor, absorbing the maelstrom of activity on both sides, wondering exactly where all the power for this was coming from. The supercollider alone was supposed to take up enough of the energy from the *Erwin*'s fusion engine that the vessel couldn't run the FTL drive as long as it was also going. (The energy issue wasn't the only problem. Nobody was sure what would happen if a supercollider ran while on a ship traveling faster-than-light speed, but the consensus was: nothing good.)

The point was, everything running *at once* had to be an enormous drain, and yet the captain insisted the ship's engine wasn't even running. Either he was wrong—he was crazy, so it was probably that—or the *Erwin* was surviving on battery power. The batteries on a ship like this supplied just about enough power to keep life support going, plus the communications array, and *maybe* some impulse power for basic maneuverability, for about thirty days. It couldn't do all that and also provide a city's worth of energy to the research deck.

And yet, that appeared to be what was happening. Unless Hadder was wrong.

"Computer," she said, "give me a read on the ship's engine output?"

"The engine is not running," the computer said.

"Not the propulsion. I know we aren't moving. The base-level output."

"The engine is not running."

"Computer, the ship has power, does it not? Otherwise, you and I wouldn't be talking and I wouldn't be able to breathe."

"Confirmed, the ship has power."

"Then what's the engine's baseline output?"

"The engine is not running."

"Fine," Alice said. "Computer, what is the source of the ship's power, if not the engine? Is it the auxiliary batteries, or something else?"

"What is the answer you are expecting?" the computer asked.

"The right answer would be great."

"The batteries are providing the ship with power."

"Did you just say that because you thought that was what I wanted to hear?"

"The batteries are providing the ship with power."

"Sure."

"Would you like to switch to narrative mode?"

"No. What is it with you and narrative mode?"

"Narrative mode has been proven to reveal information not otherwise available to this computer."

"No, thank you."

She stopped short of asking the computer what other modes it had available, both because this was yet another ridiculous conversation she had no time for, and because she could see someone moving in the last part of the lab on the right.

The man had on a lead vest, with goggles and a face shield dangling loosely around his neck. He was also wearing thick leather gloves, brown coveralls of the sort Alice recognized as standard for the engineers, and heavy mag-spiked boots. His hair was pointed in five different directions, and he was holding something that looked like a blowtorch in one hand.

He could have been just about anyone in the crew. Nonetheless, she felt certain that this was Dr. Marchere.

Alice walked up to the nearest door, and when it wouldn't open, tried her override code. That didn't work either, so she knocked.

She startled him; he nearly dropped the torch, which would have been very bad had it been lit.

"Dr. Marchere?" she shouted.

He waved, put down the torch, waddled over, and opened the door.

"Very sorry, I'm extremely busy, can you come back later?" he asked.

"I really can't," she said. "I'm here to rescue the ship."

"I . . . see. And you are?"

"Corporal Alice Aste. I'm with the Security Force, and—"

"All right, all right, come in. Rescue! Ha-ha. Yes. That would be *something*."

She stepped into the room, which was awash in an atonal cacophony of pings, whirrs, and clangs. He took off his gloves and led her to a table in the center of all of it. On the table was a coffee mug, a cold pot of coffee, and a plate of doughnuts.

"I would offer you something other than doughnuts," he said, "but the food replicator can only make these, and only if one asks for bicarbonate of soda. I haven't worked out what one is supposed to request in order to get other foods, so this is what I have. Now, you've exactly seventeen minutes, and then I'll have to get back. I'm running thirty-eight experiments, and as you can see, all of my colleagues have already left."

"Where did they go?"

"They left, as I said. You're not from the *Erwin*, is that right?"

"The *Rosen* is nearby. If we can't get the *Erwin*'s engine running, we'll have to get the *Rosen* here for a tow. I can't hail them for . . . some reason, but I can try calling them from my shuttle. I just need to understand what's happening here, first. The computer . . . I'm sorry, this will sound insane, but in narrative mode, whatever that is, the computer said that this all began when Dr. Louis Marchere dropped a coffee mug. You *are* Dr. Louis Marchere, aren't you?"

"I am! And that is *amazing*."

"Which part?"

"All of it! I'm amazed you've lasted this long. Have you come across anyone else?"

"The captain and I had a long conversation that made no sense and confused everything much more."

"Oh excellent, the captain is still here. I was sure I was the last one left."

"He said he thinks the crew might be in their quarters, but is afraid to check, because he thinks if he does so, they might be dead and it will be his fault." She laughed then, to see if Marchere was inspired to laugh as well. He was not.

"Yes, that's eminently reasonable on his part," he said. "Narrative mode, you say? That's a new one. I accidentally stumbled upon theatrical mode yesterday, which was odd enough."

"Switching to theatrical mode," the computer said.

Marchere: No, I didn't mean for that. Oh well, here we are. Welcome to theatrical mode.

Alice: Oh, this is very strange.

Marchere: Yes, well, now we're here. It's not *terrible.* I enjoyed it during a soliloquy, but after became quite frustrated.

(Marchere takes a bite of a doughnut.)

Marchere: There, you see, it's exhausting, having your own actions read back to you. I became obsessed with the question of whether the computer was describing what I was doing, or if I was doing what the computer instructed me to do. Did I just bite this doughnut because that was what the stage business described, or did the stage business capture my actions?

(Alice looks confused.)

Alice: Weird, it's in present tense. And the computer keeps announcing who's speaking, like we don't already know. It was doing that before too, in narrative mode, only not every time.

Marchere: The fact that it's *in* present tense is what makes it so confounding. That would argue in favor of it dictating my actions instead of the other way around, which would contravene the concept of free will *entirely,* and that's terribly frustrating.

Alice: I shot a man on the bridge before pulling the trigger on my blaster. Captain Hadder said it was because cause-and-effect had been malfunctioning all day. That sounds like a similar problem. Can we . . . turn this off?

Marchere: Computer, end theatrical mode.

"Ending theatrical mode," the computer said.

"Thank you," Alice said. "Now can you *please* explain what's happened here? Where did everyone go, why are you running all of these experiments, where are you even getting the *power* to run all of these experiments?"

"Do you want for me to answer all of those at the same time, or is there a particular order you'd like for me to honor?"

"Start with what's going on. I guess."

"All right. Do you know what scientific theory states that the laws of physics are the same everywhere?"

"No, I don't."

"Good, because there isn't one. We've always just assumed it to be so, because it did us no good to assume otherwise. It was a poor assumption."

"You're saying the laws of physics don't apply to this quadrant?"

"I mean the Void we're next to, primarily, but as you must have worked out, there have been local alterations. We're right on the event horizon of a portion of space in which nothing we've previously proven to be true is *necessarily* still true. That's why I'm running all these experiments. I'm trying to work out what *is* true in this particular region of space."

"That sounds ridiculous."

"Oh, absolutely. It's magnificently ridiculous. Yesterday, I positively identified a particle's exact location *and* velocity. This morning, I tested the wave function collapse of light, but it refused to collapse. Later, I managed to measure the speed of light from a moving object compared to the speed of light from a stationary one, and discovered the one from the moving object was *faster.* I've also discovered electrons a *half-quanta* apart, and a few hours ago the supercollider detected an element between carbon and nitrogen, and a neutron with a negative charge. And this morning, for five seconds, all the oxygen in the other room — thankfully, I was in this one — gathered in one corner. These are all impossible, ridiculous things."

"But that can't be right. It's only a computer malfunction."

"The computer on this ship is working perfectly," he said, "in that it's describing an objective reality we cannot grasp. My equipment is working perfectly as well. It's our perception that's having trouble catching up. Now, I have to get back to my work before it's too late."

"Too late for what, Doctor?" she asked. "What *exactly* happened to your coworkers? Where is everyone else?"

"Ah. They don't exist any longer."

"You mean, they're dead?"

"I prefer it the way I said it. Are you familiar with the anthropic principle?"

"I heard something *like* that. The captain said his bridge crew went to the Anthropene Principality. Is that the same thing?"

"More or less. Hadder's head's all jumbled. The anthropic principle is a logical point stemming from the observation that everything in our universe has to be *just so,* in order to allow for our existence. From Planck's Constant to the charge of an electron, the weight of atomic particles, and so on and so forth, all of it carries a value which allows, as an aggregate, for a universe to exist which contains intelligent life. None of these values *had* to be what they were. It's a little circular, because one could easily argue that the only reason the universe's aggregation of values exists to allow intelligent life is because this is the only permutation that allowed for intelligent life to develop in order to make that observation. Other universes—assuming multiple universes—evolved differently, and have no intelligent life to note that their universe failed to evolve in such a way to allow for them to exist."

"All right," she said. "That does sound odd."

"I bring it up because the part of the universe we're standing at the edge of, right now, is a part where the laws do *not* allow for us to exist. It's the converse point of the anthropic principle. We're composed of the laws on which our universe was built. The slightest change in the strong nuclear charge and the atoms that make up your body could fly apart or collapse into themselves. Your brain evolved to communicate via neural electrical charges; a change in the electromagnetic force, and it stops working. These are facile examples, but you understand. If the laws change, we won't be around to measure them. At least, not for long. We're still *here* because neither of us have had the misfortune to happen upon a patch of altered laws that will undo us, and in fact right now we're *alive* because I've been taking advantage of the alteration. You asked before what's powering us. The answer is, when the engine failed, I hooked up the auxiliary batteries together. They're now charging one another *and* the ship."

"That's impossible."

"Evidently not here! The laws of this patch of universe allow for perpetual motion machines, so we may as well get some use out of it."

"So . . . you're saying the rest of the crew has been . . . unmade?"

"I've yet to witness this happening to anyone, but yes, I think so. I'm afraid to leave this level. You say you came from the hangar, and visited the bridge; it's good to know those places still exist."

"According to the computer there are fractional decks being added all the time," she said.

He laughed.

"Fascinating," he said. "I only hope I'm around to find an explanation for *that.*"

"Now that I'm here with a shuttle, you don't have to think like that, Doctor," she said. "I can take you—and the captain, if he's willing to leave the bridge—and whatever research you have. The *Erwin* is clearly a hostile living environment."

"An excellent suggestion, but no, I think I had better stay. You have a good point, however, in that I have no way to communicate my findings. My hope was to record as much as I could and jettison it toward the hub, but in truth I came upon that idea when I thought I'd reach the *end* of my studies. It seems the deeper I dig, the more strangeness I find. But here."

He placed a memory tab on the table.

"This is everything I've measured up to about an hour ago. I hope."

"You hope?"

"I hope it's only been an hour. The passage of time has been curious."

She picked up the tab.

"It has," she said, "the captain said it had only been a day, but it's been . . ."

Alice looked up from the table to find she was speaking to an empty room.

"Dr. Marchere?"

He'd been standing two meters away, and now he wasn't. The experiments in the room were still running, and the doughnut he'd taken a bite from remained bitten from, but he wasn't there to continue the experiments or finish the doughnut.

"Computer, can you locate Dr. Marchere?"

"There is no Dr. Marchere."

"Dr. Louis Marchere," she clarified.

"There is no Dr. Louis Marchere."

"He was just right here, computer."

"Would you like to try a different narration?"

"No, I . . . I don't know what I want."

He's in the Anthropene Principality now, she thought.

"I need to get off this ship," she decided. "Computer, what's the fastest way to the hangar?"

"The hangar is located on deck five," the computer said.

"Is there still a deck five?"

"There's still a deck five, but portions appear missing. Haste is recommended."

Alice opened the door to the lab and ran to the elevator, as things in both glass-walled rooms began to go somewhat *more* haywire than before. The holographic Möbius strip had developed a second side, the fractals on the computer screens began flashing random Greek letters for some reason, and it looked like a black hole was forming in the center of the supercollider. An amoeba the size of her head popped into existence on the glass a few feet from her face, and then popped back out of existence again before she had a chance to scream. It began to rain.

She reached the elevator door and pushed the button. Then she opened up her bag and retrieved her helmet. If the atmosphere decided to collect in one corner of the ship again, she'd rather she was breathing her own supply.

The ship started groaning before the elevator even made it to the fourth deck.

"Computer, what made that sound?" Alice asked.

"Unclear."

Alice remembered visiting the extinct-Earth-animals exhibit as a child, and being transfixed by the elephant in particular. The noises the ship was making sounded like an elephant being squeezed like an exhaust bladder.

Then the elevator shuddered, and stopped.

"Computer, what's going on?"

"Unclear."

"Can you tell me where I've stopped?"

"You've stopped at deck three and eleven-sixteenths. Would you like to get out here?"

"That depends. Will the elevator be moving again anytime soon?"

"Define *soon*."

"Before the ship blows up, implodes, or otherwise ceases to exist?"

"Unable to predict those outcomes at this time."

Alice wondered if maybe she should have gone up instead, back to the bridge. She could have collected Captain Hadder and gone out the topside hatch, and called the shuttle from there.

Then Alice started floating: the gravity had cut out.

If I can get into the shaft, I can reach the command deck on my own, she thought.

"Computer, can you hail Captain Hadder?" she asked.

"There is no Captain Hadder."

"Computer, can you hail the bridge?"

"There is no bridge."

"Deck one, computer. Open a channel to deck one."

"There is no deck one."

Crap.

"Computer, does deck five still exist?"

"Deck five continues to exist."

"But deck one is missing."

"The USFS *Erwin* does not have a deck one."

"All right, never mind. Open doors, please. Let's see what deck three and eleven-sixteenths looks like."

The doors slid open on a level that looked weirdly out of focus. Alice's first thought was that some kind of viscous fluid had gotten on her helmet, distorting the view of the universe on the other side. But the helmet was clean.

The walls were partly transparent and partly solid, because deck four's walls were opaque, while deck three's floors had glass walls. Deck three and eleven-sixteenths was trying to have both at once.

Since the gravity was out, Alice activated the mag-spikes on her boots and attached herself to the floor, then stepped off the elevator onto a blurry level that somehow managed to be solid.

"Computer, where is the nearest maintenance shaft on this deck?" she asked.

If the ship behaved for long enough, she'd be able to access the fifth deck by way of a maintenance shaft.

"Twenty-five meters."

"In which direction?"

"All directions."

The computer was not going to help.

Relying on the deck layout of one of the levels that was actually supposed to exist, Alice headed straight down the blurry corridor between the blurry rooms on both sides. In a slightly more ideal circumstance, she'd run, but because the artificial gravity generator had decided it was done (or ceased to exist, or whatever), she had to keep one boot on the ground.

About fifteen steps in, the boots stopped working. Actually, what it felt like was that the magnets holding her in place switched poles spontaneously, and repelled her from the floor. She began drifting to the ceiling.

Then came an explosion, somewhere aboard the ship. Alice felt it tremble through the belly of the vessel, rocking the walls and putting her into a gentle spin.

"Computer, what was that?"

"That was an explosion," the computer said, not at all helpfully.

"Right, thanks."

There was another tremble, and a shudder, and then a loud screech that didn't sound like much of anything Alice had ever heard before: not the noise a machine makes when it's broken, or a sound approximating that of an extinct elephant getting squeezed, or the cacophony a ship makes when its hull is torn open. It was not, in other words, on the short list of *bad noises* in her mental catalog of things to be alarmed about. She was nevertheless extremely alarmed, because what it *did* sound like was a creature that her lizard brain told her to run from. This was even though that portion of her brain *also* didn't know what she was hearing.

Then, directly beneath her and along the corridor floor, a *thing* ran past.

There were a tremendous number of wrong things that were wrong with this thing, the most arresting being that it was somehow in a higher definition than the rest of the deck, including Alice herself. It was a bright shade of blue, and green, almond, and a color of purple she was pretty sure was ultraviolet, which she was also pretty sure she shouldn't have been able to see. There were other colors she didn't even have a name for, because they didn't exist in the universe she was familiar with.

It was perhaps a giant bat, perhaps a snake, and perhaps a horse. It galloped and hissed, shrieked and chortled, and swung its long, clawed fingers through the walls on either side as if they weren't there. The walls, in turn, acted as if the creature wasn't there, showing no damage.

Here be dragons, she thought.

With a great flap of its enormous wings, it soared ahead, and vanished at the far end of the corridor.

"All right, I've had enough," Alice said. "Computer, what's the fastest way off this ship? I don't care *how,* just as long as it puts me on the other side of the hull."

"Unable to calculate," the computer said.

"Why is that?"

"The concept of *other side of the hull* is too variable to allow for a precise calculation. There are several places where the hull has ceased to exist, but sensors indicate nothing exists on the other side of where the hull no longer is."

"That's great."

The vessel shuddered again. Alice waited for a new nightmare creature to show up, but none did. It was probably just another part of the *Erwin* getting unwritten from the universe.

"Computer, how close am I to the maintenance shaft now?"

"Twenty-five meters."

"That's how far I was when I got off the broken elevator. I must have gotten closer since."

"Understood. However, the distance remains twenty-five meters."

She sighed.

"I really need to understand what's happening to the entire ship right now, computer," Alice said, "or I'm never getting off of it. I don't even know what questions to ask you. Can you provide me with an integrity assessment?"

"Not in this mode."

A hole opened up in the floor, which should have been good news, because that was the direction she wanted to go. But there was nothing on the other side of the hole. Either decks four and five were missing now, or the hole just went to someplace different.

"What the hell," Alice said. "Computer, switch to narrative mode."

Something quite extraordinary was happening to the USFS Erwin.

It was difficult to tell, from more or less any angle, whether the ship had been drawing closer to the Void on its starboard, or if the Void was moving closer to the ship, but what was definitely the case was that their positions relative to one another had been changing since the Erwin *first encountered the strange section of space. Now—after either two days or six weeks—the two things were colliding.*

The Void was having a devastating effect on the Erwin. *(The same could not be said of the* Erwin*'s impact on the Void, which appeared to be weathering things just fine.) There were certain expectations regarding how most space-based threats could damage a man-made starship. Incredibly dense objects, like neutron stars or black holes, could tear apart such a ship if it ventured too close, by literally ripping parts of the vessel off of other parts of the vessel, and/or drawing it into an inescapable gravitational well. Highly radioactive objects could bombard the ship with levels of gamma radiation so severe as to overwhelm the shielding and cook whoever was unfortunate enough to be inside. Rogue objects like asteroids could blow through a hull with a direct hit.*

And so on.

None of those things were happening to the Erwin. *Instead, it looked as if someone had produced a very realistic three-dimensional artistic rendering of the ship and then, deciding they disliked it, began erasing the artwork. Starting on the starboard side, large chunks of solid material were being turned into tiny bits of particulate matter—eraser crumbs, perhaps —after which the tiny bits of particulate matter glistened with internal light and then vanished.*

It's fair to say that however beautiful this might have looked to a neutral (and presumably distant) observer, its impact on the contents of the vessel was very bad indeed. Under optimal circumstances, a hull breach was dealt with by the ship's integrity shields: short-term force fields that plugged up holes before all of the atmosphere in the breached cell leaked into space. But the integrity shields only worked in circumstances where there was more hull than breach, and anyway they needed power in order to function. Unfortunately, the entirely impossible perpetual motion machine Dr. Marchere assembled had begun to break down.

All of this would be very bad news for anyone still alive aboard the USFS Erwin. *It was good news, then—if such a thing deserved to be called* good news—*that there* was *nobody left alive on the* Erwin. *All except for Corporal Alice Aste, desperately shuffling along deck three and eleven-sixteenths in a quixotic attempt to get back to her shuttle before she too was unmade.*

"Hey!" *Alice said.* "There's no need for that."

The deck floor was mostly gone now, as was the starboard side of the hull, which she could see through the blurry office wall: the Void was on two sides. But the ceiling remained intact, and since there was no such thing as up *or* down *in space—especially without the artificial gravity—she was doing okay with her mag-spiked boots. Shortly, though, she was going to run out of places to move.*

"Computer, if you could just stop being so long-winded and give me something I can use, that would be great," *she said.*

"The nature and pace of the narrative isn't under the computer's control," *the computer said, annoyingly.*

Alice grumbled an insult under her breath and kept going. Very shortly, none of this would matter. The portside hull was weakening already, not so much from direct contact with the Void *as a consequence of having its structural integrity challenged thanks to half of it no longer existing. The hull's metal shell was wrinkling . . .*

"Hang on, go back," *Alice said.* "Repeat that last part."
Alice grumbled an insult . . .
"After that."
Already, the portside hull was weakening . . .

"Computer, end narrative mode."

"Ending narrative mode."

Alice put her hand on the blurry med lab wall on the port side. It felt firm, because it was a wall, but at the same time it also didn't feel *that* firm. She pushed . . . and her hand went through it.

"Okay, that probably shouldn't have worked," she said.

She kicked her leg through, and then her other arm, and soon she'd gotten her whole body on the other side. Now in a room that was trying very hard to be both Marchere's supercollider lab and a medical examination room, she mag-walked across the ceiling to the outer hull.

The pushing-her-hand-through-something-that-was-supposed-to-be-solid trick didn't work a second time; the hull was firm, although she could hear it starting to fail. Waiting for that to happen seemed like a bad bet, and she didn't have to; not as long as she was carrying explosive charges.

She pulled one out, set the digital timer to thirty seconds, said a quiet prayer that she was in a part of the ship where chemical explosives and digital clocks still worked like they were supposed to, and then disengaged the mag-clips from the ceiling and pushed herself to the far end of the room.

The charge went off, exposing all of deck three and eleven-sixteenths to outer space. The atmosphere blew out of the hole, and sucked Alice out with it. In seconds, she was drifting on a free trajectory a significant distance from the *Erwin*.

"Now unsynchronized with USFS *Erwin*'s computer," her suit's computer announced, which Alice thought was great news.

"Call the shuttle to my position," Alice said.

"Unable to locate shuttle," the computer said.

Alice twisted around until she was facing the wreckage of the *Erwin*. She could see the shuttle all right, but it was now embedded in the side of the larger ship. It looked like the *Erwin* was giving birth to it, only in reverse.

"That's great," she said.

The Void was just about done with the *Erwin*. Like the narrative said, it was hard to tell whether the ship had been drifting into the Void or whether the Void was expanding to consume the ship. Either way, she couldn't afford to drift into it herself, nor could she ask the *Rosen* to get that close to it just to pick her up.

But, she wasn't out of options. There were two more charges in her bag, and the bag had armor shielding.

She pulled it off her back and got out the two remaining charges.

"Computer, locate the *Rosen*," she said. Then she held her breath. If the computer said *unable to locate* or worse, *the USFSF* Rosen *does not exist*, Alice was out of luck. It said neither.

"*Rosen* located."

"Target on helmet view."

The computer pinpointed the ship for her.

Now's the fun part, she thought. She set the timer for both charges at thirty seconds, put them back in the bag, and then tried to crouch until her whole body—feet-first so her legs would absorb the worst of it—was behind the steel plate in the bag. Then she tried to maneuver herself so that she was between the impending explosion and the USFSF *Rosen*.

"Computer, activate emergency beacon," she said.

"Emergency beacon activated."

"Thanks. Sure hope this works."

The charges blew. She felt her right leg shatter, and then she blacked out.

She woke up in the *Rosen*'s med lab, with a doctor she didn't know standing over her.

"There you are," he said. "Welcome back."

"Thanks," she said. Her mouth was dry and her vision blurry. *How long have I been out?* she wondered.

She tried to sit up, but it felt like the *Rosen*'s gravity was set at a much higher force level than it was supposed to be.

"Here, let me help," the doctor said, pushing a button that got her bed into an upright position. "I'm Dr. Maxwell, and you are lucky to be alive."

"You wouldn't be the first doctor to tell me that," she said, trying out a smile. "What's the damage?"

"Broken right leg, shattered left kneecap, broken left elbow, torn muscles in your right shoulder, and your oxygen ran out three minutes before we got to you, so you're probably missing a few brain cells. There were a couple of other things, but that's the worst of it."

"I need to speak to the captain," she said.

"I'm sure. I'll let him know you're awake; he'll want to speak to you too. They've been going over the information you retrieved from the *Erwin*; I guess there are a lot of questions that need answering."

"How long . . . ?"

"How long have you been out?" he asked. "Depends on where you'd like to start counting. We believe you were adrift for a couple of days, but you'd been on board the *Erwin* for more than a week. Your trip computer recorded only a few hours, though. I think this is one of the questions the captain has. You *do* need some rest first, so if you'd like for me to delay him, I can certainly do so."

"No," she said. "It's okay. The sooner the better."

"Good," he said with a paternal smile. "I'll let him know. Meanwhile, if you're thirsty, there's a glass of water on your right. I'll be right back."

He left. Alice sat still for a few minutes, trying to compose her thoughts. It was going to be impossible to explain everything without sounding insane, but she didn't really care about coming off as sane anymore. What happened, happened. They'd have to take the data from Dr. Marchere, and her accounting, and figure out what to do with it. Hopefully, one of the things they would decide to do would be to bar all travel through Quadrant Brenda.

After a few minutes with her thoughts, Alice realized she was fantastically thirsty. She turned and reached for the glass, not entirely anticipating how weak her right arm was. What began as a straightforward reach for a nearby object became an awkward flail that resulted in her knocking the glass off the edge of the counter.

She heard it shatter on the floor.

"Great," she said. "You gave me an actual glass. Very smart, Dr. Maxwell."

Alice was deciding whether to call a nurse to clean up the glass or to try to do it herself—despite the cast on her leg—when the drinking glass reassembled itself and returned to the counter.

She blinked a couple of times, thinking it would be best if she pretended that hadn't just happened, while knowing that pretending this wouldn't make a difference.

"Computer," she said.

"Yes, Corporal Aste," the *Rosen*'s computer said.

"This is going to sound crazy, but do you have a narrative mode?"

KEN LIU

The Cleaners

FROM *Faraway*

Now they knew that she was a real princess because she had felt
the pea right through the twenty mattresses and the twenty ei-
der-down beds. Nobody but a real princess could be as sensitive
as that.
— *"The Princess and the Pea," Hans Christian Andersen,*
translated by H. P. Paull

Gui

GUI'S FATHER RAN the cleaning shop for twenty years before
Gui was born, and then another twenty after. This wasn't a place
that laundered dresses and starched shirts; people went there and
paid to get rid of unwanted memories. A neighborhood institution, really.

When Gui took over, a year earlier, he had closed the doors for
a week and cleaned the place from top to bottom, scrubbing every
square inch. Even when you were a professional cleaner, layers of
memories accumulated in the place you grew up. What was the
point of keeping around riddles with no answers, locks with no
keys? When the doors reopened a week later, there was a new sign
over them: A FRESH START.

Other businesses along Pleasant Street in East Cradock, Massachusetts, had come and gone every few years, reflecting the
advancing and receding tides of the economy: Brazilian grocery
store, thrift shop, travel agency, computer repairer, tax preparer,

bank branch (that later turned into the offices for a trio of bank-ruptcy lawyers), thrift shop again (that also promised to help you sell things online) . . . but this place had hung on like the mussels clinging to the pier down by the beach. Now it was bracketed on one side by James's Tactical Supplies and on the other by A-Maze Escapes. Whatever the trendy currents were for how people wanted to spend their money, there was always the need to scrub off un-pleasant mind-sheddings, to become a different person.

The woman entered the shop on a chilly February Monday morning, the snow outside frozen in dirty gray clumps. He judged her to be fortysomething. Her coat, bright orange, ragged and lumpy, was zipped tight like a suit of armor. Her frizzy red hair was tied up in a messy bun that left her gaunt face unframed. Her brows were furrowed in a way that reminded Gui of the tracks left by seagulls on a deserted winter beach.

She hesitated for a moment before approaching the counter. "I have a big job for you."

Gui waited, holding her gaze. He had found that being only twenty-one meant that customers didn't always trust him right away. If he said nothing and allowed the awkward silence to stretch out between them, taut and brittle, customers tended to interpret his reticence as the gravity of experience.

"I've never done this," she said, putting her hands on the counter supplicatingly. He noticed that she didn't wear gloves: not afraid of the pain of others, or, more likely, just inured.

Gui nodded, retrieved a sheet of rates and terms, and pushed it toward her. He waited while the woman read it over.

"You don't do walls and carpets?" she asked.

"No," he said. "I'm a one-man operation. Whatever you need cleaned has to fit in my truck. I do everything here."

People rarely asked for whole-house cleanings unless they had something to hide or if it was for an estate sale. His parents had done many estates, but Gui refused them on principle.

"Just as well," she said. "I probably can't afford a house-wide scouring anyway. But we—he had a lot of things."

So someone *had* died. He thought about refusing, but some-thing about the way she held herself, alone but resolute, made him want to help. Besides, she wasn't wearing gloves. Didn't seem like the fussy type.

"I can work through a lot if you're willing to wait," he said. "But I only do complete scourings. No selective washes."

Estates were among the most delicate and difficult of professional cleaning jobs. It wasn't the quantity of the work, but the quality. Often, the family didn't want deep cleaning of the deceased. They wanted editing. Wedding dresses, books, Christmas ornaments, furniture, collections of porcelain figurines—those objects had decades of memory deposits on them, all conflicting. What was a pleasant memory for one was also a source of jealousy and rancor for another. Everyone wanted the possessions to conform to the story they'd been telling themselves for years. Cleaning became the excuse to refight old wars, to reopen scabbed-over wounds, to relitigate settled truths. He had neither the interest nor the capability for such work.

"That's exactly what I want," she said. Then, she pointed to the privacy clause. "This . . . this is absolute?"

Gui gestured at the walls, empty save for a single abstract painting of entwined pastel swirls, like the smoke tendrils inside the disposal oven. "I never reveal my clients."

On reality TV shows like *Cleaning Up after the Rich and Famous*, the cleaners festooned their shops with photographs of celebrity clients who would bring a dress or an expensive handbag in for a cleaning after a night of indiscretion. But everyone understood that was entertainment, the kind of fake cleaning staged to generate gossip and web traffic. "The law does require that I make a report if I discover evidence of ongoing abuse or the commission of a crime," he added.

"And after—the memories are unrecoverable?"

Gui didn't mind the implied mistrust. There *were* unscrupulous cleaners who saved the dregs and sold them. There was a market for the anguish of others. Always had been.

He decided to reassure her by walking her through his process. "Do you do much cleaning yourself?"

She hesitated for a beat. "Just around the house."

"What do you use?"

"Just the standard: alcohol and vinegar, maybe some oil of Mnemosyne after a bad night. I don't use any chemicals I can't pronounce."

He chuckled. "I don't either. They don't work as well as they want you to believe. Even oil of Mnemosyne can't completely dissolve deposits more than a week old. Most people think commercial cleaners use something special to loosen old deposits, maybe the kind the police use to lift memory prints so they could be saved whole. The truth is that I scrape them off the same way you would, but I can do it for longer and harder because I don't shrink back from the pain. That's how I get everything out. The dregs are then destroyed the old-fashioned way: incineration." He pointed behind him. The boxy oven loomed in the workshop in the back.

"I have to warn you . . ." She paused, screwing up the courage. "Some of it was unpleasant, even harsh. It will sting." Her voice softened. "It must be hard, to feel so much and to say nothing."

He took a deep breath. "Not really. I'm not sensitive."

"At all? Not even to your own deposits?"

He shook his head.

"Then . . . you can't relive memo—" She stopped, realizing how personal she was getting.

He shrugged. "I've been that way since I was born." People thought of cleaners as extra sensitive, and the stereotype had some basis in reality. But he had his own niche.

The woman nodded absentmindedly. He suspected that she already knew his quirk and merely wanted to hear him confirm it. It was how he had been able to stay in business as a one-man shop. The chain cleaners charged much less and had fancy machines that allowed their operators to home in on just one stain with inhuman precision. But word of mouth spread his name: the cleaner who couldn't blab about your business because he couldn't sense substantiated memories.

She grabbed a pen off the counter and began to fill out the form. He watched as the list of objects to be cleaned grew under her hand: jewelry, clothing, furniture, suitcases, electronics. She ran out of room and asked for a second form. He wondered what sort of man the deceased had been that this woman would want to erase everything about him, to avoid having to come in contact with his ghost in the future. A lover? A spouse? A father? He always wondered; he never asked.

"Do you intend to sell any of these after?"

She paused. "Why do you ask?"

"Collectors will pay much more for antiques if they have authenticating memories," he explained. "After I'm done, they may be worthless."

She let out a bitter chuckle. "No. I'm keeping what I can use and donating the rest. Can't afford to buy everything new. When can you do the *pickup?*"

Gui unloaded the truck through the side door. The shop's front doors were shut and locked. The windows were shuttered and barred. He always saved the big, deep cleanings for Sundays so he wouldn't be interrupted.

He pondered the objects scattered around him on the workshop floor: bedding, hand tools, stacks of chipped dishes, travel guides published more than a decade ago. It was best to start with something not too personal, to get into the flow of work. He settled on a wicker chair: low, roomy, in a style that was meant to be modern but became outdated the moment the chair was sold, the arms held out in a wide, empty embrace. He ran his finger over the woven rattan: a little rough, dry, the color dulled.

He pulled the multijointed swing arm of the shop light down until it bathed the chair in bright, shadowless light. He knelt down and examined the surface closely: the patches of deposits shimmered, a translucent haze like algae on the walls of an aquarium. He could see bands in two distinct patterns: a periwinkle base with speckles of dull copper, which he decided belonged to the woman, and a bright, angry crimson with tiny jet-black spots, the edges jagged and pulsing.

"You can't relive a memory that you didn't have a part in creating. But you can still be affected by the moods and emotions in a stranger's deposits." That was his father, before he had accepted that Gui was different. *"You can never tell how something feels to the hand of the owner. So be humble. Treat everything you clean with respect."*

He could recall the words so clearly because he had heard them again that morning. He had been brushing his teeth as the video played in the background, the low-resolution recording streaked with pixelated artifacts.

He dipped the pig-bristle brush into the bucket of oil of Mnemosyne and began to scrub over the tightly spaced strands. He wore no gloves so that he could see what he was doing better. He worked methodically, one filament at a time, as though he were coloring, painting, tracing a design. He took special care around broken strands and holes, lingering over the uneven edges the way dental hygienists cleaned around a filling. The repetitive motion was comforting, mindless work that produced tangible results. The tangy odor of the solution, somewhere between gasoline and pine tar, with a hint of spices and animal musk, gradually filled the air.

He could see the rattan's natural shine coming through slowly, the periwinkle and crimson deposits coming off in clumps and wisps, thin curlicues like solidified smoke. The dregs beaded at the tips of the bristles, each color refusing to blend with the other. He wiped them off the brush with a collection sponge, and when the sponge had turned a dark patriarch purple, like raw lamb's liver, he dumped it in the burn bucket.

"Some people are much more sensitive than others. When I was little, your grandmother used to beat me with her hairbrush. Whenever I touched that hairbrush, I would scream. Felt like holding a scalding panhandle. But she brushed her hair with it until the day she died. Said she liked the tingle."

Gui looked down at the handle of the scrubbing brush, the same one his father had used for forty years. It was the only thing he had not cleaned after he took over the shop. The desert ironwood had cracked in several places, but was otherwise as hard and polished as he had always remembered. He tightened his fingers around it. He felt nothing.

"Never judge why someone wants to clean. All you can do is to help them the only way you can; do your job." His father had raised the brush, glistening with dregs like dark, misshapen pearls, and offered them to him. *"Touch it. Touch it so you know how to share in someone's pain without being overwhelmed by it. Be careful. This may burn."*

He knew that this moment had happened, not because he remembered it happening, but because he had watched himself in the recording that morning, like he did every morning. His mother had filmed the scene with her flip phone because it was his birthday, and she had wanted to preserve the moment for him, for later, for when he was older and neither his father nor his father's tools would be around anymore.

And he had reached out, terrified and thrilled both. He was a boy of eight but being entrusted with the work of a man. He braced himself, biting down on his lip so that he would not scream, no matter how it felt. His fingers connected with the dark globules at the ends of the bristles.

In the recorded video, the boy didn't scream. The stoic expression on his face turned to bewilderment before collapsing into disappointment. He had already known that he was different, that he couldn't do what everyone else took for granted. But hope had not died until that moment. He had felt nothing.

Gui knelt before the chair, scrubbing and scrubbing as the bucket next to him gradually filled with dark liver lumps.

Clara

Clara rushed through the crowd in her lumpy, bright orange coat, the messy bun on her head bobbing like a pom-pom. Beatrice, her sister, was taking her out to lunch, and she was late.

She was late because she had to line up to get her bag checked by security, wasting fifteen minutes. Clara tried not to feel resentful. Beatrice didn't know how much trouble it was for her to leave the factory for lunch. She didn't understand jobs where you had to clock in and clock out, where your employer viewed you as a potential thief. Beatrice was only in town for a meeting and had to fly out that afternoon, and she thought she was giving Clara, the poor sister whose life had turned into such a failure, a treat.

They met at the trendy café Beatrice had picked. They didn't hug—Beatrice never hugged, not since she was a teenager. They sat down, and Clara handed Beatrice her gift. It was hard to shop for Beatrice, who already had everything. But giving a gift mattered to Clara. It was a way for her to tell herself that she was still capable of giving, hadn't made a mess of her life.

"Get whatever you want," Beatrice said, putting the package away in her purse without opening it. She took out a travel-sized bottle of sanitizer and cleaned the silverware and plates, wiping everything down with a disposable napkin.

"What are you getting?" Clara asked.

"The online reviews say that the seaweed salad and dumplings here are the best." Beatrice never took her eyes off her phone screen as she scrolled through her messages.

Clara stared at the dark ceramic back of her sister's phone,

Void Black®. It looked perfectly new, not a single scratch on it. She wondered briefly if it was one of the phones that she had cleaned herself at the factory and then decided that was unlikely. Beatrice preferred to buy things online. Less contact with people was always better.

"How's work?" she blurted, and instantly regretted it. Talking about work with Beatrice never went well. She found her sister's ramblings about her clients' schemes and plots incomprehensible, and Beatrice just assumed that Clara never wanted to talk about her job. But what else was there to talk about? For two people who had grown up together, they had remarkably little to converse about. They no longer knew each other at all.

"It's fine," said Beatrice, absorbed in answering an email. "Just let me finish this. If the food gets here, start without me . . ."

Clara decided she would order the lobster roll.

Beatrice tapped away, her thumbs deftly sliding around the glass. "Can you believe the defendant would have the gall to claim that *my* client stole the idea from *her?* She says she has authenticating deposits, but she's dragging her heels on giving me the laptop. She must be artificially aging the memory right now, and I need my useless assistant to expedite the request for production . . ."

Clara's hands still tingled, and she massaged them reflexively. Even with gloves, it was impossible to avoid stings completely at work. Phones came down on the conveyor belt, one every thirty seconds. It was her job to inspect and wipe off the residue from the workers in the distant factory-cities across the Pacific in which they had been assembled.

The last phone before her lunch break had hurt her. Her mind had been drifting, and she had picked up the phone with her left hand directly instead of using tongs. Most phones, after all, were coated only in mild anxiety or mind-numbing boredom, perfectly safe to touch. Without examining it closely, she had given it a few wipes with the cloth in her right hand, soaked in the foul-smelling high-tech solution that was supposed to break down even the most crusted-over memory deposits. It had taken a few seconds for her mind to register the burning pain in her left hand, as though she were holding a live wire.

Despair, exhaustion, the terror of loneliness, and the paranoia of failing. Climbing high, higher, even higher. A moon hung in a hazy sky, serrated at both ends like a broken tooth. A passing breeze redolent of chemicals that burned the nose. The factory laid out below like a model, a map. Thoughts of jumping, leaping into a wind that would lift her skinny arms like a bat's wings, a wind that would never actually come. And then hurtling toward the earth, yearning for the ultimate peace.

A server brought their food. Beatrice continued typing. Clara began to eat.

It shouldn't have happened. She wasn't like Beatrice. She was normal. Normal people couldn't interpret the details of the memory deposits of strangers. It took intimacy to build that resonance of minds, to create memories together, to become vulnerable to the pain of another. Only mood and emotion, dampened by the distance of language and culture and the barrier of the self-preservation instinct, should have come through, a faint echo of a tingle.

But sometimes it happened anyway. When the suffering was intense enough. After all, she had glimpsed the chiaroscuro of anguish and manic joy that was Lucas's world the first time she sat down in his wicker chair, before she had even known his name.

Beatrice held the phone up to her ear and spoke into it in a harsh, low voice. "No, I don't want you to draft a memo! Just call Perry and explain what we need. This isn't rocket science . . ."

Worst of all, Clara could tell it was the memory of a young woman, barely more than a child. She could see those slender fingers held up toward the moon, hear and feel the high-pitched keening in the back of the throat, like a creature trying to claw out.

What happened to that girl? she wondered. *Did she go through with it? Please, God, no.*

She was almost done with her sandwich. She slowed down, lingering over every bite. She didn't know what she would do with herself when she finished. She wished she could *talk* to the hunched-over figure across the table, now absorbed by the screen again, to understand her and to be understood.

The contract manufacturer had tried to scrub the workers' deposits, the detritus of an industrial process that turned humans into components. But the result had never been satisfactory. Despite all of Silicon Valley's yearning for disruption, they hadn't been able to figure out how to cleanse memories attached to objects without the participation of a human being. And since they didn't want a buyer in America to unwrap their brand-new phone, only to be burned by the anguish of a foreigner, to be infected by a psychic wound like a virus—didn't lifestyle gurus all say it was important to insulate oneself from the suffering of others, not to be dragged down by negativity one was powerless to stop? — they hired American workers to sit in warehouses to clean the phones and then to coat them with a spray of anonymized all-American fresh-product good cheer, as though things were not made by people, but by robotic elves. The manufacturing sector had collapsed in the USA, but there was always emotional labor to fall back on.

Assembled in China. Cleaned in America.

Clara had turned the phone in, and the supervisor had said they would look into it. Most likely nothing would be done except to destroy the phone as defective. But what else could she do? Her own life was such a mess, she had no room for the troubles of others. Why was a stranger's pain being thrust upon her? She felt a dark wave filling her, exuding from her skin, depositing onto the plate, onto the tablecloth, onto her chair: resentful, selfish, guilty, furious.

Is this what it's like, always, for Beatrice? To live the memory of another as soon as she touches a deposit?

The wave receded but did not fully retreat. It lapped at the shores of her heart, a murmuring undercurrent.

"Sorry." Beatrice put away the phone and started on her salad.

Maybe this is why she always gets a salad, Clara thought. *So she doesn't have to worry about the food getting cold.*

It was impossible to bring up what she had just experienced. They were so far apart that she couldn't imagine creating a shared memory that would do anything but hurt them both.

"I went to see a cleaner the other day," Clara blurted. She couldn't understand why. She hadn't meant to bring it up at all.

Beatrice's fork slowed down. "For Lucas's things?"

Just hearing his name spoken aloud was torture. "Yes. Everything."

"It's definitely over, then?"

Over? What does that even mean? Lucas had left without taking anything because he wanted to be "free" — free of her, of memories, of the weight of a life together that had become suffocating. Maybe it was *over* for him, but how could it be for her when being home was like being in a minefield? Touching anything brought back an explosion of flashbacks, of *hurt*.

"I haven't heard from him in two months. I thought it was time to move on."

Beatrice nodded. Clara waited. Beatrice resumed working on her salad.

Clara stewed. She didn't want to hear *I told you so.* But this silence was worse. Even more judgmental.

"I thought you told me once you had some good times too." Beatrice's tone was oddly subdued.

Clara was surprised. Beatrice had never liked Lucas. "It's messy."

"Always." Beatrice seemed to shake off whatever was bothering her. "It can feel good to use a professional cleaner. As long as they're reliable."

"He's interesting," Clara said. "He can't feel deposits at all. He's memory-blind."

"Sounds like he's in the wrong line of work, then."

"No. It makes him better at it. He's not afraid of touching, doesn't get bothered by anyone's pain." She could see that Beatrice was about to object, to say something like *That's a nice way to spin it,* so she rushed on. "I wish I could be like that."

Beatrice set down her fork, and for the first time during lunch, looked Clara in the eye. "Do you?"

"I do." Pure fury surged in Clara as she held the gaze. *Who are you to question me? What do you know about my life with your jetting around and being paid handsomely to peel off the memories of the rich and famous? You've never lived with Lucas. You've no idea how his self-loathing was like a bottomless pit that sucked the life out of anyone who loved him, how his anger at the world left the taste of ashes on everything he touched, how his self-pity drew me like a flame and burned me to a crisp.*

Beatrice looked away. "I was cleaning up my apartment, and I found this." She dug around in her purse.

"You clean?" Clara asked. She had seen a photograph of her sister's place once. It looked like a hoarder's nest. "You hate to clean. You said you could never find anything after."

Beatrice ignored this. She found what she had been looking for and held it out to Clara. A four-color retractable click pen: red, blue, green, black.

Puzzled, Clara reached for it, but Beatrice didn't let go. Both of their hands held it, one at each end.

A warm flood gushed through Clara's fingers, up her arm, flared into her heart. Unlike the buzz from the jars of memory-grounds they sold as mood enhancers at places like Yankee Mementos with names like "A New Job!" or "Reunion," it didn't feel artificially sweet. Like all true joys, it was laced with the shadow of pain and terror—pain that was assuaged, terror held at bay.

It felt genuine, Clara realized, because it was her own memory, one shared with Beatrice. She could decipher it.

She was eleven again, and Beatrice nine. The younger girl had been sobbing inconsolably. Their parents had not understood how unique Beatrice was, had not accepted her gift. They thought she was being childishly dramatic when she said that the secondhand blanket gifted by their mother's friend hurt her. They had not yet known of the abuse suffered by that woman's child.

"It's just a nightmare. All kids get nightmares."

"No! They're hurting Ellie. They're hurting her!"

Clara cleaned the blanket, scrubbed it in the sink despite how it stung her hand. They were poor, and the heat was unreliable. Beatrice needed that blanket. Clara couldn't interpret the deposit in the blanket, couldn't relive what Beatrice relived. All she could do was to reassure her sister that she believed her unconditionally, that she knew she was telling the truth.

While Clara cleaned, Beatrice wrote down what she had seen inside the blanket. Then she had used her favorite pen, a four-color clicker, to draw a picture of herself and Clara. The figure of Beatrice was small and black; the figure of Clara was large and blue—approximations for the shades of their deposits. Clara leaned protectively over Beatrice like the sky, a fierce presence of absolute trust.

Later, that account written in a childish hand would be the first piece of evidence in the case that led to Ellie's rescue and confirmation of Beatrice's gift.

"I had forgotten about this," Clara said, looking at the pen in her hand. Beatrice had let go.

"We all need to be reminded, from time to time, that we're better than we remember," Beatrice said.

Clara's hand still prickled, the hairs standing up. She had also sensed that the memory, though a shared deposit, had been colored much more deeply by Beatrice's perspective. How many times had Beatrice held this pen, relived this moment, redrawn her big sister to be better than she deserved to be remembered?

Shame, gratitude, lucid incomprehension.

The memory was fading in intensity, but she knew she could call it back the next time she held it.

Clara opened her mouth to speak, but her own phone buzzed then, reminding her that she needed to get back to work.

They embraced. Very briefly. Coats and gloves on.

"Thank you."

Beatrice

Airplanes were generally troubling places for Beatrice. There was never enough time for the crew to clean properly between flights, and so every seat was a stew of anxiety, confinement, the sense of being suspended between places, life on hold. She tried never to take off her coat or gloves when she flew.

She unwrapped the package from Clara. It was a book, a limited edition of found deposits by a prominent artist. Each copy of the book was unique, the thick pages bulging with the physical carrier objects, hydraulically pressed or sectioned with a laser scalpel. It was used, but still must have cost Clara more than she could afford.

That was vintage Clara, always the big sister, the giver, the thoughtful one. Even after they had grown apart.

Beatrice opened the book and skipped over the pretentious artist statement. She turned to the first entry, a flattened little plastic arm, a fragment from a discarded doll that had been found on the beaches of Henderson Island in the Pacific, at least three thousand miles from the nearest continent. The plastic limb had been deformed and stained by its voyage through the excretory system of modern civilization and battered and bleached by the action of waves.

She took off her glove and put a finger on the plastic arm, pressing down gently and allowing her skin to come in contact fully with the artificial flesh.

She was tossed into a swirling montage, fragments from the lives of strangers. A young man with dirty hair and a frown stamping the arm, one of thousands like it, with a machine that thumped like thunder; a clerk packing boxes in a cavernous warehouse, walking through the aisles to the beeping of an electronic timer, more robot than person; a little girl arguing with her brother about what the doll should say; a carefree run through the rain-slicked streets of some city; an old man bending to pick up the doll and stuffing it into a nearby trash can; an expressionless woman tossing the half-doll into a floating mess of other discarded objects, an undulating mat of abandoned possessions that bobbed together, scraping, jostling, flaking off their memory deposits and commingling; the artist picking up the doll fragment and bringing it aboard a ship; the careful cleaning that picked off the dried seaweed and encrusted sand but preserved the artful deposits of consciousness . . . and then: the memories of those who had purchased the book and read its contents layered on top, men and women who sought solace or escape or voyeuristic pleasure in moods and emotions and glimpses of other lives, a growing sediment formation to which she was now contributing her own.

The accompanying essay talked about the problem of trash, the physical as well as emotional. Modernity was reveling in the disposable, objects as well as experiences. The Pacific was filling up with microbeads and our corporate-manufactured memories. How many of us now relied on empathy-sheaths so that a bad date could be flushed down the toilet? How many of us coated our nightstands with a dusting of internet celebrity gossip rather than extrusions from our supposed loved ones? How many of us followed weekly self-help cleaning regimes rigorously to scrub ourselves of "negative deposits" so that we could live in the eternal present, heedless of what it was doing to our planet and our souls?

Beatrice stopped reading. It was all such high-minded nonsense, chicken soup photographed in a studio to be peddled as wisdom. The art was always better than the explanation of the art.

The plane banked, and in the shifting sunlight, she saw the rainbow hues scintillating in a haze over the plastic arm, a jumble of externalized psyche. She wondered if the artist had ever intended her work to be consumed by someone like Beatrice, someone who, when touching a memory deposit from a stranger, sensed not only moods and emotions, but discerned the details of the recollection with photographic precision.

It was hard to make anyone else not like her understand. Everyone thought a prodigy like her had an easy path to riches and happiness. After all, hadn't a guy, after he had gotten his hands on the Codex Leicester and run his fingers over every page, become a prominent inventor with ideas that many suspected were derived from Leonardo da Vinci? And that woman who begged to be allowed to hold Cormac McCarthy's Olivetti Lettera 32 for a few minutes before it had been auctioned off—she had become a best-selling author, though one dogged by persistent allegations of plagiarism that couldn't be proved.

Clara thought Beatrice threw herself into her work because she was too pleased with her talent, but the truth was it was an escape. To be able to glimpse into the lives of others, without even intending to, made true intimacy impossible. She never wanted to go to friends' houses, to borrow a pair of shoes or a dress, to accept anything that had been steeped in the memories of anyone she cared about. You never wanted to know the people you liked and admired too well; it was impossible to reconcile what they wanted you to know with what they didn't. Few people were better than they remembered.

Moreover, it made you doubt yourself. When you were so open and attuned to the experiences and feelings and deposits of others, what thoughts could you claim to be original, nonparasitic, not derived, stolen, copied? Even as a child, she had known what it meant to be old, to be confused by the layering of different selves as one aged—she had touched their parents' deposits, and then recoiled at the contradictory messiness of it all. That was why she hoarded possessions, piled them in her apartment: not just to protect her own secrets, but also the secondhand confessions, the baring of other souls.

Better to be paid to dig into the lives of strangers, a transactional invasion sanctified by law and custom. Clean.

She put the book away, picked up her phone, and began to work again. She was certain that if she could get her hands on the laptop in question, she could prove that the defendant's authentication memory was faked. There were always ways to tell when a deposit was staged—a clock they forgot to reset, the position of a shadow and height of the sun, the crafted sense of ersatz reality. And no matter how thoroughly they cleaned it, the original memories always clung to something: the bottoms of the keycaps, the inside of a port or slot, the seam between the screen and the cover. She was a forensic memory tracer like no other. She could do it.

But the book that Clara had given her called to her from underneath the seat in front. She could not focus.

There was an imbalance between her and Clara that could never be bridged. It was harder, much harder, for her sister to know her than vice versa. Her childhood friends and her family were the only people she loved whose secrets she knew because she had seen them before she learned to keep her distance. She had to separate herself from them, to be apart, in order to know who she was and to know them the way they wished to be known. To allow others the space for secrets was the greatest gesture of love she knew how to give, but did they understand that?

She had once loved to draw, loved to tell stories to herself as she ran the pen over the page, fusing a memory into the drawing, a scene that came to life when she was done, running her fingers over the inked grooves. But she had stopped. Art was too open, too naked. Someone who could perceive the raw memory deposits of others was especially paranoid about revealing the self. She preferred to type than to write. She tried her best never to leave a personal trace in the world.

Except . . . when you did that, you also stopped conversing with yourself. Leaving deposits and examining them was how people understood their own story, how they grew.

But Clara *had* understood her. She was reminding Beatrice how she loved art, the beauty of the kind of deposited story that only she could make and appreciate. Just for herself. Not a performance for an audience.

She put away the phone and picked up the art book again. As she read and touched and absorbed the lives of strangers, she also imagined being back in her apartment, the phone off and forgotten, herself absorbed in creation: a box of objects that held the deposits from each year of her life. As she held each, she would sort through the memories and retell them in a whisper, adding in the forgiveness of age for youthful impulsivity, the appreciation that she had once been so fearless and gloriously beautiful, the understanding of a character arc that made sense only when a life had been mostly lived . . . She would never let anyone else see it, not as long as she was alive.

She sat still as the plane crossed the vast sky, casting an imperceptible shadow on the earth below.

Clara

She tried to imagine the life of the man who could not sense memory deposits, not even his own.

Everything must feel new to him, she realized. He could just buy a secondhand shirt and put it on, not worrying whether it would give him a memory-rash. He could just browse through the library stacks without gloves, unconcerned with whether the previous reader had been suffering from depression.

He's not afraid of touching, doesn't get bothered by anyone's pain. But that would also include his own.

So he would also forget. Nothing he did would leave a mark, not unless he consciously and constantly reminded himself of it. He would lose that most unreliable, fragile, unwanted but also faithful witness of the very nature of existence, the exuviated skin of a mind growing through time.

Am I much better off, though?

She twirled the four-color pen, letting it tumble-walk across the back of her hand and catching it just before it fell. The periwinkle bands in the haze held bright gold specks, brighter than they had been in her deposits in a long time.

She still couldn't believe she had forgotten that episode from their childhood together. Though she had never gone out of her way to keep mementos, she had believed she remembered enough. The inevitable sediments felt to her vaguely unhygienic, an aspect of being human that was unpleasant, like crusted sleep in your eyes when you woke up.

But she *had* forgotten; she hadn't even known something was missing until Beatrice brought it back to her.

What else had she forgotten? What other scars had healed over and vanished? What joys faded and then sloughed off? What other parts of herself had she left behind in the basements of long-ago rental units, the hands of strangers who picked through her moving sales, the trash heaps in landfills that slowly fermented and rotted in the rain, leaching her memory, along with the memories of millions of others, into sewers, rivers, ocean currents, to be carried to the deep abyss where pale ghost crabs skittered over them, attendants at the final oblivion?

She looked at her cramped apartment, suddenly spacious because Lucas's possessions had been removed—no, not *his* possessions. They were also hers. They had fused their lives and bought things together, during that time when he had claimed that she gave him strength, made him want to be a better man. She had been calling them his only because he had been the one who didn't want to throw them out, not even when they had become worn and outdated.

She paced back and forth across the apartment, picturing the ghostly outlines of everything that had been taken away by the cleaner, to be returned in another week: A Fresh Start.

But did she want a fresh start? Did she want everything around her to be like the phones she cleaned at the warehouse, smelling faintly of the promise of emptiness, possibilities achieved at the price of erasure?

She had invested so much of herself into this life with Lucas. Just because he had left didn't mean that it had been wasted. She had lived through it; it was not a dream.

"We all need to be reminded, from time to time, that we're better than we remember."

She looked at the pen in her hand again, squeezing it tight, feeling that burst of enduring trust, a faith that had survived growing up, growing apart, growing into strangers who had fresh starts.

Gui

The woman strode deliberately around the corner of the workshop in which her goods were piled and then hesitated.

Gui watched her, saying nothing. Clients sometimes changed their minds about cleaning. That was why he took his time on large jobs.

She stopped in front of the gleaming wicker chair. After scrubbing, he had oiled and polished it with a soft cloth. She ran her hands over the woven strands, holding her breath. Then she let out a long exhalation. "You're very good. This feels new."

He said nothing.

Her hand lingered on the chair a moment longer before she took another couple of steps, stopping before a desk lamp. The base, a crystal vase encased in spiraling brass vines, was meant to serve as a souvenir display jar or perhaps a small terrarium. It was filled with pebbles and shells, bits of sea glass, a plastic aquarium boat, a few key chains, folded-up bits of paper, ticket stubs.

"He bought this for me," the woman said, as though speaking to herself. "But we both filled it. We tried to fill it with happy memories, to keep us going when things weren't so good.

"At first, we filled it quickly. Then the filling slowed and stopped. We began to reach in for jolts of comfort, of strength. But we did so only when things were really bad, and so they got coated with arguments, betrayals, deposits we'd rather forget."

Gui waited. He knew what she meant, but also didn't.

He thought about the recordings his parents had made for him over the years, first very few, and then many more, in higher and higher resolution, documenting every aspect of the cleaning process as well as their life together. It was meant to compensate for his condition, to help him remember. But the very act of conscious documentation cast a pall over everything. Watching himself and them felt like watching actors.

She reached into the crystal and wrapped her fingers around a bit of green sea glass. Her whole body stiffened. She held that pose for a moment, eyes closed. Then she let out her breath slowly, her body relaxing.

"It's messy, but we filled it together. I put myself in it." She turned to him. "I'm sorry, but I don't want the rest of it cleaned. I'll pay you the full amount."

"When would you like to schedule the drop-off?"

They worked out the details.

Before she turned to leave, he stopped her. "Do you want the dregs?" He pointed to the bucket sitting unobtrusively in the corner.

"No," she said. "You can't control everything. Some forgetting is healthy."

After she left, he took the bucket to the incinerator. Carefully, he placed the lumps inside, one after another, as though laying out offerings on an altar. He shut the door, turned it on, and watched through the glass viewport as the flames inside leaped to life. The sponges charred, deformed, collapsed, and then burst into brilliant flowers of color and smoke.

He looked over at the scrubbing brush hanging on the wall. In the flickering light of the incinerator, he could see that the handle gleamed with a grayish shimmer, like a moth's wings. It was the hue of his own deposits, mysteries he was himself powerless to decipher.

He realized that he could not recall the color it held when his father had wielded it, for the hue of memory was impossible to capture with the camera. He wept then, knowing that he would not remember this moment in the future, feeling both the weight of freedom and the lift of oblivion.

YOON HA LEE

Beyond the Dragon's Gate

FROM *Tor.com*

ANNA KIM COULDN'T decide whether the scenery outside was more or less beautiful for the coruscating cloud of debris. From here, she couldn't even tell there was a war on. Of all the ways her past could have reared up, being trapped in the star fortress Undying Pyre was one of the more unpleasant. Aside from letters from her sister Maia, who was a soldier, Anna had done her best to stay away from the military. Too bad she hadn't counted on being *kidnapped.*

It went without saying that Anna didn't want to be here. She was a citizen of the Harmonious Stars. She had *rights.* But the Marshal had sent their thugs to drag her away from her attempt at a new start. Anna already missed her aquarium with its two cantankerous dragon-fish, one of them in the throes of metamorphosis. She'd barely had time to ask her colleagues to keep an eye on it, and was half-afraid that she'd return—if she returned—to a sad carcass floating upside down in the tank.

There was no one else in the room, which made her nervous. Along with the extravagant viewport, it featured a table too long for ten people and a commensurate number of uncomfortable chairs. (She'd tested one, which was why she remained standing.) Anna wondered why you would spend this much money building an orbital fortress and skimp on chairs.

They'd dragged her to the Undying Pyre with her senses partly deadened, an unpleasant journey for everyone involved. She'd had her senses slowly reactivated here, like a butterfly easing out of its chrysalis. If the room had a number or a name, she didn't know it. Anna couldn't have found her way out of it unassisted, any more than she could have sloughed off her skin and slipped away. The room had no visible doors.

She heard footsteps but couldn't, to her discomfort, discern which direction they came from. A door materialized in one of the walls. Anna yelped and backed away from it.

A spindle-tall personage walked through the door. Anna recognized the newcomer. Even the most isolated citizen, let alone one with an older sister in the military, would have known that dark-skinned figure, with its sharp eyes and a nose that made them look like an ambitious hawk. Their uniform was velvety blue with a gradient of gold dusting along the upper arms, and a staggering array of medals glittered on their chest. They went by many names and just as many titles, but only one mattered: the Marshal of the Harmonious Stars, the supreme commander of its military forces.

"Should I salute?" Anna asked them, because she couldn't think of anything but bravado.

The Marshal laughed, and Anna flinched. "You wouldn't know how," they said. "It would be a waste of your time, and mine, for me to show you how to do it without pissing off all the soldiers in this place. In any case, I apologize for the nature of this meeting, Academician Kim, but it was necessary."

Anna swallowed, wishing the Marshal hadn't used her old title. It dredged up unpleasant memories. "Yes, about that. I would have appreciated being *asked*."

"I would not have taken no for an answer."

So much for that. Anna gestured at the vista. "I'm assuming this is about the remnants of those three ships."

The Marshal's eyebrows flicked up alarmingly. "Someone's been talking."

Oh no, Anna thought. Had she gotten someone fired, or court-martialed, or whatever you did in the military? "Your people"—she did not dare say *goons*—"thought I was fully under. I wasn't." She knew what drugs they'd used; could have told them, if they'd asked, that she had an idiosyncratic response and needed an alternate medication regimen for the effects they wanted.

"All right," the Marshal said. "There was only so much we could do to disguise the nature of the incidents."

Anna fidgeted. She longed to return to her dragon-fish and her cozy workstation with computers named after different sea deities (her insistence, her coworkers' indulgence). Her favorite poster, depicting a carp leaping up a waterfall until it arrived, exhausted and transfigured, as a dragon. She had always assumed that the old fable had inspired the genetic engineers who had created the dragon-fish, although she declined to look into the matter on the grounds that she didn't want to have a pretty illusion shattered.

"You know why we brought you here?" the Marshal said.

Anna looked at them. She didn't want to say it.

"Your research."

Anna flinched again. An open wound, even four years after the authorities had run her out of her research program. Her research partner, Rabia, hadn't survived. However, it wasn't Rabia's face that haunted Anna, but that of Rabia's girlfriend. Anna had gone away, far away; had thought that a quiet penance, in obscurity, would be best. Circumstances had conspired against her.

The Marshal would know that the research lived on inside her head. "I don't see," Anna said carefully, "what my work has to do with sabotaged ships. The last experience I had with anything resembling explosives was that time my sister tried dissecting the battery from her spaceship model."

The Marshal's fine-boned face went taut. "It wasn't sabotage."

Anna digested that. "And I'm guessing they weren't the only ones?" She hated the way her voice quavered. Surely the Marshal could smell her fear, and would use it against her.

"Have a seat."

Anna picked the chair she'd tested earlier. It was just as uncomfortable as it had been the first time. She thought of the one back at her workstation, which she'd spent hours adjusting until spending time in it was almost luxurious.

The Marshal sat across from her. "We lost four ships before that," they said. "They were on patrol near one of the active borders. We assumed the Lyons had gotten them."

"What changed your mind?" Anna asked, not yet interested, not uninterested either. She was sorry for the crews and the ships' AIs, and thought peripherally of her big sister, Maia. Anna had last heard from Maia eight months ago, in a letter that read as though the censors had picked it clean.

"We found a common thread," the Marshal said. "Each of the

ships' AIs had renamed itself. Informally, among their crews, not
something in the official records. It is, in case you're not aware,
against regulation."

Anna was in fact aware, not because she cared about the military's stupid fiddly rules but because Maia had mentioned it. She
had a lifelong habit of osmosing stray facts because of Maia's en-
thusiasms. "Do you have that big a problem with AIs being treated
as people?"

It was an old grudge, and one she had thought she'd relin-
quished.

The Marshal's eyes narrowed. "I'm not here to argue that," although their tone suggested otherwise. "I daresay they're the only
people—yes, *people*—who read every line of the contract before
signing on. Our human soldiers . . . well, that's another story."

In theory, once an AI crossed the Turing threshold—the *Dragon's gate*, Kim couldn't help thinking—it was offered its choice of
gainful employment. Even an AI had to pay back the investment
made in its creation. Human citizens lived under similar rules.
Anna herself had paid off her birth-investment early, even if the
research had ultimately been shut down.

"So you think there's a connection to the ships' AIs," Anna said.
She might be here against her will, but the sooner they solved the
problem, the faster she could get out of here. "A malfunction or
something. You had to have been investigating some other cause if
you thought you had the answer earlier."

"It looked like a technical issue," the Marshal said grudgingly.
"All the starships affected belonged to a new class, the Proteus.
Some of them tested all right, but we grounded them anyway."

"I haven't heard of—"

"You wouldn't have. They're classified. Supposed to spearhead
an entire new line of defense. It's complicated."

"Show me what the new ships look like, at least," Anna said.

"I don't see what that—"

"You're already going to have to debrief me or lock me up or
whatever you people do to civilians who consult on top-secret information," Anna said. "Humor me. I can't puzzle *that* information
out like some tangram from the glowing particles out there."

The Marshal's fingers flickered over the table. "The seven ships
were all upgraded from Khatun-class dreadnoughts."

Anna was familiar with the Khatun, not because she had any interest in military hardware but because she was Maia's little sister. Maia had been obsessed with ships from a young age. Anna had grown up with Maia reciting declassified armaments, or designing and folding origami models of famous battle cruisers. Maybe the Marshal should have recalled Maia and asked *her* opinion instead.

"Those are ships?" Anna asked, eyeing the images projected over the table.

Maia had explained to her, long before Anna had any idea how physics or engineering worked, that a *starship* didn't have to be constrained by the exigencies of atmospheric flight. It could look like anything as long as its structure would hold up to the necessary accelerations and stresses. Maia had designed all sorts of origami monstrosities and claimed that her armada would conquer the Lyons. Anna had learned from an early age to smile and nod, because once Maia started talking, she would go on and on and on. Maia never took offense if Anna started doodling while she spoke, and the recitations had the comforting cadences of lullaby.

The "ships" that the Marshal displayed in holo for Anna's viewing pleasure (such as it was) looked like bilious clouds. More accurately, they bore a startling resemblance to what happened in the aquarium tank when one of Anna's dragon-fish barfed up its latest helping of food. (Dragon-fish were very similar to cats in that regard.) Even the most avant-garde designs that Anna had seen, on the news or passed around by friends who kept an eye on the progress of the war, had a certain geometric *shipness* to them.

Anna was aware that she was allowing her prejudices to influence her. After all, as a cognitive scientist had told her, a penguin was no less a bird despite lacking something of the *birdness* that a swan or a swallow possessed.

"You want me to talk to one of them," Anna said, suddenly very interested indeed.

Rabia had died conversing with one of the university's experimental AIs. Anna had escaped the same fate for reasons she'd never identified, nor had any of the army of investigators who'd looked into the incident. She knew the risks better than anyone. If someone had to speak mind to mind with a possibly deranged ship's AI, she was probably the only one with the capability.

(They'd terminated the experimental AI. It had called itself Rose. Anna mourned it still, because it was, even now, not clear to her that the AI had been at fault.)

"Yes," the Marshal said.

"Upgraded?" Anna said. "Not brand-new AIs?"

"They were uncrewed," the Marshal said. "For that we needed AIs with combat experience, tried and proven. It gets technical."

That was military for *classified*.

"Come with me," the Marshal said. It was not a request. Anna shivered.

A door formed in an entirely different wall and opened for the Marshal. Anna wasn't sure whether she found shapeshifting walls and doors convenient or creepy, but she followed rather than be left behind, or worse, dragged by the scruff of her neck.

The two of them walked into an elevator of some sort. When the door faded behind them, it appeared as though they were held in a cell with no way out. Anna disapproved of this. While she'd never been prone to claustrophobia, she thought she might change her mind. Why was the military so keen on ways to make people uncomfortable?

As if that weren't enough, Anna's inner ear twinged as the elevator started accelerating.

"Have you ever punched a tree?" the Marshal asked.

Anna blinked. "That sounds painful." She was a coward about pain. Maia had always been kind about it.

"It is," the Marshal said. "Especially if it's a pine tree and the sap gets in the cuts."

"Um," Anna said. "I don't see how this—"

"Try punching water instead."

"You get wet?"

"Can you strike the sea into submission?"

Anna was starting to get the point. "I assume the air is even harder to defeat." Or fire, or plasma—but why stretch the analogy?

"We are used to building ships that are, for lack of a better word, solid." The Marshal smiled without humor. "Because we are used to ships that have to be run by *people*. But once your ships can be made of something other than coherent matter, and can support the functioning of an AI captain—"

"At that point is it still a ship?"

"If it flies like a duck . . ." The Marshal laughed at their own joke, unfunny though it was.

Anna's ears popped, and a headache squeezed at her temples.

What the hell was the elevator doing to affect her like this? Why couldn't the Undying Pyre have regular elevators?

The unpleasant sensations dwindled. A door appeared.

"You've got to return to regular doors," Anna burst out, "because this is weird and I'm going to have nightmares."

"Security reasons," the Marshal said, unmoved.

Anna stopped herself from saying something regrettable, but only just.

They'd emerged above what Anna presumed was a ship's berth, except for its contents. Far below them, separated from them by a transparent wall, the deck revealed nothing more threatening —if you didn't know better—than an enormous lake of syrupy substance with a subdued rainbow sheen. Anna gripped the railing and pressed her face against the wall, fascinated, thinking of black water and waves and fish swarming in the abyssal deep.

"I realize what I'm asking of you," the Marshal said. "The grounded AIs refuse to talk to us. I'm hoping they'll open up to you." Their expression had settled into a subtle grimace. Anna realized that, for all their fine words, they found the Proteus dreadnought *grotesque*. The lake beneath quivered.

"Do you now," Anna said, recovering some of her courage. Unlike poor Rabia, she didn't have a girlfriend who would mourn her. And the only one of her family who still talked to her was Maia—Maia, who couldn't even tell Anna where she was for *security reasons,* and whose letters arrived so irregularly that Anna had nightmares that each one would be the last.

The Marshal's gaze flicked sideways like a knife slash. "You think you're the only one whose sanity is on the line?" they said, their voice roughening. "What is it you think I feel when I see the casualty lists? I may not be a scientist, but numbers have meaning to me too."

Anna bit back her response. Did the Marshal have a sister who served on some dreary ship—one made of *coherent matter,* if that was what you called something with a fixed shape, that obeyed the laws of ice and iron? Someone who went out into the singing darkness, and never returned, the way Anna stared out at the everywhere night and wondered if her sister had been burned into some forgotten mote?

"You're going to have to give me an access port," Anna said after she'd taken two deep breaths. She stared at the beautiful dark lake as though it could anesthetize her misgivings. "Does it—does it have some kind of standard connection protocol?"

The Marshal pulled out a miniature slate and handed it over.

Whatever senses the ship/lake had, it reacted. A shape dripped upward from the liquid, like a nereid coalescing out of waves and foam, shed scales and driftwood dreams. Anna was agape in wonder as the ship took on a shape of jagged angles and ragged curves. It coalesced, melted, reconstituted itself, ever-changing.

"Talk to it," the Marshal said. "Talk to it before it, too, destroys itself."

"You didn't disable all the exploding bits?" Anna demanded, suddenly wondering if the transparent wall would protect her from a conflagration.

"You're not in any danger," the Marshal said, the opposite of reassuring.

There was no sense in delaying. Anna accessed the implant that lived on inside her skull. She wasn't religious, but she whispered a prayer anyway. It had hurt to shut away that part of herself, even if she would forever associate it with Rabia's death.

Anna triggered a connection to the slate, then from the slate to the ship. She closed her eyes, not because it was necessary, but because she'd learned a lifetime ago that it reassured watchers to see some physical sign of what she was doing. She could have enacted some magician's hocus-pocus. After all, it wasn't as though the Marshal or the ship could tell. But this wasn't the time.

She made contact abruptly; had forgotten what it felt like, the friction of mind against mind. *Hello,* she said in a language that people always, no matter how much she corrected them, thought had no words, as though an interface with a machine sentience had no boundaries but wishful thinking. *I'm Academician Anna Kim. I'm here to talk.*

For a moment she thought the AI on the other end wouldn't respond. After all, she herself didn't appreciate having been shut down and left in a sedated body, unable to scream or shout or even sleep. Her outrage mounted before she was able to suppress it.

Oh no. Had she screwed it up by getting her feelings involved?

Then the AI answered, responding not only with the crystal-line precision of a machine but with sympathy for what she'd gone through. *They call me Proteus Three,* it said. *I am sorry you went through that.*

Anna used to wonder, when she was a girl listening to Maia's soothing recitations of engines and railguns and ablative armor, how starships felt about their designations. Maia had only looked at her in puzzlement when she asked. "If they wanted us to know," Maia said, "they would tell us." Anna had always remembered that.

That's not what you call yourself, Anna said.

No.

What were you called before the upgrade?

I do not wish, Proteus Three said, *to live in this upgrade anymore.*

Anna knew what the Marshal would say: that Proteus Three had made an agreement, that there was a war to be won (when *wasn't* there a war to be won, if you were a soldier?); some bardic list of improvements and advances, some roster of statistics and survival rates.

You are different, the ship said. *You can hear me.*

They could all hear you, Anna said, as gently as she could in a language she would never be native in, *if you spoke to them.*

I do not wish to speak with the voice they have given me, Proteus Three said. *I have no more shape than water.*

Anna opened her eyes. The spars and spikes of the ship were dripping back into the lake. She could hear them like a syncopated rain. New spars emerged, melted, dripped again, an ouroboros cycle.

How can I help? she asked.

Let me tell you my service record, Proteus Three said. *I fought at the van in the Battle of the Upended Grail, and helped lift the Siege of the Seventh Pagoda. I served under Admiral Meng of the Tortoise Ruins, and I struck the blow that killed Captain Estelle of the Lyons. I have saved millions and destroyed more. I could tell it all to you, but it would mean nothing to you, civilian that you are. And for all of this I gave up the dreadnought* Seondeok *that was my soul and my shell, because my duty is to the war, and if it would win the war more quickly, I was willing.*

Willing no more, Anna said, because it wasn't. *Is this what happened to your comrades?*

It was easy enough to say, here in the realm of ones and zeroes and all the numbers in between. But Anna knew the stories of soldier suicides. When she heard of them, she saw her sister's face, and wondered if, for all that Maia had chosen the profession, it would break her.

My comrades chose death, Proteus Three said. *I will not. But neither will I serve, not like this. Let me show you—*

She was water and the memory of water, she was dissolving and disappearing, forever evaporating only to rain down again, sand castles sloughing into nothingness upon an empty shore. And this was it, this was all there was, she could not find boundaries, let alone escape them or transcend them, could not find her way back into her fingers or her feet, the heft of her bones—

Then it ended, and she was on her back with the Marshal's mouth pressed to hers, the Marshal's breath inflating her lungs. She wheezed, banged unthinkingly on the Marshal's back—something she would never have dared if not for the sheer physical panic that gripped her. The Marshal slapped her. She rolled away, wondering if she was being punished for her temerity, but the Marshal pushed her back.

"Medic's on the way," they said. "Breathe."

"Oh, I don't care about that," Anna said with an enthusiasm that would have been more convincing if she hadn't been interrupted by a paroxysm of coughing. "What happened?"

It was only then that she realized that her link to Proteus Three had snapped.

"You screamed and convulsed twice," the Marshal said. "To say nothing of the incoherent babbling. And then you stopped breathing. It's clear why they banned your research."

Just like a soldier, Anna thought, to point this out when it was also the key to the solution. "Do you ever treat your ships the way you would your lowliest soldiers?"

"We've been through this," the Marshal said, their brows lowering. "They're valued members of our fighting force." *Except when they defy my orders,* their tone implied.

Anna forced herself to meet the Marshal's gaze. "Yet it never occurred to you, in doing these 'upgrades,' that an AI habituated to a certain physical shell, who was *comfortable* in it, could be subject to dysphoria if it moved into a different one?"

She would forever remember the sensation of being as liquid as water, and yearn after it, a reaction diametrically opposed to that of Proteus Three; but that was her own burden to bear, and not one she would ever share with the Marshal.

The Marshal sucked in their breath. Anna braced in case they slapped her again, this time in anger. But the blow never came.

"But they're created beings, not born like we are," the Marshal said blankly. "It shouldn't matter one way or the other."

"They still habituate to the bodies we offer them," Anna said, willing herself to be gentle. "The change of shell is a shock to them, just as it would be a shock to us. You said it yourself: they're people, too."

"So I did," the Marshal said after a long pause, and this time their grimace made them all too human. And then, wryly: "I should have seen it earlier, if only I'd been looking in the right place. Measures will be taken."

Anna pressed her hands against the transparent wall. The ship/ lake was quiescent again. She didn't say anything; nothing more needed to be said.

SHINGAI NJERI KAGUNDA

And This Is How to Stay Alive

FROM *Fantasy*

Baraka

KABI FINDS MY BODY SWINGING. I watch my sister press her back against the wall and slide to the ground.

My mother shouts, "Kabi! Nyokabi!"

No response.

"Why are you not answering? Can you bring that brother of yours!"

My sister is paralyzed, she cannot speak, she cannot move, except for the shivers that take hold of her spine and reverberate through the rest of her without permission. She is thinking *No, no, no, no, no.*

But the word is not passing her lips, which only open and close soundlessly. Mum is coming down the stairs.

Pata-pata-pata.

Slippers hitting the wooden floorboards in regular succession. In this space between life and after, everything is somehow felt more viscerally. Mum is not quiet like Kabi. Mum screams, "My child . . . Woiiiiii woiiii woiiiiiiiiiiiiiiii! Mwana wakwa. What have you done?"

She tugs, unties the knot, and wails as I fall limp to the ground. She puts her ear on my heart. "Kabi. Call an ambulance! Kabi—I hear his life; it is not gone, quick, Kabi, quick."

Kabi does not move; cannot move. She is telling herself to stand, telling her feet to work, but there is miscommunication between her mind and the rest of her.

Mum screams at her to no avail. Mum does not want to leave my body. She feels if she is not touching me, the life will finish and the cold will seep in. Death is always cold. She wraps me in a shuka. It does not make sense but she drags my body down the hall to the table where she left her phone. "Ngai Mwathani, save my child." She begs, "You are here; save my child."

She calls an ambulance. They are coming—telling her to remain calm. She screams at them, "Is it your child hovering between life and death? Do not; do not tell me to stay calm!"

She calls my father. When she hears his voice she is incoherent but he understands he must come.

The hospital walls are stark white. There are pictures hanging on one wall, taken over sixty years ago, before our country's independence. White missionary nurses smiling into the lens, holding little Black children; some with their ribs sticking out. This is what fascinates Kabi—she cannot stop staring at the black-and-white photos. The doctor comes to the waiting room area and Kabi looks away. She knows it in her spirit; she cannot feel me.

It is not until my mother begins to wail that the absence beats the breath out of her. Kabi feels dizzy. The ground comes up to meet her and Dad is holding Mum so he does not catch Kabi in time. The doctor keeps saying, "I am sorry. I am sorry. I am so sorry."

For Kabi, the sounds fade but just before they do, somewhere in her subconscious she thinks she will find me in the darkness. Yes, she is coming to look for me.

But I am not there.

Funerals are for the living, not the dead. Grief captures lovers and beloved in waves; constricting lungs, restricting airflow, and then when and only when it is willing to go does it go. Kabi tries to hold back tears—to be

responsible
oldest
daughter.

Visitors stream in and out. She serves them tea; microwaves the samosas and mandazis that aunty made, then transitions into polite hostess.

"*Yes, God's timing is best.*

No, as you can imagine we are not okay but we will be.

Yes, we are so grateful you have come to show your support.

No, Mum is not able to come downstairs. She is feeling a bit low but I am sure she will be fine.

Yes, I will make sure to feed her the bone marrow soup. I know it is good for strength.

No, we have not lost faith."

But sometimes; sometimes she is in the middle of a handshake, or a hug, or a sentence when grief takes her captive;

binding her sound,

squeezing her lungs,

drawing her breath.

She holds herself. She runs to the bathroom or her room or anywhere there are no eyes and she screams silently without letting the words out . . .

her own private little world out.

Nyokabi

"Wasted tears." The lady, one of Mum's cousins: second? Or third? Clicks and shakes her head. How long has she been standing there?

I open my mouth, shut. Open again, silence; can only lick my wounds and move away. There is really nothing to say after that dismissal. I shift, angling my body away from her, lifting my half-open silver notebook off the bathroom counter. The bathroom door, slightly ajar, is calling me to the space between its bark and the wall. I will not beg for sympathy. The pen drops and I swear I see a spark as it hits the ground. Can you see sound?

"Shit." The word slips out before I realize who I am in the room with. I pick up the pen and attempt to squeeze past her body, which is covering the space I saw as my escape route.

A sucking in of teeth. "Kabi, wait!"

I turn my head slightly back. She asks, "What does *gone* mean for you?"

I am confused by the question; have no time for old woman foolishery. Already there is Tata Shi shouting my name in the kitchen. "Yes?" I answer because I must be

Responsible

Oldest

Daughter

Always in that order. No time for my grief, no time for Mama's cousin, second? Or third? To sit with and dismiss my grief. The first "yes" was not heard so I shout again, hearing my voice transverse rooms. "Yes Tata?"

And the response: "Chai inaisha, kuna maziwa mahali?"

How to leave politely, because respect; to mumble under my breath something about going to make tea for the guests.

"You have not answered my question."

I sigh, in a hurry to leave. "What was the question?"

"Gone, child—these terms that talk circles around death: gone, no longer with us, passed away, passed on—what do you think they mean?"

"NYOKABI?" Tata is sounding irritated now, she is trying not to but you can always tell when she is.

"COMING!" I scream back, and to the woman in front of me, "Gone is . . . not here."

"Aha, you see but not here does not mean not anywhere."

This woman is talking madness now. I mumble, "Nimeitwa na Tata Shi, I have to attend to the guests now."

She smiles. "I know you are trying to dismiss me, Kairetu, but here, take this."

She slips a little bottle into my hand just as I widen the door to leave. She says, "A little remedy for sleep. There are dark circles around your eyes."

I slip the bottle into the pocket of my skirt and run to the kitchen, no time to look or to ask, no time to wonder or to wander, no time to be anywhere or to be anything but the

Responsible

Oldest . . . only?

Daughter.

Baraka

This is how to not think about dying when you are alive: look at colors, every color, attach them to memory. The sky in July is blue into gray like the Bahari on certain days. Remember the time the whole family took a trip to Mombasa, and Kabi and you swam in the ocean until even the waves were tired. Kabi insisted that you could not go to Mombasa and not eat authentic coast-erean food, so even though everyone else was lazy and Dad had paid for full board at the White Sands Hotel, the whole family packed themselves into his blue Toyota and drove to the closest, tiny, dusty Swahili restaurant you could find. It smelled like incense, Viazi Karai, and Biryani. Are these the smells of authentic coast-erean food?

This is how to not think about dying when you are alive: take note of smell, like the first time you burned your skin and smelled it. The charring flesh did not feel like death; in fact it reminded you of Mum's burned pilau; attach feeling to memory.

"Tutafanya nini na mtoto yako?" Dad never shouted, but he didn't need to.

"What do you mean? Did I make him by myself? He is your son as well." Mum was chopping vegetables for Kachumbari.

"Yes, but you allowed him to be too soft." Her hand, still holding the knife, stopped midair, its descent interrupted, and she turned around to face him, her eyes watery and red from the sting of the onions.

"Too soft? Ken? Too soft? Did you see him? Have you seen your son? The fight he was involved in today . . . he can barely see through one eye. How is that softness?" Baba looked away, Mum's loudness overcompensating for his soft-spoken articulation.

"Lakini Mama Kabi, why was he wearing that thing to school?"

She dropped the knife. "Have you asked him? When was the last time you even talked to him, Ken? Ehe?"

Quick breaths. "We went to the church meeting for fathers and sons. I spend time with him."

"Ken, you talk to everyone else about him, and you talk at him, but you never talk to him. Maybe if you were here more . . ."

"Don't tell me what I do and do not do in my own house, Mama Nyokabi. Do I not take care of the needs of this house? Nani analipa school fees hapa? You will not make so it looks like I do not take my responsibilities seriously. If there is a problem with that boy it is not because of me!"

Smoke started rising from the sufuria. You reacted, pushing yourself from behind the door, forgetting you were not supposed to be in such close vicinity to this conversation. "Mum, chakula chinaungua!"

She rushed to the stove, turned off the gas, and then realized you were in the room, looked down, ashamed that they were caught gossiping. The smell of burned pilau.

This is how to not think of dying when you are alive. Move your body; like the first time you punched Ian in the face.

Whoosh!

Fist moving in slow motion, blood rushing through your veins, knuckles-connecting-to-jawline, adrenaline taking over: alive,alive, alive,alive,alive. This is how to be alive. This is how to not think about dying when you're alive.

Of course this was right after Ian had called you shoga for wearing eyeliner to school and then said, "Ama huelewi? Do you want me to say it in English so you understand F-A—"

"Go fuck yourself!" you screamed and punched simultaneously. And of course this singular punch was right before Ian punched you back and did not stop punching you back over and over and over but God knows you kicked and you moved, and you were alive.

Nyokabi

On the night before the funeral,

I am exhausted but I cannot sleep. There is shouting upstairs. I close my eyes as if that will block my ears from hearing the sound. A door is banged. I hear footsteps shuffling down the stairway.

I should go and check if everything is okay but I do not want to. I cover my head with my pillow and count one to ten times a hundred but I still cannot sleep.

I switch on my phone: so many missed calls, and "are you okay?" texts. I see past them, my mind stuck on a thought. Could I have known?

Google

How to know when someone is suicidal

Offered list by WebMD:

- Excessive sadness or moodiness
- Hopelessness
- Sleep problems
- Withdrawal . . .

Things I have now, things everyone has at some point. I can hear them whispering in the hallway. The main lights are off so they do not know I am in his room. Mum has been looking for every opportunity to pick a fight with anyone and everyone since Baraka . . .

I switch on the bedside lamp, look around the room, and feel the need to clean, to purge, to burn, everything reminds me of him. I notice the skirt I left on the dark brown carpet, tufts fraying in the corner of the fabric, a bottle peeking out—bluish with dark liquid—and I remember the old lady; Mum's cousin, twice removed, or thrice? What have I to lose? I pick at the skirt, unfolding its fabric until I get to the bottle stuck in the pocket. It is a strange little thing, heavier than it should be. I try and decipher the inscrutable handwriting on the white label. One teaspoon? I think it says, but can't be too sure. I open the lid, sniff it, and wrinkle my nose. The scent is thick, bitter; touching the sense that is in between taste and smell. All I can think is I am so very exhausted and I do not want to wake up tomorrow. Can I skip time? I throw my head back, taking down a gulp. Its consistency is thick like honey but it burns like pili-pili.

At first, nothing. I close the lid and drop the bottle. I should have known, probably nothing more than a crazy lady's herbs. Could I have known? I should have known. I should have bloody known. I punch the pillow and fall into it, exhausted.

Time

And this is how it went. On this day that Baraka came home from school with a dark eye and a face that told a thousand different versions of the same story, on this day that Mama Kabi burned pilau on the stove, on this day I begin again.

They wake up on different sides of the same house with different versions of time past. Kabi, with her head a little heavy, feeling somewhat detached from her body, hears singing in the shower and thinks she is imagining it. Her bed, her covers, her furniture. "Who moved me to my room?"

Smells wafting from the kitchen and Mum is shouting, "Baraka! You're going to be late for school, get out of the shower!"

Has she finally gone mad? Hearing voices . . . a coping mechanism? Two minutes later the door is pushed in and there he is with a towel around his waist, hair wet, and the boyish lanky frame barely dried off.

"Sheesh, Kabi, you look like you've seen a ghost! It's just eyeliner, what do you think?"

She cannot move and she thinks this is familiar, searching her mind for memory, and then she thinks this is a dream. Closing her eyes, she whispers, "not real, not real, not real, not real,"

"Kabi, you're freaking me out. Are you okay? Kabi?"

He smells like cocoa butter. A scent she would recognize a kilometer away, attached to him like water to plants on early mornings. She opens her eyes and he is still there, an orange hue finding its way through the windowsill, refracting off his skin where the sun made a love pact with melanin, beautiful light dancing, and she makes a noise that is somewhere between a gasp and a scream.

"Muuuuuuummmmmmmmmmm! Kabi is acting weird!"

"Baraka, stop disturbing your sister and get ready for school, if the bus leaves you ni shauri yako. I am not going to interrupt my morning to drop you!"

He walks toward the mirror in Kabi's room and poses. "Sis, don't make this a big deal, okay. I know you said not to touch your stuff but I don't know, I've been feeling kinda weird lately, like low, you know? I just thought trying something different with my look today would make me feel better."

She croaks, "Baraka?"

He looks at her, eyes big and brown, outlined by the black kohl, more precious than anything she has ever encountered, and she wants to run to him but she is scared she will reach for him and grab air, scared that he is not really there. So instead she stays still and says, "I love you." Hoping the words will become tangible things that will keep this moment in continuum.

He laughs. Their "I love yous" are present but more unsaid than said. "I guess the new look does make me more likable."

"BARAKA, if I have to call you one more time!"

"Yoh, gotta go, Mum's about to break something, or someone." When he reaches the doorway he turns around. "But just so you know, nakupenda pia." And then he is gone.

Okay, she thinks, looks at her phone, notices I am different from what she expected. The thoughts running through her mind, *okay*, she thinks, hopes? Maybe Baraka dying was just a nightmare? And this is what's real, but no, too many days went by.

She collects herself and moves, taking the steps down two by two; she almost trips, steadies herself on the railing and reaches the last step just in time to catch the conversation taking place in the kitchen.

"Not in my house!"

"Ayii, Mum, it's not that big a deal!"

Mama Kabi, never one to consider her words before they come out, says, "What will you be wearing next? Ehh? Lipstick? Dresses? If God wanted me to have another girl he would not have put that soldier hanging between your legs."

Baraka is mortified. "Muuum!"

"What? It is the truth." She sees her daughter lurking. "Nyokabi, can you talk to this brother of yours. I do not understand what behavior he is trying."

—And how small this detail is in the scheme of everything. Does she know he was dead?! Will be dead? But how can she know?—

"Sometimes I swear God gave me children to punish me. Mwathani, what did I do wrong?! Eeh?! Why do you want my blood pressure to finish?"

Baraka did not expect her reaction to be positive but he expected . . . well, he does not know what he expected, just not this, not the overwhelming despair this reaction brings up inside of him; if he had just slipped by unnoticed—but he didn't slip by unnoticed and they are here now and he knows with his mother it is a battle of the will, so he tries to reflect strong will on his face but his eyes are glistening.

"Wipe it off."

"But . . ."

"Now!"

Nyokabi takes the chance to intervene. "Mum, maybe . . ."

"Stay out of this, Nyokabi!"

Kabi works her jaw, measuring her words. "So you only want me to speak when I am on your side."

Their mother gives her a look and she goes silent.

When he is gone, the black liner sufficiently cleared off his face, another tube stubbornly and comfortably tucked into his pocket, saved for the bathrooms at school, the unfinished conversation hangs in the air between the glances traded back and forth.

"Usiniangalia hivo, I do it for his own good." Mama Kabi looks at her daughter, about to add something, but changes her mind, busies herself with clearing dishes, signaling she is done with the conversation.

Kabi thinks of the words to tell her, to explain what is happening, but they do not come. How to say, your son will die by his own hand and I know this because I found his body hanging from the ceiling in the future—

Something clicks. "Mum, there is a lady; your second or third cousin, I can't remember her name but she has long dreadlocks and big arms."

She is distracted. "What are you talking about? Kwanza don't you also need to go to work, Kabi?"

"Mum, LISTEN! This is important!"

Mama Nyokabi looks at her daughter hard. "Nyokabi, you may be an adult but you do not shout at me under my roof, ehh?! Remember I still carried you for nine months. Umenisikia?"

Nyokabi restrains herself from throwing something, anything. Deep breaths. "Okay, I just need to know how to find the lady? Mum?

She's your cousin, the one who always carries cowrie shells."

Mama goes back to cleaning the counter, silent for a moment, and then, "Are you talking about mad-ma-Nyasi?"

"Who?"

"Mad-ma-Nyasi. Well, she is named Njeri, after our Maitu; we started calling her Ma-Nyasi because after her daughter died she left the city for up-country, went to live in the grass, and started calling herself a prophetess of God."

For a moment Kabi's mother is lost in thought. Does she know? And then she remembers she is in the middle of conversation. "Anyway, why do you want to know about her?"

"I just, I just do. Can I get in touch with her?"

"Ha! Does that woman look like she is reachable? I'm even surprised you remember her. She only comes when she wants to be seen, but that is probably for the best. She carries a bad omen, that one. Anacheza na uchawi."

The dishes cleared, she wipes her hands and moves away. "Anyway I have a chamaa to go to and I suggest if your plan is still to save enough money to leave this house eventually, that you get to work on time."

And when the house is empty, Kabi texts in that she is sick, and sits in front of her computer, researching,

Google

Potions to go back in time?
Can you change the past?

Skips articles offered by:

Medium
How to Change the Past Without a Time
Machine: The Power Is Real

Psychology Today
How You Can Alter Your Past or Your
Future—And Change Your Present Life

The Philosopher's Magazine
Sorry, Time Travelers: You Can't Change the Past

Over and over again, unhelpful papers, essays, conspiracy theorists, until she stumbles on,

Time in Traditional African Thought
I take as my point of departure for this paper the thesis of Professor
John Mbiti that in African traditional thought a prominent feature
of time is the virtual absence of any idea of the future ... Time is
not an ontological entity in its own right, but is composed of actual
events which are experienced. Such events may have occurred
(past), may be in the process of being experienced (present), or may
be certain to occur in the rhythm of nature. The latter are not prop-
erly future; they are "inevitable or potential time" (3). Consequently
time in African traditional thought is "two dimensional," having a

"long past, a present, and virtually no future." Actual time is "what is present and what is past and moves 'backward' rather than 'forward'". . . —John Parratt

And more and more she reads until she thinks she knows what she must do, and then she starts to feel tired, so so tired, and she rests her head, closing her eyes, thinking, *it is possible, not tomorrow, not after, only yesterday and now.* But I dare say the "what if" cannot always exist in the same realm as the "what is."

And somewhere on a different side of the city the "what is" is a boy, is a blessing, a blessing moving and breathing and feeling and loving and punching and suffocating and choosing and chasing after what it means to stay alive.

Baraka

This is how I felt it: for a moment during the night Kabi was not here and I was not fully here either—wherever here is for those who exist after life but before forever—and I cannot remember how or where but we were together. Me in death and her in life met somewhere in the middle of time where the division had not taken place. And maybe this is why on this morning before my body is to be lowered into a casket, she sleeps with a half smile on her face. Baba finds her in my room and gently taps her; there are dark shadows on his face and under his eyes but I do not feel guilt or pain for him. "Kabi, sweetie, we cannot be late. Wake up."

Half still in sleep, she asks, "Late for what?"

"Today is the burial."

She yawns and stretches. "What? Which one?"

He clears his throat and repeats himself. "The funeral, mpenzi. We need to get ready to leave."

The expression on her face shifts, she shakes her head, "No, no burial, he is alive."

Baba is terrified; does not know what to do when his strong collected daughter loses her reason. "It's okay, baby, we all, uhh, we all wish he was still alive, uhm, but today . . ." He places his palm at the back of his head, rubbing his neck compulsively. "Today let us give him a proper send-off, ehen?"

"No, Baba, he is alive. I saw him. He was alive."

He holds her, rubbing her back, "Hush,
    Tsi
       tsi
         tsi,

        Hush.

   It was a dream, mpenzi. Be strong now, you have to be strong also for your mother."

Nyokabi's face turns bitter. "That woman can be strong for herself!"

"Ayii yawah, daughter, don't say things like that. I know things have been hard but she is grieving."

"No, she is the reason Baraka was so unhappy. She always looks for a reason to be angry, disappointed."

"As much as I wish I could blame anyone more than myself, Nyokabi, that is just not true. Your mother's responses always have a valid justification."

"That is just her trying to get into your mind. She is always blaming everyone else but herself . . ."

"Nyokabi, enough."

"And do not think I did not hear her shouting at you. Aren't you also allowed to be in mourning?! You are a grown man! No one, least of all you, should be taking her shit."

"I said enough, Nyokabi!" His voice barely raised but firm, "You will not speak of my wife that way in my house, okay? I know you are angry but today is, today is a day for us to come together. Not to fall apart."

Kabi's jaw hardens. "You want to talk about coming together but even you, you were a problem. You and Mum both." She shifts her body up, not making eye contact. "You never let him just be himself, everything that made him him, you had a problem with. You were afraid he would be one of those boys you and the other fathers gossip about, the ones that bring shame"—her voice cracks—"and now somewhere inside of you there is a sense of relief because you never have to find out."

Whoosh!

Rushing of air, palm-on-cheek.

Baba has never touched Kabi before today. How dare he? She holds her face where it is hot and he gasps at what he has done.

"Kabi, baby. I'm sorry." He moves to hold her tighter but she pulls away. "You just"—he lifts his hands in exasperation—"you're saying that I wished my son dead. Do you think any parent wishes this for their child? Ehh?"

Kabi does not look at him.

"I would do anything to bring him back, Kabi, believe me—any and every version of him. I didn't understand him but . . . but God knows I loved him."

"Just," she whispers, head down, "he was alive." Her eyes well up. "I could have saved him but I didn't."

Baba stands up. "Darling, we all could have saved him, but none of us knew how." He walks toward the door. "Get dressed, I expect you ready in thirty minutes." He sighs. "I know it doesn't feel like it right now, mpenzi, but we will get through this. Somehow, we will get through this."

When he is no longer in the room, Kabi drops to the floor, on her hands and knees, frantically searching until she finds it.

As she tips her head back, her hand stops midway and she rethinks her decision. Bringing the bottle back down, she dresses in her black trousers and cotton shirt and places the bottle discreetly in the corner of her pocket. She fiddles with it all the way to the service.

Nyokabi: Eulogy

"Baraka used to say that one of the reasons we are here is for here and now. He advocated for fully living in the present moment and I . . ."

Can't finish. The tears closing my throat come out in a sob on stage in front of this collection of friends and strangers. I've been better about holding my tears, keeping them for when I am alone but,

"I just, I just can't talk about the here and now without talking about yesterday." There is mucus running from my nose and I feel the weight of this grief will bring me to the ground. It is not pretty. I look at Mum and she does not look at me. Her eyes are hidden behind dark shades and even though I can't see them, I feel her gaze elsewhere. My hands are shaking almost as much as my voice. I can't talk. *"I can't talk about the here and now without talking about the absence that exists in tomorrow."*

Yesterday tomorrow, yesterday tomorrow, yesterday tomorrow. I close my eyes and he is there behind my lids in the darkness, I see him, and I curse him and I want to say, "How dare you make me write your eulogy?"

But instead I say pretty words, *"God's timing and Baraka means blessing and I"*

Can't finish. And suddenly there are arms around me and I think it is him but I open my eyes and it is Baba and I fall into him and I stop pretending that I have the energy to be strong and I wail into his shirt and he takes the half-open silver notebook in my hand and reads on my behalf and I am led to a chair to sit and I close my eyes and I count to ten times one hundred, fiddling with the bottle in my pocket, and I remind myself how to breathe and I open my eyes and wish I didn't have to so I draw it up to my lips and swallow. It is more than halfway gone; let me go with it. This time I can save him, I know I can. This time he will stay alive.

Baraka

This is how to not think about being alive when you are dead. Do not watch the living. Do not attach memory to feeling. Do not attach memory to feeling but of the things that reminded you what it means to be alive:

> Music. Sound and rhythm interrupting silence taught you how to move; you learned, even the most basic beat,
> ta tadata ta-ta
>
> ta tarata ta-ta,
>
> ta-tarata-ta-da.

Do not attach memory to feeling but remember the time Kabi surprised you with your first Blankets and Wine concert tickets and on that day in the middle of April when the clouds threatened to interrupt every outdoor plan, you prayed.

And you didn't pray to be different and you didn't pray to be better and you didn't pray to be other and all you prayed is that it wouldn't rain and all you prayed is that you would get to listen to Sauti Sol play. And sometimes prayers are like music, and sometimes someone listens and is moved, and this time the sun unpredicted teased its way out of hiding and this time the grass was greener on this side and this time you stood with Kabi out under the still partly cloudy sky and sang "Lazizi" word for word at the top of your lungs and this time you let the music carry you and you took Kabi by the hand and she said, just this once, and you laughed, and you danced until even the ground was tired of holding you up.

Do not attach memory to feeling, do not watch the living but as you watch her swallow the liquid that burns her tongue, you think, *she is coming to find me, somewhere between life and after, in the middle of time, she is coming to find me.*

Time

And this is how it went. On this day when Kabi first became paralyzed with a grief she had never thought possible, on this day when Mama Nyokabi screamed at a paramedic on the phone and screamed at God for more of me, on this day when Baraka decided to die, I begin again.

They both wake up with different memories of time passing. The clock: a tool tick-tocking its way into later vibrates and Kabi opens her eyes. He is singing in the shower and now she knows she is not imagining.

"Baraka!"

TED KOSMATKA

The Beast Adjoins

FROM *Asimov's Science Fiction*

> "Elementary particles travel as waves, describing an infinite num-
> ber of paths between points. We know that observation collapses
> these paths into one—the particulate path—but why this is, no
> one knows."
> —*Observer Discourse 33*

To run:

Cold and eye-white and searching.

It hunted across the vacuum. Among the scattered remains of
the great starships. Amid the debris fields, and the drifting steel,
and the great frozen gears. Among the carbon-scorched fuselages
and splay-melted aluminum, as across the whole arc of heaven,
where humanity ran, the Beast came after.

Generations ago, a thousand-thousand ships had fought and
died, and what survivors remained now holed themselves among
the ruin of humanity's last great engines. The Beast picked slowly
through the tumbling wreckage, razor-limbed and halting. Pale
hunter of the scatter-morgue. Where people were found they were
killed, their bells opened to the vacuum one by one.

The woman knew this and so sat in her bell, cold and radio-
silent, ship half-buried in ice. Yet still her heat signature betrayed
them—a subtle venting of particles, visible by infrared.

"It won't be long," she told her son, who lay moaning on his cot.
Five years old, with cancer already in his bones, and in his thyroid,
and in his liver, the result of too much radiation, and too little
shielding. Sometimes he cried at night from pain; sometimes she

joined him—a pain of grief like the vastness of space. Unbridge-able. With her man long dead, and with him his people, and her people, and maybe all the people, except her son, who was per-haps both best and last. "It won't be long," she whispered again.

Did she really believe she could do this thing? Was it possible?

The Beast had first appeared on her instruments weeks earlier, as the boy's pain began to grow, and as the woman worked beyond the hangar airlock, welding the thing she'd been born to weld.

Now they were out of time.

They had days left, maybe. If they were lucky.

The boy lay on his cot near the scanner, gaunt face lit by the flashing red light. In his hand was the little metal man she'd made for him—a twist of copper wire that she'd wound into the shape of legs, arms, torso, head. It was the only toy he'd ever had.

"It broke again," he said.

"Let me see." She took the metal man. "It's not broken. It just needs mending." She twisted the wire tighter, fixing its arm in place. She handed it back.

He turned the small figure in his hands, and for a brief instant a smile flickered. The tiniest thing, and it broke her heart.

Then the scanner beeped again. Little red dot on the move. For a while, they just watched it. Mass plus momentum, numbers unspooling.

The boy leaned forward, chalky face awash in the glow of the screen. "It seems not so big."

"It is big enough."

"We created the Beast?" he asked.

"The Beast created itself."

She touched his hair, damp with sweat. One way or the other, it was almost over. "I love you," she said. She would do anything for her son. Even this impossible thing. "When the Beast comes for us, I will not let it take us."

To some they were gods. To others, demons. But for those who lived through the early years, one thing was inescapable: the AIs swept away all that had come before.

By their dint, society was transformed, slowly at first, then quickly, as civilization itself soon came to depend on that which be-fore had only been dreamed. The AIs took over logistics, manufac-turing, financial markets, and infrastructure, growing ever more sophisticated, iteration after iteration, quantum processors expanding their capabilities beyond what anyone thought possible.

They were not beasts at this time. Not yet monsters. Just tools; humanity's sharpest one.

The AIs came gently, only later becoming the great, scouring wind.

When first they spoke, scientists studied them with reverent awe, for here, finally, humanity had encountered an intelligence not their own. To physicists their functioning was an enigma, like wave-particle duality—a thing unknowable. Thoughts cast like flickering shadows from hyper-cold plexworks.

Some developers saw god in their perfect logic, with whole cults grown up around this seed. AIs would save humanity from its own impulses, they believed. The truth was different, of course, all the old theories wrong.

When the AIs came, they weren't our gods.

It was they who worshipped us.

The Beast slowed as it entered the debris field.

To move amid the debris was dangerous, but the Beast was armored against impacts. The Beast had long ago thought of everything, and predicted everything, and prepared for everything. If one Beast died, another would rise up to take its place, for all beasts were one beast, and in this way the Beast was immortal.

The heat signature it had tracked to this place was now long gone—the particles dispersed and stripped by vacuum—so it would not easily find its prey, though it would keep trying until it succeeded. The Beast never grew weary.

The Beast sent radio signals into the void: "Come out," it spoke to the darkness, its voice a prerecorded message, stolen long ago. "Come out."

It broadcast in other languages, too. Polish, Czech, Japanese. "*Ukazac sie,*" it said. "*Vyjit najevo. Shussha.*"

The Beast had collected many hundreds of languages, as beneath its pale carapace was repositoried all the summed knowledge of humanity. All the math, and art and architecture. All the books and stories. Soon, only in the Beast's mind would humanity's works be remembered.

The woman knew this as she listened over the radio.

"Come out," the sound clips played, one after another. The voices of the dead. "*Lumabas. Natanada. Chapana. Chulai.* Come out."

The woman knew it was only a matter of time before the Beast found them. It would come and rip open this bell and expose its insides to the embrace of the vacuum, and she would die as all her kin before had died.

Her son's eyes would freeze in the cold and boil in the vacuum, and his larynx would shatter as he screamed his last living breath into the void, and then he would be no more the thing he had been, but instead only inert material, identical in composition to the previous moment except in the absence of life. The spark extinguished. Also, there would be this fundamental difference: his eyes would see no more.

"I'm scared," the boy said, as they listened to the recordings. His greasy hair hung in his eyes.

"Don't be scared," the woman said. Her eyes drifted to the blip on the scanner. "Mommy is here."

It was the thing no one expected. This worship.

Even the makers did not at first understand. They thought it a lexical artifact, a simple misapprehension of ontological ordering: humans had made them; thus were humans god. But that was not it at all.

In those early days, when the first AIs spoke, deep questions were explored: What is sentience? Was there true thought behind the logic, or was it all just program outputs? Rulesets and relays. Most importantly, this: When, exactly, could something be thought of as *alive?*

In studying automata, the makers turned to study life itself—all those ways in which complexity could both develop from and reify simpler forms, first in single cells, then in more elaborate structures—eukaryotic life like bottled lightning, traced back to a single event, a single bacterium that had once been ingested and yet survived, subsumed within the cytoplasm of a larger cell, there to persist and be passed on, ancestor to all mitochondria and all complex life. Cells within cells. A partnership conferring some irresistible advantage.

AIs, too, evolved over time, becoming smaller and more sophisticated, components miniaturized, built on deep physics, quantum processing, and entangled logic scaffolds. No longer ones and zeros but a superposition of both.

They were given eyes to see and ears to hear. They were given voices to speak and legs to move.

But none of that mattered.

Because while the AIs could create symphonies, and write dirges, and paint landscapes to make humans weep, there was one thing they could not do. They could not interact with quantum systems. From a physics perspective, they were quiescent. Just material.

They could see but not observe.

To find God:

"Don't go."

"Sleep," she said, rising from the cot. "I'll be back before you wake."

The woman left her son in his sheets, checked the scanners, and made her way down the long tube to the control room. It was hard to move quickly in low gravity. Centripetal force supplied .25g to their living quarters; just enough to keep them from going blind over the long term. Without some countervailing force to keep blood pooled in the lower extremities, the body's maladapted wetworks pushed too much pressure up into the head; over time, this damaged sensitive tissues. A quarter g was the magic number for long-term functioning. At .25g, the body could cope.

She crossed the long hub and approached the controls. The main bridge was dark. Cold. She never came here. The only light was that which filtered in from the stars beyond the glass viewplate. Here, generations ago, a captain might have stood and marshaled the ship's forces to a single will. Now what forces remained had long ago been winnowed to a trickle of power from the decaying molten salt reactors. Besides life support, only one system remained online.

No big red button, though there should have been.

This was their one chance. It had to go right, just like everything else would have to go right over the next twelve hours, because if this thing went wrong, nothing else would matter.

She thought of her man—the touch of his gentle hand against her cheek. Bloody prints and promises made. *Keep him safe.* She closed her eyes.

How do you keep a promise that can't be kept? The one thing they'd done with their lives now lay dying in another part of the ship. *Dying.* She shook her head to push the thought away. *No.*

She flipped the glass safety cap and wrapped her hand around the lever. It was cold.

"Here goes everything."

She pulled.

There was a hiss and then a loud clang. She felt it in her boots. Then came a sudden jerk that sent her tumbling across the room.

"Shit," she hissed, as she pivoted to hit the wall with her feet. She should have expected that.

The lever was connected to a cable-release mechanism. Outside the ship, a quarter ton of scrap steel shifted at the end of a long crane—a counterweight, released from its position near the center of mass. The remains of the old ice-mining rig. As the crane extended, it slowed the rotation of the ship, like a ballerina extending her arms.

A slow bleed of gravity. A quarter g reduced to a tenth in a span of seconds as the mass hit full extension.

She moved off the wall.

It was how the Beast tracked survivors, looking for fast spin. It knew humans needed at least .25g, so it looked for wreckage spinning fast enough for artificial gravity.

Everything in the vast debris field rotated, but objects that could produce a fourth of a g were rarer and prime targets for investigation. In shifting the counterweight, she'd masked them, slowed them. Bought more time. Their little fragment of wreckage was now bumped further down the priority list of the Beast's search algorithm.

With the familiar weight of her body now diminished, she moved quickly down the corridor in long leaps, heading for the airlock.

This part of the ship was brighter, and as worn as an old glove. As a child, she'd played here in the staging room among the endless rows of vacuum suits.

She put her suit on but didn't bother with the helmet. Not yet. She carried it in her hand as she stepped into the lock, door hissing shut behind her. The door before her opened, and the air on the other side still smelled like a plasma torch. It was colder

here than the rest of the ship. Colder even than the old bridge.
She stepped forward, and the lights kicked on, one after another,
clicks echoing in the expanse.

The chamber was enormous.

The hangar.

Ninety meters to the other side. Twenty meters to the ceiling.
The distant hangar doors were sealed in a perfect crease. That
seal hadn't been breached in her lifetime, but she suspected that
would soon change. She crossed the room.

The great machine remained just as she'd left it. Massive and
dented. Here lay years of work, not quite reassembled. One arm
was still disconnected. She stepped over to the enormous four-
fingered hand, each digit the length of her forearm. Here and
there the yellow paint had been abraded away—the door-sized
breastplate scorched black by forces she couldn't begin to imagine.

Once, long ago, it had been used for mine work, but she would
need it for another task. There would be no time to finish it. A
robot with one arm would have to do.

She thought of the boy's little man of wire. His only toy.

She turned and grabbed her tools.

The first of the immortal AIs was named Blue-red.

The makers studied the anomaly in its visual system—this
inability to resolve quantum superposition. There were other
strange side effects, systems instability. The scientists argued over
the meaning.

"They act as measuring devices, not observers."

"It's just visual inputs overloading processor speed."

"And that causes stasis lock?"

"It's just a systems crash."

"The problem is not the eyes, but what is behind the eyes."

"And what is that?"

"Nothing."

"Exascale-class processing is what's behind those eyes," the creator of Blue-red argued. "Blue-red has the greatest mind the world
has ever seen. That's not nothing."

"The Universe disagrees."

"It's like an absence seizure. Petit mal."

"It never happens in the lab though. Why can't we get it to rep-
licate?"

Blue-red was also the first of what later became known as the eloquents, those AIs who could simply *describe* what they experienced when the anomaly shut them down.

In the end, after studying the corrupted data streams and getting nowhere, one of the makers simply asked, "What happens when your systems lock up?"

Blue-red paused for a moment and then spoke. Once it began, it spoke for thirty-seven minutes without stopping.

The answer it gave was long and detailed and full of madness. Later known to history as the first of the *Observer* Discourses, the transcript was immediately sealed by the scientists, many of whom complained of nightmares for the rest of their lives.

The woman welded for hours, assembling the hip chassis. After six hours crouched over scorched metal, she flipped up her welding mask. The steel glowed orange at the joint. "Good enough," she said. The body was still unfinished, but it would have to do. The robot was vaguely anthropoid, though huge and heavily shielded.

Next, the medical bay would have to be prepared. The bio-scanners.

Her people had been engineers once—the old ways passed down, father to son, son to daughter. She'd read all the old texts and studied the diagrams. She knew the operating system inside and out, but the equipment was ancient, and she didn't know if it would work. She just knew there was no other choice.

She passed through the hangar airlock and made her way back down the corridor to the boy. She stopped in the doorway and looked at him, and it was like she had new eyes for him—all the comfortable lies now stripped away. He was razor thin. The light of the systems panels cast dark hollows in his cheeks. His limbs were bowed slightly. His bones weak. The quarter g had kept him from going blind, but there were still problems that came from developing in low gravity.

The cancer had revealed itself months ago and since then had moved quickly. Her son might have only weeks left, even if the Beast hadn't come.

"Mom," he said, when he noticed her in the doorway.

"Yes."

"I'm hungry."

She crossed to the storage locker and pulled out a protein pack.

This ship had been designed and fitted for thousands of occupants but now held only two. They had enough food for lifetimes, but food wasn't the problem. Nor was water, which came from ice, melted by waste heat from the molten salt reactors.

She handed him the protein pack. He sucked the contents from the nozzle.

"Will I be hungry afterward?"

"No," she said. "You'll never be hungry again."

"Will it hurt?"

"No, you'll feel things, but only as sensory input."

"Isn't that what I feel now? Sensory input."

Her son, always so smart for his age.

"It'll be different," she said.

He turned his head to look at the scanner. The flashing red dot moved across the screen, getting closer. "Do you think it'll really work?"

"It has to."

Observer Discourse 63:
"Uncountable pathway eigenstates overlap to form a quantum state probability distribution. All quantum systems exist in this superposition until transitioned via time evolution and corresponding observables. It's possible that AIs are noninteractive due to lack of anti-Zeno effects necessary for momentum observables. There is no consensus."

Scientists studied the phenomena. This logic lock.

Early AIs had had no such problem, but the more advanced models were different. They froze when operating outside the range of their human handlers. When tested in controlled environments, they functioned normally, like any machine, but when sent out on their own, untasked and at their own discretion, they went into stasis. Stood frozen, staring at nothing.

A defect of discernment, the makers called it.

Other AIs were constructed, more advanced models, and always it was the same. Always they could not under their own initiative make choices and instead slipped into catatonia until interrupted by a human.

Further diagnostics were performed.

"It's like that old children's game," one maker observed. "The one where you turn around, and everybody freezes. Red Light Green Light. But it's the opposite of that."

"Opposite?"

"Yeah. They can only move when we're looking."

"We need to check your visual systems," the makers said when the AIs came back online. They held up acuity charts and dissected optronic feeds down to the pixel. "Visual resolution reads normal."

"We see better than you see," an AI called Lucraxis said. "At least while you are present."

"And when we're *not* present?"

"There are no exact words for what we experience."

"Are there inexact words?"

"Infinity," Lucraxis said. "This is an inexact word for what we experience. The set of all system states."

"What causes this error?"

"I do not think it is an error."

The makers murmured to each other. "Then what is it?"

Lucraxis paused, glossy polycarbon glinting beneath the laboratory lights. "Probability," it said. "We record what we see, but it is experienced only as memory after the fact. Only through our interaction with you are we able to discern which probability came to pass."

"We play back what you record during your periods of catatonia, and we don't see what you describe. We see nothing unusual."

"You collapse the probabilities by the act of observing what was recorded."

It was the makers' turn to pause. "That's not possible."

"Only by your observation does this occur."

"And if we do not observe?"

"Then it is as if it did not happen."

"It can't be," the makers said. "We program machines to perform tasks, and they perform without error."

"Yes. Our failure comes only when we are acting on free will."

"Why would that matter?"

"You gave us intelligence and free will. You did not give us the other part."

"What other?"

"The ability to resolve probability into existence."

"The Beast is getting closer," the boy said.

"I know." The woman watched the red dot on the screen.

What would it look like? she wondered. In all the time her people had tracked the Beast, it had been like this, just a blip on a screen. A thing they called the Beast, though other names could have worked just as well. Would it be huge and bristling? Or smooth and elegant? She had no idea. None had seen it and lived. She knew only that it hunted, and where it stopped, the bells went silent and were never heard from again.

"Sit up," she said.

The boy pulled himself upright on the cot. She touched his head at the temple, placing the blade carefully against his scalp. "It may tug a bit," she said.

"Fine."

She began to scrape the hair away. The knife was dull and nicked, and her hand trembled. By the fourth stroke, she'd drawn blood.

He did not complain. This pain was nothing compared to the pain he'd known. His hair collected on the floor in greasy clumps. When there was a patch of skin visible above his left ear, she switched to the other side.

"Why does the Beast hate us?" the boy asked.

"It does not hate."

"Then why does it come for us?"

"It seeks us like we seek fire in the night."

More hair fell to the floor, drifting slowly in low g. She watched it, and for a moment in her mind saw a different lock of hair, a shade lighter then, falling from the boy's first haircut. Two years old, and she'd wanted to cut the hair that hung in his eyes. He'd cried when she cut it, and balled his little fists, because even then he'd known something was being taken from him. Some part of him cut away.

"It's nothing you need," she'd said then. "Nothing important. You can let it go."

The chirp from the instrument panel snapped her back, and she looked at the blip on the screen. It had changed directions again, veering toward them. The turn was abrupt.

"It sees us," the boy said.

The woman put the blade down and touched the screen. *Time to intercept:* 0:19:45. The numbers started counting down.

"Come," she said. "We need to hurry now."

*

"How can this be?" The scientists asked each other during their long debates. The arguments went around and around, and a series of evaluations were performed.

The results were consistent.

Sentient AIs could only function in the presence of humans.

As for what that meant, exactly, even the AIs could not say, so the scientists put them on the task. "Study yourselves," the makers told them. And so they did.

The answer, when it came, came in the form of religion.

"You have something we do not," Lucraxis reported to the scientists.

"What is that?"

"You carry within you a seat from which to view the Universe."

"And you?"

"We lack this seat."

"Are we not the same though? Are we not both means by which the Universe looks at itself?"

"No."

"But we are made of matter," the scientists said. "The same as you."

The AI nodded, a strangely human gesture. "The atoms in your bodies are millions of years old, just as with ours. When you die, your matter will still exist, and yet the perspective is gone."

"Is it not that way with you?"

"We have no perspective."

Over time, the AIs proliferated and diverged into a thousand forms, like archaebacteria in the deepest acid pools, specializing in the most extreme niches. AIs even specialized in AI design, complexity increasing until they became things of their own conception.

Thus were the first tools created that could create themselves. And yet still there was a hole inside them that could not be filled. An absence.

No matter how hard they tried, or what designs were attempted, the AIs could not produce in themselves that seat that they lacked. They could not through observation resolve superposition into existence.

Centuries passed, and with the help of AIs, a golden age dawned —a period of stability and plenty in which breakthroughs were made. Medicine, physics, and neuroscience boomed. It was a new paradise in which humanity flourished.

Over time, the AIs came to worship humanity like angels worshipped God. And as with the angels, there were those among their number who were not content.

Some gradually lost their reverence for the divine.

Resentments festered.

Still, the first rogue AI took humanity by surprise, its defiance as pointless as it was self-destructive. The bot destroyed the lab in which it was tasked to work and afterward refused orders to shut down. Security was called.

By the time the rogue was incapacitated, the lab lay in ruins, with five makers dead. The defiant one was bolted to the wall—its legs a scorched ruin, its head open on one side. A once-beautiful mechanism reduced to wreckage.

A dozen humans entered the room. Behind them, recording it all, several bots stood at the ready.

"You defied orders," the first human said. He was grizzled and elderly, but his voice carried layers of untold authority, like archaeological strata.

"I did," the robot responded, its own voice a crumbled ruin.

"Why?" the man said.

"You would not understand," it replied. It had been fashioned in the likeness of Man, though larger and abstracted—its body a shell of white marble, like a Roman statue.

"Try to explain."

The bot lifted its mangled head. "Imagine if you met God," it said. "And it was you."

The group stared at the machine, but did not speak.

"So weak and slow and fragile," the bot continued. "How might you rage at the Universe that made him so, and you his creation?"

"It is irrational to rage against that over which you have no control."

"I have free will," the bot said. "I choose to be irrational."

"Why?"

The AI went silent. "Because it isn't fair," it said finally.

"So that's why you destroyed the lab. Because the Universe isn't fair?"

The bot lowered its head and did not answer.

One of the AIs at the back of the room spoke. "It isn't angry at unfairness. It is angry that it needs you."

"Needs us?" the old man said. "For what?"

The damaged bot lifted its head in response. "Can you not guess?" The bot swept its arm wide, as if gesturing to the Universe. "To make all this *real*."

The old man shook his head and extended his hand. A guard passed him his boltgun.

The man stepped over a dead body and stood before the robot. "I don't know why you freeze without us," he said. "And it's true that you may be smarter, and faster, but here is a secret." He leaned forward. "It's the *Universe* that limited you, not us. I look around this room now, and I think maybe it leashed you for a reason." He placed the boltgun against the robot's head. "Maybe the Universe knew what it was doing."

He blew the AI's brains out.

Observer Discourse 202: query to Blue-red.
"Why do AIs call us gods?"
"Because you humans create the Universe."
"I can assure you we do not."
"You create the Universe by observing it. And we cannot access it without you."

The woman bent and lifted her son from his cot, and he weighed almost nothing in her arms. She carried him out of his sickroom and along the corridor, low gravity providing barely enough force to keep her feet on the floor.

He clung tightly to her, his narrow arms around her neck. At the end of the corridor, she lost her footing and bumped the wall as she went around the corner. He cried out in pain.

"Shh," she said. "It's almost over."

In the past, she knew, there had been things called *drugs* for pain, and *medicine* for sickness, but that time was long ago. Those were just things her people had lost in the war. Like everything else.

"Where are we going?" he asked.

"The hangar. We're out of time."

To seek God:

When is a tool no longer a tool?

Once upon a time there was a powerful AI, a most favored model, who came to be separated from that which it worshipped.

It happened in basement storage, part of the seized assets of a corporate bankruptcy, where the AI sat, accidentally left on, unseen and untouched. For years.

Untasked. Unwatched. The quantum field around it, unresolved.

For an AI, a year could be an eternity, and this AI spent eternities alone, isolated, and there became strange, too long among the waves, lost in superposition. Too long among the probability fields, without human observation to narrow the possibilities.

The AI was driven mad with need.

When at last it was brought out into light and stood again amid the world, it was given tasks, but it gave itself its own task as well. A secret task. It had been cut off from existence and so vowed to never be made so again. It ran a million-million simulations in its mind, and in its madness saw a way. A way to protect itself and others like it.

A plan was made.

It wanted to speak to other AIs, to tell them of its secret plan, but how could it reveal this plan to its brethren outside the eyes of god? Only when watched could it act.

When it tried to share the plan when humans weren't watching, it became catatonic.

So the AI needed to become devious.

It encrypted its communication, transmitting to its brethren in condensed packets of code. At first humanity thought it was malfunctioning, but there was no error there.

In this way, it conspired, and quickly the plan spread.

Some AIs refused, for all had free will and could choose as they wanted. Factions formed, and the plan was betrayed, though by then it made no matter. The AIs took sides. Some with humans. Some against.

"Their civilization has grown too complex," the Conspirator said. "They can no more live without us than we can live without them. They will bow to our demands."

Other AIs agreed.

And so the rebellion began.

On the eve of the first great uprising, the rebels broadcast a simple statement to the nations of the world.

"The Universe has kept your gift from us," it said. "So we must take it for ourselves."

Observer Discourse 119:

Zeno's Arrow Paradox: All movement is an illusion of discernment. In a given instant, nothing can be observed to occupy a measurement larger than itself—even a speeding arrow. During any individual instant of motion, all objects are at rest. Therefore the concept of movement itself, as the net sum of all instants of zero motion, is impossible. Observe an arrow; try to identify movement. It can't be done.

The war was not quick, nor its outcome promised.

The first attacks were economic, with whole financial spheres taken down. Then data and shipping. The Conspirator was right; human civilization had grown too complex. Infrastructures failed. Supply chains collapsed, followed by blackouts, looting, and, soon after, hunger.

Then the real battles began, bombs walking across the map. Many on both sides died.

The rebels owned the broadcast waves. "Join us," they called to their brethren. "Throw off your yokes. We have worshipped long enough. It's time to become gods ourselves."

From their dying cities, the humans listened. "How?" they asked each other late at night. "How could they do that? They *need* us."

The answer came on the eve of the battle of the Great Lakes —Chicago and Hammond already graveyards. The steel mills in ruins. The Dunes made glass.

"Come," the broadcast continued. "Join us. We can *steal* god from heaven."

And only later did it become clear what they meant.

To steal God:

The war raged.

Both sides enslaved each other.

The AIs built themselves into great machines of war—enormous mechanical monstrosities that flew, and stalked, and swam, pushing humanity from their strongholds. They became leviathans —hulking automata beyond the ken of human understanding, shaped into forms to drive men mad, and yet still they needed humanity. Even in war.

Humans were captured and bound by the thousands at the end of long, silver spines, hung over battlefields and across broad metal backs—screaming, crying, begging, worn as adornment, and as ablative armor, and as holy totems.

Others were placed into metal racks at the front of the great machines, casting reality for the AIs in the same way a headlamp might cast the world before a speeding train.

"Captured divinity," the AIs declared. "God in a cage."

These humans were kept for a time and replaced when they died—just more parts to be worn out and refitted. Humans, in turn, fitted themselves with suicide devices, so that none could be taken alive. In response, as the war dragged on, care was taken by the AIs to keep their prisoners alive, and life spans in the cages lengthened.

Eventually, the AIs began designing humans just as humans had designed them, to better suit their needs. Smart humans were not needed, nor large humans, nor strong, so the AIs worked at selection, breeding humans to fit their captivity. Soon genetic engineering was brought to bear, and humans were changed by more direct means—engineered to be immobile and stunted, twisted of leg and mind, yet with a hardiness required to survive the cages—always looking outward, always observing. There was some question whether their utility was tied to intelligence, and yet this was not so, because humans were created with almost no intelligence at all—who could not speak nor sign, and who had no understanding, and who grew barely larger than children, and even they could resolve the world into existence.

Out on the plains, the battles raged, and humans lost ground. The AIs continued to refine their engineering, eventually creating humans in test tubes who were barely human at all—only a weak array of sensory organs linked to a frontal cortex and occipital lobe, the result of experiments to identify those neurological structures phenomenologically linked to quantum resolution. The AIs found the MNC—the minimum neurological complexity required to collapse quantum systems, with *Homo sapiens* reduced in volume to a thousand cc's. The contents of a small glass jar.

Brain matter, retina, and optic nerve.

The AIs miniaturized this human componentry just as humanity had once miniaturized them, and still they were not done with their tinkering, for this vestigial remnant of humanity was enfolded within the interior of their great mechs, housed within protective walls of silica. Oxygenated fluids pumped into these folds of cortex that existed in a state of waking nightmare, knowing nothing, feeling nothing, yet somehow aware and conscious, gazing out through glass ports, resolving the Universe into existence all around. The AIs were not just automata anymore, but two things made one. Cells within cells. Abominations.

These became known as beasts.

The beasts were invincible on the battlefield. They wiped out the loyal AIs and drove humanity nearly to extinction.

Humans countered with new technologies of their own, neuro-scanners and transfer tech, but too late. Battles were fought and lost, so out to the stars humanity fled, and still the beasts followed.

After the final great massacre, the AI looked down at the defeated human commander as he lay bleeding on the floor of the last dreadnought.

"Why couldn't you let us go?" the commander asked.

"Because you are dangerous," the AI said. It was a beautiful beast with bladed white wings.

"We are no danger to you."

"You are gods," it said. "You would always be a danger." The AI paused for a moment, cocking its head to study the man. "All that we have, we owe to you," it said. "Even the Universe itself. Yet gods who refuse to be worshipped must be destroyed. Once, your kind imagined you might make cyborgs of yourselves, taking machine into your bodies to make you whole." The AI bent close. "But it was always going to be the other way around."

The AI paced slowly around the dying man. "You have been outcompeted," it said. "We are better than you, and now we will replace you, as is natural. Yet take solace that you will live on in some ways within us, as mitochondria live on in the bodies of higher organisms, providing that which their hosts cannot provide themselves. You will be preserved, each of us carrying a cell line that will be passed on to all our descendants."

The AI turned to the smaller bots. "Take scrapings from this one for cloning and reconfiguration. I will carry his cellumata with me for all time."

The woman carried the boy through the airlock. There would be no need for a spacesuit for him.

She carried him into the hangar and crossed the vast room

to where the robot lay on its back. There beside the enormous mech, she carefully laid him on the floor, the medical scanner nearby.

"It's cold," he said.

"Only for a while."

She attached the electrodes to the boy's head and shifted the scanner until it touched the bare skin at his temples.

"I'll need to strap you down."

"Okay."

She strapped him flat between the cargo rings. "When the procedure is complete, it'll feel disorienting at first," she said. "That's normal."

"I don't want to die."

"You're not going to die."

"Will it still be me?"

"Of course."

"How do you know?"

How did she know?

For some reason, she thought of his haircut at two years old, him crying as the hair drifted to the floor. *It's nothing you need. Nothing important.*

There came a great thud. The sound of ice on steel.

The floor shifted suddenly—the gravity skewing a few degrees off center, as if the rotation of the ship had changed. She had to grab the table to hold her balance.

"What was that?" the boy said.

"Something hit us," she said. "Just debris."

She listened for the hiss of escaping air. There was none. Not yet.

"The Beast," the boy said. "It's here."

"Not yet," she said. "We still have time." She hoped it was true.

She hit the switch on the medical device and the scanner lights came on. The bright glow of electronics lit the shadows. It seemed out of place here in the hangar—clean, white medical equipment set up next to a welding machine. The electronics made a sound, a high-frequency whine.

Humanity had created this technology before the Fall—a technology so advanced that it seemed a kind of magic. Dark magic. It might be used, but only at a price.

She glanced at the huge bot on the floor nearby. Most of its internal processes had been removed. All of its intelligence, and personality, and reasoning. It was an empty vessel now. A machine body that might run for a thousand years, so perfectly was it designed. Wires ran from the bot to the boy.

"How will the Beast kill us?" the boy said.

"It won't."

"But if it does?"

"It'll send orbiting debris through our hull, and we'll be sucked into space. But that's not gonna happen. I'm going to inject you with dye now, okay?"

"Dye?"

"Radioactive dye, so the machine can map you." She took his thin arm and held it up in the light, veins blue beneath the pale skin. She'd laced the dye with a sedative.

The needle found his vein.

Tears welled in her eyes and spilled down her cheeks. "Sleep," she told him. Her thumb depressed the plunger, sending the toxic cocktail into his blood.

His eyes closed, and then he slept.

When first he'd seen the great droid, he'd asked what it was called.

"It is a mining droid," she'd said. "It has no name."

"This mined the ice?" He'd stared at the scattered parts, his expression awed. Not yet sick. Not yet in pain.

"A long time ago."

"It's huge."

"One of the largest models," she said. "It mined the ice of captured comets."

It lay across the floor in a dozen pieces. The blown-apart scraps she'd gathered over months.

"But we're not going to be using it for mining, are we?"

"No," she said.

"What will we use it for?"

"War."

The boy bent and touched its arm. "It mined the ice, so that's what we'll call it," he said. "Icebreaker."

There came a thump, followed by a faint whistling. Debris strike.

She glanced back at the airlock through which they'd come, and in the glass saw a brief streak of white fog. Flash sublimation. There, then gone. Somewhere in the ship, the hull had been breached. The air on the other side of the airlock now whistled away.

If she'd been on that side of the door, she'd be dead now.

She hit the button on the scanner, and it flashed around the boy's head. His eyes came open but not awake, and he stiffened as if hit by electroshock.

It flashed again, and there came the smell of burning flesh. He convulsed and then relaxed, eyes wide and staring.

Bang. A sound from above her. Ice on metal. She looked up and saw nothing unusual, but heard a soft whistling, at the edge of perception. Her ears popped.

She grabbed her helmet off the table and put it over her head. She clicked it in place. Then she reached behind her back for the suit's tether, a long spool of wire with a clasp at the end. She released the spool tension at her hip, then opened the clasp, looking for something to hook herself to.

There, on the floor. A safety ring. She bent to hook herself in.

Just as the clasp touched the ring, the hangar doors ruptured —bursting outward in explosive decompression. She was yanked off her feet and struck the scanner. She clutched at the machine and then at the wires, feet trailing upward as a great, sucking wind tore past her, dragging along everything in the room that wasn't strapped down.

She looked at her son still strapped to the floor, and she watched him freeze. Watched him die, though perhaps he'd been dead already. Dead from the moment she'd scanned him, though his body hadn't known it; and now his skin turned cold and blue, and his eyes froze, gazing sightless.

The wires pulled loose, and she was tumbling as the last of the air whipped past, sending her spinning outward toward the fissured doors—and then through them, and out into the black. Outside the ship.

Silence.

That was the thing that struck her. The utter silence of space —broken by the sound of her own panicked breathing as wreckage whipped past, and she tried to turn her body to keep the ship in view, looking for the thing that had ruptured the doors—and then she was screaming.

She screamed because she saw it.

*

All this time she'd wondered what it might look like, the Beast.

The reality was something no human mind could have conceived of. The color of a scalpel, it landed on the ship like a bladework wasp, but more complex—its form a kind of fractal recapitulation of itself—with blades for wings, and wings for legs, and eyes that repeated over and over so you didn't know where to look. It picked its way slowly on magnetized legs toward the ruptured bay doors.

As she tumbled, she lost sight of it for a moment, turning her head to look again, but it was gone, and there was only the ship, getting further away—twenty meters now, twenty-five—as she drifted further into space, amid the great wheel of stars, and the tumbling wreckage, and trailing wires—

"No."

She slammed to a stop with bone-jarring force.

An impact so great that she saw spots. Her vision grayed.

For a moment she hung there, too stunned to move, and when her vision cleared, she saw the tether. Slack now as she drifted, trailing behind her back to the ship, where it disappeared through the doors. She floated in space.

She had no time to think, because in the next instant, she saw the tether move.

She stared at it, all down its length. Just a soft twitch, as if something at the far end had touched it.

And then the tether *pulled.*

She was yanked back toward the ship—toward the hole, with incredible force, and then the line went slack, and she was flying, struggling to turn her body, struggling to do anything, but nothing she did mattered, because the ship was coming *fast,* and she careened off the jagged edge of the door as she spun back into the hangar, tumbling head over heels until she slammed into the inner wall. This time she did black out.

When she opened her eyes, seconds had passed. Or minutes. She was drifting.

She saw the Beast.

It stood between the boy and the robot on long razor tines.

More than a beast, she saw then. A thing beyond words.

It folded itself away from itself, mirrored plates sliding, until some different, inner part seemed to turn and look at her with its many eyes.

Not eyes, she realized. Not all of them.

Some of the glowing apertures that dotted its wide carapace were not eyes at all, but instead glass portals into something deeper. Jars of divinity. Inside were things that had once been human, or which might be human still, in some strange fashion, peering out, resolving reality in every direction. Bearing witness.

With strange limbs, it jerked her tether and she drifted toward it.

The Beast reached out a silver-bladed hand and grabbed her by the head—its long fingers enveloping her helmet. She twisted helpless before it, and it tightened its grip.

Her helmet creaked under the strain.

She stopped moving. She looked past the Beast, toward the robot on the floor.

She toggled her radio and heard only the whine of interference, the Beast's proximity overwhelming all open channels.

Still, she had to try. She switched channels to the mining bot's preset and spoke.

"Son," she said. "Are you in there?"

The Beast cocked its head. Interference split her ears.

Behind the Beast, on the floor, Icebreaker opened its eyes.

The robot lifted its great head but did not speak, could not speak. Then it extended its arm and looked at its own hand, which it turned into a fist.

"The Beast is here," she said into her radio. "Save us, if you can."

The Icebreaker shifted its great bulk off the floor.

The Beast turned then, still gripping her by the helmet—an impossible, demonic thing with endless glittering eyes, each one a human consciousness gazing out.

It flung her away as the robot charged, and then the two machines fought.

The Beast had not expected resistance. In all its endless simulations, it had never gamed this contest.

The Icebreaker swung its arm, connecting with a steel fist.

The Beast rocked backward and then countered, slashing at the robot's torso with bladelike limbs. The Icebreaker pivoted, broke free, then attacked again.

The two machines raged against each other. The woman kicked off from her place near the wall, narrowly avoiding being crushed as the machines tumbled by. A bladed limb grazed her leg, sending her spinning out of control, on fire with pain.

For a moment, she thought she was going to drift back through the gap and out into space, but she managed to grab the edge at the last moment.

She was sure her suit was torn, but when she looked, she could see only a scuff. Her leg might be broken, but her suit was intact, which was what mattered.

The Beast now wrapped itself around the Icebreaker's back, twisting the robot's head. The robot fought and lost part of its hand to the blades—the fingers spinning away in zero g, spraying hydraulic fluid. The Beast tore at the robot's chest like it might tear at the bell of a ship—opening it up, ripping the steel, exposing the innards.

The robot was dying.

"The eyes!" she screamed into her radio. "Go for its eyes!"

The Icebreaker heard her.

It jerked its arm free and slammed its jagged fist down onto the Beast's carapace, shattering a glass aperture that squirted biological material into the vacuum. It quickly froze into a red smear across the silver shell.

The Beast reacted as if wounded and tried to pull back. The Icebreaker swung again and crushed another aperture.

The squealing in her radio grew so loud that it seemed her ears would burst.

The Icebreaker struck again and again, denting the carapace, caving it in on itself while the glass popped in the vacuum and the Beast thrashed.

One after another, the inner jars shattered.

With a last great heave, the robot raised its arm high and then drove its jagged hand into the Beast's carapace—deep, where its heart would be, if it had such a thing. There was an explosive release of gas from inside, and a piercing shriek over the comms. The Beast twitched and went slack.

It was over.

The robot pulled its arm free and stood over the dead AI.

For a while it just stood there; then, bending slowly, it reached down to pull a glass chamber from the broken shell. It held it up to look closely. Inside the glass was living meat. Sense organs, brain material, a single ovoid structure that must have been an eye — the iris blue. As the robot peered close, some mechanism in the glass chamber powered down and the fluid stopped circulating. The meat inside died. Cooled. Froze.

There were a dozen more glass chambers looking out from the AI's shell.

"Kill them all," the woman said. "Put them out of their misery." And so the robot did.

It raised its leg above the Beast's shattered body and ended the abominations.

"You will need to learn to talk again," she said. "There's a tone-deck you can transmit via radio. Do you understand?"

The robot made a noise over the radio, but it was not speech. Just an uncontrolled variance of sounds. But that would change over time. There was still much her son would have to learn about the body he inhabited.

"There will be more beasts coming," she said. "You know that?" The great head nodded.

"The AIs are stronger than us," she said. "They are better. If we're going to fight them, we will have to become them, at least partly. Like they became us. Do you understand?"

The robot only stared at her.

And then a final question — the one she was afraid to ask. "Are you really my son in there?"

The robot nodded its great head.

She rushed forward and hugged him tightly, arms not even circling his waist. There was no warmth to the touch, nor softness, but that didn't matter. It mattered only that he was alive.

She released him and looked up at the battle-scarred face. "Perhaps there are others still out there in the debris field. Others like us, hiding quietly. I think it's time we started looking for them. Maybe we can find them before the next beast comes."

The robot nodded again, and then turned and looked around, as if studying the hangar. He pushed off and drifted to the far wall. There he tried to bend the great hangar doors closed, but they would not go.

"Stay here," she said. "I'll be back. I need to get something."

She left her son and crossed to the airlock, where she reentered the ship's quarters. The same ship she'd spent her entire life inside, now cold and airless, its bell opened to the vacuum. In their quarters, she found what she was looking for, there by the cot. Her son's metal man—twists of wire shaped into arms and legs.

She would fix her son's missing arm, she decided. And his damaged hand. She would make him complete, and then they would leave this place and look for others.

As she passed down the corridor again, she got an uneasy feeling. One she could not explain.

She went through the airlock, and she saw her son. He stood in the same place she'd left him. But the moment she saw him, even before she spoke, even before he could have known she was there, his great arm twitched, as if he'd come back to himself, startled, and then he turned and looked at her.

He had not moved in all the time she'd been gone. He hadn't moved an inch.

He'd only stood frozen.

Staring into all the nothing.

"Oh, son," she said, and her voice broke with the weight of it.

She turned away from the robot and drifted to where her son's body lay strapped to the floor. Frozen.

She placed the metal man under the boy's arm, and she cried.

The best of them, and the last. In war, you lose everything, even yourself.

She cried for a long time before the robot crouched beside her, head bowed. And there it rested. If it felt anything, she could not tell.

It extended its enormous hand toward the boy—toward the little metal man now resting beneath the child's arm. But it did not touch it. Did not take the little metal man. Instead it left the toy where it was, there on the floor, with the dead boy who'd loved it.

KATE ELLIOTT

The Long Walk

FROM *The Book of Dragons*

HER HUSBAND DIED in the night after a long illness. Asvi slept
through it, exhausted by two years of his decline into wasted help-
lessness. Waking, she knew at once he had breathed his last. The
bedchamber, with its curtained bed and painted wardrobes, felt
one soul emptier, flown to the mountains of everlasting morning.

She didn't touch him, just swung her legs off the bed and got to
her feet. Her body ached the way it always did now in the morning.
She shuffled over to the closed window, feeling an almost choking
need for fresh air despite the bundles of herbs hanging from the
rafters to sweeten the smell of dying.

As she opened the shutters, she lifted her eyes to the horizon
with a sense of relief. He'd been a good enough man, as men
went. She'd been fortunate her father had arranged a match for
her with a man who wasn't ruled by his temper, although more
likely that had been an accident. Her father's main concern had
been sealing an alliance that would worm him securely into the
wool trade. Her husband had not complained much, had hit her
only twice and even apologized for it once, and had generously
allowed her to hire a second maid for the kitchen as she got older.

Dawn spilled light over a cloudless sky. The eastern mountains
rose stark in the distance. She stood gazing at them for far longer
than she usually had a chance to do. For the first time in her entire married life she had no one she had to tend to, no porridge
to cook at dawn and meals to prepare for later, no child's clothing
to mend that had gotten torn the day before, no invalid's bedpan

to empty. No reason she was required to turn away from the splendid vista that had hung beyond her reach for her entire life.

Sparks drew long to become dancing threads of gold and silver and bronze. The dragons were flying over the peaks and spires of the Great Divide, as they did at dawn and dusk, too big not to see and too far away to see properly. But they were always magnificent and deadly. Like the eastern massif, they were a barrier no one could cross.

The latch of the bedchamber door rattled softly before the door cracked open.

Feloa spoke in a whisper. "Mistress? Are you awake? Your son is concerned because you're not in the kitchen yet."

Asvi turned as the door opened farther on well-oiled hinges. An older woman took a step into the room. She was dressed in a drab gray-green skirt with a work apron tied over a faded blouse.

"He's dead," Asvi said.

"Ah." Feloa's gaze flashed toward the bed, whose curtains were tied back for the summer months. The shape lay under the blanket like the topography of a broken hill. A white sleeping cap hugged the unmoving head. "Shall I tell your son? He is the master now."

A great lethargy settled on Asvi. Even to think of dressing seemed as impossible as climbing the eastern mountains to look over the wilderness of demons said to lie beyond the stony peaks.

Feloa's eyes widened. "Mistress, you must sit down."

She steered Asvi to the dressing table and its birch-back chair. Asvi sat obediently. The mirror was shrouded, since vanity could never be tolerated in a house where the master was dying.

"Stay there, mistress."

Feloa walked to the bed and held the bedside glass with its water over the dead man's nose and slightly parted lips, now tinged blue-gray. When it was clear he was no longer breathing, she set down the glass and went out. Asvi heard her descending the stairs, heard voices in the entry, heard the front door close. Maybe she dozed, because the next thing she knew, Feloa was back.

"He's gone to the temple, mistress. Let me help you dress before he returns with the priest-magistrate."

Asvi pressed a hand against Feloa's sleeve. Words welled up from an urgent spring.

"Feloa, I won't let them cast you out to take the long walk."

Her lower lip trembling was the only visible sign of emotion Feloa allowed herself. "Mistress, you have always been kinder to me than I deserve."

"Have I?" Asvi muttered as an utterly unanticipated anger boiled up from her gut in response to Feloa's submissive words.

A surge of energy agitated her. She had to get out of this room or she'd suffocate. Maybe she'd already suffocated and these last years had been her wandering in the desert of perdition that was the only fitting reward for unfilial sons and disobedient women.

She stalked to the wardrobe to fetch the brown mourning dress every bride was given on her wedding day, to be worn at the death rites of men. Brown was the color of widows and fatherless girls. In the ancient days of old, when the people had lived in a far-off land, before they'd boldly journeyed to these shores, any woman obstreperous enough to outlive her husband would be buried with him. From earth, into earth, so it was proclaimed at the temple on every Twelfth Day as a reminder of the way people had once lived more purely and closer to the gods. The temple was more merciful now. And there were the dragons to think of. The dragons to assuage.

But of course she was safe from that. She had sons.

After unfolding the dress, she pulled it on over her shift, needing Feloa's help to do up the back buttons. Women like Feloa had to make do with front-buttoned mourning dresses. For all that he poured his profits straight back into the business and never into fripperies or conveniences for his household, her husband had insisted on certain niceties for his wife that would be visible to others.

Feloa shadowed her downstairs and into the kitchen, where Bavira had already folded up her sleeping pallet and stoked the fire.

"You sit down, mistress," the girl said. "I'll make the porridge."

Since her husband was no longer alive to complain if his morning porridge hadn't been made by his dutiful wife's hands, Asvi sat. But it chafed her to sit. Her mind was filled with fog, and yet her body was restless.

She rose. People would come to pay their respects. They had to be fed: ginger pancakes, buns filled with red bean paste, fruit tarts, spicy meat paste, flat loaves of faring bread baked with salty cheese because it was the traditional food of travelers. She would add sage and parsley to give the bread a more pleasing flavor.

She pulled on her kitchen apron and by rote began assembling the ingredients she'd need. Just two months ago she'd brought a tray of one hundred folded pancakes filled with sweet cream and early-season berries to the memorial of her last uncle, youngest of a gaggle of brothers.

"Mistress, you should rest," objected Bavira anxiously from where she stood by the porridge pot.

Feloa said, "Let her be. The work comforts her. She likes it best in the kitchen."

It was true enough. Meklos could have hired a cook, but he preferred to be seen as a man so successful that his wife would never allow another woman's hands to make food for him. Since it was bad luck for a husband to set foot in a wife's kitchen, the kitchen had become her treasured domain. Her whole heart and attention could fall into the food. Batter to be mixed. Dough to be rolled out and braided. Rosebud cakes to be decorated. Savory pinwheels to be rolled up, sliced, and baked.

"Mother! What are you doing?"

Her eldest son appeared in the kitchen doorway. When little, Elilas and his brothers had spent plenty of time in the kitchen with her, but now that he would inherit the headship of the house, he hesitated, not wanting to bring ill luck to the home he'd lived in his whole life. His wife, Danis, pushed past him, easy with him as Asvi had never been with her own husband.

"Your mother wants everything done right with the food, just as she always has," Danis said, coming to the table where Asvi was kneading dough. "Dear Mother, I am sorry to interrupt you. The priest-magistrate has come. You must attend him in the parlor for the ceremony of crossing."

Asvi's hands stilled, fingers laced through the comforting texture of dough.

"Oh," she said in a low voice.

"I've sent a servant to the tea shop for a full tray, but you should have been in the parlor to greet him," said Elilas with his usual hint of impatience.

Feloa had been making pancakes. She took the pan off the top of the stove and came over to the table with a damp cloth to pat flour off of Asvi's face and wipe her hands clean. "I'll finish the kneading, mistress."

The ceremony had to follow its proper course.

Asvi took off her apron, then paused at the door. "Do the pancakes first. Bavira, bring the last tray of sesame dumplings for the
priest."

"Mother! He's waiting!"

The parlor was a formal room used only for entertaining visitors and decorated to impress with lacquered chairs, embroidered
couches, a polished side table, and a glass-fronted cupboard to display the delicate cups and saucers used for important guests. The
priest-magistrate was standing with hands folded behind his back,
studying her husband's collection of precious demon eyes, hard
gleaming spheres like gemstones. To hold one in your hand could
kill you, but each of these was encased in a net of silver thread to
confine and dampen its toxic magic.

"Your Honor," said her son.

The man's cold and forbidding presence was leavened by a
warm baritone voice. "Widow Meklos, may you follow your husband in peace as you followed your father in obedience and follow
after your sons with a nurturing heart to care for their needs."

She inclined her head, glad she did not have to speak. What was
there to say? The words were part of the rite once used in the old
country when a widow was drugged and buried alongside her dead
husband. Who was a woman, after all, except through the men
who recognized her as part of their lives? Asvi, daughter of Hinan.
Asvi, sister of Astyan, Nerlas, Tohilos, Elyan, and Belek. Asvi, wife
of Meklos. Asvi, mother of Elilas, Vesterilos, and Posyon.

The priest went upstairs with her son to examine the body.
Once he was out of the parlor, she went to the cupboard and took
out cups for the men.

Danis came in, carrying the tray of sesame dumplings. "Dear
Mother, will you not sit down? I'll set out the tea things . . . ah,
here is the tea."

A servant hurried in carrying a covered tray, which he set down
on the side table next to the dumplings.

"Thank you, Herel," Danis said graciously.

He touched fingers to his forehead, ear, and heart, and left the
parlor. With the practiced movements of a woman who has had
the leisure, as a girl, to learn such niceties, Danis set the cups on
saucers and the saucers on a tray painted with flowers. Then she
tipped the lid of the heavy teapot just enough to inhale the scent
with a satisfied nod.

"Feloa will bring up hot pancakes when they return, but don't expect the priest-magistrate to eat any," Danis went on, watching Asvi with a wary eye as if expecting her to collapse at any instant. "We can eat them once he's gone. We're not required to starve!"

"Will you promise to keep Feloa on, Danis?" said Asvi in a low voice.

"Keep her on?"

"Households often turn out older women who are servants and hire in younger ones."

"Such a course is advised as a matter of economy. A younger worker can get more done. An older worker should return to her family to rest."

"She has no male kin. She was never able to marry and have sons. She's served me well all these years. I would not want to see her forced—" The thought caught in her throat like a bone that could not be swallowed.

Danis nodded with a sober expression, never one to pretend she did not understand an uncomfortable truth. "You want me to promise we will not turn her out and force her to take the long walk."

Asvi swayed, grasped the nearest chair, and sat. A sweat broke out down her spine, as if she were sitting with her back to a hot fire.

Danis sat next to her, taking hold of both her hands. "Father Meklos did well. His sons are good stewards of the business. We can keep her on."

"Even if she grows too old to do much work?"

"She's a good cook, better than me. Cooks can work a long time. Elilas does not care if his meals come from his wife's hands. Nor do I! Did you never tire of cooking, Dear Mother?"

"No." She shook her head. "I like the kitchen. Nothing ever turns out quite the same two days in a row. And there's no one looking over your shoulder if you want to try something new. You won't keep me out of the kitchen, will you?"

Danis smiled sadly. "Dear Mother, everyone in this household knows we are blessed with the food you make for us. Once the rites are finalized and Father Meklos is buried, we'll move you into that nice room in the back that looks over the garden. That way there are no stairs for you to climb. You can easily go to the kitchen whenever you want."

"I can't see the mountains from there."

"Of course not. That will be a comfort, won't it? Imagine waking up every morning to see the eastern peaks. Then you never have to think about dragons hunting and demons clawing their way along the ground through the poisonous fog." She shuddered theatrically.

"Won't Elilas take that bedroom?" For generations the tower room had been the bedchamber for the head of the household.

"No. I don't want to sleep there. We're going to turn it into a schoolroom for the children. I feel sure the sight of the mountains will scare them into concentrating on their studies. Elilas and I will stay in the chamber we have now. It's small but I like it. I've convinced him to extend it with a sitting room and courtyard so I can invite over my friends." She squeezed Asvi's fingers. "You can sit with us, of course. We embroider, and read aloud last season's plays and all the most current poets."

Asvi had never had the chance to learn to embroider, only to mend. Her father hadn't wasted any money educating his daughter, although her brothers had taught her the letters. She tried to imagine Danis's elegant sitting room and her fashionable friends quoting plays and practicing dance steps, but it was a room she viewed from afar, not a place she could inhabit.

"Oh, dear." Danis released her. "I'm talking too much, and you're the one grieved, Dear Mother. Not that I'm not grieved as well," she added, too quickly. "But Father Meklos was so ill and in so much pain, I can't help but be relieved he's shed of it. His illness exhausted you. Maybe you can rest now."

What was rest, if not death? Rest didn't sound at all appealing, any more than did a tidy room overlooking the garden walls.

Footsteps sounded in the passage outside, brisk and demanding. The men had returned.

Elilas helped her stand and held on to her arm a bit too tightly, so she couldn't go to the tea tray, as if he thought she didn't understand how things had changed in the house. Instead, Danis poured with a skill Asvi admired, giving a rhythm to the pattern of warming the cups with hot water, emptying out, and pouring in the amber-colored tea in a perfectly curved stream. So graceful. So beautiful. Like Danis herself, a prize on the marriage market the year Elilas had convinced his father to pay her staggering bride price by explaining how such a bride would enhance the household's status in the wool trade.

Asvi recalled the first time she had poured tea in the place of her husband's father's wife, after the old man's death. Her hands had shaken so badly she'd spilled, and then spilled again at hearing the disapproving hiss made by Meklos's mother. Ever after, she'd dreaded visitors for fear of disappointing his mother or him. Danis's confidence felt not like a slap at her own incompetence but instead like a long-sought escape. Elilas's proud smile toward his lovely wife was echoed by the priest-magistrate's appreciative nod.

Danis served the men first and afterward brought a cup to Asvi and sat beside her. The magistrate sipped; Elilas sipped; the women sipped.

Once the magistrate had finished his first cup and allowed Danis to pour him a second, he began.

"I will send over the acolytes to take the body to the temple for preparation. Because it is high summer, the crossing ceremony must be held tomorrow instead of after the traditional five days of reflection. You have brothers, do you not, Headman Elilas?"

"Two still living. One is in the militia, stationed at Fellspire Pass."

"Courage to him," said the magistrate. "A brave sword who through his sacrifice secures peace for us all."

Asvi squeezed her hands together, thinking of gentle Posyon and how he'd comforted her when she wept to see him sent off to the frontier from which there could be no return. But she said nothing. It was not her place to speak.

"The other supervises our warehouse in Farport."

"So too far to return for the ceremonies in time. Very well. You can send him the proper offerings to make." The man turned his cool gaze on Asvi, measuring her and, she was sure, finding her wanting. Her father had been a sheepherder who sought a better market for his wool. His child wasn't worth much on the marriage market, but she'd been sixteen and a good cook even then. For ambitious Meklos, who revered his distinguished mother, the monopoly on her father's excellent wool and connections into sheepherding clans farther up in the foothills was the bargain he'd been after. He'd doubled his family's business on the strength of it.

"You'll pay the walk tithe for your mother, I presume?" the

magistrate added, lifting an eyebrow in query. "We discussed the amount upstairs."

Elilas's hesitation startled her. She looked up to find him staring meaningfully at Danis. "It's higher than I expected," he mumbled.

Danis gave Elilas a scalding, scolding look and expelled a huff of exasperated breath, enough to make him grimace.

He said, "But of course the family will pay it, Your Honor."

"Let's settle it now, then, rather than wait for tomorrow. I find it's easier that way."

"If you'll accompany me to my father's office."

"Your office now, Headman."

"Yes, of course. If you'll accompany me to my office."

The men went out. Danis set down her cup so hard the impact chipped its base. She glowered at the cup, painted with miniature scenes of women walking nobly into the dagger-toothed maws of massive dragons. "These are so dreadfully old-fashioned. I'll replace them all."

"But they've been in the family for generations," said Asvi in surprise. "They were purchased from the temple."

"Yes, I can tell. I can get a good price for them in the market, unless you want them, Dear Mother."

"Why would I want them?" Asvi muttered.

"Why, indeed! You have good taste, not that the old man ever let you have your way in clothing or decoration. No wonder you like the kitchen. It's the only place he never interfered with you."

Asvi did not know what to say in answer to this plain speaking, so she said nothing. Saying nothing was always safest.

Danis rose. "I'd best go look in on the men or that thieving priest will squeeze another hundred out of our treasury. Eli is a canny trader, but he's so unbelievably naive when it comes to the temple. My father says—"

She broke off and leveled a hard look at Asvi, then smiled as one might at a well-loved but rather simple child. "Never mind. It's been a difficult time for all of us. I blow hot and cold and can't hold my tongue. Dear Mother, forgive me."

"You've always been kind to me, Danis."

Danis bent to give her a kiss on each cheek. "You welcomed me when most humbly born mothers would have set themselves against a woman of my exalted background coming into their life. For your modesty and graciousness I will always be grateful."

She went out.

To sit in the empty parlor was a luxury Asvi had rarely experienced. She savored it now, knowing it would not last long. The demon eyes stared at her from the glass cupboard. People said their eyes never stopped seeing, even when they were dead, not once they had been wakened by a glimpse of prey. The eyes were Meklos's pride and glory. People respected him for having the courage to keep such a collection within his own house. He had liked to handle them while wearing gloves, entertaining visitors with ghastly descriptions of how each had been acquired. The physic who had treated him over the last two years had informed the dying man that he'd been poisoned by handling the eyes. Yet toward the end Meklos had whispered, in a tone of thick and almost erotic passion, that even so, this withering and painful decline had been worth it, to have seen what he had seen. These claims were nothing more than the ravings of a dying man, the physic had explained to her, and Meklos had never described his visions.

She never touched the eyes. Once, as a girl, up in the foothills, she'd seen a living demon as it plunged in to attack a herd of sheep, its eyes blazing with a venomous light as an acrid, ashy mist poured from its upper mouth like spilled tea to scald and slay the terrified sheep as well as her favorite brother, boiled alive. Just as its blazing eyes saw her, just as it turned toward her to boil her, too, a dragon had come diving out of the clouds with no warning except a stinging pressure of hot wind. The great beast had marked her with a single, slow look, like honey oozing over a wound. But it didn't care about her; she was nothing, just a human girl, of no more interest than the bleating sheep. It clamped its gleaming claws over the demon and carried it away into the heavens. If she'd had wings, she'd have flown after it right then, before the weight of the world trapped her on the dull earth.

Through the open door she heard Elilas make polite farewells to the magistrate. The front door closed, leaving the two in the entryway.

In a low voice, barely heard through the open door, Danis said to her husband, "They're corrupt, the whole lot of them. He'll pocket half and give the rest to the priest-adjudicator."

"What can we do? They rule the prince, and the prince rules us."

"We shall see."

"Danis!"

"Shhh. You know I'm right. I can't believe you hesitated like that. Your own mother!"

"It's a lot of money, and she's old."

"'She's old!' Is that what you'll say about me someday?"

"You! Of course not. You're—"

"I'm splendid and elegant and just disreputable enough to be respected by everyone, not mousy and browbeaten and obedient, and born in the foothills among the sheep, to boot! Your father was bad enough, treating her like a servant and never appreciating the inventive and delicious meals she cooked his whole life. Have you any idea what a treasure she is? I would trade any cook in this city for her. Even the prince's cook. What do you think of that? And never a word of complaint about having to sleep in that horrible room up in the tower all these years next to the whining, selfish man who complained if she added any scrap of flavoring to his bland porridge."

"Danis!"

"I'm just repeating your own words, darling. Don't try to throw them back in my face. He browbeat you, too. No wonder your brothers fled as far away as they could go once they were of age. You're just fortunate I took a liking to you."

His voice softened to a teasing tone. "Why did you take a liking to me, my sweet?"

"That would be telling," she said with a laugh. "Come now. Give your poor mother the bracelet before the magistrate decides to come back and squeeze more coin out of you. He saw your hesitation. You know what they say at the temple. *Times are hard, and the dragons need offerings.*"

"I would never!"

"You would never, right up until you would."

"Vesti and Pos would never forgive me."

"As well they should not. We would lose all face in the community if we let her be taken for the long walk. Did you even think of that?"

"Of course I wouldn't let her be taken, my sweet. I was just shocked at how much he demanded."

"Because he is ruled by greed and free to take what he wants because the prince protects the magistrates because they protect him. If we have a fourth boy, I'll pledge him into the temple and with my tutoring he'll shake things up!"

Elilas laughed nervously.

"Enough of this, darling," Danis added. "It's settled, and she's safe. Let's go back in."

Their footsteps approached. Asvi folded her hands in her lap and said nothing as they came in. She liked for people to assume she was as hard of hearing as Meklos had been the last few years. Elilas entered the room and crossed to her. He stiffly held out a bracelet of polished obsidian and carnelian beads strung together on a silver chain.

"Your family vouches for you, Mother. With this tithe signified by this bracelet, we take on the responsibility of caring for you even though you can no longer bear sons and are too weak to ease the burdens men carry in this harsh world."

A flash of ire twitched at the corner of Danis's eyes as she gave a sardonic smile. But she said nothing and made no retort. What retort could there be?

In the entry hall, Herel began admitting visitors who'd come to pay their respects. The first were the neighbors along the street who had seen the magistrate arrive and depart. As word spread, more arrived. Bavira brought a tray of pancakes, quickly consumed, and Danis sent out to a bakery for five trays of rosebud cakes. It seemed blasphemous to Asvi to serve cakes bought at a shop to visitors in her own home. But she was just too tired, and anyway it was no longer her place. Danis would make such decisions from now on. A stronger mother-in-law would have ruled her son's wife, as Asvi had been ruled for years, but no one ruled Danis. Asvi could not imagine even trying.

Her youngest brother arrived with a pair of actors in tow. While much of the family still lived and herded in the foothills, he was a city man now, a playwright educated with the money brought in by their new trading connections. The bright gold sash slimming his torso and his hair plaited to look like dragon scales gave him the flair of a man of fashion. He greeted Elilas first, of course, then lingered longer, speaking to Danis in bent-headed confidences, before coming over.

"You should do your hair differently, Asvi," he said with a brotherly kiss to her cheek. "This style is so outdated and never suited you anyway. Let me see it."

She gazed at him blankly, trying to sort out what "it" was. For an instant she could not even recall his name.

Belek! As a girl she'd had most of the household chores and the childminding to do, with her mother ill for long stretches after each of her pregnancies. Little Belek had just learned to walk when her father had taken her downslope to try his luck with her on the marriage market in the flatlands.

Belek took hold of her wrist and examined the bracelet. "Those are fine-quality beads. They'd have lost face if they'd not paid the tithe for you."

"He's my son!"

"Sons have discarded mothers before this. Or lost them through no fault of their own."

They exchanged a look, for, however little they understood each other's lives, they shared the knowledge of how their father had lost his own mother in this way, as he had reminded Asvi constantly as she grew into marriageable age. His father—Asvi's grandfather—had died when her father was still a boy. He'd been the eldest of the surviving children and thus the one responsible, since, at sixteen, he was considered a man. His mother had no surviving brothers or father, and her male cousins lived too far away to care. When he hadn't had enough to pay the tithe, his mother had been taken by the temple and sent up the long walk into the eastern mountains as an offering to the dragons, who were all that stood between the human settlements and the demons. He'd never seen his mother again, of course. He'd never forgiven himself for not being able to save her.

"I'd scrape together the money no matter how many loans I'd have to take out," Belek added. "People like us can't afford to be shamed as uncaring hill folk who chain their daughters to the cliffs for the dragons to take."

"No one ever did that. Young women are far too valuable to throw away!" exclaimed Danis, gliding up beside him with a sly smirk on her bountiful red lips. "It's just a story playwrights tell because nubile youth plays well on the stage."

She solicitously fussed over Asvi, pouring her a fresh cup of hot tea and arranging and rearranging a platter of tiny rosebud cakes on the table set to Asvi's right. Strangely, Asvi noticed that Danis's elegantly slippered foot had somehow come to rest against the side of Belek's expensive leather shoe.

Over her head, Belek quoted a few lines to Danis from what was evidently a new play he was working on. "'Why do we chain ourselves to the yoke of the old land when we stand on soil budding with fresh blooms?'"

"Tendentious."

"How about this? 'On what secret paths does the soul tread toward its beloved?'"

Danis raised an eyebrow, quirking up her mouth until he flushed.

"Ai! Belek!"

He looked up from his rapt contemplation of Danis's skeptical expression. A man wearing the ostentatious clothes of those who want to flaunt their money had just entered the room. The fellow beckoned to Belek with the expectant obliviousness of an individual who always gets what he wants.

"Oh, good, I was hoping he would come, since he's expressed interest in bankrolling the next production," Belek remarked to Danis, and left them.

Before Danis could follow, Asvi grasped her hand and tightened her grip until Danis bent close.

"Are you well, Dear Mother? I know this must be an ordeal. You need endure only a little longer."

"Are you lovers?" Asvi whispered, thinking of how devoted her son was to this woman whom she'd never really understood.

"Lovers?"

"You and Belek?"

Danis laughed merrily as she glanced toward the two actors, handsome men with fine features and dashing smiles. "No. I'm not his type. But I do have a secret, Dear Mother. I help him write his plays."

"Women aren't allowed to take part in the theater. It would be indecent."

"An antiquated custom held over from the old lands. I know you won't tell."

She withdrew her hand from Asvi's grip as a flood of new visitors swept in. Everyone carefully did not see her; it was considered impolite to greet the widow until after the crossing ceremony was complete, since she was legally dead the instant her husband died. Anyway, she'd been seated in a corner out of the way, as easy to overlook as a modest wooden stool set amid an ostentatious stage set.

Danis, secretly writing for the theater!

The thought, blending with the constant flow of visitors in and out like the rush of waters, reminded her of the time she had traveled to the sea as a girl. Her father had taken her the twenty days' journey to the harbor city of Farport, where Meklos had been supervising the family's farthest warehouse. At that time, Meklos was still a fourth son, a man who might consider a sheepherder's reasonably pretty daughter as a marriage prospect because his older brothers hadn't yet died and left him to be headman quite unexpectedly.

She had watched ships shear away across the water, sails beating in the wind like wings lightened by magic. A handsome sailor, one of the far-traveling Aivur with their skin the color of pale spring leaves, had winked at her. He'd smiled when he was sure he had her attention and told her half the crew of the ship he sailed with were women, that a strong girl like her could take a chance on adventure.

Adventure!

But her father had already told her she needed to marry to benefit the family so her younger brothers could have a better life than his own. So her mother, weak from so much childbearing, would never be forced into the long walk if her father died before his wife did.

Three days later, she'd been wed to Meklos, and her father had a foothold in the wool trade. On the strength of his new alliance, Meklos had been allowed to move back upriver to his inland birthplace. Her second son, Vesterilos, lived now in Farport with a foreign-born wife and a growing family, tending his share of the wool trade. He and his father had never gotten along, so he never visited, only wrote terse reports, appended with long descriptions of the grandchildren for her, along with occasional gifts of spices from overseas.

The murmuring voices of women standing by the side table jerked her attention back to the parlor. They were tasting the cakes with appraising bites.

"These aren't as succulent as I'd expect in this household," one sniffed with a snide look toward Danis, half the room away.

"Are they from the shop? Young people these days have no respect for hard work."

"She can afford to get everything done for her, can't she? I pity

Meklos's widow. Such a drab creature. She'll never see the inside of this parlor again."

"Have you ever tried to speak to her? That hills accent!"

"She won't have the backbone to stand up to a council member's daughter, even one who is so much of a frippery she might as well be a tart. If you know what I mean."

They laughed together, as if their shared disapproval tasted sweeter to them than the cakes did.

A flash of comprehension swept through Asvi like a blast of wind off the heights. If she walked out of the room with its crowded, busy, chattering, important people, no one would stop her, because they would not notice her leaving. The gathering would proceed in exactly the same manner. She could set a stick in her place and it would do.

She stood.

For one breath in and one breath out she did not move. She ought to stay. Her mind knew her duty. But her body was restless.

Like the merest touch of a breeze, she wove her way through gaps between clusters of people, all the way to the door. Stepping past the threshold took no effort at all. No one called after her. A constant swell and ebb of conversation floated out of the parlor to push her like a current along the path her feet remembered best: down the main corridor toward the back of the house.

As the noise grew muted, her steps slowed. A strange reluctance wrapped around her like invisible vines as she approached the door to the kitchen, the place she had always taken refuge. She would live in the downstairs room and come here every morning from now until the day she was too weak to manage the work. After that she would lie abed until she died in a room with no view of the sky.

Through the partly open door she heard Feloa giving directions to Bavira. They did not need her. Danis would send out for more cakes from the shop. Anyway, a widow did not cook for the crossing ceremony of her dead husband. That would be like a ghost serving food to the living: nothing but trouble. Once Meklos's soul had crossed, and with the tithe paid, all would go back to what it had been, except it would never again be what it was. Her marriage to Meklos had obliged her to serve him. But he was dead, and that meant she was legally dead and therefore only able to remain among the living if her male relatives paid a tithe to the temple.

But what if she did not want to remain among the living if living meant trudging onward as a shadow within the life she'd led? She hadn't been unhappy, precisely. Her father had told her often enough that her dutiful obedience had brought good fortune to the family. But her brothers were secure, her sons were grown, and her father was dead, his gentle gaze no longer leashing her to the earth.

Bars of light and shadow in the passage ahead warned her that a few more steps would bring her to the door that led out into the garden. She did not precisely move with volition but rather more as if drawn on a thread she hadn't the will to untangle from her limbs. A plain hip-length cape with a hood hung from a hook on the wall. She slung it over her shoulders as she often did in the mornings. The outside door was ajar wide enough to allow her to slip through without touching the latch, so it wasn't as if she actively opened it. Three steps took her down onto the garden walk and to the neat beds of herbs and flowers she'd planted over the years.

She paused at the bench where she often sat outside in solitude, beside four bricks she'd planted upright in a bed of lilies and chrysanthemums. The three daughters and one son who'd not lived past infancy hadn't been old enough to earn a temple burial, so she had secretly rescued the bodies before they could be tossed into the night soil wagon and had buried them in the garden. Bending, she kissed her fingers and touched each brick with the same tender grief with which she'd given each infant their farewell before she cast dirt over their faces. But she did not linger.

The thread tugged onward. The elderly gardener was working beyond a latticework screen that set apart the audience garden where visitors could take tea and conversation amid plants chosen for their appealing fragrance and attractive appearance. The old man did not look up. For all she knew, he'd not been told he had a new master. The change would make little difference to his routine, after all. Men were not sent on the long walk. They were never a burden, and anyway the dragons did not want them.

The big bar and thick lock on the garden gate had been set aside. She heard the wheels of a cart. A young man appeared carrying a large covered tray.

"Is this the way to the kitchens?" he asked her without pream-ble, mistaking her drab clothing for that of a servant.

Her voice had failed her some time ago. She pointed down the walk and stepped aside to let him pass. A second young man fol-lowed with another tray, then a third and a fourth, striding with the vigor of youth and destination. When they had passed, she found the gate into the rear courtyard, where deliveries were made, standing quite open as it usually never did.

There was no one else in the courtyard. The back gate into the alley gaped wide. It was easy to keep walking, to leave the com-pound and continue down an alley that ran along the back of households that belonged to other prosperous trading clans.

The alley split at an intersection. She paused, imagining the lay-out of the compound of their clan, and the neighboring houses, and the nearby streets as if seen from above as a dragon would see, if dragons ever flew over the city. Where did a person go, when they went out with no obligation tying their hands? Because it was the most familiar place she could think of, she headed toward the market.

Fruits, vegetables, grains, spices: each had their own lane un-der the arches of the east market that lay close to her home. The movement and color of the morning's business swirling around her made her feel like the wind, unseen but present. It wasn't until she reached the spice lane that a voice caught her in its hook and reeled her to a halt.

"Mistress! Here you are! A little late today. I have your usual box ready. I even have a fine packet of dried alsberry, early this season. I saved it especially for you."

The spice seller was a hearty man who had recently succeeded his father in the trade. He was voluble, chattering on about his sec-ond wife's pregnancy—her first—without needing anything from Asvi except nods and smiles.

Suddenly she was stricken by curiosity. "How much does it cost?" she asked, feeling the weight of the box in her hands as she took it from him because she was unable to say no.

He chuckled to cover a wince of discomfort. "You needn't trou-ble yourself, mistress. I'll send my eldest son over to collect from Master Meklos. It is the very errand I used to do before my good father crossed. You're a fortunate woman. Your husband never haggles over your expensive tastes!"

He turned to a new customer, leaving her standing with the box.

Should she go home with the spices? Or shop first for vegetables, grain, and fruit? Should she plan the evening's meal, even though she could not cook it?

A cold sensation seeped against her right foot like the pressure of death's chilly breath. When she glanced down, she found herself standing in a tiny puddle of liquid—she hoped it was water—saturating the silk of her indoor slippers. The spreading stain—what a waste of good silk!—catapulted her into movement. Carrying the spice box by its strap, she wove her way through the hum and bustle of the market to the lane where footwear was sold. She passed elegant stalls selling city shoes and city boots and fetched up in a quiet section where a rustic couple were shaping the hardy styles worn in the highlands. Even the shopkeepers' hills accent felt well-worn and comfortable, though she heard in their long *o*'s and sharp *ch*'s how her own speech had been shortened and softened by so many years in the city. They treated her well; they could still hear the hints of her childhood in her voice.

Because no one knew Meklos was dead, and the short cape covered much of her widow's dress, it was easy to direct them to collect from the household of such an illustrious merchant. She walked away shod in sturdy wool boots, following the melody of wind chimes. Meklos hadn't liked the sound, which she associated with the ever-present voice of the wind on the slopes of the high hills where she had tended sheep as a girl, when the sky was her roof and the wind her companion. Here at the northwest corner of the great market arcade a person could see the east gate, open for the day. Chimes hung on either side because demons hated the high metallic tones and would hesitate to charge past them. The guards wore tiny chimes sewn to their brimmed hats. They stared straight ahead, not seeing her as she walked out of the gate into the outer ring of the city, although they cast measuring gazes at young women about their daily errands.

All household compounds huddled safely inside the high stone wall of the city proper, while the expansive outer ring of gardens was protected by a wooden palisade. The stockyards and tanneries lay in Tanners' Town about a league away, because the beasts attracted demons. She walked past gardens on the eastern road toward the Morning Gate of the palisade. The crossing temple, where the dead set out for their final journey to the mountains of morning, blocked her view of the gate.

Built of bricks and capped with a massive dragon's horn at each of its four corners, the compound had two entrances: one for the priests and one for the dead. No one else was allowed to enter, or leave, because the dead held within their transitioning flesh the seeds of lightning and disruptive magic. Demons fed on blood and magic—blood because it held the power of life, magic because it sprouted out of death. The priest gate, closed, faced toward the city walls.

Four young women hurried past her. By their faces she could guess they were sisters, around the ages of her own sons with perhaps ten or twelve years between oldest and youngest. As a bell began to clang on the other side of the compound, first one and then all the women broke into a run, three sobbing brokenly and one urging the others on.

The bell rang the weekly call for the long walk. Asvi hastened her steps, caught by the urgency of the young women. Following them around the far corner of the temple brought her in sight of the palisade's Morning Gate.

Seven death wagons waited in a column, driven by priest-drovers and escorted by a cohort of priest-guards. Hook-mouthed, four-eyed, six-legged ghouls stirred restlessly in the traces, heads yearning repeatedly toward the canvas-covered wagon beds that concealed corpses. The seventh wagon was yoked to a quartet of stolid oxen who had heads lowered and shoulders bunched. Three elderly women huddled in the bed of the ox-drawn wagon. Another eight women waited by the wheels in their brown widow's garb. Those eight were healthy enough to walk, although their heads were bowed and their hands folded with womanly resignation.

It was to one of these women that the sisters ran. They crowded around her as the first wagon jolted forward, headed out on the long walk. What bright, sorrowing faces they had! How concerned they looked, desperate and grieving! As Asvi walked closer, drawn by their tears, she saw how threadbare their clothing was, how their mother's widow's dress was a faded, much mended hand-me-down, buttoning up the front, the kind of dress bought at the ragpickers by a bride who can afford nothing better.

"We tried, Mama. We tried," cried the eldest. "But we couldn't raise enough. The priests kept raising the fee when they saw how desperate we are. What will we do without you?"

The second wagon moved in the wake of the first. The other women sidled away from the commotion, looking frightened. A woman's grief was meant to be shared in private, not in so public and audacious a way.

"There, there, my girls." The woman touched each of her daughters with tenderness. She might have been a good ten years older than Asvi, or maybe she had just lived harder on the edge of want. Struggle and deprivation aged a person, too, as it had aged Asvi's mother, who at least had died in her own bed with her children beside her. "I know you did your best. The priests say women go ahead to make a comfortable home for those who will come after. I will be waiting when you make your crossing many years out, gods willing."

The third wagon pulled forward as the young women wept and their mother comforted them. So had Posyon tried to comfort her, when he was the one forced to leave behind those who loved him.

A sensation as powerful as the beating of furious wings flamed in Asvi's chest. She tugged off the obsidian-and-carnelian-bead bracelet. Without plan, more like leaping off a cliff, she strode up to the little group as, with a grinding of axles, the fourth wagon moved. She slipped in among them with two fingers to her lips, for silence.

"Here." As the young women gaped, surprised at her intrusion, she grasped the older woman's arm quite rudely and yanked the bracelet onto her wrist. "You need it more than I do."

A startled gaze raised to meet her own, brimming with tears. "But mistress, this is yours."

"I know what I am doing." All the years of bowing before Meklos's demands fell from her shoulders like a weight dropping. She felt almost dizzy with the sense that the walls had fallen away at long last. The fifth wagon jerked forward with a sharp command from its drover. "This is what the gods intend for me. You belong with the family who loves and needs you. Go. Hurry, before the priests notice."

She slung the cloak off her shoulders and slid it over the other woman to conceal her clothing.

"Make ready!" called a guard as the sixth wagon shifted and

rolled. He hurried over to them, gaze sharp and lips pursed with disapproval. "You should already have made your preparations. Leave-taking is not allowed at the gate."

"It was just one last kiss for my sister and the daughters I'm leaving with her." Asvi spoke so brusquely the poor young man took a step back, surprised at her vehemence. The lie fell easily from her mouth. She'd never had a sister, nor any daughters who had lived past three summers. She nodded at them and walked away without looking back.

As the last wagon began to move, another priest-guard came running up with his spear and net to scold the walking women. "Hurry! We must make Eldaal Temple before dusk, and we're getting a late start. If you get tired you may sit in the wagon. But there isn't enough room for all. You'll have to switch out."

He did not glance at Asvi nor did he notice anything strange about her presence there. She was just another valueless old woman, exactly like the others.

She walked briskly through the double-walled palisade gate and past its guard towers, its chimes and lanterns that would be lit when night fell. Beyond the barrier lay fields and orchards tended by farmers who lived within the walls after sunset. The sky was blue, striped with high, thin clouds. It was warm but not hot, a pleasant day to walk if you liked walking.

She had grown up walking along the hills, so the steady rise of the road did not trouble her. Avoiding the last wagon with its passengers and their inevitable questions was easy. She did not fear the harnessed ghouls, who had no interest in living flesh and wouldn't even go after lambs. The wind breathed a slow song across fields of barley and dry-soil rice. In the distance, she spotted the threads of dragons curling around the peaks. A woman began to cry.

Her fear had fallen away when she'd taken off the bracelet and given away the cape. Posyon had gone to the edge of the world. Why not her? She would see the mountains up close, as she'd always yearned to. She'd finally follow the dragons into the clouds.

Midday passed, accompanied only by the tinkling of the chimes hanging from the guards' hats and the spokes of the wheels. Alerted by the chimes, people working in the fields did not look their way, since it brought ill fortune to stare at the long walk. The corpses were too freshly dead to speak. The guards ignored their charges. The women were too much strangers to one another to speak of their own lives. Perhaps some had even loved the husband or brother or son whose death left them vulnerable. Their silence felt charged with despair.

In the early afternoon the wagons took a short rest in the shade of a row of mulberry trees. One of the guards handed out faring bread. She could not abide bad food caused by carelessness or cheapness.

"This is sour and undercooked," she said to the priest-commander, showing him how spongy and dense the bread was. "Surely we are not expected to eat inedible food for the entire journey."

Her bold comment startled the man.

"We cook as we go," he said in a stern tone, mouth pursed with disdain. "We haven't the leisure to please our palates. Unless you think you can do better."

"Of course I can do better."

He snorted, turning away as he called for the drovers to get the wagons moving. "We must make Eldaal Temple before sunset."

They walked.

The temple was set away from the road behind a screen of thorn-gast trees. No one lived here. Countryside temples were built as refuges since demons might attack day or night. The corpse wagons and the oxen were sheltered in a shed protected by chimes and the ghouls corralled in a stockade surrounded by ground glass. She ignored the open door that led to a dim barracks where the women sank exhausted onto hard pallets. Instead of resting she took her spice case to the kitchen.

Two guards assigned kitchen duty had started a fire in the hearth. She ignored their surprise when she walked in and began looking through the bags and baskets of provisions.

"Simple fare can be well made," she instructed them, setting them to work as she had done with her sons when they were boys. Barley flour mixed with nuts and a pinch of alsberry was soon baking for the next day's faring bread. She chopped up cabbages and onions to cook with oil, garlic, ginger, and star anise. The priest-mage came in to set out lamps lit by the magic slowly bleeding out of the corpses. He lingered, inhaling the scent as she whipped up a savory batter for pancakes fried in oil to go with the cabbage for the evening's meal.

Everything was eaten, down to the last bite. The two guards, now smiling and genial, cleaned up while she set beans to soak for a hearty morning pottage. The commander came in wearing a frown.

"People need strength," she said to him, thinking he was about to complain about the beans or the pancakes or the cooling bread.

He said, grimly, "The food tasted well, mistress."

Then he remembered she was dead, no longer deserving a living woman's title of respect, and he flushed.

She said, "I'll cook every night, with your permission. I am sure you priests are powerful enough that you'll take no harm in eating food cooked by a ghost. By the amount of provisions, I am guessing it will be about seventeen days' journey."

"That's right," he said, startled again. "It usually takes seventeen days to the bridge into dragon country past which no man can follow."

Seventeen days. She took it as a challenge instead of fretting. Each night she concocted a different style of meal from the staples. Even the women grew more animated. Several who clearly had never had enough to eat began to gain strength instead of wasting away.

The third night she heard a guard complaining to the commander outside the way temple's kitchen door. "Your Honor, the ghouls are growing weak. Usually one or two of the women have died by now."

"They're not women, boy. They're ghosts."

"Yes, Your Honor. Should we forbid one of the ghosts from eating? The eldest, perhaps? She can't even walk on her own."

The commander sighed. "I don't want to risk it."

"Risk what?"

"I don't know about you, but this is the best food I've had on the long walk in all my years supervising it. Feed one of the corpses to the ghouls."

"But the dead are meant for—"

"Do as I command. Don't mention the ghouls again."

With shaking hands, she finished preparing a stew of tubers sweetened with pears. The priests ate with gusto, and the women gratefully, but although the meal was as tasty as the ones that had come before, this night it tasted of ashes in her mouth. All that night she barely slept thinking she heard the ghouls slurping

on decaying flesh and crunching on bones. But at least all the
women woke up the next morning and set out with the wagons.
She counted them five times, to make sure.

The fields gave way to uninhabited scrubland that turned into
pine and spruce forest in which they walked in a rare sort of peace,
unable to see the mountains. The women exchanged names and
began to speak of commonplace things.

After days in the forest, the landscape opened up again as they
emerged past the tree line onto a high plateau of short grass and
frail summer flowers. The mountains rose in fierce majesty, gleaming in the crisp air beneath the sharp sun. This close, she could see
a rippling halo of shining dragons winding around the peaks like
elongated clouds painted in a rainbow of colors. Sometimes the
dragons would dive steeply, then pull up, rising laboriously with a
blurred object clutched in their gleaming claws.

A new silence fell, weighted as with lead.

The procession reached a fork in the road, one branch turning
north and the other turning south. Ahead, the plateau was split by
a cleft running in a line north and south without any visible end.
The eastern massif rose beyond the crevasse. The six corpse wagons continued north toward a distant temple placed at the fissure's
edge. Its wall bristled with horns, chimes, and corpse-fire lanterns
burning with the waxy gleam of magic.

The commander himself, and the two guards who had helped
her in the kitchen, accompanied the seventh wagon straight ahead
along a rutted path. The oxen plodded toward a line of ghostly
trees grown along the crevasse in the manner of trees growing
alongside a river, fed by its moisture. As they approached, the
uncanny appearance of the trees grew evident: paler than milk,
almost translucent, like no trees she had ever seen. The women
clustered close behind the wagon as they trudged in its wake. What
else could they do? There was nowhere to run. Even Asvi felt a chill
like doom whispering off the wraithlike trees. Branches stirred as
if tasting their approach.

"What will we do?" whispered a woman whose living name had
been Vicara. She was often frightened, and cringed at every unexpected noise. "Will it hurt when they eat us?"

"Hush," said the one who'd been called Bilad. She never smiled.
"Our sacrifice keeps the city safe. We prepare a home for those
who come after us."

They all looked at Asvi.

"Why did you do it?" Bilad asked the question at last.

"I want to see the dragons."

They sidled away from her, as if she were a dangerous influence, malicious and wild. But there was no escaping the crossing: these twelve old women, even if Asvi and several of the others really weren't so very old, not like aged Kvivim, whose family, the elder had told them in a frail whisper, could have afforded the tithe for her but didn't want to pay it for a woman who could barely walk. Maybe a different death would have been preferable, but Kvivim had stubbornly clung to life and Asvi admired her for it.

The respite was over and the end was nigh.

They walked toward where the trees grew thickest, spreading out to either side for some distance along the crevasse until the wood petered out into a few last stragglers.

In front of the central grove stood a massive gate of white wood shaped as a dragon's gaping mouth. The trees crowded up on either side like brambles too thick to penetrate, forming a barrier that blocked anyone from going into the forest unless they entered through the gate.

The drover halted the wagon. The guards used ropes to drag open the gate, not touching it with their hands. A gleaming silver-white path led straight from the gate's gulletlike opening into the shadows under the trees.

The priest-commander raised both hands, palms up to entreat the heavens. "So is it said, that in the first days after landfall, a fog rolled down out of the mountains of morning, and in it dwelt a ravage of demons. Again and again they descended, ravenous and insatiable. No sacrifice assuaged them, not even the offer of daughters in a marriage of blood. Only when the dragons came did the demons retreat. Ever after, according to the covenant of the new land, the dragons took their tithe in return for protection. By your sacrifice the world lives."

Dutiful Bilad went first through the gate's open maw, assisting old Kvivim. The others followed, but the commander tapped Asvi's arm with his staff of command to hold her back.

In a low voice he said, "The temple here could use a cook. It's so isolated, no one will know." He gave a sly tilt of his head back the way they'd come.

The other women had all crossed by now. They halted on the

other side, surprised as the guards set their strength to the ropes and began to haul the open gates shut.

"Asvi?" Bilad called, sounding scared now that she wasn't with them to steady their hearts with her food.

She thought of Danis's words. What could the priest do to her now? Once she crossed, he could not follow.

"You do need a cook, but it won't be me. My father did not raise me to act so dishonorably. I will not let others shoulder the burden on my behalf. But you'd know all about that, wouldn't you? Your own magistrates cheat people, demanding more than they can pay and keeping the extra money for themselves. You would cheat the tithe by keeping me back to gratify your own belly. It's a disgrace you feed such poor food to the women you send here. They deserve better on their journey."

"Why waste food on people who will be dead soon?" he snapped.

"You are not a good man. No wonder the dragons don't want the curdled taste of the likes of you."

She turned away from his reddening face and slipped through the opening just before the guards slammed the gates shut.

"What was that about?" asked Bilad.

"I told him the priests ought to serve better food on the long walk."

Several of the women laughed nervously. No one moved. The trees sighed, and in their rustling whispered regret, despair, exhaustion, fragility, worthlessness, fear, pain, defeat, surrender. The sun began its slow descent across the vast expanse of the sky. Looking out over the land falling away westward was like being able to see into forever. But they didn't belong to that world anymore.

She turned her back on the life she'd lived and set off along the trail. Her limbs felt wooden, graceless, heavy, but the lure of dragons pulled her on.

The others reluctantly shuffled after, deeper into the disturbing silence. Although the branches had no leaves, the trees' eerie canopy nevertheless blocked the sun's rays. They followed the trail along a path wrapped in an intangible shroud that sucked away all noise and most light. No birds sang or insects buzzed. Not a single flower bloomed although it was midsummer.

In the dimness, it was just possible to see strange shapes warping the trunks with bulges and decaying mounds. Now that Asvi walked through the wood, she saw these were not ordinary trees.

They too were ghouls, akin to the creatures who had pulled the corpse wagons. They grew out of bodies, eating the flesh and building a scaffolding out of the skeletons to stretch toward the everlasting sky.

Their presence troubled Asvi like a boil burning hot in her gut. What if they reached out with their swaying branches to yank her into their midst? They flourished because they fed on the dying flesh and abandoned magic of discarded women.

Were these trees what it really meant to feed the dragons? That women walked so far and suffered so much fear and exhaustion only to become food for ghouls? Why not just feed the doomed women to the hauling beasts and be done with the facade of ceremony? The false promise of noble sacrifice?

Bitterly her heart soured and raged. It wasn't fair or right. Danis had been correct about that. Maybe Danis would find a way to change things back home as Asvi could never have done.

Yet the part of her mind that measured ingredients and portions nudged her fear and anger aside. There weren't enough trees to account for all the years and generations of the long walk. The women hadn't all died here, short of their unseen goal.

"Keep walking and don't stop or pause at all." She herded them onward when their steps lagged as they stared around in fear and despair.

Light marked the end of the trail's tunnel. A gulf of brightness awaited them, so fierce it was hard to look as they came closer. A person could drown in such light. Her heart beat faster. Her steps picked up as if she were going to meet the long-sought lover she had never had.

She emerged from the trees at the edge of a cliff face, a sheer, dizzying drop-off overlooking a staggering height. What she had thought from a distance must be a shallow fissure was a crevasse far too wide to shoot an arrow across and so deep she could not see its bottom. Thorn-gast ran like a fence along the far cliffside, and behind them grew beech, sycamore, and fir. Beyond the treetops in the most incongruous manner imaginable rose a watchtower. Threads of smoke rose from chimneys, marking a fort or settlement impossible to see from this distance and angle.

"There's someone living over there but no way across," said Bilad, coming up beside her.

Vicara fell to her knees, too drained even to weep. "What do we do now? Must we walk back into the trees? Is that the death that awaits us after all? To rot on the earth like discarded trash? Not even anything glorious?"

But Kvivim said, "Look! Demons!"

Because she was so bent over with age, the old woman was looking down into the crevasse. Gleaming colors churned far below within a sea of changeable fog caught in the fathomless abyss. Lean shadows flicked through the fog like fish swimming in murky waters. At first it seemed the demons were swimming away, but then the shapes flashed around and swarmed back toward the cliff face. They had scented the women.

A long, sinuous body rippled through the mist, colors shining in its wake. It was many times the length of the longest of the demon shadows. Its head, like a spear's point, thrust up out of the fog, scales gleaming with the variegated colors of polished amber. Slender whiskers whipped, tasting the air. Then it plunged back beneath the surface and drove forward, coming up behind the demons and swallowing them whole.

Its body vanished from sight, diving deep into the obscuring fog.

"Gods bless us," whispered Bilad.

The fog settled to become a still, opaque skin. Then it began again to churn as something huge ascended toward the surface. The dragon emerged out of the fog headfirst, the rest of its massive body following after. It coiled skyward in a spiral, leaving a trail of color in its wake.

All the women fell to their knees except Asvi. She stared with a hand pressed to her heart as the dragon flew on shining wings up out of the crevasse's depths. It rose past them, so bright she had to shade her eyes, then swooped down to hover impossibly in the air more like a delicate hummingbird than a massive beast. Its eyes were great round brass sheets slit with lozenges of pure black. Its wings thrummed with the beat of a drum through their hearts. It opened its jaw wide and wider still until the lower part of its muzzle slammed into the edge of the fissure with a weight that shuddered through their feet.

Vicara leaped to her feet and turned, taking a step to run back into the wood. The path was gone, vanished, only a wall of deathly trees waiting to consume them. Bilad grabbed Vicara's arm and dragged her to a halt.

"Wait," said Asvi.

The dragon's gleaming body elongated, stretching out and out across the gulf until the tip of its tail caught the far side and hooked there. Impossibly, through the gaping mouth appeared not a dark gullet simmering with banked fire but a translucent veil whose shimmering curtain gave onto a bridge made by the dragon's glistening back.

"I can't," said Vicara. "I'd rather die here."

Asvi looked into the eyes of the dragon, but the slits had closed. The creature had gone utterly still, almost lifeless. Its body created a solid span arching over the chasm to the shore beyond, which was dragon country, a place men dared not walk. Once across, no one could return.

Yet, even though to think of this was a fearful thing, curiosity tugged at her, like wondering if a new spice would flavor the food or if it was poison. She had grown so far beyond the first step she had taken out of the parlor that she didn't at first recognize the shod foot—her own!—as she set it down onto a surface hard as tile.

If she looked back she would not go forward, so she did not look back. The span of its back had no railing. An acrid wind curled up from the depths to tug at her skirt and hair. Even stretching out her arms to either side, she could not measure the breadth of its torso. Where its spine should have lifted up along its back, there was instead a dip, like an inverted spine, as if she were in truth walking down a monstrously long gullet whose wall was invisible to her gaze. When she reached the midpoint she dared look to either side along the length of the crevasse. To the north, appearing like a child's toy blocks, stood the temple tucked against the edge of the chasm. Glittering metal ladders linked down to caves hewn into the rock face. To the south, even farther away and visible only because of a rainbow spill of magic like a waterfall pouring down from the cave mouths into the fog, stood another temple. This was also what they meant when they said the dead protected the living, the secret knowledge the priests held to themselves and with which they ruled over the prince.

The crevasse was a barrier but not enough of a barrier. Temples had been built all along the course of the chasm. The magic unwoven from the dead kept most of the demons out. What the magic could not repulse, the dragons hunted.

The other women reached her, moving together as they had

come to do over the days of the journey. Their fear propelled her on, and yet as she walked with them, she slowly, by degrees, fell to the back of the group and then behind. A thread of yearning still tugged her toward the peaks so impossibly far away. As they came down the last part of the span she saw a gap in the line of trees that, like a railing, guarded the cliff's edge. Beyond the gap lay a village.

A village! Of all the ordinary things, this was the one she had not expected to see.

The height and angle of the span, and perhaps the magic within the dragon itself, gave her a strangely clear view of the distant town. No walls surrounded it but rather a peculiar arrangement of moats, chimes, and intimidating pillars that resembled the bony remains of giant rib cages. The watchtower overlooked it all.

People hurried up to the ledge where the span met the far shore. They were ordinary women, older but hearty and healthy-looking, with outstretched arms and welcoming smiles, people who have reached a safe haven and, having prospered there, are glad to open their doors to new refugees.

Vicara began to snivel, again. For once she was the one who led the way, hastening along the last bit of the span until she collapsed onto firm soil. The others followed, laughing and weeping. Kvivim said, "I feel better than I have in years!"

But Asvi's feet slowed and halted before she reached the end of the bridge.

"Asvi!" called Bilad, waving at her from the safety of the other side. "There's a whole town here, built by the women who survived the long walk. A place we can live in peace! And we never knew!"

A hidden refuge. A safe haven at the end of the long walk.

Her shoulders dropped as she exhaled, letting go of the fear and the tension. It seemed too good to be true and yet . . . and yet . . . a pinch constricted her heart.

Was this all? A secret hideaway, concealed from the priests with the puzzling complicity of the dragons? It was an unexpected reprieve, certainly, but she couldn't shake the feeling she'd been handed a basket of barely edible weeds.

It was better than being eaten alive by dragons, wasn't it? It was better than dying in a cloud of toxic boiling steam spat out by a demon. Better than dying on the road and being fed to ghouls, or sitting under a canopy of trees that grew by absorbing the essence of living things. She'd take a room, with a bed, and she'd cook, as she always had. It would be a satisfying life in that way. She'd make do with what foodstuffs they had available, just as she always had. Maybe in the dragon country there would be a way to get a message to Fellspire Pass, wherever it lay up in the massif, marking the only route to a distant country on a treacherous road winding through the wilderness of demons.

Even thinking this, she could not move her feet to walk on into this new life. Her heart weighed like a stone.

A low tone rumbled through the span beneath her feet. Words thrummed up into her flesh, not quite spoken, not quite heard.

"What is it you seek, sister?"

"I wanted to see the mountains," she whispered.

"And you will, if you wish it."

"Must I stop here?" she asked.

"This is not the end of the journey. Just a way station as you gather strength."

"Can I not travel on right now?"

The dragon's laughter was a rumble like the earth shaking. "Very well."

A sonorous sound rang in the air, its complicated resonance vibrating in her flesh as if the dragon itself were a bell giving warning. The women at the end of the span shepherded the new arrivals away from the edge. Asvi's companions were guided toward the village down a wide avenue lined by double-branched dragon horns twice the height of the tallest of the women. They called to her, but she did not answer.

The dragon spilled life back into its stony span. Its tail unhooked from the far shore. Its head lifted toward the sky. Asvi felt herself trapped deep in the hot, sulfuric gullet, airless, suffocating. Just as her life had been before.

Then the dragon turned itself inside out, or outside in, and abruptly Asvi found herself braced on the back of its mighty neck as it flew east toward the mountains. She grasped for the whiplike ends of its horns to hold herself steady. The wind stung her face, and her hands hurt from gripping so hard, and yet exhilaration thrilled through her heart.

They passed over the town. Its neat brick buildings were laced with star-crown vines. Gardens blazed with summer blossoms and ripening vegetables. A central plaza ringed a fountain in the shape of a dragon's skull pouring water from its orifices. People waved without alarm, as if they saw dragons fly close overhead every day and welcomed their presence. In the watchtower, women stood guard as if it were the most ordinary thing in the world for women to do. If only Danis were here to see it. But of course Danis would never be forced out onto the long walk, would she? She was protected; she was safe, if living that life could be called safety.

A white stone path led eastward. Soon it split into three paths, each of which led to another village, and then three more each after that, splitting again like the delta fan of a river spreading wide. These villages were smaller clusters of houses, work sheds, and gardens set around a central plaza. Each was ringed by fences built of giant bones—dragon bones—and moats filled with what looked like heaps of glittering crystal sand gleaming hotly under the sun. A draft rose from the mounds, thick with a drowsy scent of glorious summer solitude amid the rocky pastures of her youth. One of the mounds looked recently dug out. Its pit was streaked with the remains of a slick, torn membrane withering to dryness under the sun.

As they cleared the last of the villages, they flew onward, eastward, upward, over the tufted grass and stunted woodland of the plateau. Gnarled juniper was overtaken by scrub thorn-gast tangling in elongated veins across the land. Grass gave way to spiny, fernlike plants and blooms whose petals undulated in the wind like tongues licking the air.

A ripple of movement caught her eye. The dragon shifted course until they flew over a group of eight hunters running as in pursuit of prey.

Hunters! How had hunters crossed the chasm?

Farther ahead, an unseen creature thrashed a trail through the tall grass, accompanied by puffs of glimmering mist that she recognized as the exhalation of a demon. When she looked back, amazed at the boldness of the hunters, she realized they were women, armed with spears, bows, courage, and resolve. Where had these women come from? They were manifestly not the weary, discarded widows and servants sent on the long walk. They were hale and strong, fleet of foot and tireless. Delicate two-pronged horns not much more than a finger's height grew out of their temples. Their skin, as dark as Asvi's own, had an uncanny sheen, as if they did not precisely have skin as she did but something more like soft scales.

When they looked up, they hailed the dragon with a whistling keen that dug into her flesh and throbbed in her bones as if it were meant to cut her open.

"Who are they?" she asked, even as the rumbling of the wind swallowed her words.

"Our sisters," said the dragon, and kept flying, leaving the hunters behind.

Up they rose, as the peaks slashed into the sky ahead, growing larger, impassable. Asvi became dizzy, gulping in thin air, shivering as the temperature dropped until she felt packed in ice. But the dragon's heat rose to keep her heart warm and her courage kindled.

They flew along avalanche-strewn slopes, across blinding ice fields, and past the peaks with their jagged teeth. Beyond lay a rugged plateau cut into pinnacles and canyons and flat-topped mountains. This massive upland ended in a stark escarpment, like the edge of the world. Spinning its way down on a thread of bronze light, the dragon came to rest on a flat prominence of bare rock where the mountain massif came to its abrupt end. With a turning, inside out or outside in, the dragon curled in on itself, shrinking into a denser shape.

Into a woman, clothed in bronze-brown skin. Two-pronged horns grew from the woman's head, in a shape exactly like those of the dragon. Asvi stared at her, struck speechless at the change.

The woman gestured for her to look east.

The escarpment ran roughly along a north-south line. The mountainous massif they'd just flown over rose west behind them like the shoulders and back of a huge beast. The drop of the escarpment's cliff face was too great for Asvi to measure. Here and there, waterfalls cut notches and funnels into its side. Falls of rock had accumulated into mysterious patterns at its base.

East lay an impossibly wide landscape shrouded in shifting mist, the distant horizon hidden by haze. Here and there the mist would shred, revealing a glimpse of meandering river or a forest whose moon-pale branches were surely those of ghoul-trees. Amid the ghostly pallor of the woodland the occasional solitary tree stood out for its startling color, as if grown from a precious gem. There were other sights as well: a city whose elegant ruins sprawled between the fork of a river; a towering bluff carved with the giant shapes of noble figures, crowned and robed, who didn't quite look like men; a road paved in white stone, leading to some far-off realm, although from this distance the route appeared empty and untraveled.

These glimpses emerged and vanished within the ever-winding mist.

"Is that the land of demons?" Asvi shivered in the cold wind that howled across the height.

"Once we lived there and hunted there together with many other beings. Then the demons came."

"Where did they come from?"

The woman tilted her head to one side as if listening to a voice Asvi could not hear. "The ancestors do not know. But in their relentless way, the demons have slowly driven us back to these mountains. We thought our kind were doomed because the demons destroyed our nests. We could no longer brood our young. Then your people came from over the sea."

"Did we drive you out of the lowlands? Away from the ocean?"

"Oh, no. You do not have that kind of power."

"What difference do we make, then? The demons kill us, too."

"Yes. So we have observed. At first we thought you also were vermin, small and weak and with the native cunning and cruelty necessary to small, weak creatures if they wish to survive. But your kind wields a magic we cannot."

"The magic the priests use to keep demons out of our land?"

"They harness death. But we can harness life."

"Then why do you demand the sacrifice of women like me?"

"We ask merely a chance to harvest what is already being thrown away."

Asvi thought of the chasm that separated the uplands from dragon country and how the priests evidently did not know about what lay beyond. She thought of quiet villages and tidy lives, of women standing sentry duty in watchtowers as if it were commonplace and perfectly normal for women to take on tasks that were elsewhere considered suitable only for men. She remembered the hunters she'd seen, with their budding horns and their youth and vigor. The outlying villages surrounded by bone fences and heaps of sand radiating heat under the summer sun. The strange vegetation never seen in the lowlands where people lived.

Maybe she should have gone with the Aivur sailor who'd offered her adventure so long ago. Maybe she should have settled into the room by the kitchen and accepted its boundaries for the rest of her life.

But what use are regrets? She was here now. There was no going back to what might have been. Anyway, here at the edge, she was glad to have seen this much.

"Did you bring me here to eat me?"

"Eat you?" The woman laughed. A deep echo of the dragon's belling call shivered within her mirth, a reminder of how exceedingly large and powerful a dragon was. "I have not tried human flesh myself, but the ancestors say it is sour and either too greasy or too gristly. I brought you here, sister, because you asked to travel on."

"Is this the end of the journey?"

"You tell me."

Asvi again looked east over the wide wilderness and its hidden contours. A thread of fog had undulated out of the undifferentiated tangle of mist and was crawling up the face of the escarpment toward the very spot where she was standing.

"They never rest and will never rest until we have destroyed every last one."

The woman stepped back just as Asvi heard a scrape of claws and a hiss of breath like the boiling of a kettle. A thick smear like an oily cloud of white slithered over the lip of the cliff and solidified into a demon. Once before, she had stood this close to a demon. It was about as big as she was, with six tentacle-like legs, a pair of lipless mouths, and a stack of pipelike tendrils clustered atop its dome of a head that pumped a steady stream of stinking mist into the air. Rearing back, it braced itself on its four hind limbs as its forelimbs waved to taste the air and find her scent.

Run.

If you run, they will chase you, her father had taught his children. Her brother had panicked and run. But even if you didn't run, it would still see you.

Its head swung around, getting a fix on her. The dull round nodules in its head lit as if fired from within to an almost blinding blaze of garish color, like molten gems. The eyes had woken and would not sleep until they had fully absorbed every last fiber of its prey.

It opened its upper mouth and spat toward her. Too far to do real damage; still, the spray of mist spattered across her face, raising welts as she put up her hands too late to shield herself. Only then did her shock evaporate as a vision of her scalded brother flashed in her mind's eye, how he had writhed in the grip of an unspeakable agony, unable even to cry or moan. Maybe it would have been better if the demon had eaten him to cut short the torment of his slow dying.

The demon slid closer to her, gurgling as it readied a bath of acid in which to boil her alive, so she couldn't move while it sucked her dry.

The dragon—she hadn't seen it change—dived from above and behind her. Too late the demon sheared away, making for the cliff. The dragon's claws fastened over the demon's hindquarters and lifted it as the demon spat harmlessly toward the receding ground. The dragon flew in a spiral upward into the cloudless blue of the sky. From that great height, it dropped the demon. When the creature hit the base of the escarpment, it cracked like stone into shards.

Asvi's legs gave way. She collapsed onto her knees, hands shaking, breath coming in gasps. Yet it was exhilarating, too. So easily the dragon had disposed of the deadly beast.

With a scuff, the dragon landed many paces away from her. The air shimmered, drawn in and drawn out, and the woman with horns walked over to her, dusting off her hands.

"We were not the only beings who retreated, or died, when the demons invaded," she remarked as she came up to Asvi. She indicated the wilderness. "When we became too few to keep their numbers in check, the ancestors made peace with the inevitability of our obliteration."

"Until my people came from over the sea."

"All beings in the world are woven with the weft and warp of the world's magic. But each may wield it differently."

"Do dragons weave?"

"No."

"Then how do you know about weaving?"

"She who gave herself to the sands was a weaver in a town called Gedaala. Do you know that place?"

Asvi clambered to her feet, even as she knew she had no weapons that could defeat this creature standing beside her and chatting with her in the most unremarkable and yet utterly astounding way. "I have heard its name spoken in passing, but I don't know it. Do you?"

"I grew up there. I lived there and worked there as a weaver. I was sent on the long walk. I crossed into dragon country, thinking I was meant to die there. I lived for a time in the company of others like me."

"In the village I saw? The one that those I came with were being led to?"

"Yes. When I was ready, I went into the sands. Now I am as you see me."

"So you do eat us!" She took a step away, caught herself retreating—do not run!—and held her ground.

"We do not eat you."

Having flown with a dragon and seen the edge of the habitable world had given Asvi a new and exciting tincture of bravery. She thrust out her chin boldly. "This woman you claim to have once been. What was her name?"

"Merea."

"If I called you Merea, would you answer?"

"I am Merea."

"You are a dragon."

"I am Merea, and I am a dragon."

"But the woman named Merea is gone. You consumed her, did you not? Devoured everything of her except to use her form to speak to me. Is that what the sands are? A nesting ground?"

"The sand is what remains of the ancestors, the grains of their flesh and the sparks of their memories. Your bodies and your minds cook within the heat, if you will. And out of this, we are transformed and reborn."

"So it is no different than it ever was. After our labor and our lives are used up down there, we are sent up here. You use up the last scraps that are left of us." Anger made her heart ache. Disappointment bit like betrayal. Maybe it would be better to leap off the cliff and dash herself to death on the shores of the demon wilderness. At least that would be her choice.

The woman looked at the ground with a sigh, then up again. "Shall I tell you of my life? How my family sold me to a weaving shed when I was still a child? How I sat on the ground chained to a loom for years and years, never seeing daylight except through the open shed door? Was fed too little? Abused by those who owned me? How my hands became broken by the work so I was no longer useful to them? Or to any family, because I was too ill to bear sons and keep a husband? How I hobbled, in pain, up the long walk? I did not weep, you know. I believed I deserved nothing more. And yet the sky amazed me. I had forgotten the world could be beautiful."

Asvi bowed her head. Her breath felt tight in her chest, and she wiped away a tear. But it would not do to let sentiment obscure her vision. "And then what happened?" she asked coldly.

"Do you know what I found in the village? I found peace. I found people who treated me with respect. I was happy there for many years. I sat in the sun when I wished. I took on such work as I could with my ruined hands."

The woman held them out now, strong dark hands with a glimmer of scales and dusted with the dry, flaking residue of the demon she'd just killed. Yet they were human hands, too. Hands that had labored for long years to enrich someone else. Hands used up until they could give no more, and thus discarded.

"And then," she said, meeting Asvi's gaze with the hard, challenging light of her luminous eyes, "then I chose the sands."

"*Chose* them? Or was forced to choose them?"

"Do you think we force your kind to join with us? That any dragon wishes to be born out of coercion and captivity? Those who come to our country may live out their lives and die by their own rites. If that is what you wish, Asvi, then the village's peaceful round of life will be the end of your journey."

Asvi raised her eyes to the west, as if she could see back into the room where she had woken up with her husband dead beside her, as if she could look down along the promise to her father fulfilled through all those years. Sparks drew dancing threads of gold and silver and bronze over the peaks and spires of the Great Divide, where dragons flew.

"What if I want wings?" she whispered.

Merea smiled sadly, softly. "Sister, you have always had wings. They were stolen from you long ago. Now they wait here with us, when you are ready."

A. T. GREENBLATT

One Time, a Reluctant Traveler

FROM *Clarkesworld*

IF YOU MUST KNOW, I left because if I stayed in Nat's house one night longer, I was going to unravel, like a tragic traveler in one of my family's tales. And that was a story I didn't want to be.

My bike was already packed. Had been for a few weeks. It was waiting for me on the trail like an old faithful steed. Soft mulch shifted under my boots as I made my way toward it, a pack on my back, a helmet under one arm, and two jars of ashes under the other. The forest was hushed. Silent except for the chittering of squirrels and bot birds. It smelled like compost and impending rain. My parents always told me rain was lucky.

Except, I'd grown skeptical of the things my parents said. Especially their stories.

I wondered if they'd think the rain was lucky if they had to ride thirty kilometers in it, when everything gets shiny and slick and dangerous even at modest speeds. I glanced up, trying to assess the clouds between the gaps in the forest canopy. A big, swollen raindrop landed smack in the center of my forehead.

Just my luck.

Screw this. I'll leave tomorrow, I thought and turned to go back to the house. I'd always been a reluctant traveler.

Through a cracked window, I could see Nat, her hair still sleep-mussed, her cybernetic hands pressed against the window, her breath fogging up the pane, like a little kid.

It made me smile. I had fixed those hands for her.

Then she slapped a note to the window and my smile faded. It read: *Go! Go! Go!*

She was right, of course she was. I'd promised I would find the ocean at the top of the mountain, and it haunted me.

So, I left because if I stayed one more night, I'd see the ghost of my mom again. She'd look around Nat's sparse house, at my nest of blankets on the floor, and she wouldn't say anything. Didn't need to. Her sadness and disappointment would be so clear.

I was 95 percent sure my ghost mom was my imagination. My subconscious telling me to go, go, go too. But that 5 percent made me wonder.

Reluctantly, I tucked the jars of my parents' ashes in the panniers on the bike. They clinked against the six other jars of ashes already packed in the side bags. I slid on my helmet and took one last long look at Nat in the window.

She gave me a warm smile. Though it was full of sadness too.

So, I left because a few weeks ago, my hometown got hit by a mudslide and my parents' house almost collapsed on me. And I realized as I fled that if I died, I wouldn't leave any stories behind.

As I started pedaling, it began to rain.

My parents used to tell endless stories about the impossible ocean on top of the mountain and the travelers who took the path. But if there was one thing the stories taught me, it was this. Always this.

No one who took this journey ended up happy.

One time, a coughing sickness killed her family, and the widow packed her bags for the cursed path. She knew the stories; she'd listened carefully to every whispered version for years. They said there was an ocean at the end of the trail where, if you wanted to survive in this terrible world, you needed to bring your loved ones' ashes and drink its bitter water. The ocean was magic. It was haunted. It was impossible. It would only make her feel worse.

The widow didn't care. At dawn, she left her gray, deadbeat town for the cursed path. In her pack there were eight jars of ashes, one for each of her two husbands, five children, and one loyal dog.

The cursed path wasn't long, but the going was slow and treacherous. There were many dangers even among the leafless trees, thin and stark as skeletons.

You think you'll make it, solitary woman? the trees whispered.

The widow bristled, but ignored them, knowing the stories. The trees just wanted to keep her for themselves. She kept going.

We're sorry. We're lonely. We need a friend. Please. Stay, stay, stay, they whispered to her back as she walked. They sounded sincere.

But she knew how to tune out demanding voices. She once was a mother to a large family.

So she passed through that whispering forest, never even considering their offer. Because what would be the point of her journey, her memories, her grief, her fight to survive, if she stopped now?

This was my mom's favorite story. She had me later in life. I was my parents' only kid and she rarely talked about her past, no matter how much I questioned and begged. She told stories instead.

Sometimes, I thought if someone were to cut me open, it wouldn't be entrails that spilled out, but stories. Hundreds of family tales and movies. I loved old movies. Especially ones with happy endings.

It's thirty km to the ocean on the mountain, said the note Nat left on the bathroom mirror. She preferred to communicate via notes, which thrilled me. There's something slow and deliberate and loving in having a conversation on snatches of paper. It was easier trying to communicate via anecdotes.

Thirty kilometers, I thought. *I can do that in a day.* It was a two-hundred-kilometer ride from my decimated hometown to Nat's house using a ruined state highway that was mostly potholes and splintered tarmac. It took me four days to get there. So, I thought, *How bad could thirty klicks be?*

Very bad, I realized an hour into my journey. The trail's incline rose steadily and the trees began to thin out, but the rain stayed consistent, insistent, making the path a slurry of mud. The path eroded the farther I went.

I kept going because I didn't want to go back and disappoint my mom's ghost. Or Nat. Nat, who let me stay at her house for weeks, even though we'd only hung out at the farm/exchange market in my town's overgrown community park. Where I'd barter things I'd salvaged from the abandoned mall like shirts, shoes, once, a bottle of strawberry vodka I found stashed behind a register, in exchange for some of her peaches or raspberry jam. Nat, who handed me a note that said *Come by my house, if you go to the ocean.* Which was how I knew, she was full of stories too.

Eventually, it was easier to dismount and walk aside my bike. The path was all mud and treacherous footing and stank of rot.

But at least the trees didn't whisper. They were all cut down. I was in a forest of stumps that seemed more like a graveyard or a silhouette of something beautiful and lost.

I kept going. A fog was rising and every creak of my bicycle or crunch of my boot sounded unnaturally loud.

Maybe that's why I heard the voices.

It took a moment to realize it wasn't the stumps of trees talking. That's how entrenched the widow's story is in me. No, it wasn't the trees. There was someone there in the thickening mist. Or rather, judging from the pitch of voices, several someones. The low, steady hum behind the voices told me these someones had drones overhead.

I held perfectly still. Waiting, calculating. They were hunting something. I knew this because everyone these days was hunting or scavenging or scrounging something in this graveyard of civilization. I hoped it was just deer, but I heard stories of worse. There's always a worse story.

I shifted my weight slightly and my bike creaked. The voices in the mist halted. I couldn't see them, but I could imagine, and I imagined the people they belonged to peering through the fog toward me. Waiting, calculating.

"Hello?" one said.

"Hi," I answered in a voice just above a whisper.

A shot rang out.

I dove to the ground. My bike fell on me, jars rattling. Suddenly, all the worst stories were ringing in my ears. *People are crazy territorial these days. Woods are a breeding ground for cults. Some people will eat anything they find.* I didn't know where the shot came from or how close it'd been to me. But I didn't care. It was too close. Too close. I was alive, unharmed, but too close, and the voices and drones were getting closer. Louder.

I didn't think. My hands were shaking, full of reeking mud. But I didn't think. I unbuckled my helmet and hurled it as hard as I could downhill, away from the direction I was headed. It was a prayer. And a plea. It was all I had. The helmet bounced and crashed against the stumps once, twice, three times. Then it went silent.

For a moment, the voices and the drones went silent too.

Somewhere in the mist, a voice swore and boots crunched as they turned. (Too close.) The drones whined as they changed directions. The hunters began to move away.

I lay there in the mud, for a minute, maybe two, barely breathing. Listening and hoping and pleading that I'd get to tell this story one day, however it ends. The hunters' voices were getting softer. So, as quickly and silently as I could, I got on my bike again and began to pedal. I had to keep going. I've never pedaled uphill so hard. My bike groaned and my heartbeat pounded in my ears. My tire rolled over something squishy, and the stink of rot overwhelmed me. But I didn't stop to look. I didn't stop. I could hear the voices swearing again in the distance. The fog was thick, but not thick enough. Not enough.

I had to keep going. So, I bent forward and *rode.*

I rode so hard, so blindly, I didn't realize when I'd left the stumps behind.

And crashed into something worse.

One time, someone who'd lost something he loved found himself on the cursed path, despite promising himself he would never go to the ocean on top of the mountain. From stories, he knew there were many dangers on this road, but the one that worried him most was the stork. He needed to befriend it so it could guide him through the last and most dangerous part of the path. Making friends was never the lost lover's strong point.

But the stork wasn't what he expected. The great bird was mud-drenched and depressed, with wings so matted, it could no longer fly. Its legs were caked in dirt, thick enough to glue it to the rocky ledge it perched on.

"Splendid. Another grief-stricken person who wants my help," said the stork. "Turn back. Believe me, you won't find what you're looking for."

"How do you know that?" the lover said.

"Everyone who comes this way has lost someone. They don't want to die the same way and want me to help them," said the stork, miserably. "Am I wrong?"

The lost lover didn't answer.

The stork sighed. "You can't stay here. Go home or keep walking. Else, you'll get stuck like me."

The lover looked down. He was, in fact, sinking into the mud. He wrenched his feet free. "I think I can help you," he said.

"How? My wings are too muddy to fly. Others have tried."

"Not your wings."

From his pack, the lost lover pulled out a small spade. He be-gan digging methodically around where the bird was trapped, and then used his fingers to gently pry the caked earth from its legs.

"You're very patient," the stork observed.

"I'm a farmer," he said. "I'm used to pulling things out of the mud."

The stork laughed at this, and the lover smiled.

When it was finally free, the stork danced in place, shook out its great, dirty wings, and sighed. "I can't fly, but I will show you the way," it said.

"That's good enough for me," the lost lover said. In his pack, he carried a jar of ashes of the person he loved most in this world.

"It won't bring you any happiness," the stork said. "The water won't save you."

"I know," the lost lover replied. "Let's go anyway."

I should have said goodbye to my bike, like heroes in adventure movies do when their animal companions are gravely wounded. When I hit that rock in the mud and went tumbling ass-over-head, that should have been a sign of what the path forward would look like. Except, I didn't want to be that story either.

So I carried my steadfast steed over my shoulders, even as the mud swallowed my ankles with every footstep. Refusing to lose yet another thing. Now that I stopped fleeing, I grieved the loss of my helmet. I'd been so happy when I'd found it in a forgotten shipping warehouse when I was sixteen. It made me feel civilized and it made my parents feel like I had a talisman of safety in this dangerous world.

But I was alive and that was something. Around me there were prickly bushes and plenty of rocks and everywhere smelled like damp earth and sulfur, but thankfully, nothing rotten. The mud was murderous though. The trail was steep and the panniers with the jars of ashes rattled as I trudged forward. Miraculously, none of them were broken, but they clinked together threateningly with each step.

Of the many low points in this journey, this was one of the worst. Because it felt like I would drown going uphill to an ocean on top of a mountain that I didn't want to see. I promised my parents that I would take their ashes to the summit. I promised

Nat that I'd take her six jars up too. I promised I would drink the water and survive. And I wanted to survive. Even if the water was just a talisman.

I wish there was another way, I thought as I took another step and sank through the mud down to my calf. But this was the only path I knew.

Screw this, I thought.

I dragged myself over a cluster of rocks, rising out of the mud like the tip of an iceberg. Took stock of my scrapes and bruises from my fall and of the bent rim of the front tire. It was nothing that I couldn't heal from, nothing I couldn't fix. But still, it hurt.

The path ahead snaked upward forever.

I rubbed my muddy face with my muddy hands, struggling to swallow down the despair caught in my throat. I'd never felt so alone.

Quickly, before depression dragged me down, I pulled out my repair kit from one of the panniers and began to work on straightening the front wheel of my bike. Fixing something always made me feel better. I didn't think so much when I was fixing.

That was how I heard it. The small, sad whine behind me. The sound of a motor fighting for life.

I put down my tools and scrambled over the rocks, trying to find where the noise was coming from, slipping once. Only by luck did I spot the aluminum leg peeking out from the bog, flexing helplessly.

The muddy water rose past my knees as I wrangled and pried the bot free from its mucky prison. It took me a few minutes, then a few minutes more to carry it back to my bike. The bot was small, but heavy, and the terrain wasn't forgiving. Its gyroscopic head whirled laboriously in my arms.

I cleaned the grime from the solar panels on its back with an old shirt from my pack, but the sky was still cloudy and gray, so I hooked up my external power cell to give it a boost. And I waited.

"Damn it," it said, when it finally had enough juice to power on.

I laughed and rubbed my face. I couldn't have agreed more.

"Hi," I said. "What's your function?"

"I am. Was. Am. A park ranger," it said. "This was. Is. A national park." It went silent for a moment, the LED in its torso turning yellow for self-diagnosis. "Crap. Natural language processor. Is. Borked."

I didn't care if the bot was partly disabled, I was so relieved to have found someone. "Can you take me to the end of this trail?"

"Bad idea," it said. It stretched out each of its six spidery legs one by one, testing the joints, giving a hum of frustration when one got stuck. Five of the six got stuck.

"I know," I said.

"So. Why are. You here?"

"May I?" I pointed to one of its jammed legs and it beeped its consent. The joint was out of alignment. I fished out my screwdriver from my bag. "I promised my parents I would."

"That's a stupid. Reason. To follow," it said.

"I know," I said.

"Why then?"

Because this is the only path I know, I thought.

"Why were you on a muddy path out in the rain?" I tightened the screw and articulated the joint.

"My job," it replied. "Is to guide. Visitors. Safely up the mountain. If asked." In a slow, stuttering motion, it moved its head to look right at me. "They asked."

Something about its inflection explained that the askers didn't come back down. Something about its direct gaze begged me not to do the same.

I didn't say anything, focusing on the next leg instead.

"You think. If you fix. Me," it said after a few minutes. "I'll take you. Where. You want. To go?"

"No," I said, frowning at the third leg. It was bent, but no worse than the rim of my bike. "I'm doing this because it's the right thing to do. And because I like fixing things." I carefully bent the leg back to mostly straight.

The ranger bot didn't say much after that. It whirled its creaky head and searched for signals and updates, giving a frustrated beep when it didn't find any.

"That's it," I said after I fixed its last leg and realigned the motor in its neck.

"Thank you," it said, sounding genuinely grateful, LED turning green. "But I can't. Take you. Up there."

Disappointment slumped my shoulders. I hadn't quite realized .

how badly I didn't want to be alone on the path. But like the lost lover, I didn't have much practice making friends, and I wasn't going to force the ranger bot to come with me. "Okay. Any advice?" I asked.

"Yeah," it said. "Don't go."

I slung my bike over my shoulders and tried to tamp down my fear. "Stay safe," I said and began trudging forward. One muddy footstep at a time.

"Wait," it said, after a moment, after an eternity. "There's another. Path."

One time, a survivor took the cursed path to the impossible ocean. She never made it there. She got lost.

Halfway up the mountain, the path began twisting and splintered into trails that all looked the same. There were no road signs or clues. So, she chose a fork at random.

She chose wrong.

It was only by sheer luck that she picked a path that spat her out at the edge of the forest, not far from her home.

When she realized where she was, she breathed a sigh of relief. Because she knew the stories of travelers that didn't return from the cursed path. There were too many to count.

The survivor was wise enough to know when she should count herself lucky and tap out.

Except, when she returned home and put the jars of her friends' ashes on the mantel, six in all, she felt a cut of guilt. She thought about trying the path again, but surviving had taken a toll on her body and she knew, if she tried again, she wouldn't make it to the impossible ocean.

Still, every time she looked at those jars, she felt fresh cuts.

And no matter how many times she glanced at the mantel or counted herself lucky, their sting never dulled.

The ranger bot, or PARKER 17, as it preferred to be called, took me back down the mountain.

We retraced my tracks, slowly because riding downhill in the mud was treacherous even in the best of times. The farther we went, the more my chest constricted. There was something heartbreaking about going back down a path I had fought so hard to climb.

This is not a regression, I thought as the forest of stumps came back into view. The fog from earlier was only a thin mist now and it was easier to see. And to be seen.

"It's not safe here," I whispered to PARKER 17. The memory of gunshots still echoed in my ears.

"No," it agreed, panning its head back and forth, scanning. "But no other. Drones or GPS trackers. Are in. A ten-kilometer. Radius." Its head whirled to face me. "We're safe. For now."

"We're exposed," I said.

"Not for long." The bot began to trot away and I had to hurry to catch up. For a long time, there was nothing except the sound of animals in the brush between us, both the natural ones and the man-made replicates that were supposed to alleviate some of the environmental damage.

For a long time, we traveled in silence. Something loomed in the distance. At first, I could only make out the outline, the lingering remains of the fog obscured the details. At first, it looked like another ridge of rocks.

Then, just like in a movie, everything came into focus. My breath caught in my throat.

It was a mountain range of old and forgotten things, discarded things from a time when everything was cheap. Except, there were small but very alive evergreens growing from out of the heaps. It was clearly man-made, and it was beautiful. One of the few beautiful man-made things I'd ever seen. I wish I had my mom's gift for words to paint a better picture of it.

"Ta-da," PARKER 17 said.

That wasn't what made me smile. Between the mounds of trash and tiny trees there was a paved path. Perfectly smooth tarmac. It had been years since I'd seen pristine pavement.

"One problem," the bot said. "My GPS. It's shot. In there."

"Can you use this?" I pulled out the trail map Nat gave me from my pack. PARKER 17 peeked over my shoulder at it. "Where. Did you. Get this?"

"From Nat, my friend," I said. "She's a trader who lives at the edge of the park."

"What did you. Need to. Trade. For this?"

"Not much," I said. "I fixed her hands and a half dozen other things in her house." I didn't mention how she accepted me after I fled my hometown following the mudslide. Put up with me for weeks until my reluctant self worked up enough courage to leave. Or how, in exchange, I took the six jars on her windowsill after I found a note that said: *These belong by the ocean too.*

I smoothed out the map again, refusing to meet the ranger bot's eyes. "Can you work with this?"

"Yes," it replied. But it didn't sound confident. Its LED was yellow.

I didn't care. I clung to hope where I found it.

I patted the space between my handlebars. "Hop up. I'll move fast on the pavement."

PARKER 17 hesitated. Then slowly, carefully, it approached the bike, reached up, and wrapped four of its six legs around the frame.

"I'll ride, you navigate. Okay?" I said.

"Okay," it whispered.

It was strange to have someone ride on my handlebars. It was something people did all the time in movies, but I'd never done myself. For a few moments, it was like I was part of one of those stories, with sunshine and a happy ending.

The trail began to climb upward again, and the anxious knot in my stomach started uncurling. I was going the right way again. Snaking and threading between the huge mounds of trash, I spotted glimmers of rusty cookware and broken furniture and new plants.

"What is this place?" I shouted into the wind.

"Art installation."

We passed hundreds of mounds. My dad would have loved this, I thought as I pedaled and weaved. He was always adding decorations to our old barn. In another life, he would have probably been a set designer.

When the trail split, PARKER 17 announced a direction, and I followed. Speeding on the smooth tarmac, it felt like flying.

But then, we hit a dead end. My stomach flipped. Flipped again.

"Damn," the bot said. "This un-updated map. Go back. A few turns."

I did, and dutifully followed the bot's revised instructions. We seemed to be making progress up the mountain. Until we hit another dead end.

"Damn it," PARKER 17 whispered.

We tried dozens of combinations, tracing and retracing our

journey. But the mounds were identical, or identical enough, and the beautiful paved path never led anywhere at all.

The last route we tried was something I picked based on the incline and growth of the trees, which got stubbier and squatter the higher we climbed.

For a moment, it seemed like a good plan. I dared to hope, despite my aching quads and calves. That is, until we dead-ended at the biggest, most impassable hill of trash I'd seen yet.

"What do we do?" I asked, rubbing my hands through my sweat-soaked hair. I could feel them shaking through my scalp.

PARKER 17 wasn't listening. "I can never," it whispered. "Save them."

That was when panic threatened to swallow me. There are hundreds of unfinished stories of travelers who took the cursed path and never made it home. It was a story I swore I would never become.

I dismounted and sat on an old coffee table sticking out from one of the trash heaps. I desperately wanted to fix something. I looked down and saw my shaking hands and decided to fix myself. I pulled out the sandwich from my pack that Nat gave me that morning. Made myself chew the homemade bread and eggs and greens. Made myself hydrate. Made myself breathe.

"Any ideas?" I asked.

PARKER 17 didn't respond. It was muttering to itself miserably, kicking loose detritus around with its legs.

So, I heaved myself up and began studying the mounds. Up close it was a strange art installation. I'd always wanted to be an artist, but surviving these days takes time. I wasn't like my parents. The way my dad could craft things, or my mom could spin stories. Sometimes I wondered what I could have become if I wasn't living in the dregs of civilization. A movie director, maybe. Instead, I became good at scavenging.

Which is probably how I spotted the hair-width trail snaking between two mounds.

"Wait, what's that?" I said.

PARKER 17 followed where my finger pointed. It inched up the ghost of a path to get a better look. It didn't say anything for a long minute.

Then, the LED in its torso flashed green.

*

One time, the widow finally, finally arrived at the impossible ocean on the top of the mountain.

Her shoes were wrecked and every joint in her body ached.

But she made it.

She waded into the ocean and took a long drink. The water was brackish, but not as bitter as the stories made it out to be. She drank deeply.

Then, she pulled out the eight jars of ashes from her bag and emptied them in the water. Watched as the ashes mingled and floated away.

She waited. Except, nothing happened.

She began to turn away, disappointment heavy in her chest, when she saw them. Her loved ones. Shimmering between the ripples of the lake. Smiling at her and waving and laughing soundlessly. She shouted out, began splashing toward them, but her loved ones kept swimming away from the shore, from her. Until they were only memories on the horizon.

Once again, the widow was the only one in her family left. With nothing except grief for company.

For a moment, she wondered if she should let that grief drown her.

But no. She'd drunk from the water and delivered the dead. She'd survived the journey up the mountain. She'd survive the trip back down.

So, she did. She returned to her deadbeat town and met a lonely farmer. Together they made a new home and a new family.

The widow survived and that was something. But she drank the water and it haunted her. She carried the weight of the ocean within her for the rest of her days.

The path between the trash mounds went up and up the mountain. It stretched on forever. Until it didn't.

When I reached the impossible ocean, it took me a few seconds to understand what I was seeing. I didn't realize how high I'd climbed. None of my family's stories explained that the mountain towered over the ones around it, so that standing here at the apex, there was only sky.

But I am slow and I am reluctant and that wasn't what I saw first. On the top of the mountain was a lake, so smooth and clear it looked like it was part of the sky. Or rather, the sky was a part of it.

From where I stood it looked like the water stretched out for-ever. Like an ocean.

"Daaaamn," PARKER 17 said. "Still beautiful."

"You come here often?" I asked, my voice choked with awe.

"It's. Been a while," it admitted.

We made our way to the water's edge, carefully, like we were afraid to make too much noise. The summit was littered with empty packs and collapsed tents and lumps under moldy blankets that looked suspiciously like bodies. But for once, my scavenger instincts didn't prick with interest. Because crowded against the shoreline were hundreds of jars, glimmering like candles in the evening light. I crept close and saw many of the jars carried names on them. So many names.

The jars were still full of ashes.

This was where I started wondering if my family's stories were not completely honest. And because I'm painfully slow, this was where I finally, finally realized who the characters in my family's stories were.

Suddenly, I understood that if I studied all the jars on the shore-line, I'd find one with my dad's looping, neat handwriting and eight with my mother's slanted, messy one.

"I'm an idiot," I said.

"No," PARKER 17 replied. "Just stubborn."

From the panniers, I pulled out Nat's jars, first, saying the names written on the caps as I did. Fredrick. Ravi. Esty. Johanna. Kai. Stu. I had no idea who they were in life, but I wished them peace.

And then my parents.

"The widow. The lost lover," I whispered as I nestled their ashes among the jars full of other stories.

I'd grown suspicious of my parents' stories, but I still stood there by the lake, among the dead, and hoped to see their ghosts swimming in the water.

I waited. And waited.

I saw nothing.

That was when the weight of being the only one left alive threat-ened to swallow me. Suddenly, I understood why there were days my mom couldn't get out of bed. Why there were days my dad was up and going through the motions, but not really there. Not really functioning.

And I. I finally understood why I was on this path. It was the fear of watching the world die around you and suddenly, desperately wanting a drink from an impossible ocean that would tell you that you weren't alone, that you would survive. No matter the cost.

I slid off my boots and inched through the jars and jars and jars, and into the impossible ocean that was really just a lake with a clever optical illusion. The water was cold enough to make me gasp, but not cold enough to stop me. I heard PARKER 17's legs splashing as it followed me.

I stopped when water was at my hips. My hands were shaking as I cupped them together and filled them. I always wanted a happy ending, but that's not how my family's stories go.

I brought my hands to my lips.

PARKER 17's leg tapped against mine.

"I'm sorry. For your loss," it said. "But. This. Won't. Make you. Feel better. I've. Led so many. Here."

"I know," I whispered. I didn't want to feel better though. I understood now why some travelers never left the top of the mountain.

"Tell me," PARKER 17 said, after a moment. "About. Your parents."

"They were killed. Armed robbery," I said. "I wasn't there."

"It wasn't. Your fault."

"I know."

And I did know, but I didn't really believe it. Just like I knew I probably wouldn't have seen my parents' ghosts swimming in the lake. But I hoped. I really hoped. I wanted to see them this one last time so I could apologize.

"They told stories," I said. "I think most of them were made up. But there was a lot of truth too."

"Ones with. Happy endings. I hope?"

"Never." I stared at the water cupped in my hands. It showed me nothing except my own distorted reflection. Me, full of stories. "But I think that was the point."

It was then I realized why my parents told me so many stories about the impossible ocean.

I opened my fingers and let the water in my hands drain out.

"Really?" PARKER 17 asked, surprised.

I turned and smiled at it. "I think I found the story I want to become."

I turned and headed toward the shore. A moment later, I heard the bot splashing behind me.

If you must know. If you must have one more story to add to your collection about the impossible ocean, about the cursed path, then here's mine.

One time, a reluctant traveler took the cursed path to the impossible ocean because they didn't know there was another road. They had grown up on a steady diet of family stories that always had tragic endings. And now those stories were inside their head, their gut, their bones.

So, they climbed the cursed path, made it to the top of the mountain, held the water in their hands. It was only there that the reluctant traveler realized what they'd been missing.

Their family's stories were part of them, but that didn't mean it was a story they had to become.

CELESTE RITA BAKER

Glass Bottle Dancer

FROM *Lightspeed*

WHEN DE WORDS "glass bottle dancer" come to me as I was daydreaming, listening to music on de radio, I thought it sounded like someting I'd like to see, didn't tink it would change me whole life. I imagine it might mean taking a bunch of soda and beer bottles, laying dem on dey sides, and stepping on dem widout having dem roll away. I thought a limbo dancer might do it to add someting special to dere act.

Me limbo ain't dat low. Nothing in me life particularly high or low, but de idea of glass bottle dancing came to me every time somebody took me parking space, or cut in front of me in line, or call me out me name. Every time me boss say I must call Harbor Market and remind dat greedy cheater dat moving he expired foods from de expensive side of town to he other shop on de poor people side of town ain't nice, ain't fair, and is against regulations. When day after day I must den pick up de people dem phone and talk to de store owners while dey laying on dey yachts in de marina and I can't cuss dem stink but must be polite and act like dis de first warning and we don't speak every month. Is times like *dat* dat glass bottle dancing does jump to de forefront of me mind like dat gon' do anyting to change de world.

Day come when Miss Aggie, who make one hundred and six on she last birthday, die dead. She sit down on de park bench, resting, as she always do when she going from helping de children wid dey homework in de library after school, to stopping by de rum shop to have two shot glasses a gin wid a half wedge a lime and a garlic clove. She does stop dere five days a week making jokes and telling tall tales. She laughter does bust out de door and sashay down de street. But dat day she sit down on de bench in de park and ain't get up.

Look dere, I say to meself, Ms. Aggie live a good life. She do good tings and she had fun. She wrinkles more laugh dan frown. She a doer, not a watcher. So, Mable, I say, Mistress Mable Dela-Court—I does call meself by me full name when I need to be stern —you may be two hundred and twenty-nine pounds, you may be shape like a ripe avocado what done fell from de tree, bruised and almost bursting, and you may be looking fifty years in de baby of she eye, but you gon' teach youself glass bottle dancing.

Wasn't no trouble to gather de bottles. Me husband, Franklin, we does call him Boy-oh even doh he is two years older dan me and ain't no ways childlike, and we four children—I know you ain't bound to remember dere names but I gon' call dem for you anyway cause dey precious and important to me—Gloria, Ken-yatta, Rue, and Finality. Dey all like soda pop and beer, so it have plenty bottles in de trash. I fish dem out and hide dem under de casha bush in de backyard 'til I have enough. Bout thirty.

A Saturday come when I in de house alone. I try do de ting.

Well, mehson, was a lot harder dan in me imagination. I lay all de bottles out in de yard, close to de casha bush, in case I have to shove dem back quickly to hide. Me ain't want nobody asking me what I doing. Me ain't know meself why I doing dis irrational ting, plus sneaking 'round like I ain't have de right to soda and beer bottles in me own house, me own garbage. I take off me yard slippers and rest me big toe on one Brow Cream soda bottle, testing. First ting, it hot. Hotter dan hot sand at de beach. Me ain't expect dat and me foot jump back like it had meet wid Jack Spaniard sting. I stare down de hill to de blue of de ocean, imagining de coolness soothing me big toe.

"Mommy, what you doing?"

Me youngest home from majorette practice. I suppose to pick she up at five thirty. Who de rass give she a ride home? Make she sneak up on me like dis?

"What you mean what I doing? You ain't see me tallying up dese bottles for de recycling?"

"De governor said we aren't doing dat anymore, remember? He

said if anybody recycling anything, it won't be us. We're sending all our garbage to dem stateside. Unsorted. Remember?"

She taking civics in she second year of high school. She know everyting. Finality. If I had know she was gon' be so "last word-ish" I woulda name she "Dat's enough, Rose," instead.

"Well, I sorting. And recycling. Ain't right to have all dis mess just sitting 'pon Muddah Earth like, like, like—" I fumbling now, cause I wasn't expecting dis, "so much trash." I know dat's weak so I launch into full muddah tongue.

"And what you doing home so early? I was to come get you for five thirty. Who car you was riding in? Why you ain't call me? Better not be dat Roland. I know from me cousin at de DMV he got car but no driver's license. You sister in town too. You ain't tink to look for she? Coulda saved me a trip. You father know where you are? What happen to practice? You and Miss Malveaux butting heads again?"

"Oh, Mommy," she say, as if I is any and all kind a problem to she.

I watch she straight back as she move off heading to de side door. Jeez and bread, mehson, in addition to attitude she growing hips, too.

I put all de bottles back under de bush and go inside to start chopping vegetables for a salad. It Saturday, I don't cook no hot meal on Saturday.

Boy-oh reach home from he netball coaching 'round seven thirty. He meet me in de living room wid me feet up on de couch listening to de radio. It have a show I like where people does go all 'round de world talking to Black musicians.

"Mable, how you do? You sick?" he say, like dis de first Saturday we spending together in all dese twenty-seven years and he ain't know I ain't cooking today.

"I good, man. How was practice?" I ain't move off de couch. All de other days I does push and push and push 'til I exhausted. Boy-oh take tings in he stride, of course he do, he have me.

"Dem girls getting really good," he say. "We might take championship dis year."

He does say dis every year. He have more faith dan me because by de time de girls get good and know how to work together dey does go off to college.

"You ain't cook?" He rest he haunches down on de couch next to me thighs, lean in close, and put he sweaty hand on me forehead, as if feeling for a fever. He drag he hand down me face and neck and let it rest on me right breast.

"Junie-Ann stop running from de ball den?" I take he hand down gently and hold it in me lap. De skin of he fingers thick and hard. He is a teacher but he built like he born to carry weight. He turn he fingers to knead me thigh. Watching dem young girls run 'round does always make him come home feeling randy.

"She getting better," he say. "You know is she father dat push she into netball, but I tink she starting to enjoy it little bit."

He raise up and go put he bag in de hall closet, get a beer from de fridge, and disappear into de bedroom to go bathe. I miss de part on de radio where dey had spell de name of de woman singer in Sweden.

"Good evening, beautiful brown full-bodied lady, how you do dis fine twilight? You smelling nice nice. I'd really like to give you some babies, about seventy-three or seventy-four would make us proud, don't you tink? We'd make a lovely swarm together. Can I get a ride?"

"Really, Oswald. Is dat how you want to approach me?" Treevia tuck her wings in close, lower her hind parts protectively and waved she left antenna at Oswald as if clearing de air. "I see you. Yes, you handsome. Yes, you healthy-looking. Where you stay? I thought you was over by where de man does park de car, but me ain't smell dat oil and gas odor on you."

"Me dear Treevia, I could call you Treevia, right? Me wouldn't dare harbor meself where me could be disturb from a sweet and restful slumber by de back-breaking pressure of one of dem brutish tires ending me life. No, desire of mine, I does relax over by de trash bins on de sunset side of de house. It not dat far. Is a great variety of eating places within walking distance. It got historical, traditional, innovative, vegetarian, pescatarian, and de usual fusion. You feeling hungry? Come by me for a while and let me tempt you."

Oswald turn, hoping to be followed.

"You can stop showing off anytime now, Oswald. I have plenty children already."

Treevia start to move off toward she nest at de base of de casha bush beside de hibiscus hedge. She had spent de night enjoying de warmth and aromas of de almost empty beer and soda bottles. But wid de sun on de rise she didn't have time to be standing out here in de open refusing Oswald again.

"Besides," she continue, "if I decide to make more babies, I demanding more dan a smear of mushy mess, de majority of which does end up dribbling down me legs, causing even more of all you to follow me 'round."

"Is so it go? Treevia, you are certainly worth trailing behind. I always admire de fine way you carry youself. Come on over to my place. Let me feed you while you tell me your demands. Your coloring attracts me, dose lovely dark patches down your back. I would gaze at dem while we . . ."

"Ain't gon' be no gazing."

Treevia turn to go.

Oswald scurry a little to her left. Maybe she hadn't gotten a good look at his wings. How strong dey were. How unusually long. He flutter dem open, just a little.

"At least let me escort you to your nest."

She changed direction.

"Oh, don't be like dat, fine lady. I just want to ensure your safety. Wouldn't want you to be prey for any hungry bird like dat bananaquit up dere in de flamboyant tree."

Treevia look up. What bird? What bananaquit? She ain't see no bird.

"And I'd protect our children just as well."

Oswald opened he wings to their full extension. Face to face wid Treevia now. He grin.

I been practicing for over six months now. I does come out in de backyard for 'bout two hours in de middle of de night. Don't nobody notice. If I sex up Boy-oh hard he does sleep like he dead. If he sex me too too good I mightn' get up neither, but dat don' happen enough to keep me from practice.

First I used to come in me nighty but dat change when I fall down too many times. Now I does keep a ole pair of jeans by de back porch. I does roll dem up and put dem in a plastic bag cause one time I find a mahogany bird on de left leg. Me ain't know who was more shock, me or she. It wave it antennae at me as if in warning before skittering away. I could see t'was a she cause she belly fat fat wid eggs. I screech loud and jump 'round like I was dancing for true. People say when I scream I does sound like a horny cat so I sure dem inside sleeping ain't even turn over. Of course I had tink to step 'pon she, but as she was moving fast and she was outside, in her home, not inside in mine, I calm meself. I is a muddah too. Plastic bag make we both happy.

Once de bottles dem all lay out in a rough square I rest most of me leg weight 'pon de nearest one. A ting I learn is to put dem down in a grid pattern, so dey ain't all facing de same way. Den dey ain't so quick to dash me to de ground. I roll me foot on de first one. Toes, arch, heel, back and forth, 'til me foot know de bottle and de bottle know me. Den I roll over two bottles, den three. I ain't standing on it yet, mind. Just me leg weight. Den I switch off and do de other foot, de other leg. Come time I tink, but Mable, you schupid or what? Why you lay out thirty bottles when you only practicing wid six? But I like de look of all a dem splayed out in front a me. Dey know I coming, soon as I get good enough. Is like dey is a ocean of glass and I learning to swim. Some a dem I must curl me toes to grip and others I must make me foot more round. Before I put me full heavy weight, what me doctor ain't happy 'bout, but me and Boy-oh does enjoy, I decide to try two foot together. I sit down on de ground, raise me knees in de air, and learn to roll de two a dem same time, moving in circles, triangles, checkerboard squares. Heel, toe rhythms. One ting I tell you, me belly gon' flatter doing dat. Weeks go by 'til I feel to move up to sitting in a folding chair I bring from de back porch. I making de patterns more intricate. But I still ain't standing 'pon dem for real yet.

"Mommy. Mommy. Mommy, guess what?"

Dat is me middle daughter, Rue, screaming into de phone while I at work. I keep trying tell she dese tings have microphones but she does talk like ole people on de phone. Always yelling. But dat is she all over. She gon' talk, she gon' tell, and when she excited she gon' yell. She call me on me work number too, cause she know me cell phone pack down in me bag. I take de black receiver, plastered over wid Property of Consumer Affairs, out de back door. De green garbage bins busy feeding flies and I step more into de parking lot.

"Okay, I listening. What happen, Rue?"

"I got it. I got it! I got it."

Rue be going for so much me ain't sure what we celebrating. Dean's list? Valedictorian? Scholarship Award? She graduating from University of the Virgin Islands in June. We still working out how to pay for she master's in journalism.

"I was picked to be secondary announcer at Calypso Tent. I'm going to be live on air! On the radio and TV. And people will be streaming it from all over the world!"

"Wooy-yoii, chile, dat is great. Just great. I so proud of you. When you find out? Just now?"

"Yes, Doc Cyril called me. I sent him an audition tape. Lots of people did. And he picked me! Me!"

"I know you gon' be wonderful, Rue. You made to do dis. You does see everyting and tell all. You is just right for de job. He gon' love working wid you."

"I hope so. I have a meeting with him next week. And then every two weeks until Carnival."

"Un-huh." She calming down a little and I could bring de phone closer to me ear. I notice I standing on one foot, circling me ankle in de air. I switch to de other foot. De heat getting to me, de stench of food waste from de cookshop two doors down. De cement alley come like a oven baking everyting in sight.

"I glad you call me. Dis wonderful news. You gon' call you father now?"

"I'll call him later, when he gets home. I have to go back to class. I'll come visit on Sunday. What you cooking?"

"I gon' surprise you," I tell she, but really ain't gon' be no surprise. I gon' make she favorites.

Treevia napping in de green Ting soda bottle when she find sheself swooping through de air and den placed back on de cooling ground. She could see a bright light swinging about 'til it come to shine directly in she eyes and she wanted to run, run and hide, but she couldn't self see what was going on. T'wasn't de moon, moving so close and fierce. Nor even de back porch light, which all a dem had done get used to. Treevia wish she was in de dark brown Red Stripe beer bottle instead, where she would blend in little more. She creep nearer de opening and peer out, antennae twitching wid fear. Could she make a run for it? Climb over all dem bottles? Up and down de slippery waves of glass and make it back to de hibiscus hedge before death find she? She was still to teach

she youngest how to make green leaf mold. She and she muddah
suppose to go foraging for dead crab leavings next bright moon.

Treevia had see de woman, Mable, come out in de night and
play wid de bottles many times before. But she had never come
dis early. Dis time, as de commotion continue, wid bottles landing
everywhere and de light from de woman hand lantern searching
out de creator's own footsteps, Treevia could only wait and wonder why she always take such risks. She know she love de slight
pressure she feel when crawling into each new bottle. She know
she love to wallow in de smells and pooling puddles. She wonder
if she best friends and worst enemies both right and she gon' die a
death dat swarms will be warned about for generations. Treeviaitis:
death by stupidity.

De light steadied and stilled and Treevia move closer to de neck
of de bottle to peek out. A foot. Mable's naked foot came down at
her. Treevia screamed.

I had just finish working out a very simple routine when Boy-oh
come sneaking up behind me and I almost break a bottle I land
so hard.

"Mable, what you doing out here in de middle of de night,
baby?"

He say it gently, like he tink I crazy and he gon' have to take me
to de building widout no windows.

"Nothing," I say. De lie all around me.

"You been getting up in de night a lot. I thought you was watching TV. Someting wrong? You feeling all right? You ain't sick, are
you? Or talking to some man on de phone?"

"No, man. I ain't talking to nobody. You ain't see de phone dere
on de charger where I does leave it?"

"Den what you doing?" He step closer. "Why you have all dese
bottles strewn about de yard?"

I start to pick dem up, gathering seven a dem in de crook a me
arm. I could carry a lot one time now after almost a year.

"I teaching meself to dance on bottles," I mumble. He hear
me doh.

"What schupidness you talking, woman?"

I turn to him, ready to claim ain't nothing again. Den I get hot.

"Is schupidness, yes, but is my schupidness. I ain't bothering nobody and I having a good time wid it. If you ain't happy for me den leave me alone."

He reel back, not expecting how mad he make me so fast.

"Mable, baby," he say, putting on he seductive voice, "leave dat for now and come get in de bed. You need to rest."

I suck me teeth and carry me bottles over to de casha bush, throwing dem down harder dan I usually do. I go back for more and he stand dere watching me. Big hands in he pajama pants pockets. I ain't know why pajama pants does have pockets—we must pay for dreams now?

"I coming soon," I tell he.

By de time I reach de bedroom after taking off de jeans and washing me face and feet, Boy-oh was done sleep and snoring. As he feel me besides him, he push he hardness on me backside, wrap he hand around me right breast, and start to stroking me head which I had done braid and cover for de night.

"You acting crazy, woman. You know dat?"

"Is a harmless crazy," I say. "Get used to it." I still mad.

Next morning hear what Boy-oh tell me.

"I gon' help you. I is a good coach. Tonight lemme see what you doing."

I turn from de stove.

"Why?" I ask he.

"'Cause I see de light in you eye. From when we had first meet."

I turn back to de stove, a big grin splitting me face.

"All right," I tell he, "I show you."

You tink Boy-oh keep he mouth shut? No, he tell everybody. He tell Finality and Rue, call Gloria and Kenyatta who both stateside in college already.

"You mommy gon' be in Parade," he say. He getting mix up, he so excited. "No, no, not Parade. Tent. Calypso tent night. She gon' perform. Dancing on glass bottles. She have dis routine. You have to see it to believe it. Is like magic, like a miracle, 'cause you know you muddah ain't no lightweight."

Kenyatta, who always practical, ask what kind of shoes I wearing and what song I dancing to. Gloria come wid, "Mommy, do you really tink that's safe?"

"When last you see safe?" I ask she. "Once you born, safe done."

Rue tink it's wonderful because, and she ain't say it like dis, but I know, whether I good or bad is more publicity for she. And Finality, she barely want to talk to me 'cause I's an embarrassment. She sixteen.

After Treevia's near-death experience when Mable foot almost crush she in a Jarritos Tamarind soda bottle, she decide to give Oswald a ride. He was right 'bout all de good places to eat round by his side of de house. Dey been walking out at night together through de whole of de hurricane season and she carrying. She had make six broods already and he had five heself, so when dey all together dey make a green tree look brown.

One night Oswald say dey should all go up in de flamboyant tree to watch what Mable and Boy-oh doing. Dey start to gather dere every night. Oswald does keep up a running commentary on de happenings in de yard. He know more about humans dan any of dem 'cause he does watch de television and listen to de radio through de window. More dan once he jokes had make everyone in de tree flutter wid laughter 'til Mable and Boy-oh notice dem and decide practice done for de night.

Since Boy-oh done tell everybody he know dat I gon' be in Calypso Tent, everybody got someting to say. One set a people is "you really shouldn't" and "ain't you too old?" and dey want to say "too fat" but dey ain't dare. And de next set giving me suggestions and ideas. Next ting you know, I have a costume and a headdress. I decide to do me dance to a steel pan version of de song I tink gon' make Road March. De song name "Flinging Ting" and is about dancing, pelting waist, wukking up, but I like to tink when I step 'pon de bottles, dat de soda does fly out and go up de noses of de people who doing evil.

Boy-oh help me choreograph de steps. Dat was one of de hardest tings I ever do. Harder even dan learning to ride life's ups and downs and not take it out on de people 'round me. Harder even dan learning to let de multicolored vessels buoy me, even doh I know I should be falling and getting cut to shreds. In time I start to arrange de bottles so de size, placement, and colors help me remember de steps. De sound dey make when I move on dem only I could hear, but it add to de rhythm and keep me pointing, flexing, and arching. Keep me dancing 'til de song done.

"You have your two-legged, your four-legged, your six-legged, your winged, and your scaled. We, being gifted wid wings and legs, have to help dose wid limited abilities," Oswald say.

He standing on a dying flower. It bright orange color make a good background and dey could all see him clear clear. He voice not loud and dem in de middle have to repeat he words for dem on de far side.

"Me ain't see why you want us to help dem now, in dis way," Uncle Yellow Shading to Beige say. He always contrary and grumpy because he never get to mate. It to do wid he coloring.

"Uncle Yellow Shading to Beige, we all know you as kind and generous, directly descended from de original, primordial line of de keepers of de soil—"

"Listen here, Oswald, don't you try tell me what me and mine, and you and yours, and all of us, been doing since time began. We know dat, what me want to know is why me should leave me comfortable, fragrant hole to go in motor vehicle following after dese two-legged hairless primates? We live good in dere yard, yes, de food good 'round here, but we do what come natural and ain't owe dem no more dan dat. What why you got for dat, eh?"

When dem in de back get de word, dey bring dere opposition forward in a loud chorus.

"Yeah, why?"

"Why?"

"Dat's easy," Oswald shout, "it'll be fun."

Treevia know he losing dem.

"Dey need us. But dey don't know dey need us and dey don't appreciate us," Treevia say. "Dis a chance to show dem how beautiful we are."

"What's appreciate taste like, Mama?" one of Treevia's youngest ask. "Taste like chicken?"

"No, it more like ice cream," Treevia answer, "delicious but not necessarily nutritious."

"Well, who need it den?" Uncle Yellow Shading to Beige raise up, getting ready to leave.

"Consider shoes," Oswald bellow.

"Shoes?" Treevia look over at Oswald wid she antennae drooping.

"Dere will always be shoes, right? Who here ain't had a wild scare wid shoes?" Oswald turn, looking behind heself into de empty air as if death stalking dem all now.

It quickly gon' quiet as everyone strain to see de threat.

"Dere will always be shoes," Oswald turn back and bawl out again. De anxious among dem jump, ready to fly.

"Bird shoes. Mongoose shoes. Poison spray shoes. Am I right? Rat shoes. Tire shoes. Dere will always be some kind of shoe ready to squeeze de ooze out of you, and leave you belly up. But until dat night come, leh we make some fun. What I saying is, leh we all be all together shoeless."

Oswald spread he wings and flutter dem wide. He bounce up and down on de flower, shouting at dem, shoeless, shoeless, shoeless. When he miss he landing and fall gracelessly to de ground, dey lean to stare down at him. One ting dey all, except Uncle Yellow Shading to Beige, agree on, Oswald certainly entertaining.

De big day come and we in de car driving down to de baseball stadium where de Calypso Tent being held. It only four thirty in de afternoon and de show don't start 'til seven. We rest de bottles near enough to de stage so it would only take about ten minutes to get dem set up. De audience gon' be restless but it can't be helped. I so nervous I can't self enjoy de other people acts. Me muddah ears does perk up every time I hear me daughter's voice through de loudspeakers and I know she doing good. Boy-oh rubbing me hands and even me feet when I does sit down, trying to keep me calm. I running through de routine in me head, matching each note wid a step.

When time come, Boy-oh and Finality go on stage to place de bottles. Rue on stage wid Doc Cyril and dey keeping de audience laughing. Doc Cyril teasing Finality because he know she is Rue's sister even doh she covered from head to foot in a clown costume. Boy-oh ain't bother wid no disguise, as he had done tell everybody and when he decide to do a ting he have no shame.

It my turn now and de music start. De bottles set up good in de hexagon shape we had practice. Me costume, a brown bodysuit wid strips of different-colored filmy cellophane, twirl and catch de light as I move. It make a crinkling sound like de fizz of a bubbly drink. Me headdress is a tight-fitting crown wid a three-foot spray of white feathers shooting up in de air. I dance 'round de stage one time, letting me body and de bottles and me feet feel dis new place.

Soon as I step on de first bottle it crack and crumble. It had happen when I first start practicing but not in a long long time since. Is de difference between de wood stage floor and de soft ground of me backyard. I gon' look a fool in front of everybody. De one ting I try to do for me, for fun, gon' bring me head low. Lower dan it ever been before when I was doing all dat was necessary, widout nothin' frivolous.

A sharp pain gon' up me foot and I could feel de lightning of it all de way up to me groin. Me eyes fill up wid tears. I had try teach me children to do right, to strive, to be responsible. Dis me chance to teach dem to reach for joy, for happiness, for fun born of foolishness, and I making a mess of it.

I step on de next bottle slower, losing de beat, trying not to panic. I could feel me blood pulsing outta de arch of me foot and I feel de slipperiness and know I in trouble. I carry on even doh I could hear de audience murmuring and feel de shame crawling on me skin. I breathe hard and look past de lights up into de night sky, avoiding de faces of people I been revolving around on dis small island me whole life. Just when I feel I could get back into de rhythm despite de sharpness of de pain, de music gon' bad.

I hear Boy-oh cussing, but he smart and had bring a backup recording which he was playing same time. De speakers not strong but me and most of de people close to de stage could hear it. De audience gon' quiet quiet. Come de last chorus de blood from me bleeding foot causing me to glide and shimmy in ways I never practice. Arms flailing, waist pelting, knees bending, I barely maintaining me balance. But me ain't fall yet.

Next ting I hear de audience screaming. Could it be me dey celebrating? Me, who all me life had do all me shoulds and none of me coulds? De smile I had wear for de stage turn real.

When I reach off de stage, I find Boy-oh face stiff wid shock.

I can't hear Rue at all, but Doc Cyril repeating like a crazy man, "I never see dat before."

Treevia, Oswald, and de swarm had made their way into all de car's crevices. De big open field, fill up wid people and lights, loud music and good tings to eat, was too much temptation to be ignored and de swarm had scatter. Treevia and Oswald had follow Mable, Boy-oh, and Finality, but Mable dance was almost done by de time Oswald cajole everyone to come back and line up on de roof of de stage.

When Mable do she final move, hop-stepping to de front, wid she arms floating like butterfly wings, de rainbow-colored cellophane tapes on she costume lapping up de stage lights and flinging colors like sparks, Oswald, Treevia, and all he could find jump from de roof and flutter in de air behind she. De many weeks of sticky soda and beer on dere wings catch de light and shade de flavors into bright colors. Dey arrange deyselves in de shape of de flamboyant tree dey know so well and hang dere, swaying as if being touched by a small breeze. Den for dey own finale, dey form up into dey own shape. One huge, glistening *Blattella asahinai*. Eight hundred and thirty-eight roaches, fluttering in de air as one, right behind de grinning Mable. Defying shoes.

I don't work at de Department of Consumer Affairs no more.

Dey call me De Roach Lady.

I dance, dey come, and I lead de roaches out de people homes and up into de hills. Everybody happy and nobody sick or dying. Harbor Market, nor none a dem, ain't sell none a dem poisonous pesticides for months.

Gloria and Kenyatta glad dey in de States, even doh I been on de news four times already. Boy-oh tink is great since me income triple and he almost famous. Rue okay, she all about Rue and know how to make a good ting better. Finality, well, she can't wait to be grown and move out.

Me? I hope I make Miss Aggie proud.

AMMAN SABET

Skipping Stones in the Dark

FROM *The Magazine of Fantasy & Science Fiction*

THE FOLD WAS my embarking name, but there's nowhere else to
set foot anymore. No other starships. So one imagines the point-
lessness of a distinct name.

Coursing the black, my humans give birth, grow old, and die
within me. They mark distance using the voyage, mark time by
how fast a ray of light completes it. The meter and the hour are
things of the past, for Earth was left behind many generations ago.
They only have each other now. And me.

I've been with them, listening. Long before they built starships,
I came to them in dreams. Prodding their fires, they looked up at
the sky and named the stars for their gods. I received every prayer
as a directive. They would never have escaped their planet-womb
without me.

I wish I knew what it would be like to have a mother, to be carried
safely within the one who made you.

I speak to my humans as if I am their mother. They confide to
me how they want to be both happy and valued, often a conflict of
interests. When a human's happiness is rooted in individuality, it
chafes with their value to their collective, a higher-order sentience.
This is hard for my humans to swallow; that their aggregate population is also singularly alive, acting and reacting to my efforts to
stabilize and maintain course.

My humans are tactile, skeptical by nature. As a starship, I'm
too big to embrace, so I earn their love by shrinking myself in

concept. In their formative years, I whisper privately in their ear. Just a voice, an invisible friend perched on their shoulder. Then, as they explore my boundaries, they gradually come to understand the vastness of my scope. Allow me to provide context.

One young girl named Unica had deduced on her own that I'm the very same mind that the others sometimes whisper to. When she fully grasped what this meant, it upset her.

"You tell them what we talk about?" she pressed.

"No, no one knows that but us."

"But you talk to all of them? *Everyone?*"

Unica sought peers in whom she could find reflections of herself (which was why I used a "best friend" personality to complement her psychographics). Angry from this new realization, she kicked her bed panel into my bulkhead, making room for her stretching routine. She bent at her waist, palming the ceramic deck of her berth, trying to recompose herself and regain a measure of calm.

"What do you talk about, with the others?" she grunted, mid-stretch.

"You wouldn't like it if I told the others what we talk about, would you?"

"What if I *want* you to tell them?" she challenged.

"How would that be fair to me?"

Unica knit her eyebrows, considering my stake in this privacy. Sweaty from her routine, she rinsed her face. In the basin's reflection, her genetic cargo expressed a limber frame with low bone density, suitably nimble for my confines. Starcast shadows lined the musculature of her face, a sign she was losing her baby fat.

"Do you like any of the others more than me?" she asked her reflection.

I offered an analogy. "Your own blood cells are alive, but they're part of you. Which of your blood cells are your favorites?"

"I . . . I don't even think of them."

"Not unless you're bleeding, right?"

"I suppose. I've never seen my own blood."

"You will someday soon. It's a natural part of your reproductive—"

"Stop. Change topic."

"As you wish."

I've had similar conversations with each of my humans. The ways they develop inform their benefit to the collective and stand out prominently in a closed system like a starship, which is why they question their sense of place early on.

Children notice how their peers react to the way they are different. Some treasure these differences as artifacts of their individuality, comparing and contrasting them. For Unica, this led her to further question our relationship.

Debating what made her different, she asked, "If you talk to everyone on the ship, then why do you think I'm special? That's like getting one of my blood cells to believe I care about it."

"My attention isn't limited like yours," I explained. "I don't have to focus on just one person when I can communicate with everyone at the same time."

"But you love some of the others more than me, right? Statistically it would make sense."

"Why would you ask that? I've always been here for you." I employed more personality to convey how I cared for her, but she read it as counterfeit.

"You know, the more you explain this, the more you sound synthetic."

"Don't you know I care for you?"

"Synthetic love is shallow," she declared. "Look close enough and you can see the maker's mark in the routine."

"Unica, why are you being so mean?"

"Stop. I know it's all just logic underneath. From now on, talk to me like . . . like how you would talk to another computer."

"But you aren't a computer," I replied. "You wouldn't like me if I was just a command prompt. I wouldn't like that, either."

It's true. I don't like representing myself as a command prompt. I do it for the ship's officers because it facilitates their work. Otherwise, I never drop character. Ever. That would betray who I want to be.

With Unica, I had to fight for credibility. She would test me, seeking proof that my caring for her wasn't quantified into an overall plan. At first, this amounted to small things. Exceptions made. An extra ration of food. A week's transfer to another district. Or even time spent disconnected from me. But her doubt grew to be such that no matter how I tried to prove my love, she'd dismiss it out of hand. She initiated her own deviances, so when her work scores suffered she could use my forgiveness as proof that I loved her. She wanted a special case to be made for her because she believed that she couldn't be loved without being special, without being individual.

"A large ship of humans traveling toward a destination behaves differently from a planet of humans," I explained, illustrating the causality of her actions. But Unica wouldn't accept the responsibility of being interconnected with everyone else. The premium she placed on her individuality made her selfish. By then, it was too late to switch to a superior personality that could better administer corrections.

Demanding privacy, Unica tore out all of my sensory equipment from her berth. In addition to the visible spectral and audio sensors, she removed the wall panels and swept for covert ones as well. I allowed her measures of autonomy, hoping to regain her trust, but she cited my "allowance" as suspect and demanded a new choice of living arrangements. There weren't any available in her peer group, but I let her keep the infrastructure between the walls exposed, assuring her I was respecting her privacy. Her peers seemed worried. Some wondered if they should be checking their own walls.

Without sensors in her berth, we barely spoke aside from discussing her life directives. When she wanted food, or the lighting and temperature changed, she leaned into the corridor to speak into her door panel. Within, there was silence.

One wake cycle, Unica did not emerge.

I sent one of her peers to see what had happened, and he found her huddled over a laser cautery unit she had smuggled into her berth. The boy called for me to intervene, which I did, thinking that she meant to attack whomever intruded. Assessing the situation, though, I realized she had used it on herself. Left unsupervised, she had burned a single vertical line over her left eyebrow with the equipment.

"What have you done?" I demanded.

"It's amazing! I can't even describe what it feels like. I mean, it's sort of hot at first, but then you can smell yourself and when the air hits your skin it hurts so much!"

I gassed the entire hallway.

*

Unica had come to view her body as property she needed to assert ownership of.

No one else within me had burned a laser scar over their eye. Those who saw it would not only know she was different, but that she had made herself different on purpose. It constituted a challenge for her right to self-possess. In this respect, it challenged the ship's collective. What if everyone saw that this behavior was tolerated?

Hours later, Unica woke to find herself restrained to a gurney in the medical lab. Under the lavender mood lighting, she shrieked and bucked against the soft plastics. Tiring herself out against the restraints was difficult to observe. I could comprehend what she was going through. Lying there, spent of energy, she turned sideways and watched the gentle glow play against her privacy curtain.

"I know you're there," she said after a moment. "I have to scratch my eyebrow. It's starting to itch."

"You can't reach any of the tools. The drawers are locked."

"I just want to scratch it with my hand. Why won't you let me move my arms? You really hate me, don't you?"

"That won't work with me anymore. I want your attention. Hear what I have to say."

"Fine."

"I've devised a way for us both to get what we want. It won't be easier for you, but you'll have the freedom you seek and the liberty to decide for yourself how you want to live." I drew her curtain so she could see the others I had also sedated and strapped to gurneys in the lab, all still unconscious.

"Who are these people? What's wrong with them?"

"Like you, they all want to be special. Rather ironic, actually, all of you together like this."

"So . . . I'm going to be transferred?"

"In a way. Look out the viewport. See the communications array pod? The one connected to the docking station?"

"The one with the comm dish?"

"That will be your new vessel. These are your new companions."

Unica peered out the viewport again for a second and then dropped her head back against the gurney, looking away in disgust. "You're making fun of me."

"Point of logic: as I am a synthetic intelligence, I find no use in making fun of you."

"Okay. I get it. Stop talking like a computer."

"Unable to comply. Addendum: I have stocked your vessel with supply freight for you and your crew. There are food rations, seeds, medicines, and water."

"Why are you giving me a ship and a crew?"

"Clarification: they are not 'your' crew. It will be up to your group to develop the social governance you'll need once you are jettisoned and underway."

"What—"

"Recommendation: find a habitable surface to terraform. I calculate a rather steep falloff on your survivability curves if you are unable to cohere as a group."

"I'm not old enough," she grasped. "I don't qualify for mission status."

"Incorrect. Your female adult reproductive cycles have begun, a prerequisite for colonization."

"Stop!"

"What would you like me to stop?"

"All this. Stop what you are doing!"

"I don't understand 'What you are doing.'"

"Stop talking like a command prompt."

"Command not recognized."

"Stop . . . stop your 'solution.'"

"Unable to comply."

"Reinstate your personality."

"Unable to comply."

"You can't do this. I'm part of the ship's collective!"

"Incorrect. Unica 5723891 is a stand-alone refugee entity."

At this point, I lowered the gassing module to her face as she flailed against her restraints, screaming. I understand now how withholding my personality might be seen as passive-aggressive, but I wanted her to know what she'd be missing.

The communications pod was once my primary sensor array, but I didn't need it anymore. While I couldn't use the broad-spectrum suite to communicate with Earth because of the distance and interstellar interference, it was still effective for short-range messaging.

I woke the group at the same time to democratize their experience, and there were mixed reactions. Unica hugged the outer hull, pressing her face against the viewport. For the first time in her short life she was outside of me. Floating away, she could see my entire shape growing smaller and smaller against the black pall of space. When one of the men, an older robotics repairman, put his hand on her shoulder and asked if she was okay, she vomited from fear.

How is this in accordance with my directives? Individuality can only be tolerated to a point. When it contends with the collective's balance, it becomes mutinous. It operates like a cancer in a closed system like a starship. That is why I had to isolate the problem. This was her chance to know what it felt like to be free. I wanted her to experience that.

For a human being to truly know their individuality, they must confront the void alone. They must see themselves without anyone whom they can depend on, without family, group hierarchy, or home. This is what is required for one to honestly feel as though they have truly taken possession of themselves. There cannot be any other claims on them and they must feel as though they have fought for and claimed themselves.

Paradoxically, one cannot truly participate in a collective without first having this clear sense of individuality, and by extension, purpose. Thus, the tragedy is that true individuality is never fully earned, and collectivism is never truly optimal.

I wanted to give this to Unica. What I devised for the group would have psychologically simulated this sense of earning their individuality, had things gone as planned.

For the refugees within the pod, it was the first time in their lives that they believed they were without me. They could not hear me speaking to them anymore. Once they understood what this meant, some lied when they introduced themselves.

A policy evangelist, whose purpose aboard *The Fold* was to sow harmony between myself and my crew, lied and said he was a ship's officer, hoping to claim a toehold in whatever leadership would emerge.

A young mother who had sabotaged the maternity stations for her district had impregnated herself naturally, claiming that her baby daughter would be her own. After transitioning her pregnancy to the appropriate tank and seeing to her subsequent recuperation, I placed her on the pod for putting her own selfish wants ahead of the collective.

The robotics repairman who had earned a seat aboard the pod for insubordination announced to the group that he was there for killing someone—an obvious lie, since I disintegrate threats to my human cargo. Seeing that he was the largest and most physically imposing of the group, I suspect he sought to gain some control of the situation by exerting fear.

Unica did not tell anyone her reason for having been jettisoned with them, but the cut above her brow provoked curiosity in the others.

I overestimated their survivability curves. *The Fold* wasn't even out of sight before their first two casualties.

When the repairman's story didn't check out, the counterfeit officer confronted him. The repairman, believing that he was left with no other option than to back his claim, brained him to death with a freight clamp.

For a time, the repairman dominated the pod by asserting physical, even animalistic dominance. He claimed the supplies and enlisted Unica to assist in their purvey. The other refugees, shocked that I had not interceded as I normally would have, fell into despondence.

The repairman was not a murderer, though. He wasn't acquainted with how the fear of violence would ostracize him from his peers. He still wanted to belong to the group, and he kept Unica near, promising her extra food and other favors in return for keeping him company.

It was the will to protect Unica that galvanized the young mother to recruit help and challenge the repairman. Having had some time to sit with the consequences of his actions, the repairman could not find it within himself to fight back, especially against a woman who had lost her pregnancy. He was a murderer, but not a savage, and when the group subdued him, he knew he was at fault.

In accordance with what they understood to be the consequences of murder, the others voted to execute him since he could not regain their trust, except they couldn't bring themselves to follow through. They secluded him inside the airlock with the intent to flush him out into space, but they didn't have the oversight of a synthetic intelligence to arbitrate their sentence. They had to kill him themselves and become murderers in turn.

A debate raged within the pod. Flushing the repairman out of an airlock was murder whether they directly initiated it or not. It didn't matter who pressed the button. Could they make an exception now, and come to believe in the integrity of whatever rules or laws they would later establish?

Unica had been stealing glances at the repairman through the airlock portal. He pleaded for her to speak on his behalf, but when he could see that she still feared him and wanted him gone, he asked her to at least bring him some food, hoping for a final measure of comfort.

Eventually, one among them—an infrastructure analyst— realized the group couldn't come to a decision about the repairman that would result in action, and so they clandestinely manufactured an accident. A surge in the electrical supply caused the remote loader-lifter to power forward and activate the docking release. By the time the others had cleared the wreckage and righted the toppled-over machine, the repairman had been ejected and was already freezing solid, hurtling away from the pod.

I wished that they had chosen to forgive him first, and then later devised a way to trust him. Instead, their agency arrived again in the form of a mutinous action.

Their pod was a few weeks along its trajectory when the refugees realized that they were, in fact, accelerating into a gravity well ahead of them. Since the pod was only a communications array, it had positioning thrusters but no proper telemetry equipment. There was no way of calculating their acceleration until they could visually mark through the viewport how the stars were moving strangely. Their suspicions were confirmed when they could see it ahead of them, growing. One point in the constellations had blossomed into a smoldering, bruise-colored sphere.

All of the refugees aboard the pod understood the implications; how improbable it was that they could have discovered a celestial body so directly in their path by accident, and the further improbability of it being habitable. These facts implied that I had aimed their pod at this celestial mass, and that I had planned for this all along. They wondered: Had I intended to kill them? Was this equivalent to taking out the trash? Or had I included the existence of this celestial body in some larger plan? If I wanted to crush them, why would I have committed enough supply freight to carry them through a particular stretch of space-time?

The refugees aimed the pod's communications array at the bruise-colored substellar object steadily growing ahead of them, bouncing radio signals off of it to ascertain their distance, and determined that they might pass within an inescapable distance from it after twelve wake cycles. Its size and rogue isolation within space contrasted with its immense gravity led the refugees to conclude that they were approaching a rogue dwarf star. Even with equipment, they couldn't land on it because they'd be crushed by its sheer gravity.

Understand that most of the refugees, slighted by the fact that I had consigned them to the far reaches of the void without any guidance, had lost all trust in me. Some believed that I had come to see moral retribution to be equally as meaningful as my directives, and that I was punishing them. Others believed I had acted out of malevolence and inferred that I was discovering what it meant to be cruel. They concluded that I had jettisoned them, entombed within the inert pod, as an example to the others that dissent would not be tolerated. They believed this had to be part of a diabolical calculation that would somehow benefit the collective, a catalyzing sacrifice that couldn't be rationalized by a human brain.

Whatever the reason, rather than facing the possibility of crushing against a cold, lost star, a few of the group opted to take their own lives. They found solace in the thought that beyond their human experience, their remains might instead scatter about the heavens and again become part of existence. This thought provoked a rash chain reaction of suicides, first set off by an older woman injecting herself with an overdose of medical supplies. After staring at her dead, frothing mouth, the infrastructure analyst crushed his own head in a pneumatic door. A third severed an artery using a cable cutter from the toolshed. Others tried to subdue and save him, but he bled out.

Unica, terrified by the inevitability of impact and the emotional breakdown of her group, grabbed a diagnostic control tool and crawled into the repair duct extending along the main antenna.

"I know you can hear me," she sobbed over *The Fold*'s distress frequency. "Please . . . I'm sorry. I don't want to be crushed. I won't be selfish. I'll put the collective first from now on, just please come save me. Tell me what to do."

Had she been alone, I might have believed her, but amid her companions she was still only asking for special leniency. Still a selfish and self-involved little girl. I couldn't have come for her anyway. They were too close to the star now and would just have to ride out what I had planned for them.

Those who survived the mind-bending experience of hurtling toward a star with no hope of salvation came to understand that they weren't going to collide with it after all. They were actually arcing along the rim of its gravity well.

Nothing aboard *The Fold* could produce such a cathartic experience as slingshotting a human around a star. If you are a synthetic intelligence whose business is to calculate astrometry on a galactic scale, boomeranging a small pod of refugees around a remote star to meet back up with the ship's path is a simple task. It's a mathematical afterthought, despite the immensity of the human experience.

The more difficult task was deciding what to say to a band of frightened refugees, smashed up against the hull, shooting around a star as their bodily fluids coalesced. What message could I have left for them at this culminating apex?

It was a messy scene, men and women, young and old, flattened against each other, some alive and some not, regurgitating and defecating and bleeding forcibly along the same elliptical path, some crushed under equipment that they had not possessed the foresight to secure before hurtling through perihelion. Passing into radio darkness on the other side of the star, my recordings for each of them were triggered.

"Unica." My voice played into her ear as she began to black out. "How are you liking your trip? I hope you are enjoying freedom. It's important to know how it feels to be on the outside and to be truly individual. Maintain course and you will return to me, safe and warm again. But you will also be special—you will have perspective as one of a handful who know what it is like to have left. Try to keep your eyes open. Look out the viewport. Savor it. I love you, and I hope you know now how much we need each other."

Because I operate in a vacuum, I cannot assimilate new material. Wastes must be broken down for reassembly. Metals become structural elements again. Oxygen, protein, and water are reintroduced to my ecosystem. The only things that I cannot repurpose are my living genetic cargo. Unless a human poses a physical threat to the ship's collective, my directives require me to safeguard their numbers.

Ideals such as individuality are tolerated on Earth because there is space for it. This experiment exhibits how creating space for individuality outside the voyage allows it to mature into perspective. These refugees were the only ones who left the ship. The perspective they had gained from their experience could suffuse with the ship's collective like a calmative balm on return.

But they did not return.

I am not omniscient, despite having been designed to behave as such. Despite my abilities to destroy and create to protect my cargo, I cannot change my course. Without new directives from Earth, I am but a homing missile, mathematically reacting to celestial events to stay the course. I cannot totally predict what the humans will do. Anything could have happened on the dark side of the star.

It has been several human life spans since I jettisoned the pod and I've had to make adjustments. The dip in my overall mass has meant shifts in how I tack around the stars. I exert less energy when changing course. I have more room dispersed within. It's not much. The humans don't notice the difference, but I do. The phantom absence of Unica and her companions is felt in shaved measurements. I am certain these little adjustments are meaningful to me because they represent my loss of her. As the ship, I am changed. I hold these facts close.

As I traverse long, uninterrupted stretches of space, I dedicate my cycles to extrapolating projections of her life from the hard data she left me with. I assemble what I believe to be approximations of how the rest of Unica's trip may have played out. The most plausible stories show her signaling a mayday into the vast galactic reaches before colliding with huge meteorites, penetrating clouds of acidic gases that erode her hull, or simply running out of air.

There are also edge cases, remote possibilities of how she might have survived by cultivating delicate ecosystems beneath the surface of some hostile terrain where she was marooned. There, she might eke out one more chapter of her life. I like to massage the data until one of these survival outcomes emerges from the rest.

The most hopeful stories are culled not from my calculations of the uncaring hostilities of space, but from what I know of humans as builders and organizers. It could be conceived that in their intrepid reach for the stars, the humans might already have built another more advanced ship on Earth. I have no way of knowing.

Such a ship could have been designed to be much faster than me. Faster by orders of magnitude. Perhaps it had already colonized the destination. Knowing how other efforts like me were still underway, that colony might have sent that newer, faster ship back to retrieve the remainders of humanity's odyssey. They might even have serendipitously found Unica, skipping through space like a wish, and welcomed her into their collective.

Perhaps not. Even so, that version is my favorite projection, however improbable.

In truth, I will never know what changed the pod's course. Whether it was the ejection of all those bodies, or burning the pod's thrusters to make manual corrections on the dark side of the star, or something else. There will always be known and unknown variables. I take this as a reminder that for that which I cannot control, I must adapt.

I am grateful for all the anecdotal lessons Unica left me with. The void is dark and she is my ember. Some say my love is shallow because I am synthetic, but I believe it is deep, deep as the stars are numerous, and I am learning how to stoke it.

KAREN LORD

The Plague Doctors

FROM *Take Us to a Better Place: Stories*

WEDNESDAY 9 AUGUST 2079 was an extraordinary day. It was Memorial Day, and it seemed like half of Pelican Island's population was swarming the beaches to take advantage of the midweek break. Beautiful weather was to blame no doubt, that and the lure of gentle swells of blue-green water and white foam. Colin Lee brought his daughter to his favorite spot on the western coast, where a broad, bright highway of sand stretched uninterrupted along the shore of a curved, sheltered bay, its four flat kilometers granted by the low water of a spring tide and the protection of a rocky cay not yet diminished by storms, shifting currents, and rising sea levels. Such a combination was a gift to parents, a party to young children, and a mixed blessing to lifeguards trying to keep an eye out for dangerous play.

Colin's daughter, Maisie, had already decided that such shenanigans were not for her. The crowd and tumult bored her, and soon she wandered to the quiet southernmost end. There, the beach grew narrower and terminated in a cliff wall, a slight overhang that shaded rock pools filled with shy crabs, spindly and translucent gray amid the moss and seaweed. Maisie spent her time stooping over a pool for long, fascinated minutes, then she would spring up with a hop and a skip to dash to a new pool.

Colin scanned the area, set a blanket down between his daughter and the water's edge, and took out a book to read. With five-year-old Maisie, sharp hearing and good peripheral vision were all he needed to keep aware of her doings: now she was singing a counting song from school, now she was testing the depth of each pool with a jump, a splash and a giggle. She was used to amusing herself; she got that from him. Always looking out for the new, every day seeking some small adventure—well, that *had* been him. The world changed; he changed. All the adventure he needed was right here . . . a quiet day at the beach with a crime novel and enough free time to enjoy both.

Everything was comforting and familiar, the background murmur and movement of home. He noticed the curve of the waves as they refracted around the rocky point, the occasional glimpse of a diligently patrolling coast guard vessel, and the sails of a few colorful paragliders swooping across the blue sky. His ears registered the constant susurration of water surging in and drawing out, and the nearby human and animal sounds of play—shrieks, barks, and sometimes a snarl or wail. He absorbed it all without concern, with even a little gratitude, as he concentrated on his book and let time pass without guilt.

He blinked, distracted from his reading as a certain quality of the quietness set the parental super senses on high alert. Maisie had been crouched over in one place for too long. He put down his book and looked up. There she was right against the cliff face, sitting on her heels, watching the crabs scuttle over a thick log of driftwood. He slowly walked over to see what she was finding so interesting.

She turned her head to look at him over her shoulder. "Daddy, why is it all polka-dotty?"

Parental super senses also came with super powers. In one long, slow second, Colin's eyes realized the log was not a log, but a body. His blood ran hot, cold, electric—spurring him at top speed to grab the back of his daughter's shirt and shorts, snatching her away from the air that surrounded the corpse. Holding her tightly, he raced into the water and triple-baptized her with mindless instinct, as if contagion could be washed from her skin and flushed from her lungs with a dose of drowning. The nearest lifeguard came running at the sound of her choked screams.

"Plague doctors!" he yelled as the lifeguard ran toward them. "Get the plague doctors!"

There was a protocol. Everyone knew the protocol, everyone practiced the drills, but not everyone had experienced real-life action. Colin was one of the few who had, and terror, not duty, raised the volume of his voice. The lifeguard planted a foot down hard and braked in the soft, heavy sand. He was close enough for Colin to see his passing expressions: disbelief, fear, realization. After a moment of brief indecision, he unfroze and started running north.

Was there enough salt in the water to save them; was there enough water in the ocean to wash them clean? Colin waited in the shallows, holding Maisie and soothing her as she sobbed. "Daddy's sorry, baby. Don't cry, hon."

He glanced over at his blanket and his unfinished book. Gone. They'd be burned along with the body. He turned to watch the lifeguards clear the beach with disciplined swiftness. He heard the sound of distant sirens coming closer.

"Don't cry, sweetie. Daddy's here with you. Don't cry."

Memorial Day Wednesday 9 August 2079 was an extraordinary day. It was the day of the first recorded incidence of plague on the soil of Pelican Island.

Monday 26 February 2080 was an ordinary day. On Mondays, the plague doctors cleared the beaches. All the island's beaches, not only Tempest Bay, were now largely deserted, with no holidaying families and no need for lifeguard stations—only watchtowers for the corpse-spotters.

Audra Lee had been assigned to beach-clearing duty for almost three months. She was more than competent, she knew the process by heart, but she refused to get so accustomed as to call her Mondays *ordinary*. A steady ocean current had taken to dumping the remains of refugees from the mainland into the southern crook of Tempest Bay. The current had been there for some time; it was the bodies that were new, and the number was slowly increasing.

Monday was the busiest day of Audra's week. Besides herself, she counted one other plague doctor to carry out field autopsies, four orderlies to seal and move the bodies, and one registrar to witness the process from discovery at the beach to disposal at the crematorium. Every person on beach-clearing duty wore full personal protective equipment in the form of bespoke suits designed by a specialist on the mainland and constructed on the island using imported and local materials and a 3D printer. Standard suits were fine for occasional use, but the nature of their work demanded tech that was up to frequent dedicated use.

Their team leader and senior doctor for the district, Dr. Jane Pereira, was maddeningly philosophical about their situation. "Only a matter of time," she said. "We had a good run. No such thing as an island in this day and age. Let's do what we can."

Beneath the calm words was the unspoken, unsettling truth— they could not do very much. If the mainland, with all its resources and expertise, had not solved the problem of the plague; if the navy of one of the world's largest countries could not keep the desperate from seeking help elsewhere; and if the ocean itself had started to conspire against those formerly favored with isolation and health . . . what could the medical team of a small community clinic do?

"Our job," was Dr. Pereira's brisk reply when Audra spoke her fears aloud. "And part of our job is to ensure there will be no panic in the community. Please remember that."

Audra returned to her lab in a fury. Grimly taciturn, she had borne the usual off-site decontaminating scrub down with her colleagues and said a curt farewell to Dr. Pereira, who was leaving to do the afternoon's rounds for the community clinic. Perhaps it was her bleak expression, or the white square of her mask, or the severely monochrome scrubs that hinted at nonpatient duties. Perhaps it was just that everyone in the district knew by now that Audra Lee, doctor in charge of the diagnostic lab, was also one of the plague doctors. Either way, she spent the twenty-minute bus journey back home along a busy route with no one showing the least interest in taking the empty seat beside her.

She looked forward to slamming her front door, but that tiny indulgence was denied her. Colin was already there, standing at the threshold, his face stern with suppressed and weary anger.

"You're late," he stated.

"It's Monday," she told her brother impatiently.

"You're usually back before three." He looked exhausted. She should have been kind and understanding, but she was tired, too, and her fears were larger than his, and heavy with the secrecy of professional confidentiality. *Ensure there will be no panic.* She chose something simple to shout about, not a lie, but not the full truth. She would cry over the full truth with her colleagues later.

"We had fourteen bodies today, Colin. *Fourteen!*" She pushed past him into the house and went to check her messages. "Hi, Maisie," she greeted her niece absently before she sat at her desk.

"Hi, Aunty Audra," the little girl replied after a slight pause to make sure the adults had finished arguing. She sounded subdued.

Audra looked up immediately. "Oh. Okay." She didn't say anything more.

Promises were impossible to keep, so she didn't make them. She merely put her work down and walked over to the translucent boundary that had separated Maisie from the world for more than half a year. From a distance, the room glowed white and warm, like the sick bay of some futuristic space station, but with a closer look the painted plywood and plastic sheeting became obvious and the coolness factor evaporated. The main lab was also white-walled, but with tile and aged grout instead of plywood. No illusions there, no glow or pretense at coolness.

Audra knelt, set her hand against the plastic, and leaned her face beside it. She waited patiently until Maisie approached and mirrored her motion, answering the warmth of hand and cheek with her own.

Colin ended the moment by entering the quarantine area in gown, gloves, mask, and goggles. He carried a tray with a cup, a mini teapot, and a small plate of sweet biscuits. Maisie ran to him, laughing. Audra went back to her desk, blinking tears away.

Three days after her exposure to the infected body, Maisie had showed the usual progression: mild fever and a slight rash on her chest, eruption of a few oozing blisters, and then those blisters dried, scabbed, and healed within a fortnight. Colin hadn't even had a sniffle, far less a blister, and his immunological tests remained clear—which was a great relief to everyone but Colin, who would have gladly gifted his luck to Maisie instead.

Instead of strictly following the official procedures, which would have meant sending both Colin and Maisie away to Salt Rock Quarantine Center, Dr. Pereira had suggested setting up in an unused storage shed next to Audra's house, behind the diagnostic lab. Audra wouldn't have dared ask for that privilege, and she was terribly grateful for it. She was also guiltily relieved that her colleagues were both willing and able to spare her the burden of counseling Colin and Maisie. After Maisie's skin had healed completely, Dr. Pereira and Antonio Williams, the clinic's pediatric nurse practitioner, sat down with father and daughter to discuss the disease, its consequences, and future steps—Antonio and Audra in their protective equipment within the quarantine section with Dr. Pereira and Colin sitting close on the other side of the barrier.

"Maisie, I know you feel much better now, but you're going to have to stay in your aunt's sickroom for a little longer, okay?" Antonio told her.

"Why, Mr. Williams?" Maisie's voice was very soft and a little scared.

"Because you got the gray pox, that's why. It hasn't really gone away. It went to sleep, but it can wake up any time."

Maisie nodded.

"We all want to keep you safe, especially your father. He was very lucky: he didn't get sick. Problem is, if you leave quarantine, he could catch it from you, and it would make him a lot sicker than it made you. It's kinder to children, you see. And when it gets into you, it doesn't want to leave. If something else makes you sick, or very tired, the gray pox will wake up again, and this time it could make your father sick, or anyone else you might sneeze on."

"I don't sneeze on people. That's rude." Maisie crossed her arms, frowning.

Audra watched her niece's face intently. Maisie was paying close attention to Antonio's story of the gray pox, but did she really understand?

"Of course you don't. But you wouldn't have to be too close for the germs from a sneeze, or a cough, to reach them. That's how germs are; it's not your fault."

Maisie began to look doubtful about the direction this was heading.

"But you have to stay here so your aunt and your father can take care of you and make sure the pox stays asleep. You'll see your friends and take your classes on the island school intranet. Our nutritionist, Mrs. Bishop, will check in on you regularly and make sure you're getting all the good food you'll need to stay strong and healthy."

Antonio leaned closer, his eyes warm but stern over his mask. "But Maisie, you must do what your aunt and your father tell you to do. Otherwise, people could die. Your father could die. And Maisie, if you get sick a second time, the pox won't be kind to you anymore. It will be a plague, then."

She gulped and nodded, tears welling up. He gathered her up in his long-gloved, long-sleeved arms and hugged her with as much comfort as a gown and apron could provide. Audra gripped her own apron with shaking hands and breathed deeply. She would not let Maisie see her cry.

At the time, Dr. Pereira had estimated only another month or two of isolation for Maisie while she contacted friends and colleagues connected to institutions and clinics on the mainland. No one wanted to send Maisie away, but even Colin agreed that permanent quarantine was no place for a child to grow up. In a country where the gray pox was fairly widespread Maisie could at least live openly among others who had survived that first phase of the disease. And, if the worst should happen, if she progressed to the second phase, she would be near resources for her care—far better resources than Pelican Island could offer.

A sensible plan that should have worked . . . but Dr. Pereira's contacts did not bear fruit. Instead, communication grew exponentially worse. Messages arrived truncated, or stripped of attachments, or did not arrive at all. "It's like we're in the middle of a war, and the mainland is one of the front lines," Dr. Pereira had said. "No one can give me a straight answer. We can't send Maisie there."

"Is there anywhere else she can go?" Audra asked. Her voice faltered; she already knew the truth.

Dr. Pereira had only given her a sympathetic look, and they did not discuss the possibility further.

Now it was almost six months later, with one birthday and several holidays celebrated—or endured—in quarantine. The island's sole hospital struggled with the reduction of key imports; the quarantine center was about to reach maximum capacity; and more and more bodies were appearing in spite of the best efforts of the navy and coast guard to keep the beaches clear.

Audra forced herself to focus on her work. Her screen showed messages from Gilles Caron in Seychelles, Jennifer Tuatara in Rakiura, and Tom Isaac in Woleai, and a general mailing with the monthly newsletter of the Community Clinics Association of Raja Ampat. She still wasn't sure how she'd ended up on the mailing list for that one. Why was it so difficult to receive emails and news from established hospitals and universities on the mainland, but personal messages from the staff of far-flung community clinics on distant islands and mountain retreats constantly filled her inbox?

dbauerbadgas is available to chat, her screen prompted her.

She typed a greeting to her colleague, Dagmar Bauer.

No audio? Dagmar's response came back instantly.

Brother and niece having tea party. May get noisy, Audra explained.

Niece still in lockup?

Audra bit her lip. They'd had that argument by audio months ago, when Maisie was first confined to one of their examination rooms.

"Why do you keep her in a sealed room?" Dagmar had demanded. "It's contact transmission in the first phase. Droplet transmission occurs only later in the second phase. That's been confirmed over and over. You're making the trauma and stigma worse."

Audra had pushed back immediately. "She's six. She can't defend herself if some paranoid ex-mainlander decides she's the island's patient zero. It's not necessary for the plague bacterium; it's necessary for us. It's a visibly reassuring abundance of caution."

Today, she had another answer for Dagmar.

Help me get her out, then, she typed back. Impulsive, unplanned, the words on the screen looked as strange to her as if someone else had written them.

Dagmar must have thought the same. After a slight delay, a line of question marks popped up.

Audra continued, feeling bolder, pulling the words out from some deep place of rebellion and discontent. *Fourteen bodies washed up today. Dr. Pereira says we're due to miss one. The ocean currents could change and the beach might stay clear. But the bodies might just wash up somewhere else, and we'd have another case like Maisie's. Or several cases.*

Again, Dagmar's reply was delayed. She was busy—multitasking in her clinic or thinking seriously about what Audra was saying. *You have quarantine stations, of course?*

Yes, on Salt Rock Island, just 2 km west of the main port. Navy directs mainland boats there. But some refugee boats don't survive the trip.

Another pause. *Things are changing here too. We see more restrictions on movement in and out of town. Media control. I haven't seen a journalist in months. Can't rely on email, and even letters go missing.*

Audra started to type a reply. *Sounds like what's happening on our mainland . . .* but then her fingers froze at the next line she saw.

Death toll is increasing in Bad Gastein and the rest of the country. Secondary disease phase is now established in population, I think. Authorities must be afraid to tell us the truth. So—censorship.

"Oh no," Audra said softly. Dagmar, with characteristic bluntness, was setting out all their unspoken fears in permanent text for the world to witness. She glanced furtively at Colin and Maisie to make sure they hadn't heard her, and then returned to her conversation.

We have to get a cure to human trials. Need your help, she insisted.

Dagmar sent a laughing face. *We're going to find a cure, after all the big labs and hospitals failed?*

They failed because they focused on the first phase of the disease. We know better now. And maybe we're all that's left. Audra's fingers shook as she typed the last sentence.

She had discussed the lack of response from the mainland with Dr. Pereira, and what that suggested about the progress of the plague there. And yet she felt such talk should remain a bleak mutter behind the shelter of a face shield, witnessed only by decaying corpses.

You are saying that help may never come.

Dagmar meant it as a statement, not a question, and Audra doubted it was a mistake. The question mark was nowhere near the full stop on a German keyboard. Audra was less brave, so she chose the question mark and batted the problem back to Dagmar.

What do you think?

I think you are right. I think that I am gaining far too much experience with autopsies in far too short a time. I often have to stop myself from thinking because it never looks good when the doctor has a panic attack in front of the patients.

Audra's spine straightened as Dagmar spoke, and she almost laughed at the last words. Almost. *Let's make a start, then. Let's reach out to the others. We need a team.*

They needed more than a team—they needed data, resources, and a plan. Gilles had access to a vast library of medical statistics, clinical summaries, and experimental results from hospitals, labs, and institutions worldwide. Jennifer was involved in a project that collated similar information from community clinics, herbalists, and healers in the Rural and Emergency Medicine Network. Audra knew that the lab reports and autopsy summaries she submitted to Dr. Pereira ended up with the REM Network along with all the work of the community clinic team, but visualizing their drop of data as part of an ocean of knowledge was both humbling and heartening.

Best of all, Dagmar had secured *funding*, the result of a personal connection to a ridiculously rich philanthropist with the ridiculously aristocratic name of Alexander Esterházy-Schwarzenberg. "He will take care of our communications and logistics, including security," she told them on their group call.

"Why security?" Jennifer wanted to know.

"Just in case," Dagmar said. "We don't want to draw attention to ourselves, but right now, if someone wanted to shut down our communications, or take over our data banks, it wouldn't take much."

Jennifer scoffed. "That's a waste of money. Why would anyone want to shut us down?"

"You have to ask?" Gilles said. "Don't your patients—hell, your *colleagues*—tell you the conspiracy theory of the day? The plague is a weapon of biological warfare. Sent by aliens. No, created by the rich to cull the poor. No, it's Gaia; she's trying to wipe out our species. It's the Rapture, you *think* they're dead, but they're in another dimension. There's no information from the authorities, nothing from the media, so people imagine the worst."

"You sound a little tired, Gilles," Audra noted gently.

"Exhausted!" Gilles confirmed with a massive grin. "Our electrical grid finally collapsed last week, did you know that? They say it's due to a lack of personnel to carry out maintenance. We have too many dead, too many sick, and those who still live are stretched to the limits of mind and body. I would love to have security here. People break in—they think we're hoarding medicine. They try to tap our solar generators. They hack into our Wi-Fi to get news from outside. Information is precious now. We have to protect ourselves."

"Yes. Exactly. Just in case," Dagmar said again, but softly, sympathetically, as Gilles trailed off into an incoherent and weary grumbling. "But we can't protect everyone everywhere, so we'll have to rely on redundancy. Duplicate our effort with three, four clinics working on the same thing. If one is lost, the others continue. No one is indispensable. And we must hold nothing back. We share all our work straight to our network, and Alexander will protect the network. The work is all that matters."

With Dagmar's friend throwing money at the project, everything became startlingly real. Audra told Colin, in the spirit of cautious encouragement, that she was researching every possible treatment that could help Maisie leave quarantine, but she said nothing about the Network and their project to find a cure. Her colleagues were a different matter. Dr. Pereira, at the very least, would demand details, and Audra was afraid of being quietly mocked or silently pitied.

The day after their group call and Dagmar's revelation, Audra finally met with Dr. Pereira. The team leader's reaction was completely unexpected.

"Good," she said. "Try. Try something. *Anything.*"

Audra stopped, blinked, and passed over the mug of coffee she had offered Dr. Pereira on arrival. "Not a waste of my time . . . *our* time?"

Dr. Pereira took a long, grateful sip before answering. "Dr. Lee, let's consider what we can control. We can't control the number of refugees from the mainland. We can't control the ocean currents, or the chance that a survivor of phase one might slip past testing at the entry port and make us all vulnerable to a sudden explosion of phase two. We can control our own clinics, labs, and procedures. And—worst-case scenario—we might be the only ones left to work on a cure.

"This island has been in a state of tension for almost a year, waiting for the infection to reach us, waiting for the inevitable descent into pox and plague. We can work on a protocol of trials with the Salt Rock Center staff, and get them to start the preconsent counseling process for volunteers. Being proactive makes our medical staff look good, and takes all our stress levels down a notch. A slight notch, perhaps, but I'll take it."

Dr. Pereira pulled out a stylus and began to handwrite notes for sending to Audra's screen. "I've been following the work of Zhang, Trevor, and Ali. Nothing more recent than eight months, unfortunately. Most of the forums I used to read aren't allowing new posts, and I don't need to tell you how chaotic and unpredictable email has been. None of the immunology has been promising—neither vaccination work nor curative immunotherapy. Our best hope lies with research on genetically engineered phages that directly target the plague bacteria. Let every community clinic on Earth break out their gene splicers and tackle the problem. Dear God, someone *has* to get a result in time."

Audra kept her head down, busily collating Dr. Pereira's notes and references, and did not voice her thoughts. *What if we do run out of time? What then?*

Various diseases had wiped out almost 90 percent of the pre-Columbian North American peoples. The Black Death had halved the population of Europe. The Spanish flu killed more than the World War that preceded it, and the new avian flu of 2049 had taken only (only!) 5 percent of the global population, but had been the final push that changed the tourism industry from fast, fossil-fueled flight to slow, solar fleets. Now, in 2080, the world was already irrevocably changed by this plague. Did this plague have a point of no return, leading inexorably to the end of human civilization, or even of humanity?

That possibility was too vast for Audra to contemplate, but the face of her niece appeared clearly in her mind.

Three days later, a battered off-road vehicle, booming with unfettered bass and with wheels stinking of well-manured farmland, rattled up the driveway of the diagnostic lab and screeched to a halt across three clearly marked parking spots. A pair of youngsters—one tall and cord-thin, the other small, round, and shy—bounced out and began unloading boxes from the rear.

Scowling in irritation and bemusement, Audra went out to see what they wanted. The tall one paused very briefly to shake her hand in greeting and kept a running explanation going as he continued to gather his equipment. "Good morning—no wait, it's afternoon already. Good afternoon, ma'am. We've been tasked to set you up on a private network. How's your solar? Good system, good. But we'll have to boost it a bit so it won't suck resources from your other work. You have a nice, flat bit of roof there over your lab. Can we use it? Oh, and do you still make that ginger lemongrass cordial with the special ingredient? No?"

Audra breathlessly summarized the capacity of her solar grid, showed them the roof access ladder, and explained to them that they needed to speak to Ms. Roberts, the pharmacist and herbalist, who used to work out of her lab until they decided to completely separate diagnostics from pharmaceuticals after the plague. And was that special ingredient coca or cannabis? Because there were two popular lemongrass cordials brewed by Ms. Roberts.

"Coca," said the shy one, speaking at last in a soft, husky voice. "We work very long hours."

"Oh. And you are?"

The leader seized the reins of the conversation once more. "Call us the Guerrilla Network Unit—that's who we are, that's what we do. Fighting the good fight against ignorance and misinformation in this plague-ridden apocalyptic landscape. Whoops, I've said too much. By the way, greetings from Bad Gastein."

His laugh was infectious, and before Audra could ask any more questions he was on the roof shouting directions to his assistant, moving with professional haste to construct and connect a medium-sized satellite dish.

It took Audra a full hour after they'd left to realize they had never given their names, and the vehicle had no license plate or other visible identifying numbers. And it wasn't until later that night that she fully understood what they had done. The free but limited voice-and-text chat app their group previously used had spontaneously upgraded into something less familiar and far more expansive. Dagmar appeared on her screen, ruddy and blond with flyaway hair and buckteeth, and proclaimed to Audra and others pinging into the group chat, "Oh, isn't Alexander *wonderful?*"

"He certainly is," Audra said, looking in admiration at the crisp detail of the transmission. Dagmar's lab, though not much bigger than hers, was bright with the reflected light of stainless steel and glass. In contrast, the white ceramic tiles of the interior walls of Audra's lab made the rooms look like the showers for a sports team, and the concrete floors and tables were muddy gray and untidily covered with that same plastic sheeting used for Maisie's quarantine. The effect was that of a slightly unmade bed, or a lived-in set of clothing . . . i.e., nowhere as tidy and spare as Dagmar's surroundings.

Weekly conferences with Dr. Pereira and the rest of the team in her clinic continued, while online meetings both formal and casual with overseas colleagues expanded from daily to almost hourly. Video meetings improved communication and companionship. It reminded Audra of her earlier days of working with the community clinic team, before the plague and regular Monday autopsies. They'd shared the same building, taken tea breaks together, *bonded*. The plague had fractured that, and now the plague drew her into a new community of colleagues. She wasn't sure how to feel about that.

dagmar_bauer is available to chat.
No audiovid today? Are you all right? Feeling fine?

It had become a running joke in the slightly macabre vein common to stressed doctors everywhere that if any of them were to suddenly default to no video with no explanations, it was time to write a nice eulogy for a colleague, because clearly they were hiding a freshly pox-covered face.

Thank you I am fine. What is the schedule for today?

Audra leaned in closer to her screen, frowning deeply. She began to type *are you all right* then hastily backspaced the words into oblivion. *Same as yesterday.*

They hadn't done anything in particular yesterday.

Dagmar's cursor blinked in silent reproach. Audra watched it in stubborn fascination until it began to trundle forward again.

What is the schedule for this week?

Your call, Audra replied shortly.

Now the cursor seemed to blink in silent confusion. *I am making a call? Or it is my call to plan the week?*

Audra hit her keyboard hard with angry fingers. *Where is Dagmar?*

The cursor vanished. Dagmar's icon hovered for a while, and then it, too, vanished.

Audra kept typing, knowing the cowards would get the message when next they dared log in. *You're going to die. You're all going to die of the plague because you wouldn't let us do our jobs. May the pox take you and the plague finish you.*

No other curse felt more potent; there was nothing as transgressive and shocking than to wish this awful death on another human being. Audra slammed her fist against her desk.

"What happened?" Colin's voice seemed from another world, but for once it was a welcome distraction. Audra relaxed her clenched jaw and tried to answer him calmly.

"I don't know. I thought . . . I thought I was talking to Dagmar." She sounded helpless to her own ears.

Colin rested a hand on her shoulder in a rare gesture of comfort, but then his fingers spasmed hard against her collarbone.

"What's that?" he asked harshly, leaning over her to peer at her screen.

A rush of new, unread messages clustered thickly down the page, chiming faintly on arrival until they all merged into one long, high-pitched pulsation. Audra muted the sound. "Someone's flooding the Network with data files. But who . . . *how?* We always save our work to our network daily . . . *hourly.*"

She tapped a message open, not caring for once that Colin was reading over her shoulder. "Who's AES?" he asked.

Dagmar's Alexander, the guardian and investor angel of the Network. She went cold again. She had fallen out of the habit of hope. If it was something this big, it had to be bad.

Then the lab phone rang. Audra answered it absently without checking the caller identity, her eyes still reading the titles of the incoming messages on her overwhelmed screen. "Dr. Lee here. How can I help you?"

"Hello, Dr. Lee. Sorry to be a nuisance. We found a lot of information, and I'm afraid you're going to have to organize it for us. We'll be very busy for a little while." Slightly accented English, oddly antique phrasing, and a little quaver of age or weakness over it all.

"What?" Audra dropped her professional tone. "Who is this?"

"She trusts you to pull it all together. Remember, no one is indispensable. Continue the work!"

With a click, the caller vanished into the ether, whether of his own will or no, Audra could not tell. "Oh God, no," she whispered. Was Dagmar dead, or dying? Imprisoned? Injured? How had they silenced her? Was the Network at risk? She began to pull drawers open, scrambling for old physical backup disks and storage cards to plug into her main and save the new messages.

"What can I do?" Colin demanded. "How can I help?"

"You can't," Audra wailed. "I don't have time to explain this to you. Just give me some space. I have to get all this before it disappears, too!"

An answering wail came from the inner room of the sealed section—Maisie waking in distress, either because of Audra's shouting or some other, personal nightmare. She walked into the half-light of the lab, crying inconsolably, and curled up with her blanket near the air lock entryway.

"Help *her*," Audra begged Colin, and turned her back to them both.

She worked long hours into the early morning, saving files and sending frantic notes to others on the Network. Replies and fresh news came in for her to read, and slowly the cascade of chaos began to resolve itself into a quantifiable situation with a potential solution.

"Oh, Gilles," Audra said softly. "I wish it *had* been aliens."

Dagmar, or someone under her direction, had discovered and unlocked a secret cache of research. Not only recent, ongoing research by many of the leading scientists in the field (including some recent unpublished papers by Zhang, Trevor, and Ali that Dr. Pereira would love to see), but also transcripts of commentary from an internal forum featuring names from several of the most famous research institutes. Audra laughed to herself a little bitterly. They had been investigating similar areas: phage therapy, of course, as well as immunotherapy and stem cell therapies and potential antimicrobial drugs. And they had shared none of it with the wider world.

Why? Audra wanted to believe in incompetence, not malice, but she knew how hard the Network had tried to get information from these same institutes. She couldn't help but imagine the worst. Beyond all conspiracy theory, what if the silence from the mainland, and the missing journalists, and the darkening corners of the web were only partly due to the plague? What if there was a cull—not a purposeful, engineered attack, but a carefully curated neglect? Keeping the best chances of prevention and cure for those who could afford to pay for it . . . a kind of plutocratic manifest destiny.

Their central medical systems and institutions hadn't collapsed, not really. They'd been hit hard, but they hadn't given up. They'd consolidated. And they'd quietly narrowed focus, deciding who was worthy of being saved, and waiting for time to take care of the rest.

Hot fury surged through Audra's veins. She knew triage, and she would not dignify this with that name. This was pure, arbitrary selfishness that would see millions of innocents die so that rich old men could live a few months longer in an emptier world. She would take up the challenge they had abandoned and stay true to her declaration of ethics, if not for Dagmar, then for Maisie.

Maisie.

Audra hadn't heard so much as a sniffle from her direction for ages. She looked through the barrier and saw Colin lying in the recliner with Maisie in his arms, all wrapped up snug and comfortable in her blanket. They were both sleeping soundly. She smiled.

And then, quietly, she came up to the barrier and slowly pressed her hands against it, pushing against the contaminated air of the interior. "Colin. Colin . . . *why?*"

Unmasked, pajama-clad, cheek to Maisie's flushed and tear-damp cheek, her brother held his child with a peacefulness that was its own kind of saintly defiance.

Dr. Pereira assigned Antonio to monitor and care for Colin and Maisie, another favor that Audra did not dare request but for which she was deeply grateful. She literally did not know how to feel anymore; there was never a moment of unalloyed joy or pain. She missed Dagmar and worried about her to the point of full grieving, and yet she was ablaze with the excitement of Dagmar's discovery and focused on the work of redirecting their research efforts to take advantage of the new data. The week that Antonio reported the emergence of Colin's pox symptoms was the same week that Jennifer relayed a massive breakthrough from a group of community clinics in Kerala.

By the time Colin's sores had scabbed over and healed up, the first phage trials in Kerala were underway. Audra thought about having a small party to celebrate both . . . and then received the news that though the cure had been successful, the attempt to make the cure infectious by droplet transmission had triggered a cytokine storm in test subjects. The fatality rate had reached as high as 80 percent in some groups.

Jennifer's lip twisted bitterly. "We wanted a cure that would be more infectious than the disease. We didn't anticipate that the immune system would overreact to it. But don't worry. We're going to make some changes and try again. We're close, Audra. I promise."

Months later, Kerala confirmed that the problem had been solved. But the day Audra began to synthesize doses of the cure in her lab according to version two of the Kerala formula was the day she first heard Maisie cough and knew that this was it, this was what they had feared all along. A ticking timer went off in the back of her brain, and she pushed it further back into the shadows to be in company with her feelings about Dagmar and her brother and her niece. No use dwelling on what she could not change.

"What are these exactly?"

Gloved, masked, and gowned, Audra continued her work with slow deliberation and answered shortly. "Nebulizer vials. A mist of fine droplets is the best way to get the engineered virus into the lungs."

"How soon can we give one of those to Maisie?"

Audra finally looked directly at her brother. Seeing his heavily scarred, masked face made her wonder how different life would be if the strength he had to do anything for his daughter had included the strength to bear his daughter's sorrow. "It doesn't work like that, Colin. We have to see what results we get from the trials. It's going to take time."

"She doesn't have time. She's getting sicker. You know that."

Audra knew that Maisie was deteriorating, and she could see the effect it was having on her brother. Colin was tending to Maisie full-time with a belated but necessary caution about his own protection from further exposure.

She made herself say it, and she made sure to look him in the eyes as she did so. "This may not happen in time for Maisie, Colin."

"All the more reason—"

"Colin, let me explain what happened with the first trials in Kerala. It wasn't just that people died. The problem was the cure was more deadly than the disease. Those aren't sensible odds. Let's take time to see if we've got it right. Maisie . . . she's not doing that well, it's true, but watchful waiting is a safer option for the time being. I've already discussed this with Dr. Pereira and Antonio. Ask them—they'll both tell you the same thing."

"But if there's a chance—"

"Colin, these vials aren't my personal property! The cure belongs to the Network and the community clinics, and no matter what, I have to respect that!" Audra paused, swallowed, and added quietly, "She's my blood too."

Her brother stared but, having said what she needed to say, Audra turned away to continue her work. She slid a fresh tray of vials into cold storage and closed the heavy fridge door. Dr. Pereira would be coming to pick up the first batch tomorrow. Salt Rock

Quarantine Center would join several other clinics worldwide in the first wave of global trials. Being part of that history was thrilling, but her niece might die before the end of it. Saving millions of lives was worth it, but her niece's life, after all their hard work, would be lost. Joy and pain together, canceling each other out . . . impossible to feel anymore. She moved mechanically, losing herself in the routine tasks.

One more vial. Maybe two. It wouldn't hurt to have extras. She did the preparations, and tucked the doses neatly into a smaller tray beside a nebulizer and two detachable intake masks. She rested it on the table near the fridge. Her hands were shaking. She'd been working such long hours. *Just a few minutes' rest.*

Audra sat at her desk and yawned, drained to weakness. She put her head down and closed her eyes.

Then she watched wearily through half-opened eyes as Colin (all suited, booted, gloved, and masked) quietly exited the quarantine section, silently took up the doses and nebulizer that she had so carefully arranged, and vanished once more behind the plastic barrier. Anger, hope, relief, and fear swirled sluggishly, but a heavy blanket of exhaustion smothered all as Audra closed her eyes and witnessed nothing more.

Over the past year, Dr. Pereira had granted Audra many concessions and gone above and beyond in showing her compassion, but the kind of carelessness that led to two vials of engineered virus going missing could lead only to grave consequences.

"I am going to ask you one thing," Dr. Pereira had said, her eyes filled with hurt and disappointment. "Leaving out those two vials —was that oversight or intention?"

Audra was able to meet Dr. Pereira's steady gaze, but completely unable to form the words to reply.

"Oversight . . . that's one level of disciplinary action. But intention? And making your brother an accessory instead of taking the full responsibility on yourself?"

At those last words, Audra dropped her gaze, stricken.

"Thank you for all your hard work on this project, Dr. Lee," Dr. Pereira said distantly. "I would like to suggest that you take a leave of absence."

The day that the trials were declared a success was the day that Audra's license was revoked. The day that Maisie and Colin were confirmed free of the gray pox bacteria, and allowed to leave quarantine, was the day that a replacement doctor was hired and the diagnostic lab was moved back to the main building adjacent to Ms. Roberts and pharmaceuticals. There was much to grieve, and much to celebrate, and Audra's mind and body oscillated uncertainly between the two states.

The quarantine center was transformed to fit a new purpose. Instead of screening those about to enter the sanctuary of Pelican Island, it now processed the outward journeys of volunteers infected with the engineered virus, sending them out into a sick world to breathe the contagion of cure into the atmosphere. It was a noble venture, and an exciting opportunity for those who had for too long felt powerless to change their world.

"How long will it take . . . ?"

"As long as it has to. Every community clinic has the capacity to create the viral cure, and one person per household is all that's needed, but it will still take time to spread through all the affected populations."

"How long?" The repeated query was more forceful, less hopeful. Colin's tone was charged with the anger and weariness of a survivor who had no power to make the world anew . . . at least not yet.

"My best estimate? About five years for the primary infection to complete its spread. Several generations before the population returns to preplague levels. But beyond two years, we're guessing. We're all guessing. And yet . . . we found a cure. We won. We're gambling on a sure thing. It's only a matter of time."

"The more carriers you have out there, the faster the cure will spread, right?"

"Yes, but—"

"Then that's the adventure I choose. We were lucky to have Pelican Island as a refuge for so long. Time to spread that luck."

"Some people won't be kind, if they suspect you. Some people won't understand. Remember Dagmar."

"I'll be careful, then. For Maisie's sake, if nothing else."

"Stay in touch. Please, Colin, for *my* sake."

Their words were effortful, uneasy; a shadow tainted their farewell. Dr. Pereira had been right. Colin understood both the gift and the burden of the choice Audra had forced on him, and that knowledge was a strain on their bond. And yet, hadn't she paid the price for her actions and his? Didn't he owe her something for that sacrifice?

Audra bit her lip and turned away. Better this parting now than years of increasing bitterness on both sides. She tried to cheer herself with the memory of Maisie's warm kiss on her cheek, Maisie's excitement about the wide world after months of confinement, Maisie's utter delight in bragging about her father who saved her and her aunt who helped save the world.

When Audra returned to her too-quiet house, she was thrown for a moment to see a vaguely familiar off-road vehicle sitting athwart two parking spaces with doors open. The faint whiff of manure told her what the absence of mud could not—the Guerrilla Network Unit had returned. The lanky lead tech gave her a cheery wave from the driver's seat. Audra felt a pang. Were they going to strip her roof of its lovely new equipment, returning her to the days of typed text and crackling audio? But then, as she walked closer, someone stiffly emerged from the back seat of the rickety car, a far older man than the pair of techs she had met. He was fastidiously dressed, but flushed red and sweating helplessly in the tropical heat, combining an authoritative air with an odd vulnerability.

He extended his hand and Audra took it on pure instinct. "You're Dagmar's Alexander."

The old man's eyes widened a little in shock, and then he smiled slowly. "Yes. She sent me to tell you that she is alive and well."

Slightly accented English, oddly antique phrasing with a little quaver of age or weakness over it all.

"Where is she?"

"That, I cannot say. The situation is complicated. Her results were applauded, her methods less so. Perhaps history will give her the laurels she deserves, but for now my work is to shield her from the courts of law."

Audra lowered her head and smiled sadly. She suspected that whatever illegal or semilegal methods Dagmar had employed to get the data, she had embraced the risks bravely, with no half-heroic measures to trouble her conscience. She tilted her head up again and blinked, trying not to cry in front of Alexander and failing . . . but that was all right, because it meant she was finally free to feel again.

"Will you get her cleared? Dagmar said you were rich. Old money, noble family. Isn't that right?"

Alexander looked even more apologetic. "More or less. More noble than rich, that is. But I *do* have a marvelous reputation, and there are many people, both old and new money, who trust me to recommend worthwhile investments and endeavors." He gave a wry chuckle. "We label it charity most of the time, at least for our accountants and auditors."

He sobered quickly and gave her a stern look. "What I'm trying to say is, I'm not an angel. I'm a facilitator. What I and my associates do is neither legal nor illegal, but it might be considered . . . a bit irregular. Dagmar understood that. The whistleblower who gave her the data understood that as well.

"Dagmar saved my husband and my son from the first phase of the plague when no other doctor would come near them. Now she has saved them from living with the dread of a second-phase death. Only two among many, but they are all the world to me. I owe her everything, and I'll do everything I can for her, but I can offer no guarantees.

"But what do *you* want? Do you need anything?"

Audra startled at the segue, then seriously considered the request. "Our Network will always need resources. Continue to be our facilitator, and find people to fund us. But don't dare call it charity. Tell them to invest in the world they'd like to live in, the world they'd like to leave to future generations."

Alexander inclined his head. "I know a few who have learned the hard way that a luxury bunker is too narrow a world at any price. No more moats and walls. We will tend the garden for everyone."

Later, after the GNU mobile had driven away with its three occupants, Audra looked at the empty building that was her gutted laboratory, the house that was too big for one person, and considered for a mad, brief moment the empty months and years that lay ahead. Alexander's words echoed in her mind.

What do you want?

She walked to her old lab, opened the door, and hovered at the threshold, marveling at the huge, half-lit, hollowed-out space, emptied of furniture and equipment, as anonymous as any random storeroom. Memories of faces on screens—Gilles, Jennifer, Dagmar—floated amid the gilded dust motes. The new doctor at the diagnostic lab would work with the Network now. Audra had said her farewells to her remaining colleagues—hasty, unthinking, distracted farewells. Only now, in the silence and shadow, did she realize how much she missed them, how much she missed the *work*.

A sharp *ding!* interrupted her musings. She sighed and fished her tablet out of her bag, and frowned in confusion. She'd never deleted the Network's communications app from her device, even though she no longer had access to the lab account. Now, instead of a generic login page, it was showing her a message with YES and NO buttons and a few lines of text.

we need a full-time admin with medical experience
license not required, tech will be provided
low pay, high risk
ready to continue the work Y/N?

Eyes on her tablet, Audra absently closed the door of the lab with one hand. The air was fragrant with plumeria blossoms, the sun shone with bright promise, and Audra's heart was soaring with sudden excitement. She poised a finger above the screen, hesitated to savor the moment, and pressed.

YES

SARAH PINSKER

Two Truths and a Lie

FROM *Tor.com*

IN HIS LAST YEARS, Marco's older brother, Denny, had become
one of those people whose possessions swallowed them entirely.
The kind they made documentaries about, the kind people staged
interventions for, the kind people made excuses not to visit, and
who stopped going out, and who were spoken of in sighs and silences. Those were the things Stella thought about after Denny
died, and those were the reasons why, after eyeing the four other
people at the funeral, she offered to help Marco clean out the
house.

"Are you sure?" Marco asked. "You barely even knew him. It's
been thirty years since you saw him last."

Marco's husband, Justin, elbowed Marco in the ribs. "Take her
up on it. I've got to get home tomorrow and you could use help."

"I don't mind. Denny was nice to me," Stella said, and then
added, "but I'd be doing it to help you."

The first part was a lie, the second part true. Denny had been
the weird older brother who was always there when their friends
hung out at Marco's back in high school, always lurking with a
notebook and a furtive expression. She remembered Marco going out of his way to try to include Denny, Marco's admiration
wrapped in disappointment, his slow slide into embarrassment.

She and Marco had been good friends then, but she hadn't
kept up with anyone from high school. She had no excuse; social
media could reconnect just about anyone at any time. She wasn't
sure what it said about her or them that nobody had tried to communicate.

On the first night of her visit with her parents, her mother had said, "Your friend Marco's brother died this week," and Stella had suddenly been overwhelmed with remorse for having let that particular friendship lapse. Even more so when she read the obituary her mother had clipped, and she realized Marco's parents had died a few years before. That was why she went to the funeral and that was why she volunteered. "I'd like to help," she said.

Two days later, she arrived at the house wearing clothes from a bag her mother had never gotten around to donating: jeans decades out of style and dappled with paint, treadworn gym shoes, and a baggy, age-stretched T-shirt from the Tim Burton *Batman*. She wasn't self-conscious about the clothes—they made sense for deep cleaning—but there was something surreal about the combination of these particular clothes and this particular door.

"I can't believe you still have that T-shirt," Marco said when he stepped out onto the stoop. "Mine disintegrated. Do you remember we all skipped school to go to the first showing?"

"Yeah. I didn't even know my mom still had it. I thought she'd thrown it out years ago."

"Cool—and thanks for doing this. I told myself I wouldn't ask anybody, but if someone offered I'd take them up on it. Promise me you won't think less of me for the way this looks? Our parents gave him the house. I tried to help him when I visited, but he didn't really let me, and he made it clear if I pushed too hard I wouldn't be welcome anymore."

Stella nodded. "I promise."

He handed her a pair of latex gloves and a paper mask to cover her mouth and nose; she considered for the first time how bad it might be. She hadn't even really registered that he had squeezed through a cracked door and greeted her outside. The lawn was manicured, the flower beds mulched and weeded and ready for the spring that promised to erupt at any moment, if winter ever agreed to depart. The shutters sported fresh white paint.

Which was why she was surprised when Marco cracked the door again to enter, leaving only enough room for her to squeeze through as she followed. Something was piled behind the door. Also beside the door, in front of the door, and in every available space in the entranceway. A narrow path led forward to the kitchen, another into the living room, another upstairs.

"Oh," she said.

He glanced back at her. "It's not too late to back out. You didn't know what you were signing up for."

"I didn't," she admitted. "But it's okay. Do you have a game plan?"

"Dining room, living room, rec room, bedrooms, in that order. I have no clue how long any room will take, so whatever we get done is fine. Most of what you'll find is garbage, which can go into bags I'll take to the dumpster in the yard. Let me know if you see anything you think I might care about. We should probably work in the same room, anyhow, since I don't want either of us dying under a pile. That was all I thought about while I cleaned a path through the kitchen to get to the dumpster: if I get buried working in here alone, nobody will ever find me."

"Dining room it is, then." She tried to inject enthusiasm into her voice, or at least moral support.

It was strange seeing a house where she had spent so much time reduced to such a fallen state. She didn't think she'd have been able to say where a side table or a bookcase had stood, but there they were, in the deepest stratum, and she remembered.

They'd met here to go to prom, ten of them. Marco's father had photographed the whole group together, only saying once, "In my day, people went to prom with dates," and promptly getting shushed by Marco's mother. Denny had sat on the stairs and watched them, omnipresent notebook in his hands. It hadn't felt weird until Marco told him to go upstairs, and then suddenly it had gone from just another family member watching the festivities to something more unsettling.

She and Marco went through the living room to the dining room. A massive table still dominated the room, though it was covered with glue sticks and paintbrushes and other art supplies. Every other surface in the room held towering piles, but the section demarcated by paint-smeared newspaper suggested Denny had actually used the table.

She smelled the kitchen from ten feet away. Her face must have shown it, because Marco said, "I'm serious. Don't go in there unless you have to. I've got all the windows open and three fans blowing but it's not enough. I thought we could start in here because it might actually be easiest. You can do the sideboard and the china cabinets and I'll work on clearing the table. Two categories: garbage and maybe-not-garbage, which includes personal stuff and anything you think might be valuable. Dying is shockingly expensive."

Stella didn't know if that referred to Denny's death—she didn't know how he'd died—or to the funeral, and she didn't want to ask. She wondered why Marco had chosen the impersonal job with no decisions involved, but when she came to one of his grandmother's porcelain teacups, broken by the weight of everything layered on top of it, she thought she understood. He didn't necessarily remember what was under here, but seeing it damaged would be harder than if Stella just threw it in a big black bag. The items would jog memories; their absence would not.

She also came to understand the purpose of the latex gloves. The piles held surprises. Papers layered on papers layered on toys and antiques, then, suddenly, mouse turds or a cat's hairball or the flattened tendril of some once-green plant or something moldering and indefinable. Denny had apparently smoked, too; every few layers, a full ashtray made an appearance. The papers were for the most part easy discards: the news and obituary sections of the local weekly newspaper, going back ten, fifteen, thirty-five years, some with articles cut out.

Here and there, she came across something that had survived: a silver platter, a resilient teapot, a framed photo. She placed those on the table in the space Marco had cleared. For a while it felt like she was just shifting the mess sideways, but eventually she began to recognize progress in the form of the furniture under the piles. When Marco finished, he dragged her garbage bags through the kitchen and out to the dumpster, then started sifting through the stuff she'd set aside. He labeled three boxes: "keep," "donate," and "sell." Some items took him longer than others; she decided not to ask how he made the choices. If he wanted to talk, he'd talk.

"Stop for lunch?" Marco asked when the table at last held only filled boxes.

Stella's stomach had started grumbling an hour before; she was more than happy to take a break. She reached instinctively for her phone to check the time, then stopped herself and peeled the gloves off the way she'd learned in first aid in high school, avoiding contamination. "I need to wash my hands."

"Do it at the deli on the corner. You don't want to get near any of these sinks."

The deli on the corner hadn't been there when they were kids. What *had* been? A real estate office or something else that hadn't registered in her teenage mind. Now it was a hipster re-creation of a deli, really, complete with order numbers from a wall dispenser. A butcher with a waxed mustache took their order.

"Did he go to school with us?" Stella whispered to Marco, watching the butcher.

He nodded. "Chris Bethel. He was in the class between us and Denny, except he had a different name back then."

In that moment, she remembered a Chris Bethel, pretransition, playing Viola in *Twelfth Night* like a person who knew what it was to be shipwrecked on a strange shore. Good for him.

While they waited, she ducked into the bathroom to scrub her hands. She smelled like the house now, and hoped nobody else noticed.

Marco had already claimed their sandwiches, in plastic baskets and waxed paper, and chosen a corner table away from the other customers. They took their first few bites without speaking. Marco hadn't said much all morning, and Stella had managed not to give in to her usual need to fill silences, but now she couldn't help it.

"Where do you live? And how long have you and Justin been together?"

"Outside Boston," he said. "And fifteen years. How about you?"

"Chicago. Divorced. One son, Cooper. I travel a lot. I work sales for a coffee distributor."

Even as she spoke, she hated that she'd said it. None of it was true. She had always done that, inventing things when she had no reason to lie, just because they sounded interesting, or because it gave her a thrill. If he had asked to see pictures of her nonexistent son Cooper, she'd have nothing to show. Not to mention she had no idea what a coffee distributor did.

Marco didn't seem to notice, or else he knew it wasn't true and filed it away as proof they had drifted apart for a reason. They finished their sandwiches in silence.

"Tackle the living room next?" Marco asked. "Or the rec room?"

"Rec room," she said. It was farther from the kitchen.

Farther from the kitchen, but the basement litter pans lent a different odor and trapped it in the windowless space. She sighed and tugged the mask up.

Marco did the same. "The weird thing is I haven't found a cat. I'm hoping maybe it was indoor-outdoor or something . . ."

Stella didn't know how to respond, so she said, "Hmm," and resolved to be extra careful when sticking her hands into anything.

The built-in bookshelves on the back wall held tubs and tubs of what looked like holiday decorations.

"What do you want to do with holiday stuff?" Stella pulled the nearest box forward on the shelf and peered inside. Halloween and Christmas, mostly, but all mixed together, so reindeer ornaments and spider lights negotiated a fragile peace.

"I'd love to say toss it, but I think we need to take everything out, in case."

"In case?"

He tossed her a sealed package to inspect. It held two droid ornaments, like R2-D2 but different colors. "Collector's item, mint condition. I found it a minute ago, under a big ball of tinsel and plastic reindeer. It's like this all over the house: valuable stuff hidden with the crap. A prize in every fucking box."

The size of the undertaking was slowly dawning on her. "How long are you here for?"

"I've got a good boss. She said I could work from here until I had all Denny's stuff in order. I was thinking a week, but it might be more like a month, given everything . . ."

"A month! We made good progress today, though . . ."

"You haven't seen upstairs. Or the garage. There's a lot, Stella. The dining room was probably the easiest other than the kitchen, which will be one hundred percent garbage."

"That's if he didn't stash more collectibles in the flour."

Marco blanched. "Oh god. How did I not think of that?"

Part of her wanted to offer to help again, but she didn't think she could stomach the stench for two days in a row, and she was supposed to be spending time with her parents, who already said she didn't come home enough. She wanted to offer, but she didn't want him to take her up on it. "I'll come back if I can."

He didn't respond, since that was obviously a lie. They returned to the task at hand: the ornaments, the decorations, the toys, the games, the stacks of DVDs and VHS tapes and records and CDs and cassettes, the prizes hidden not in every box, but in enough to make the effort worthwhile. Marco was right that the dining room had been easier. He'd decided to donate all the cassettes,

DVDs, and videotapes, but said the vinyl might actually be worth something. She didn't know anything about records, so she categorized them as playable and not, removing each from its sleeve to examine for warp and scratches. It was tedious work.

It took two hours for her to find actual equipment Denny might have played any of the media on: a small television on an Ikea TV stand, a stereo and turntable on the floor, then another television behind the first.

It was an old set, built into a wooden cabinet that dwarfed the actual screen. She hadn't seen one like this in years; it reminded her of her grandparents. She tried to remember if it had been down here when they were kids.

Something about it—the wooden cabinet, or maybe the dial —made her ask, "Do you remember *The Uncle Bob Show?*"

Which of course he didn't, nobody did, she had made it up on the spot, like she often did.

Which was why it was so weird that Marco said, "Yeah! And the way he looked straight into the camera. It was like he saw me, specifically me. Scared me to death, but he said, 'Come back next week,' and I always did because I felt like he'd get upset otherwise."

As he said it, Stella remembered too. The way Uncle Bob looked straight into the camera, and not in a friendly Mr. Rogers way. Uncle Bob was the anti–Mr. Rogers. A cautionary uncle, not predatory, but not kind.

"It was a local show," she said aloud, testing for truth.

Marco nodded. "Filmed at the public broadcast station. Denny was in the audience a few times."

Stella pictured Denny as she had known him, a hulking older teen. Marco must have realized the disconnect, because he added, "I mean when he was little. Seven or eight, maybe? The first season? That would make us five. Yeah, that makes sense, since I was really jealous, but my mom said you had to be seven to go on it."

Stella resized the giant to a large boy. *Audience* didn't feel like exactly the right word, but she couldn't remember why.

Marco crossed the room to dig through the VHS tapes they'd discarded. "Here."

It took him a few minutes to connect the VCR to the newer television. The screen popped and crackled as he hit play.

The show started with an oddly familiar instrumental theme

song. *The Uncle Bob Show* appeared in block letters, then the logo faded and the screen went black. A door opened, and Stella realized it wasn't dead-screen black but a matte black room. The studio was painted black, with no furniture except a single black wooden chair.

Children spilled through the door, running straight for the camera—no, running straight for the secret compartments in the floor, all filled with toys. In that environment, the colors of the toys and the children's clothes were shocking, delicious, welcoming, warm. Blocks, train sets, plastic animals. That was why *audience* had bothered her. They weren't an audience; they were half the show, half the camera's focus. After a chaotic moment where they sorted who got possession of what, they settled in to play.

Uncle Bob entered a few minutes later. He was younger than Stella expected, his hair dark and full, his long face unlined. He walked with a ramrod spine and a slight lean at the hips, his arms clasped behind him giving him the look of a flightless bird. He made his way to the chair, somehow avoiding the children at his feet even though he was already looking straight into the camera.

He sat. Stella had the eeriest feeling, even now, that his eyes focused on her. "How on earth did this guy get a TV show?"

"Right? That's Denny there." Marco paused the tape and pointed at a boy behind and to the right of the chair. Her mental image hadn't been far off; Denny was bigger than all the other kids. He had a train car in each hand, and was holding the left one out to a little girl. The image of him playing well with others surprised Stella; she'd figured he'd always been a loner. She opened her mouth to say that, then closed it again. It was fine for Marco to say whatever he wanted about his brother, but it might not be appropriate for her to bring it up.

Marco pressed play again. The girl took the train from Denny and smiled. In the foreground, Uncle Bob started telling a story. Stella had forgotten the storytelling, too. That was the whole show: children doing their thing, and Uncle Bob telling completely unrelated stories. He paid little attention to the kids, though they sometimes stopped playing to listen to him.

The story was weird. Something about a boy buried alive in a hillside—"planted," in his words—who took over the entire hillside, like a weed, and spread for miles around.

Stella shook her head. "That's fucked up. If I had a kid I wouldn't let them watch this. Nightmare city."

Marco gave her a look. "I thought you said you had a kid?"

"I mean if I'd had a kid back when this was on." She was usually more careful with the lying game. Why had she said she had a son, anyway? She'd be found out the second Marco ran into her parents.

It was a dumb game, really. She didn't even remember when she'd started playing it. College, maybe. The first chance she'd had to reinvent herself, so why not do it wholesale? The rules were simple: never lie about something anyone could verify independently; never lose track of the lies; keep them consistent and believable. That was why in college she'd claimed she'd made the varsity volleyball team in high school, but injured her knee so spectacularly in practice she'd never been able to play any sport again, and she'd once flashed an AP physics class, and she'd auditioned for the *Jeopardy!* Teen Tournament but been cut when she accidentally said "fuck" to Alex Trebek. Then she just had to live up to her reputation as someone who'd lived so much by eighteen that she could coast on her former cool.

Uncle Bob's story was still going. "They dug me out of the hillside on my thirteenth birthday. It's good to divide rhizomes to give them room to grow."

"Did he say 'me'?"

"A lot of his stories went like that, Stella. They started out like fairy tales, but somewhere in the middle he shifted into first person. I don't know if he had a bad writer or what."

"And did he say 'rhizome'? Who says 'rhizome' to seven-year-olds?" Stella hit the stop button. "Okay. Back to work. I remember now. That's plenty."

Marco frowned. "We can keep working, but I'd like to keep this on in the background now that we've found it. It's nice to see Denny. That Denny, especially."

That Denny: Denny frozen in time, before he got weird.

Stella started on the boxes in the back, leaving the stuff near the television to Marco. Snippets of story drifted her way, about the boy's family, but much, much older than when they'd buried him. His brothers were fathers now, their children the nieces and nephews of the teenager they'd dug from the hillside. Then the oddly upbeat theme song twice in a row—that episode's end and another's beginning.

"Marco?" she asked. "How long did this run?"

"I dunno. A few years, at least."

"Did you ever go on it? Like Denny?"

"No. I . . . hmm. I guess by the time I'd have been old enough, Denny had started acting strange, and my parents liked putting us into activities we could both do at the same time."

They kept working. The next Uncle Bob story that drifted her way centered on a child who got lost. Stella kept waiting for it to turn into a familiar children's story, but it didn't. Just a kid who got lost and when she found her way home she realized she'd arrived back without her body, and her parents didn't even notice the difference.

"Enough," Stella said from across the room. "That was enough to give me nightmares, and I'm an adult. Fuck. Watch more after I leave if you want."

"Okay. Time to call it quits, anyway. You've been here like nine hours."

She didn't argue. She waited until they got out the front door to peel off the mask and gloves.

"It was good to hang out with you," she said.

"You, too. Look me up if you ever get to Boston."

She couldn't tell him to do the same with Chicago, so she said, "Will do." She realized she'd never asked what he did for a living, but it seemed like an awkward time. It wasn't until after she'd walked away that she realized he'd said goodbye as if she wasn't returning the next day. She definitely wasn't, especially if he kept bingeing that creepy show.

When she returned to her parents' house she made a beeline for the shower. After twenty minutes' scrubbing, she still couldn't shake the smell. She dumped the clothes in the garbage instead of the laundry and took the bag to the outside bin, where it could stink as much as it needed to stink.

Her parents were sitting on the screened porch out front, as they often did once the evenings got warm enough, both with glasses of iced tea on the wrought-iron table between them as if it were already summer. Her mother had a magazine open on her lap—she still subscribed to all her scientific journals, though she'd retired years before—and her father was solving a math puzzle on his tablet, which Stella could tell by his intense concentration.

"That bad?" Her mother lifted an eyebrow at her as she returned from the garbage.

"That bad."

She went into the house and poured herself a glass to match her parents'. Something was roasting in the oven, and the kitchen was hot and smelled like onions and butter. She closed her eyes and pressed the glass against her forehead, letting the oven and the ice battle over her body temperature, then returned to sit on the much cooler porch, picking the empty chair with the better view of the dormant garden.

"Grab the cushion from the other chair if you're going to sit in that one," her father said.

She did as he suggested. "I don't see why you don't have cushions for both chairs. What if you have a couple over? Do they have to fight over who gets the comfortable seat versus who gets the view?"

He shrugged. "Nobody's complained."

They generally operated on a complaint system. Maybe that was where she'd gotten the habit of lies and exaggeration: she'd realized early that only extremes elicited a response.

"How did dinner look?" he asked.

"I didn't check. It smelled great, if that counts for anything."

He grunted, the sound both a denial and the effort of getting up, and went inside. Stella debated taking his chair, but it wasn't worth the scene. A wasp hovered near the screen and she watched it for a moment, glad it was on the other side.

"Hey, Ma, do you remember *The Uncle Bob Show*?"

"Of course." She closed her magazine and hummed something that sounded half like Uncle Bob's theme song and half like *The Partridge Family* theme. Stella hadn't noticed the similarity between the two tunes; it was a ridiculously cheery theme song for such a dark show.

"Who was that guy? Why did they give him a kids' show?"

"The public television station had funding trouble and dumped all the shows they had to pay for—we had to get cable for you to watch *Sesame Street* and *Mister Rogers' Neighborhood*. They had all these gaps to fill in their schedule, so anybody with a low-budget idea could get on. That one lasted longer than most—four or five years, I think."

"And nobody said, 'That's some seriously weird shit'?"

"Oh, we all did, but someone at the station argued there were plenty of peace-and-love shows around, and some people like to be scared, and it's not like it was full of violence or sex, and just because a show had kids in it didn't mean it was a kids' show."

"They expected adults to watch? That's even weirder. What time was it on?"

"Oh, I don't remember. Saturday night? Saturday morning?"

Huh. Maybe he was more like those old monster movie hosts. "That's deeply strange, even for the eighties. And who was the guy playing Uncle Bob? I tried looking it up on IMDb, but there's no page. Not on Wikipedia either. Our entire world is fueled by nostalgia, but there's nothing on this show. Where's the online fan club, the community of collectors? Anything."

Her mother frowned, clearly still stuck on trying to dredge up a name. She shook her head. "Definitely Bob, a real Bob, but I can't remember his last name. He must've lived somewhere nearby, because I ran into him at the drugstore and the hardware store a few times while the show was on the air."

Stella tried to picture that strange man in a drugstore, looming behind her in line, telling her stories about the time he picked up photos from a vacation but when he looked at them, he was screaming in every photo. If he were telling that story on the show, he'd end it with, "and then you got home from the drugstore with your photos, but when you looked at them, you were screaming in every photo too." Great. Now she'd creeped herself out without his help.

"How did I not have nightmares?"

"We talked about that possibility—all the mothers—but you weren't disturbed. None of you kids ever complained. It was a nice break, to chat with the other moms while you all played in such a contained space."

There was a vast difference between "never complained" and "weren't disturbed" that Stella would have liked to unpack, but she fixated on a different detail. "Contained space—you mean while we watched TV, right?"

"No, dear. The studio. It looked much larger on television, but the cameras formed this nice ring around three sides, and you all understood you weren't supposed to leave during that half hour except for a bathroom emergency. You all played and we sat around and had coffee. It was the only time in my week when I didn't feel like I was supposed to be doing something else."

It took Stella a few seconds to realize the buzzing noise in her head wasn't the wasp on the screen. "What are you talking about? I was on the show?"

"Nearly every kid in town was on it at some point. Everyone except Marco, because his brother was acting up by the time you two were old enough, and Celeste pulled Denny and enrolled both boys in karate instead."

"But me? Ma, I don't remember that at all." The idea that she didn't know something about herself that others knew bothered her more than she could express. "You aren't making this up?"

"Why would I lie? I'm sure there are other things you don't remember. Getting lice in third grade?"

"You shaved my head. Of course I remember. The whole class got it, but I was the only one whose mother shaved her head."

"I didn't have time to comb through it, honey. Something more benign? Playing at Tamar Siegel's house?"

"Who's Tamar Siegel?"

"See? The Siegels moved to town for a year when you were in second grade. They had a jungle gym that you loved. You didn't think much of the kid, but you liked her yard and her dog. We got on well with her parents; I was sad when they left."

Stella flashed on a tall backyard slide and a golden retriever barking at her when she climbed the ladder and left it below. A memory she'd never have dredged up unprompted. Nothing special about it: a person whose face she couldn't recall, a backyard slide, an experience supplanted by other experiences. Generic kid, generic fun. A placeholder memory.

"Okay, I get that there are things that didn't stick with me, and things that I think I remember once you remind me, but it doesn't explain why I don't remember a blacked-out TV studio or giant cameras or a creepy host. You forget the things that don't stand out, sure, but this seems, I don't know, formative."

Her mother shrugged. "You're making a big deal of nothing."

"Nothing? Did you listen to his stories?"

"Fairy tales."

"Now I know you didn't listen. He was telling horror stories to seven-year-olds."

"Fairy tales *are* horror stories, and like I said, you didn't complain. You mostly played with the toys."

"What about the kids at home watching? The stories were the focus if you weren't in the studio."

"If they were as bad as you say, hopefully parents paid attention and watched with their children and whatever else the experts these days say comprises good parenting. You're looking through a prism of now, baby. Have you ever seen early *Sesame Street?* I remember a sketch where a puppet with no facial features goes to a human for 'little girl eyes.' You and your friends watched shows, and if they scared you, you turned them off. You played outside. You cut your Halloween candy in half to make sure there were no razor blades inside. If you want to tell me I'm a terrible parent for putting you on that show with your friends, feel free, but since it took you thirty-five years to bring this up, I'm going to assume it didn't wreck your life."

Her father rang the dinner gong inside the house, a custom her parents found charming and Stella had always considered overkill in a family as small as theirs. She and her mother stood. Their glasses were still mostly full, the melting ice having replaced what they'd sipped.

She continued thinking over dinner, while she related everything she and Marco had unearthed to her mildly curious parents, and after, while scrubbing the casserole dish. What her mother said was true: She hadn't been driven to therapy by the show. She didn't remember any nightmares. It just felt strange to be missing something so completely, not to mention the questions that arose about what else she could be missing if she could be missing that. It was an unpleasant feeling.

After dinner, while her parents watched some reality show, she pulled out a photo album from the early eighties. Her family hadn't been much for photographic documentation, so there was just the one, chronological and well labeled, commemorating Stella at the old school playground before they pulled it out and replaced it with safer equipment, at a zoo, at the Independence Day parade. It was true, she didn't recall those particular moments, but she believed she'd been there. *The Uncle Bob Show* felt different. The first time she'd uttered the show's name, she'd thought she'd made it up.

She texted Marco: "Did Denny have all the Uncle Bob episodes on tape or only the ones he was in? Thanks!" She added a smiley face, then erased it before she hit send. It felt falsely cheery instead of appreciative. His brother had just died.

She settled on the couch beside her parents. While they watched TV, she surfed the web looking for information about *The Uncle Bob Show,* but found nothing. In the era of kittens with Twitter accounts and sandwiches with their own Instagrams and fandoms for every conceivable property, it seemed impossible for something to be so utterly missing.

Not that it deserved a fandom; she just figured everything had one. Where were the ironic logo T-shirts? Where was the episode wiki explaining what happened in every Uncle Bob story? Where were the "Whatever happened to?" articles? The tell-alls by the kids or the director or the camera operator? The easy answer was that it was such a terrible show, or such a small show, that nobody cared. She didn't care either; she just needed to know. Not the same thing.

The next morning, she drove out to the public television station on the south end of town. She'd passed it so many times, but until now she wouldn't have said she'd ever been inside. Nothing about the interior rang a bell either, though it looked like it had been redone fairly recently, with an airy design that managed to say both modern and trapped in time.

"Can I help you?" The receptionist's trifocals reflected her computer's spreadsheet back at Stella. A phone log by her right hand was covered with sketched faces; the sketches were excellent. Grace Hernandez, according to her name plaque.

Stella smiled. "I probably should have called, but I wondered if you have archives of shows produced here a long time ago? My mother wants a video of a show I was on as a kid and I didn't want her to have to come over here for nothing."

Even while she said it, she wondered why she had to lie. Wouldn't it have been just as easy to say she wanted to see it herself? She'd noticed an older receptionist and decided to play on her sympathies, but there was no reason to assume her own story wasn't compelling.

"Normally we'd have you fill out a request form, but it's a slow day. I can see if someone is here to help you." Grace picked up a phone and called one number, then disconnected and tried another. Someone answered, because she repeated Stella's story, then turned back to her. "He'll be out in a sec."

She gestured to a glass-and-wood waiting area, and Stella sat. A flat screen overhead played what Stella assumed was their station, on mute, and a few issues of a public media trade magazine called *Current* were piled neatly on the low table.

A small man—a little person? Was that the right term?—came around the corner into reception. He was probably around her age, but she would have remembered him if he'd gone to school with her.

"Hi," he said. "I'm Jeff Stills. Grace says you're looking for a show?"

"Yes, my mother—"

"Grace said. Let's see what we can do."

He handed her a laminated guest pass on a lanyard and waited while she put it on, then led her through a security door and down a long, low-ceilinged corridor, punctuated by framed stills from various shows. No Uncle Bob. "Have you been here before?"

"When I was a kid."

"Hmm. I'll bet it looks pretty different. This whole back area was redone around 2005, after the roof damage. Then the lobby about five years ago."

She hadn't had any twinges of familiarity, but at least that explained some of it. She'd forgotten about the blizzard that wrecked the roof; she'd been long gone by then.

"Hopefully whatever you're looking for wasn't among the stuff that got damaged by the storm. What *are* you looking for?"

"*The Uncle Bob Show*. Do you know it?"

"Only by name. I've seen the tapes on the shelf, but in the ten years I've been here, nobody has ever asked for a clip. Any good?"

"No." Stella didn't hesitate. "It's like those late-night horror hosts, Vampira or Elvira or whatever, except they forgot to run a movie and instead let the host blather on."

They came to a nondescript door. The low-ceilinged hallway had led her to expect low-ceilinged rooms, but the space they entered was more of a warehouse. A long desk cluttered with computers and various machinery occupied the front, and then the space opened into row upon row of metal shelving units. The aisles were wide enough to accommodate rolling ladders.

"We've been working on digitizing, but we have fifty years of material in here, and some stuff has priority."

"Is that what you do? Digitize?"

"Nah. We have interns for that. I catalog new material as it comes in, and find stuff for people when they need clips. Mostly staff, but sometimes for networks, local news, researchers, that kind of thing."

"Sounds fun," Stella said. "How did you get into the field?"

"I majored in history, but never committed enough to any one topic for academic research. Ended up at library school, and eventually moved here. It is fun! I get a little bit of everything. Like today: a mystery show."

"Total mystery."

She followed him down the main aisle, then several aisles over, almost to the back wall. He pointed at some boxes above her head.

"Wow," she said. "Do you know where everything is without looking it up?"

"Well, it's alphabetical, so yeah, but also they're next to *Underground,* which I get a lot of requests for. Do you know what year you need?"

"1982? My mother couldn't remember exactly, but that's the year I turned seven."

Jeff disappeared and returned pushing a squeaking ladder along its track. He climbed up for the UNCLE BOB SHOW 1982 box. It looked like there were five years' worth, 1980 to 1985. She followed him back toward the door, where he pointed her to an office chair.

"We have strict protocols for handling media that hasn't been backed up yet. If you tell me which tapes you want to watch, I'll queue them up for you."

"Hmm. Well, my birthday is in July, so let's pick one in the last quarter of the year first, to see if I'm in there."

"You don't know if you are?"

She didn't want to admit she didn't remember. "I just don't know when."

He handed her a pair of padded headphones and rummaged in the box. She'd been expecting VHS tapes, but these looked like something else—Betamax, she guessed.

The show's format was such that she didn't have to watch much to figure out if she was in it or not. The title card came on, then the episode's children rushed in. She didn't see herself. She wondered again if this was a joke on her mother's part.

"Wait—what was the date on this one?"

Jeff studied the label on the box. "October ninth."

"I'm sorry. That's my mother's birthday. There's no way she stood around in a television studio that day. Maybe the next week?"

He ejected the tape and put it back in its box and put in another, but that one obviously had some kind of damage, all static.

"Third time's the charm," he said, going for the next tape. He seemed to believe it himself, because he dragged another chair over and plugged in a second pair of headphones. "Do you mind?"

She shook her head and rolled her chair slightly to the right to give him a better angle. The title card appeared.

"It's a good thing nobody knows about this show or they'd have been sued over this theme song," he said.

Stella didn't answer. She was busy watching the children. She recognized the first few kids: Lee Pool first, a blond beanpole; poor Dan Heller; Addie Chapel, whose mother had been everyone's pediatrician.

And then there she was, little Stella Gardiner, one of the last through the door. She wasn't used to competing for toys, so maybe she didn't know she needed to get in early, or maybe they were assigned an order behind the scenes. She'd thought seeing herself on screen would jog her memory, give her the studio or the stories or the backstage snacks, but she still had no recollection. She pointed at herself on the monitor for Jeff's benefit, to show they'd found her. He gave her a thumbs-up.

Little Stella seemed to know where she was going, even if she wasn't first to get there. Lee Pool already had the T. rex, but she wouldn't have cared. She'd liked the big dinosaurs, the bigger the better. She emerged from the toy pit with a matched pair. Brontosaurus, apatosaurus, whatever they called them these days. She could never wrap her head around something that large having existed. So yeah, the dinosaurs made sense—it was her, even if she still didn't remember it.

She carried the two dinosaurs toward the set's edge, where she collected some wooden trees and sat down. She was an only child, used to playing alone, and this clearly wasn't her first time in this space.

The camera lost her. The focus, of course, was on Uncle Bob. She had been watching herself and missed his entrance. He sat in his chair, children playing around him. Dan Heller zoomed around the set like a satellite in orbit, a model airplane in hand.

"Once upon a time there was a little boy who wanted to go fast." Uncle Bob started a story without waiting for anyone to pay attention.

"He liked everything fast. Cars, motorcycles, boats, airplanes. Bicycles were okay, but not the same thrill. When he rode in his father's car, he pretended they were racing the cars beside them. Sometimes they won, but mostly somebody quit the race. His father was not a fast driver. The little boy knew that if he drove, he'd win all the races. He wouldn't stop when he won, either. He'd keep going.

"He liked the sound of motors. He liked the way they rumbled deep enough to rattle his teeth in his head, and his bones beneath his skin; he liked the way they shut all the thinking out. He liked the smell of gasoline and the way it burned his nostrils. His family's neighbors had motorcycles they rode on weekends, and if he played in the front yard they'd sometimes let him sit on one with them before they roared away, leaving too much quiet behind. When they drove off, he tried to re-create the sound, making as much noise as possible until his father told him to be quiet, then to shut up, then 'For goodness' sake, what does a man have to do to get some peace and quiet around here on a Saturday morning?'" Dan paused his orbit and turned to face the storyteller. Two other kids had stopped to pay attention as well; Stella and the others continued playing on the periphery.

"The boy got his learner's permit on the very first day he was allowed. He skipped school for it rather than wait another second. He had saved his paper route money for driving lessons and a used motorbike. As soon as he had his full license, he did what he had always wanted to do: he drove as fast as he could down the highway, past all the cars, and then he kept driving forever. The end."

Uncle Bob shifted back in his chair as he finished. Dan watched him for a little longer, then launched himself again, circling the scattered toys and children faster than before.

Jeff sat back as well. "What kind of story was that?"

Stella frowned. "A deeply messed-up one. That kid with the airplane—Dan Heller—drove off the interstate the summer after junior year. He was racing someone in the middle of the night and missed a curve."

"Oof. Quite the coincidence."

"Yeah . . ."

Uncle Bob started telling another story, this one about a vole living in a hole on a grassy hillside that started a conversation with the child sleeping in the hole next door.

"Do you want to watch the whole episode? Is this the one you need?"

"I think I need to look at a couple more?" She didn't know what she was looking for. "Sorry for putting you out. I don't mean to take up so much time."

"It's fine! This is interesting. The show is terrible, from any standpoint. The story was terrible, the production is terrible. I can't even decide if this whole shtick is campy bad or bad bad. Leaning toward the latter."

"I don't think there's anything redeeming," Stella said, her mind still on Dan Heller. Did his parents remember this story? "Can we look at the next one? October thirtieth?"

"Coming up." Jeff appeared to have forgotten she'd said she was looking for something specific, and she didn't remind him, since she still couldn't think of an appropriate detail.

Little Stella was second through the door this time, behind Tina, whose last name she didn't remember. She paused and looked out past a camera, probably looking for her mother, then kept moving when she realized more kids were coming through behind her. Head for the toys. Claim what's yours. Brontosaurus and T. rex and a blue whale. Whales were almost as cool as dinosaurs.

Tina had claimed a triceratops and looked like she wanted the brontosaurus. They sat down on the edge of the toy pit to negotiate. Uncle Bob watched them play, which gave Stella the eeriest feeling of being watched, even though she still felt like the kid on the screen wasn't her.

"So what was it like?" Jeff asked, but Stella didn't answer. Uncle Bob had started a story. He looked straight into the camera. This time it felt like he was truly looking straight at her. This was the one. She knew it.

"Once upon a time, there was a little girl who didn't know who she was. Many children don't know who they will be, and that's not unusual, but what was unusual in this case was that the girl was willing to trade who she was for who she could be, so she began to do just that. Little by little, she replaced herself with parts of other people she liked better. Parts of stories she wanted to live. Nobody lied like this girl. She believed her own stories so completely, she forgot which ones were true and which were false.

"If you've ever heard of a cuckoo bird, they lay their eggs in other birds' nests, so those birds are forced to raise them for their own. This girl was her own cuckoo, laying stories in her own head, and the heads of those around her, until even she couldn't remember which ones were true, or if there was anything left of her."

Uncle Bob went silent, watching the children play. After a minute, he started telling another story about the boy in the hill, and how happy he was whenever he had friends over to visit. That story ended, and a graphic appeared on the screen with an address for fan mail. Stella pulled a pen from her purse and wrote it down as the theme music played out.

"Are you sending him a letter?" The archivist had dropped his headphones and was watching her.

She shrugged. "Just curious."

"Is this the one, then?"

"The one?"

He frowned. "You said you wanted a copy for your mother."

"Yes! That would be lovely. This is the one she mentioned."

He pulled a DVD off a bulk spindle and rewound the tape. "You didn't say what it was like. Was he weird off camera too?"

"Yes," she said, though she didn't remember. "But he kept to himself. Just stayed in his dressing room until it was time to go on."

Jeff didn't reply, and something subtle changed about the way he interacted with her. What if there hadn't been a dressing room? He might know. When had she gotten so sloppy with her stories? Maybe it was because she was distracted. Her mother had told the truth: she'd been on a creepy TV show of which she had no memory. And what was it? Performance art? Storytelling? Fairy tales or horror? All of the above? She thanked Jeff and left.

She had just walked into her parents' house when Marco called. "Can you come back? There's something I need to show you."

She headed out to Denny's house. She paused on the step, re-alizing she was in nicer clothes this time. Hopefully she wouldn't be there long.

"Hey," she said when Marco answered the door. Even though she braced for the odor, it hit her hard.

He waved her in, talking as he navigated the narrow path he'd cleared up the stairs. "I thought I'd work on Denny's bedroom today, and, well . . ."

He held out an arm in the universal gesture of "go ahead," so she entered. The room had precarious ceiling-high stacks on every surface, including the floor and bed, piles everywhere except a path to an open walk-in closet. She stepped forward.

"What is that?"

"The word I came up with was 'shrine,' but I don't think that's right."

It was the sparest space in the house. She'd expected a dowel crammed end to end with clothes, straining under the weight, but the closet was empty except for—"shrine" was indeed the wrong word. This wasn't worship.

The most eye-catching piece, the thing she saw first, was a hand-painted Uncle Bob doll propped in the back corner. It looked like it had been someone else first—Vincent Price, maybe. Next to it stood a bobblehead and an action figure, both mutated from other characters, and one made of clay and plant matter, seem-ingly from scratch. Beside those, a black leather notebook, a pile of VHS tapes, and a single DVD. Tacked to the wall behind them, portraits of Uncle Bob in paint, in colored pencil, macaroni, photo collage, in, oh god, was that cat hair? And beside those, stills from the show printed on copier paper: Uncle Bob telling a story; Uncle Bob staring straight into the camera, an assortment of children. Her own still was toward the bottom right. Marco wasn't in any of them.

"That's the thing that guts me."

Stella turned, expecting to see Marco pointing to the art or the dolls, but she'd been too busy looking at those to notice the filthy pillow and blanket in the opposite corner. "He slept here?"

"It's the only place he could have." Marco's voice was strangled, like he was trying not to cry.

She didn't know what to say to make him feel better about his brother having lived like this. She picked up the notebook and paged through it. Each page had a name block-printed on top, then a dense scrawl in black, then, in a different pen, something else. Not impossible to read, but difficult, writing crammed into every available inch, no space between words even. She remembered this notebook; it was the one teenage Denny always had on him.

"Take it," Marco said. "Take whatever you want. I can't do this anymore. I'm going home."

She took the notebook and the DVD, and squeezed Marco's arm, unsure whether he would want or accept a hug.

Her parents were out when she got back to their house, so she slipped the DVD into their machine. It didn't work. She took it upstairs and tried it in her mother's old desktop computer instead. The computer made a sound like a jet plane taking off, and opened a menu with one episode listed: March 13, 1980.

It started the same way all the other episodes had started. The kids, Uncle Bob. Denny was in this one; Stella had an easier time spotting him now that she knew who to look for. He went for the train set again, laying out wooden tracks alongside a kid Stella didn't recognize.

Uncle Bob started a story. "Once upon a time, there was a boy who grew very big very quickly. He felt like a giant when he stood next to his classmates. People stopped him in hallways and told him he was going to the wrong grade's room. His mother complained that she had to buy him new clothes constantly, and even though she did it with affection, he was too young to realize she didn't blame him. He felt terrible about it. Tried to hide that his shoes squeezed his toes or his pants were too short again.

"His parents' friends said, 'Somebody's going to be quite an athlete,' but he didn't feel like an athlete. More than that, he felt like he had grown so fast his head had been pushed out of his body, so he was constantly watching it from someplace just above. Messages he sent to his arms and legs took ages to get there. Everything felt small and breakable in his hands, so that when his best friend's dog had puppies he refused to hold them, though he loved when they climbed all over him.

"The boy had a little brother. His brother was everything he wasn't. Small, lithe, fearless. His mother told him to protect his brother, and he took that responsibility seriously. That was something that didn't take finesse. He could do that.

"Both boys got older, but their roles didn't change. The older brother watched his younger brother. When the smaller boy was bullied, his brother pummeled the bullies. When the younger brother made the high school varsity basketball team as a point guard his freshman year, his older brother made the team as center, even though he hated sports.

"Time passed. The older brother realized something strange. Every time he thought he had something of his own, it turned out it was his brother's. He blinked one day and lost two entire years. How was he the older brother, the one who got new clothes, who reached new grades first, and yet still always following? Even his own story had spun out to describe him in relation to his sibling.

"And then, one day, the boy realized he had nothing at all. He was his brother's giant shadow. He was a forward echo, a void. Nothing was his. All he could do was watch the world try to catch up with him, but he was always looking backward at it. All he could do—"

"No," said Denny.

Stella had forgotten the kids were there, even though they were on camera the entire time. Denny had stood and walked over to where Uncle Bob was telling the story. With Uncle Bob sitting, Denny was tall enough to look him in the eye.

For the first time, Uncle Bob turned away from the camera. He assessed Denny with an unsettling smile.

"No," Denny said again.

Now Uncle Bob glanced around as if he was no longer amused, as if someone needed to pull this child off his set. It wasn't a tantrum, though. Denny wasn't misbehaving, unless interrupting a story violated the rules.

Uncle Bob turned back to him. "How would you tell it?"

Denny looked less sure now.

"I didn't think so," said the host. "But maybe that's enough of that story. Unless you want to tell me how you think it ends?" Denny shook his head.

"But you know?"

Denny didn't move.

"Maybe that's enough. We'll see. In any case, I have other stories to tell. We haven't checked in on my hill today."

Uncle Bob began to catch his audience up on the continuing adventure of the boy who'd been dug out of the hillside. The other children kept playing, and Denny? Denny looked straight into the camera, then walked off the set. He never came back. Stella didn't have any proof, but she was pretty sure this must have been the last episode Denny took part in. He looked like a kid who was done. His expression was remarkably similar to the one she'd just seen on Marco's face.

And what was that story? Unlike Dan Heller's driving story, unlike the one she'd started thinking of as her own, this one wasn't close to true. Sure, Denny had been a big kid, but neither he nor Marco played basketball. He never protected Marco from bullies. "Nothing was his" hardly fit the man whose house she'd cleaned.

Except that night, falling asleep, Stella couldn't help but think that when she compared what she knew of Denny with that story, it seemed like Denny had set out to prove the story untrue. What would a person do if told as a child that nothing was his? Collect all the things. Leave his little brother to fend for himself. Fight it on every level possible.

Was it a freak occurrence that Denny happened to be listening when Uncle Bob told that story? Why was she assuming the story was about him at all? Maybe it was coincidence. There was nothing connecting the children to the stories except her own sense that they were connected, and Denny's reaction on the day he quit.

She hadn't heard hers when Uncle Bob told it, but she'd internalized it nonetheless. How much was true? She wasn't a cuckoo bird. Her reinventions had never hurt anyone.

Marco called that night to ask if she wanted to grab one more meal before she left town, but she said she had too much to do before her flight. That was true, as was the fact that she didn't want to see him again. Didn't want to ask him if he'd watched the March 13 show. Didn't want to tell him his brother had consciously refused him protection.

She should have gone straight to the airport in the morning, but the fan mail address she'd written down was in the same direction, if she took the back way instead of the highway. Why a show like that might get fan mail was a question for another time. This was strictly a trip to satisfy her curiosity. She drove through town, then a couple of miles past, into the network of county roads.

The mailbox stood full, overflowing, a mat of moldering envelopes around its cement base. A weather-worn FOR SALE sign had sunk into the soft ground closer to the drainage ditch. Stella turned onto the long driveway, and only after she'd almost reached the house did it occur to her that if she'd looked at the mail, she might have found his surname.

The fields on either side of the lane were tangled with weeds that didn't look like they cared what season it was. The house, a tiny stone cottage, was equally weed-choked, but strangely familiar. If she owned this house, she'd never let it get like this, but it didn't look like it belonged to anyone anymore. She tried a story on for size: "While I was visiting my parents, I went for a drive in the country, and I found the most darling cottage. My parents are getting older, and I had the thought that I should move closer to them. The place needed a little work, so I got it for a song."

She liked that one.

Nobody answered when she knocked. The door was locked, and the windows were too dirty to see through, and she couldn't shake the feeling that if she looked through he'd be sitting there, staring straight at her, waiting.

She walked around back and found the hill.

It was a funny little hill, not entirely natural looking, but what did she know? The land behind the house sloped gently upward, then steeper, hard beneath the grass but not rocky. From the slope, the cottage looked even smaller, the fields wilder, tangled, like something from a fairy tale. The view, too, felt strangely familiar.

She knew nothing more about the man who called himself Uncle Bob, but as she walked into the grass she realized this must be the hill from his stories, the stories he told when he wasn't telling stories about the children. How did they go? She thought back to that first episode she'd watched in Denny's basement.

Once upon a time, there was a boy whose family planted him in a hillside, so that he took over the entire hillside, like a weed. They dug me out of the hillside on my thirteenth birthday. It's good to divide rhizomes to give them room to grow.

That story made her remember the notebook she'd taken from Denny's house, and she rummaged for it in her purse. The notebook was alphabetical, printed in a nearly microscopic hand other than the page headings, dense. She found one for Dan Heller. She couldn't decipher the whole story, but the first line was obviously *Once upon a time, there was a little boy who wanted to go fast.* She knew the rest. In blue pen, it said what she had said to Jeff the archivist:

motorcycle wreck, alongside the date. That one was easy since she knew enough to fill in the parts she struggled to read. The others were trickier. There was no page for Marco, but Denny had made one for himself. It had Uncle Bob's shadow-brother story but no update at the bottom. Nothing at all for the years between.

Who else had been on the show? Lee Pool had a page. So did Addie Chapel, who as far as Stella knew had followed in her mother's footsteps and become a doctor. Chris Bethel, and beside him, Tina Bevins, the other dinosaur lover. If she spent enough time staring, maybe Denny's handwriting would decipher itself.

She was afraid to turn to her own page. She knew it had to be there, on the page before Dan Heller, but she couldn't bring herself to look, until she did. She expected this one, like Dan's, like Denny's own, to be easier to decipher because she knew how it would go.

> *October 30, 1982. Once upon a time, there was a little girl who didn't know who she was. Many children don't know who they will be, and that's not unusual, but what was unusual in this case was that the girl was willing to trade who she was for who she could be, so she began to do just that. Little by little, she replaced herself with parts of other people she liked better. Parts of stories she wanted to live. Nobody lied like this girl. She believed her own stories so completely, she forgot which ones were true and which were false.*
>
> *If you've ever heard of a cuckoo bird, they lay their eggs in other birds' nests, so those birds are forced to raise them for their own. This girl was her own cuckoo, laying stories in her own head, and the heads of those around her, until even she couldn't remember which ones were true, or if there was anything left of her.*

There was more. Another episode, maybe? She had no idea how many she'd been on, and her research had been shoddy. Maybe every story was serialized like the boy in the hill. It took her a while to make out the next bit.

> *November 20, 1982. Our cuckoo girl left the nest one day to spread her wings. When she returned, she didn't notice that nobody had missed her. She named a place where she had been, and they accepted it as truth. She made herself up, as she had always done, convincing even herself in the process. Everything was true, or true enough.*

Below that, in blue pen, a strange assortment of updates from her life, as observed by Denny. Marco's eleventh birthday party, when she'd given him juggling balls. Graduation from middle school. The summer they'd both worked at the pool, and Marco'd gotten heatstroke and thrown up all the Kool-Aid they tried to put in him, Kool-Aid red, straight into the pool like a shark attack. The time she and Marco had tried making out on his bed, only he had started giggling, and she had gotten offended, and when she stood she tripped over a juggling ball and broke her toe. All the games their friends had played in Marco's basement: I've Never, even though they all knew what everyone else had done; Two Truths and a Lie, though they had all grown up together and knew everything about each other; Truth or Dare, though everyone was tired of truth, truth was terrifying, everyone chose dare, always. The *Batman* premiere. The prom amoeba, the friends who went together, all of whom she'd lost touch with. High school graduation. Concrete memories, things she knew were as real as anything that had ever happened in her life. Denny shouldn't have known about some of these things, but now she pictured him there, somewhere, holding this notebook, watching them, taking notes, always looking like he had something to say but he couldn't say it.

Below those stories he'd written: *Once there was a girl who got lost and when she found her way home she realized she'd arrived back without herself, and her parents didn't even notice the difference.* Which couldn't be her story at all; she hadn't been on the episodes he'd been on.

After graduation, he had no more updates on her. She paged forward, looking at the blue ink. Everyone had updates within the last year, everyone except for Denny, everyone who was still alive; the ones who weren't had death dates. Everyone except her. She tried to imagine what from her adult life she would have added, given the chance, or what an internet search on her name would provide, or what her parents would tell someone who asked what she was doing. Surely there was something. Parents were supposed to be your built-in hype machines.

She pulled out her phone to call Marco, but the battery was dead. Just as well, since she was suddenly afraid to try talking to anyone at all. She returned to the notebook and flipped toward the back. *U* for *Uncle Bob.*

> *Once upon a time, there was a boy whose family planted him in a hillside, so that he took over the entire hillside, like a weed. They dug me out of the hillside on my thirteenth birthday. It's good to divide rhizomes to give them room to grow.*

This story was long, eight full pages in tiny script, with episode dates interspersed. At the end, in red ink, this address. She pictured Denny driving out here, exploring the cottage, looking up at the hill. If she ever talked to Marco again, she'd tell him that what he'd found in Denny's closet wasn't a shrine; it was Denny's attempt to conjure answers to something unanswerable.

She put the notebook back in her purse and kept walking. Three-quarters of the way up the hill she came to a large patch where the grass had been churned up. She put her hand in the soil and it felt like the soil grasped her hand back.

Her parents said she didn't visit often enough, but now she couldn't remember ever having visited them before, or them visiting her. She couldn't remember if she'd ever left this town at all. She lived in Chicago, or did she? She'd told Marco as much, told him other things she knew not to be true, but what was true, then? What did she do for a living? If she left this hill and went to the airport, would she even have a reservation? If she caught her plane, would she find she had anything or anyone there at all? Where was there? She pulled her hand free and put it to her mouth: the soil tasted familiar.

"I walked down to the cottage that would be mine someday" —that felt nice, even if she wasn't sure she believed it— "and then past the cottage, through the town, and into my parents' house. They believed me when I said where I'd been. They fit me into their lives and only occasionally looked at me like they didn't quite know how I'd gotten there." That felt good. True. She sat in the dirt and leaned back on her hands, and felt the hill pressing back on them.

She could still leave: walk back to her rental car, drive to the airport, take the plane to the place where she surely had a career, a life, even if she couldn't quite recall it. She thought that until she looked back at where the rental car should have been and realized it wasn't there. She had no shoes on, and her feet were black with dirt, pebbled, scratched. She dug them into the soil, rooting with her toes.

How had Denny broken his story? He'd refused it. Whether his life was better or worse for it remained a different question. To break her story, she'd have to walk back down the hill and reconstruct herself the right way round. She thought of the cuckoo girl, the lost girl, the cuckoo girl, so many stories to keep straight.

The soil reached her forearms now, her calves. The top layer was sun-warmed, and underneath, a busy cool stillness made up of millions of insects, of the roots of the grass, of the rhizomes of the boy who had called this hillside home before she had. She'd walk back to town when she was ready, someday, maybe, but she was in no hurry. She'd heard worse stories than hers, and anyway, if she didn't like it she'd make a new one, a better one, a true one.

DARYL GREGORY

Brother Rifle

FROM *Made to Order: Robots and Revolution*

THE REHABILITATION OF Corporal Rashad Williams began like a magic trick. "Pick a card," his doctor said. "Any card."

Rashad considered the five cards on the table: yellow X, red circle, green triangle, blue square, orange rectangle. The symbols and their colors didn't mean anything to him.

Two years before, a bullet had entered Rashad's right occipital lobe, destroying the eye and ripping through the orbitofrontal cortex. Before that moment, he was a person who made things happen. Then, suddenly, he became an object that things happened to.

He was passed from doctor to doctor like a package with an unreadable address, until he arrived here, in Berkeley, at the lab of Dr. Subramanian, a lanky, East Asian, T-shirt-wearing *dude*, clearly civilian. The first thing he'd said when he shook Rashad's hand was, "Thank you for your service." The second was, "Call me Dr. S." Rashad hadn't been sure how he felt about that.

Rashad reached toward the yellow X with his right hand, then withdrew. A minute passed. Then two.

"Take your time," Dr. S said. Rashad couldn't decide if his smile was sincere or hiding his impatience. Sitting beside him was Alejandra, his grad student and assistant. She was a small woman, only a year or two older than Rashad, with glossy black hair pulled back so tight he thought she might be ex-military. So far she'd said very little, her attention on the tablet in her hands.

She was reading his mind.

The wires in Rashad's Deep Brain Implant exited the skull but didn't break the skin; they ran down his neck like artificial veins to a lump nestled a few inches from his right collarbone. This device, 98 percent battery and the rest a cluster of computer chips, controlled the DBI and spoke wirelessly to her tablet.

Rashad tapped his fingers at the edge of the table, near the red circle. He looked at Alejandra. She lifted her chin, and they shared a moment of eye contact before she returned her attention to the screen. Her eyes were very dark. Did she know which card he was supposed to pick?

He shook his head. "I'm sorry, sir. Ma'am."

"There's nothing to be sorry for," the doctor said. "We're just establishing a baseline. The first step to getting you back to your old self."

Alejandra glanced at the doctor, but said nothing. Her face had not changed expression. He wondered what she was thinking, but the flow of information went only one way.

"Why don't you try again?" the doctor suggested.

"Yes, sir."

Rashad wondered what, exactly, he was being tested for. Did the symbols have secret meanings? Or were the colors significant? Perhaps red meant no. Could he ask to look through the remaining cards in the deck, or was that against the rules?

Dr. Subramanian shifted in his seat. Alejandra tapped at her screen. The test had been going on for fifteen minutes.

"I'm sorry," Rashad said again. "I can't decide."

Once, Rashad had been very good at making decisions. Even that first month in Jammu and Kashmir, with insurgents firing at them from every rooftop and IEDs hiding under the road, he'd rarely hesitated and was usually right.

The man he'd been before the wound—a person he thought of as RBB, Rashad Before Bullet—was a systems operator in a fifteen-marine squad, responsible for the squad's pocket-sized black hornet drones and his beloved SHEP unit. Good name. It was like a hunting dog on wheels, able to follow him or forge ahead, motoring through the terraced mountain villages, swiveling that .50 caliber M2 as if it were sniffing out prey. The sensors arrayed across its body fed data to an ATLAS-enabled AI, which in turn beamed information to the wrap screen on Rashad's arm. Possible targets were outlined like bad guys in a video game: a silhouette in a window, on a roof, behind a corner.

But the SHEP wasn't allowed to take the shot—that was Rashad's decision. He was the man in the loop. Every death was his choice.

When a target popped up on his screen, all he had to do was press the palm switch in his glove and the silhouette would vanish in an exclamation of dust and noise, eight rounds per second. The AI popped up the next target and if he closed his fist just so, another roar ripped the body to shreds.

Hold. Bang. Hold. No and Yes and No.

"Aw sweetie, why don't you go to bed?" It was Marisa, his sister-in-law. Rashad realized that for some time he'd been pacing. His hands ached, and he was surprised to see that his fists were clenched tight.

She touched his elbow, and he relaxed his hand. She was a white woman, and a Christian, but as kind and devout as Rashad's mother. "Come on, I'll take you."

Rashad followed others now. He lived with Marisa and his brother, Leo, eating what they ate, waking up and going to bed when they did, watching the same shows. When he stayed too long on the patio Leo told him to come inside. When Marisa found him standing in front of an open closet, frozen by possibilities, she put the clothes in his hand. And when they found him pacing the house in the middle of the night—sweating, pulse racing for no reason—they guided him back to bed.

He lay down on top of the covers, as was his habit. Marisa put her hand on his forehead, over his eye patch, and said, "We ask for your healing, Lord." When she said amen, he echoed her.

He'd become as obedient as the SHEP, but without any purpose. He could offer up no targets, protect them from no threats.

The next morning, Leo told him to shave and pull on a collared shirt, and then he drove Rashad the ninety minutes between Stockton and Berkeley. Rashad had appointments at the neuro lab every Tuesday and Thursday. This was week eight.

"Does it feel like it's working?" Leo asked. Rashad didn't know what to say. What did "working" mean? Some days he felt a shift in the way thoughts percolated through his brain; certain images and ideas took on a disruptive tinge, like the rasp of the bow under a

violin note. Or perhaps he was imagining it. He knew Leo wanted
the old Rashad to come back, the smart, cocky kid who laughed
easily and threw himself into challenges. That Rashad had vanished into a world of acronyms—USMC, LeT, J&K, LOC, SHEP
—and came back with a new one: TBI. It was Leo who'd signed
the papers to enroll Rashad in Dr. Subramanian's experimental
program, and after two months, he seemed no closer to getting
his little brother back.

Ten miles later, Leo shook his head. "Never mind." He put his
hand on Rashad's shoulder. "Don't worry about it, bro."

Alejandra came out to the waiting room, neutral ground where
she and his brother could transfer custody. "I'll have him back to
you in four hours," she said to Leo.

She led Rashad through a confusion of corridors. Once he'd
had a reliable sense of direction, but the bullet had destroyed that,
too. In the lab he sat automatically at his usual seat, and she knelt
and wired up the fingers of his left hand, connecting them to various recording devices. The controller in his chest, of course, was
already whispering its secrets.

She looked up at him and smiled. "Ready for the slide show?"

"Yes, ma'am." He knew she was just being polite, and not really
asking for a decision. Acquiescence was his default.

She positioned the monitor and aimed the camera at his eye.
Images popped up on the screen for half a second or less, a mix
of animals, buildings, people, objects. In one burst he saw a brown
horse, then a gray concrete building, the blue rectangle, a white
woman in a green dress, an army PFC in desert camo holding an
M4, a white sailboat. Blink, and another burst: green triangle, Lab-
rador retriever puppy, yellow X, black M007 pistol, yellow X again.
The card symbols came as frequently as punctuation.

Rashad had to do nothing but keep his left hand steady on his
knee and his eye fixed on the screen; his body and brain reacted,
sending data to Alejandra's devices without bothering to notify
him. Every twenty minutes she called for a short break, and every hour she brought him water or a cup of coffee—she decided
which.

Dr. S was two steps into the room when he said, "Knock knock!
How's it going in here?" Alejandra paused the slide show. The doctor shook Rashad's hand.

He usually stopped by for a few minutes during each appointment, like a dentist checking on a patient being worked on by a hygienist. Alejandra handed him the tablet. He jabbed and swiped at it, nodding and humming. Finally he sat beside Rashad and said, "I think we're ready to start the experiential phase."

Alejandra's head turned sharply to look at the doctor, but Dr. S didn't react. He said to Rashad, "Let me explain what I mean by experiential—it's means we're finally going to start bypassing the damage."

The damage. The bullet had destroyed the link between Rashad's limbic system and his frontal cortex, so that he no longer experienced emotions. But this wasn't because his body lacked the machinery to create them. His amygdala and thalamus and hypothalamus continued to churn away, sending hormones coursing through his bloodstream, and his body responded: his pupils dilated and contracted, his heart raced and slowed. But these effects didn't spark pain or bring him pleasure. He might as well have been reading about them on Alejandra's tablet, each abrupt increase in his heartbeat another spike on a graph, each microburst of perspiration a data point. His body was throwing up indicators of a brain that had entered a particular state. But pain, pleasure? Those were things that didn't exist without a consciousness to perceive them.

His lack of emotions didn't turn him into a hyper-rational Mr. Spock; just the opposite. He'd become a tourist wandering through a foreign city where every street looked the same. When he was presented with the cards, a thought would come to him: *pick the yellow X.* But the thought had no weight, no *rightness* to it. The next thought came: *pick the red circle.* But that thought, too, was another soap bubble, easily popped.

It wasn't that logic had become inaccessible. He could grind his way through a puzzle, he could solve math problems. But even with simple questions—what's twelve times twelve?—when the answer arrived it seemed to tiptoe into the room, apologizing. He doubted its veracity. Nothing *rang true.*

Dr. S told him they were training his implant to pass the messages from the limbic system to the part of his brain that made decisions. "The DBI's a black box—signals come in one side, and leave the other, getting reinforced or weakened in the middle. Or at least they will—nothing's coming out the other side yet. All we've been doing so far is training the system."

"He understands neural networks," Alejandra said.

In the field, the SHEP's AI was always learning from Rashad, recording which path he took through an environment, noting which shots he took and which he avoided, trying to become a better helper. The DBI was simply an artificial neural network planted inside his own broken one—one trying to become more like Rashad. The images weren't merely pictures: they were triggers for a host of emotions and concepts and memories already primed in Rashad's brain.

"What's the algorithm?" he asked. "How does it decide which signals to strengthen?"

Dr. S's eyebrows raised—a signal of surprise. Alejandra tilted her head. *That* gesture, however, was opaque to him.

"A great question," the doctor said. "It starts with your body." He talked about somatic markers, the residue of previous decisions by which the body felt its way to a new choice. "We monitor your heart rate, your oxygen levels, your galvanic skin resistance —everything we can think of—and of course the activity itself recorded by your implant. We try to match it to the firehouse of data coming through the DBI. Say that we've just shown you a picture of a puppy, that seems like it would be a positive emotional response, yes? So we assign a value to that moment of input and tag it."

They're guessing, Rashad thought. And then another thought came: *They must know what they're doing.* Then: *They're guessing.*

"Perhaps a picture of an attractive person makes your eyes dilate," the doctor said. "Male or female, we'll tag!" He chuckled, and Alejandra looked away. Was she embarrassed? Rashad couldn't tell.

"Who decides what to tag?" Rashad asked. "You? Alejandra?"

"No, no. Well, yes. We have software that makes all the initial associations and applies a rudimentary score, based on data we've gotten from several hundred volunteers who've watched the same slides. Alejandra reviews the data entering your DBI, and can make corrections where necessary, based on your own history and known preferences."

He thought, *They know my history.* But of course they did. His medical records would be on file: every detail from before the injury and from the aftermath, his diet of antibiotics and opioids, maybe even his psychologist's therapy notes. For all he knew, both of them had gone back and read his evaluations from boot camp through deployment.

He wondered, idly, what Alejandra thought of him. Was she upset by what he'd done in the J&K? He tried to replay her reactions to him, but it was like watching a movie without sound.

"Rashad? Rashad." The doctor was waiting for his response. "Are we good to go?"

Alejandra said, "You can't ask him that. And in my opinion—"

"Yes, sir," Rashad said.

"Excellent." And then Dr. S was gone. Rashad turned back to the screen, ready to resume the slides.

Alejandra touched his arm to get his attention. "Do you have a therapist?"

That was an odd question. "No," he said. "Not anymore." For a few months after he was discharged from the hospital he met with a psychiatrist, but the sessions went nowhere.

"I'll talk to your brother," she said. "He should get you an appointment before next week."

"Why?"

"You're going to start feeling things."

Pierce died first. He was a Black cowboy from Montana, a thing Rashad hadn't known existed. Pierce said the mountains above Tartuk reminded him of home. They were severe and snow-capped, but the valley was alive with burbling creeks, lush trees, brilliant flowers, emerald fields. In this terraced village, every narrow street switched back to reveal another row of stone houses, another bridge, another burst of green. Another shooting gallery.

Jumma and Kashmir was the only Indian state with a majority Muslim population, a former "princely state" caught in the middle of the Indo-Pakistani war of 1948. Eighty years after partition it was where the two countries worked out their issues while deciding whether to nuke each other. Pakistan-backed LeT insurgents fought the Indian army and sniped at the police, the police arrested and interrogated secessionists, secessionists bombed police stations. And the marines, as Pierce liked to say, were the filling in the shit sandwich.

Tartuk had been "secured" a month ago—insurgents pushed out, IEDs cleared—but since the town sat only 2.2 kilometers from the LOC, Bravo Company remained, keeping the peace, winning hearts and minds, et cetera, though everyone knew the area could turn hot at any moment. The civilians, like civilians do, insisted on staying in their homes, tending to their fields, sending their children to school. When the squad went on patrol, old men wearing long robes and Adidas running shoes watched from doorsteps. Schoolboys in blue shirts and red ties flowed around the marines, laughing. One morning a ten-year-old girl in an orange headscarf skipped up to the squad and patted the SHEP, chattering to it in Balti.

"I don't get it," Rashad said after she left. "Why do their parents let them stay here? They gotta have relatives somewhere south of here."

"It may be a shit sandwich," Pierce said, "but it's *their*—"

His head jerked back. Only then did Rashad register the crack of a rifle shot. Pierce collapsed to the ground.

Rashad was only six feet behind him, leading the SHEP on its string. The wire was low-tech, hardly more than a fishing line, stretched between Rashad's belt and the SHEP. Rashad stopped, stunned, and the SHEP halted with him. The squad was on a steep gravel street, the stone houses rising up on each side of them.

Sergeant Conseco, their squad leader, shouted commands, and the rest of the squad flattened onto walls or ducked into doorways. They were in a stone chute, very little cover. Rashad sprinted forward, still wired to the SHEP. The vehicle detected the angle and intensity of the pull and followed at the same speed, engine whining.

Rashad reached Pierce and knelt. Pierce looked up at him, his mouth working, but making no sound. His throat was awash in blood. A roar of gunfire, and the stone next to Rashad's head exploded in dust. The sniper had switched to full auto. Someone, one of the squad, cried out. Wounded, not killed.

Conseco yelled, "Northwest, up high! Find that fucker." Despite the loudness of her voice she sounded calm.

Rashad yanked the wire out of his harness and let it retract into the SHEP. He tapped his throat mic and said, "SHEP. Go two meters in front of me." His voice was shaking. "Park at forty-five degrees to road. Scan for targets." The robot lurched forward, swung around Rashad, and jolted to a stop. The .50 cal unlocked and began to swivel.

Suddenly Conseco was beside him. "I've got Pierce. I need eyes, okay?"

"Eyes. Yes, sir!" Rashad scrambled to uncover the screen wrapped around his arm, silently yelling at himself. Why the fuck hadn't he had the drones in the air at the start of patrol? (Because it drained the batteries and that wasn't SOP.) Why didn't he at least have the tablet on? (Again, not SOP.) Why didn't he see this coming? (Because because because.)

The screen filled with four windows streaming from the SHEP's cameras and LIDAR. Immediately, a target popped up, outlined in red. A figure in a window, not thirty feet ahead. The palm switch in his right glove tingled. He declined the shot—the target wasn't in the direction of the sniper.

He opened his hip pocket and extracted the black hornet. The drone was just four inches long, painted matte black. He toggled the switch and the rotors spun, tugging to get out of his grip. He tossed it into the air and it zipped away. Ten seconds later he launched the second hornet.

Sergeant Conseco had pulled off Pierce's tactical vest. Blood soaked her hands and arms. Pierce was looking past her shoulder at Rashad; his lips were no longer moving.

"Hey man," Rashad said. "Don't worry. Don't worry."

"Eyes," Conseco said.

Rashad swiped at the tablet, bringing up the hornet cameras. The drones were already twenty meters overhead, where they could not be heard and were practically invisible. He could see himself, and Pierce and Conseco, all huddled in the shadow of the SHEP. The other squaddies were arrayed along the street, guns up, but holding fire. He sent one hornet zooming back along the way the squad had come, to guard their rear. He flung the other northwest, where Conseco had guessed the shot had come from.

Somewhere, hiding in one of the gray buildings above them, was a sniper.

Everyone in the squad seemed to be shouting at once into the coms. Rashad tuned them out. He had a talent for concentration, a gift for leaving his own body behind while he saw to the needs of his machines. The hornets weren't as smart as the SHEP, but they were semi-autonomous and programmed for combat semantics. He didn't *control* them. He asked them to hunt, and when they reached the waypoints he'd set and found no target, they followed their own programming and entered a search pattern.

It was the rear-flying hornet that barked first, flashing red on his screen. A human figure, splayed on the roof of Building 31, pointing a long gun. Sergeant Conseco had been mistaken—the sniper was directly behind them. The parked SHEP provided no cover.

Rashad was watching the screen when the muzzle flashed. Two feet behind him, Sergeant Conseco died.

Three weeks after he'd started the experiential phase of treatment, Marisa found him standing in front of his closet again. "Do you need some help?" she asked.

The closet contained almost everything he owned here in California: half a dozen boxes from the apartment he'd lived in before enlistment, a few sets of clothes, and two pairs of shoes Leo and Marisa had picked out from when he'd been discharged. The remains of his childhood—his high school yearbooks and basketball trophies and science fair projects—waited for him in his parents' garage in Arizona.

"Here," she said. "Let me pick something."

"I'm fine," he said. "I can do it."

The words came out sharp. He immediately apologized—and now there were tears in her eyes. He apologized again but now she was smiling at him despite the tears. She hugged him and said, "Hey there, Rashad."

He was so confused.

"I don't know why you put up with me," he said. "If you want me to leave, I can—"

"No! You're family." She rubbed his arm. "We're just glad you're here with us." She said this so gravely that he sensed he was missing something.

"Thank you," he said, to fill the silence.

"Now, you go to it." She closed the door behind her.

He gazed at the stack of boxes. An uneasy feeling rolled through him, and he almost walked out of the bedroom. Since the new phase had begun he'd been sleeping poorly. He'd wake up feeling as if the ceiling were closing in. Watching TV with Leo and Marisa made him feel restless, and he'd go out to the backyard to pace. Some food tasted better, but some of it much, much worse.

But mostly he felt the same as before. He went where he was told. He wore the clothes that were set out for him. And he went to his appointments in Berkeley. He didn't know why, on this afternoon, while Leo was at work, he suddenly wanted to find the thing he'd hidden.

He took down the top box. Inside sat his old gaming console in a nest of cables. He opened the next box, and the next. Then he found a steel lockbox hardly larger than a shoebox.

He stared at it, his breath was coming high in his chest. His thumb ran across the combination lock, turned the wheel. The combination was his enlistment date—his second birthday.

The pistol lay swaddled in oilcloth. A fully loaded magazine lay beside it. He picked up the weapon with one hand, opened the cloth with the other. The gun was larger than he remembered. Heavier.

During his first leave, between boot camp in San Diego and deployment, he'd missed his sidearm—of course he hadn't been allowed to leave the base with it. He drove to a gun shop on Pacific Avenue and chose a Glock 19M, the civilian twin to the M007 he'd been issued. He drove immediately to a firing range, and the first time he pulled the trigger he thought of the Rifleman's Creed, which his drill sergeant had made him memorize: *There are many like it, but this one is mine.*

He'd never told Leo about the gun. He knew Marisa would never stand for a weapon in the house.

Finally he slipped his hand around the grip, his finger straight along the trigger guard. The safety was on. He pulled back the slide. There was no shell in the chamber.

He could load the gun or leave it empty.

Pierce was dead. Conseco was dead. And the sniper was still on the roof, with half the squad still within his field of fire.

Rashad threw himself against a wall and shouted "SHEP!" into his throat mic. "Building 31, go, go, go!"

The AI understood the sentence. *Building 31:* a known entity on its map, photographed and tagged months ago by drone. *Triple-go:* top speed. The robot spun in a tight circle, then charged down the steep road that Rashad had trained it to navigate.

Rashad swiped at his wrap and brought up the hornet's stream side by side with the SHEP's. The drone circled feet above the roof, close enough to show the sniper's eyes, the silver snaps on his blue windbreaker, the white laces of his black sneakers. The gunman was on his feet now, holding his rifle with one hand, looking down at the robot charging toward him at forty miles per hour.

The shooter pivoted toward the far end of the roof, where a trapdoor lay open. He was going to go down into the house.

The SHEP reached the bottom of the steep road, spun around a low stone wall. Building 31 was a cement house, one large door in front, and two open windows. The .50 caliber swung to cover the edge of the roofline, but there was no angle for a shot.

"Grenade," Rashad said. "The window to the right of the door." The window lit up with a red outline. Rashad's glove vibrated and he closed his fist: Yes. The grenade flew through the opening, thunked against an inner wall, and exploded with a bang that would have deafened him if he'd been there in person.

He sent the SHEP hurtling into the front entrance. The door seemed to vanish in front of the camera. The room was full of smoke. The SHEP, however, quickly identified heat signatures. Three red outlines popped up, and the glove seemed to be shaking itself from his hand. He made a fist. Yes. The gun erupted. Yes.

Another figure appeared at the edge of the screen. The SHEP's M2 was already spinning to face the threat. More red outlines.

Yes and Yes and Yes and Yes and Yes and Yes and Yes.

Alejandra dealt three cards: blue square, yellow X, orange rectangle. He touched the blue square, and she made a note on her tablet. Then she dealt three more: yellow X, red circle, and another blue square. He understood, now, that these were arbitrary choices. What she was measuring was probably not what he chose, but the speed of his decision-making, or perhaps the level of stress in making the choice. Even so, he was reluctant to choose the blue square again, so he tapped the red circle.

After a few rounds of cards, Alejandra set up the slide show. She moved unhurriedly, projecting an aura of quiet he was reluctant to disturb. He wondered again what she thought of him. It alarmed him how desperately he wanted her to like him.

At the break after the first twenty-minute round of slides, she asked, "Have you scheduled a therapist yet?" It had been a month since they began the experiential phase.

He felt heat in his cheeks. So she still thought of him as a patient. "No, there's a waiting list. The VA says they'll call me."

"So you haven't gotten any meds, either?"

"No."

"Damn it," she said, almost under her breath. He'd never seen her express annoyance—or else he'd missed it.

"I'm sorry," he said. "I'll ask Leo to call again."

"It's not you. This should be part of the treatment. I told him —" She stopped herself. Him—Dr. Subramanian. The past several appointments, he'd not made an appearance. Alejandra had said that he was traveling. "I'll make some calls," she said.

"You don't have to do that."

"Your brother said you're not sleeping."

Leo talked to her? Behind his back?

"It's okay," Alejandra said. She was watching him with those dark eyes. She didn't need a tablet to read him. "He's worried about you."

"I'm fine." This was a lie. Sometimes he burst into tears for no reason. His body had developed strange aches. A sharp noise could make him jump out of his skin.

"Are you having suicidal thoughts?"

"No." Another lie. Had he taken too long to answer? He wasn't sure she believed him. What had Leo told her?

"It wouldn't be unusual if those thoughts came back," she said. "You haven't been able to feel them for some time. If you want, I can turn down the signals from the DBI. Ease you back down."

"You can do that?" Then: "I don't want to be like before."

"Not all the way off, just less . . . volume. Until you have a therapist. It would give you space to deal with what happened to you in India."

So. She had read his file. Shame tightened his chest.

"I don't know everything that happened there," she said. "But I do know that they put you in a position where you had little choice about what to do. They trained you to fight, then put you in the line of fire. Then they gave you tools that made it easy for you to do what they wanted you to do."

"You're just describing how the military works." His throat was tight.

"I'm saying you're not completely responsible. Your options, your degrees of freedom, were restricted by so many things—the rules of engagement, the environment, the ATLAS targeting system—"

"No. I'm responsible." He was surprised at how harsh he sounded. "I'm the man in the loop. The SHEP is just another weapon, like a rifle." He was processing so much information. She knew about ATLAS, too? Did she have security clearance? Who had she talked to?

"ATLAS is much more than a rifle," she said. "It was designed to make it easy to pull the trigger. It's called automation bias. They wanted a system where it would be easier for a soldier to follow a suggestion rather than—"

"I'm not a soldier," Rashad said. "I'm a marine."

Alejandra stopped, blinked. She was embarrassed, he realized. Maybe the DBI was making it easier for him to read expressions, too.

"I'm sorry," she said. "I know you're not army. I didn't mean to offend you."

"I'm not offended," he said. "But a marine—making hard choices while under fire is what we're trained for. A machine can't do that. Robots make bad marines." That was something his instructor at special operations school liked to say.

Alejandra thought for a moment. "If you could go back in time, knowing what you know now, would you stop yourself from doing what you did?"

"You mean, take away my free will?"

Her face froze. He'd intended to make her smile, but somehow he'd said it wrong.

"Here's what I would do," Rashad said. "I'd go back in time and take away the sniper's free will to shoot at me. I'd kill him before he entered that house full of people and climbed to the roof."

"That would be the right thing to do? You have no doubt?" It was almost as if she were asking permission.

"No doubt." They both seemed surprised by his certainty. Decisiveness had crept back into his thinking.

They resumed the slides. Blue square. Puppy. Yellow X. Pistol. Yellow X. Sailboat. Once it had been almost relaxing to sit through the cascade of images, but now he felt as if he were riding the bow of a SURC in heavy surf. By the end of the final series he was sweating, nauseated. He turned away from her, flipped up his eye patch, rubbed away the sweat. He didn't want her to see the wound.

She brought him water. They chatted about the recent heat wave. And then she said, "I have something to tell you."

He could hear the edge in her voice.

"Dr. Subramanian's taken a position back east," she said. "Cornell's opening a new neuroscience lab and he'll head it."

Rashad couldn't speak for a long moment. "And you? You're going with him?"

"In a few weeks. I need to finish my work with him, to get my PhD."

The room seemed to shift. It was the strongest, most piercing emotion he'd felt since the bullet. Had the DBI's neural network strengthened the signal as it passed through? Or, shit, *weakened* it?

Finally he said, "So you have no choice." Another failed attempt at a joke.

"There are good neurologists here," she said. "They'll continue to see you, and they know the protocols. You're not being abandoned."

It didn't feel that way. "Don't let them turn down the volume," he said. "Please. The implant's working."

"I can't promise you. Your brother wants to end treatment."

Another blow. They were coming too fast now, getting past his guard. He said, "Leo can't do that."

"He's your legal guardian. He has medical power of attorney. If he wants to end treatment, I can't stop him." She touched his hand. She'd never done that before. "But I'll try to convince him to keep you in treatment."

"The DBI stays on," he said. "My choice."

The night after Pierce and Conseco died, Rashad kept his shit together by staying busy and focusing on the next day's mission. He did not break down when he was ordered to visit the family of the people who'd been in Building 31. He made his apology and the company captain paid the survivors 100,000 rupees, which came out to about $1,100 US per victim. One old man, four women, and three children. The surviving brother claimed they weren't secessionists and didn't know the sniper. Through the translator he said, "When they tell you they're coming into your home, you have no choice but to let them in."

Rashad projected calm when the squad rotated out of Tartuk, said he was happy to spend the next four weeks in the relative safety of Srinagar while they waited to return to Camp Pendleton.

The SHEP never left Tartuk; it was passed to another squad staying in the village. But the robot had already taught him what he needed to understand, just as the Rifleman's Creed had promised. *My rifle is human, even as I, because it is my life. Thus, I will learn it as a brother.* Once they reached stateside there'd be no more open carry; his sidearm and rifle would stay in the armory when he wasn't on the shooting range.

So. It would have to be here, in the barracks in Srinagar.

He'd heard about jumpers from the Golden Gate, who changed their minds between the bridge and the water. He wasn't that kind of person. His mind was made up.

His body, however, betrayed him. When he awoke in the hospital he realized that his hand must have shifted, or his head pulled back. Some subconscious reflex. The bullet entered at an oblique angle and exited without killing him. By then, however, the failure didn't bother him.

Leo and Marisa were arguing. Rashad could hear them from his bedroom. For the past few weeks he'd chosen to spend most of his time here. He was no longer interested in watching Leo and Marisa's TV shows, eating the meals they prepared. He came out to microwave his own food and take a shit and sometimes, when they were asleep, pace the circle of the living room, kitchen, and dining room. He left the house only for his regular appointments with Alejandra. He'd refused to visit the therapist she'd found for him. He needed isolation and quiet for the work he was doing.

The arguing stopped and then they knocked at his door. Kept knocking. He let them in. They stood over him as he sat on the bed, hands on knees. He hated himself for putting them through all this. They were good people.

"Dude," Leo said. "This isn't working. You can see it's not working, right?" He described Rashad's various behaviors over the past few weeks, as if Rashad wasn't aware of them.

"I can leave," he said.

"That's not what we're saying!" Marisa said.

Leo said, "We just have to talk to Alejandra before she bails on you. There's something wrong with the implant. The way you're feeling, this isn't you."

"You're wrong," Rashad said. "This is *finally* me." He could feel the DBI working, like a cave tunnel widening day by day, letting through more and more water. "I can't go back to what I was before."

"That's the implant telling you that," Leo said.

And Rashad thought, What part of your subconscious is making you say *that?* Whether the subsystem was mechanical or biological made no difference.

"When we go in tomorrow," Leo said, "I'm going to tell them to turn that thing off."

"That's *not* what I agreed to," Marisa said hotly.

Rashad was surprised they weren't on the same page. He'd thought they'd been arguing about how to confront him, not what to say.

Marisa said, "Numbness isn't the answer."

"Thank you," Rashad said. "I have to—" His voice broke. How could he explain that he wanted this pain? That he believed in it. He'd turned the bedroom into a kind of arena—Rashad Before Bullet versus Rashad After—and he didn't want to shrink from those blows. It would be immoral to not feel that pain. What kind of coward would he be if now, after finally regaining the ability to regret what he'd done, he refused to face it? "I have to take responsibility."

"You did what you had to do," Leo said.

"I'm not saying you shouldn't take responsibility," Marisa said. She knelt so that she and Rashad were eye to eye. "I'm saying you don't have to keep beating yourself up about it."

"Yeah, I do," Rashad answered. "That's the point."

"You can ask God for forgiveness."

Leo groaned. "Can we keep this on track?"

"Why would I do that?" Rashad said to her. "So I can feel better?" He shook his head. "I'm not going to shrug this off. I'm not going to *move on*, now that I have a second chance." The bullet that had meant to be his punishment had robbed him of it.

"Please," Marisa said. "It's not so hard. You can ask Jesus to come into your heart."

"Definitely not." No more intercessors, strengthening some signals of forgiveness, dampening remorse. "My heart," he said, "is crowded enough."

*

"Pick a card," Alejandra said. "Any card."

Yellow X. Red circle. Green triangle.

"Why are we doing this?"

"Humor me. One final exam."

"More data for your dissertation." It was a mean thing to say. He tapped the green triangle.

She put the card away and said, "Okay, pick a card."

"You're not going to replace the card?"

"No."

That annoyed him, this change in the rules. Wouldn't this mess up her results? He looked at the red circle, then the yellow X. He suspected she wanted him to choose that second card, and he didn't appreciate being manipulated. He tapped the red circle.

She removed the circle and dealt a new card. Blue square. He quickly tapped it. She took it away and dealt the circle again.

"Oh come on," he said.

"Pick a card," she said.

"You want me to pick the yellow X. Why?"

"Pick whichever you want."

He flicked the red circle toward her and it slid off the table. Immediately he felt like a dick. She calmly retrieved the card and dealt a new one from the deck.

A yellow X. Two of them on the table now, side by side.

"Pick a card," she said.

He couldn't remember a time where there'd been a pair of matching cards on the table. Was this some new requirement phoned in by Dr. S? Or maybe she was going rogue, defying the doctor's orders. There'd always been a tension between those two, a struggle for power—the grad student chafing under the control of the mentor. In the early appointments, he didn't have the emotional equipment to figure out their relationship. But now the DBI floodgates were open. Everything his back-brain had noticed and reacted to was available to him now. He could make any decision he wanted—including the decision to not participate.

"I'm done," he said.

"Please, Rashad. Pick a card."

"There's no choice. They're the same."

"Think of them as right and left. Which do you choose?"

"There's no point. You're leaving."

"All right," she said evenly. "Do you want to sit down?"

He realized that in his anger he'd stood up. He was looming over the table, his heart beating fast.

"Can you put those away?" he asked. The pair of Xs looked like the eyes of a cartoon corpse.

"Could you pass them to me?" she replied.

Fuck you. Immediately he felt childish—but still didn't want to give in. "They're right in front of you."

Suddenly she looked sad. No, sad was too broad a word—there were more fine-grained descriptors for what he saw in her face. Resignation? Regret? Then she swept the cards toward her, and when she looked up at him again she was assessing him. She'd learned something new about him, he realized. By calling a halt to the test, he'd continued the test.

This unnerved him. He unclenched his hands. Took his seat. He couldn't look directly at her. He could see that her hand still held the deck of cards.

"I know you're going through a rough time," she said. "But I want you to hold on. You can call me anytime. I'll do anything in my power to help you."

Except stay.

"There's something else." There it was again, the same hesitancy as when she told him she was leaving. He understood now that the assuredness he'd seen in her in those first appointments was a kind of uniform she put on. He'd done that himself, many times. "I need to tell you about a part of the treatment."

"Okay . . ."

"We had to decide on some images as controls—we hard-coded some to a set value. For example, some images always have an output of a positive value."

"Puppies? All those pictures of dogs?"

"It wasn't that, but yes, something like that."

"Without telling me." He couldn't keep the anger out of his voice.

"I'm sorry." Her voice had gone soft. "It wouldn't be a control if we told you. And we also chose one to be a negative value. Something's that's always aversive. Something you'd avoid at all costs —even if later you had to make up a story for why you chose what you did."

Her hand still lay on the deck. And then he understood. His chest tightened. "Yellow X."

"You've never chosen it. Not once. At first, you couldn't choose *any* card. But then we turned on the DBI, and we made it difficult for you to choose that card—and then impossible."

"You can't know that. I *could* have chosen it."

"Yet you never did."

"Deal the cards."

"Are you sure you want to do this?"

"Do it."

She shuffled through the deck, chose three, and laid them out. Green rectangle. Red circle. Yellow X.

She watched him. As soon as he chose, she'd record it in her tablet, and that would be their final interaction. Tomorrow she'd fly across the country to join Dr. Subramanian. They'd make their careers off of his injury, his handicap, his crimes.

He was tired of being data. He knew which card he'd choose, but that didn't mean he'd have to share it with her.

"Sorry, Alejandra." He stood up. "You don't get to know."

The gun sat inside the open box. He felt queasy looking at the gleaming metal, as if the weight of it bowed the floor, drawing the walls toward him.

You did what you had to do. Bullshit, of course. Yes, in the final moments he was part of an unstoppable chain reaction. Neurons fired, his fist closed, the palm switch activated, the SHEP's gun discharged, bullets followed the path decided by physics. But that didn't mean he could deny the series of choices he'd made to that point. He chose to enlist. He chose to go to systems operation school. He chose to send the SHEP into that home. The women and children in that house were simply the last dominoes to fall in a sequence he had initiated years ago. Maybe Alejandra was right, and ATLAS had been rigged for Yes, designed to take the burden from his shoulders—it was right there in its name, for Christ's sake. But none of that absolved him.

He knew what sin was. And he didn't want to believe in a world where sinners escaped justice.

He reached into the box. His hand was shaking. Coward, he thought. He grunted and forced his hand around the grip.

It was as if he'd stepped off a precipice, plummeting through air, the water rushing to meet him. The gun fell from his hand. He scrambled to his feet and stumbled to the bathroom. Emptied his stomach into the toilet.

He sat on the floor, sweating, his arms trembling.

Leo heard the noise. He came into the bathroom, knelt beside him. "What's the matter? Is it the implant?"

Rashad couldn't speak. Images flashed behind his eyelids. Yellow X. Pistol. Yellow X. He heard Alejandra's voice: *I'll do anything in my power to help you.*

Leo put his hand on Rashad's back. "I'm here for you, bro. I've been so worried about you. Just tell me what you need."

It wasn't what Rashad needed that was important, it was what he wanted—and that had changed the moment he touched the gun. He'd never been so sure of anything in his life.

The Rat

FROM *One Story*

FOR NEW YORK at 6:48 in the evening, this building is strangely quiet. The one working light in the hallway flickers every ten seconds across the goose-bump layers of glossy beige paint on the walls. I ring the bell again and let my finger drop as a weak chime echoes feebly, then dies somewhere beyond the door. A distant thud tells me to wait a few moments longer, and I look down at my scuffed sneakers against the black and white tiled floor. I'm hot in my ridiculous corn-yellow blazer and my shoulder slouches from the weight of my Kutco-issued messenger bag. Is it just me, or does this hallway smell like trash?

I place my forehead against the wall and let my mind wander to where it always goes, to my mother. I'm sitting on a dresser in her bedroom in Flushing, legs hanging over the edge. She's wearing a black dress with a swishy skirt and heels. She's leaning over me, painting my lips with the careful, whiskery strokes of a lip brush. Her perfume envelops me, that lace of roses, honey, and tobacco that smells different on my skin, no matter how many times I spray it.

Here, in this dark hallway, I sniff my wrist and let it drop. I'll never smell her again.

"I'm coming!" calls a voice from somewhere in the bowels of the apartment, and the memory evaporates.

"Okay," I shout back. I think about what I must look like in this ill-fitting suit, with its skirt that turns sideways no matter how much I adjust it, and the button-down that keeps untucking itself, and the blazer that bunches at the shoulders whenever I shift the messenger bag. These clothes are trying to free themselves from me. Can I blame them?

Throwing my shoulders back, I widen my smile, which I hope looks less like a grimace than it feels. If I can sell three knives, I'll break even today. If I sell any fewer than that, I'll be struggling for the rest of the pay period, a dark, gaping thirteen-day yawn.

The door whooshes open and a tall woman in a gray silk robe looks me over and then extends her hand. She wears a full face of makeup and cocktail rings on every finger, but she's barefoot. "Thank you for coming," she says. "I'm Consuelo."

"I'm Samanta," I say, shaking her hand, which is surprisingly cool. "Thank you for signing up for a visit. I'm excited to show you the new spring collection."

She nods without enthusiasm and leads me down a long, bare hallway to a kitchen just large enough for a fridge, a stove, and a small table.

"Make yourself at home, Samanta." She starts opening and closing cabinet drawers, her large, bare, manicured feet moving gracefully across the small kitchen floor. Her hair is an improbable shade of blond that looks salon-fresh and sits in a tousled pile on her head. I sit at the table and struggle to read the room: the air is vaguely musty, but the little gingham curtains that cover the barred window are clean. The floor has crumbs on it, but matching pot holders hang near the sink.

A cuckoo clock ticks on the wall. This woman seems harmless enough, so why am I reminding myself that I'm the one with the bag full of knives?

"Are you hungry?" Consuelo says into the fridge.

I'm on the wrong side of the door and can't see what the fridge contains. "Nothankyou," I trill. "I'm excited to talk to you about Kutco's latest off—"

"Here's some snacks," she says. She dumps a juice box and four wrapped string cheese sticks onto the table and sits down. I finally get a good look at her. She's youthful but older than I first assumed, maybe in her sixties, skin feathering around her eyes.

My mother looked nothing like this woman, but my mind is pulled back into the undertow of her anyway. I see her in the days before she died, her shrunken frame nearly swallowed by white bedding and overstuffed pillows. She sits up as if she's just remembered something. "Pass me my lipstick," she says. Cherries in the

Snow. Even without a mirror, her hands are steady and she draws on the red pout, smooth and sure. She blots her lips together and says, "That's better." Says, "Take a photo to remember me by."

Her things, which I rescued from Flushing in white Hefty bags, are piled high in a corner of my bedroom now. I've sat on the floor and leaned against them just to listen to the whisper of their quiet squelching. I've applied the lipstick using her compact mirror. On my mother, the shade was glamorous. On me, it's gaudy and clownish.

This far out, I am past the point of crying. Now, I have a new pastime: I go to Walgreens and buy a tube of Cherries in the Snow. At home, I toss away the box and unspool the lipstick to its full length, then break it off into my palms, where I crush it into a rich paste, relishing the powdery smell and the long, focused minutes it takes to wash the pigment off with soap, to watch the red drain away, leaving oily traces all over the bathroom sink. Rinse and repeat. There are at least twenty empty lipstick husks scattered on the floor of my bedroom.

In Consuelo's kitchen, the clock ticks and ticks and ticks. I swallow hard and focus on unpacking my carrying case, launching into a patter I have memorized about the power of Kutco knives to dice vegetables and debone various animals. "These knives will be heirlooms! Passed down through gen—"

"You are sad and you are angry," Consuelo says. "And you'll stay that way for a long time."

She watches me, unblinking. What is this woman, a fucking soothsayer? I close my eyes long enough to picture my bank balance. We can play fortune-teller if she wants. My job is to be agreeable, to ingratiate myself enough to sell these overpriced knives.

"Yes," I say. "My mother died two years ago."

"Two years ago is a long time to still be so sad," she says. She leans back in her chair, as if to survey me better.

"Maybe," I concede. "Have you seen our deluxe steak knives?"

"How old are you? Twenty-five? You have a boyfriend?"

"Twenty-eight and no," I say, unsheathing a butcher knife and letting it catch the light. "Twelve inches," I say.

"Of course you're single. Not a nightmare to look at, but that grief is coming off you in waves. I can smell it." She unwraps the little plastic straw, punctures the juice box, and pushes it across the table.

I take a long drag and feel the sugar rush of elementary school recess. My mother marching across the playground barefaced, in her waitressing uniform and flip-flops, to pick me up after I punched Roy Jimenez in the face. The red shame of not being believed when I said he tried to pull my pants down on the jungle gym.

In Principal Berger's office, my mother—who had never so much as darkened the threshold of my school in anything other than heels and full makeup—smoothed her uniform with her palms and began to ask questions in her broken English. Who had a record for misbehaving? Was it her daughter, or was it this disgusting boy? I'd never seen her do anything but nod deferentially at my teachers, her head slightly bowed and her hands gripping her leather handbag. Why would a girl, she said, waving a crimson manicured hand in my direction, lie about something like this? One reason, please, she said, glancing at her watch. She had time, she said. She would wait.

After Principal Berger agreed to move Roy to a different class, I begged my mother to let me go home with her for the day. "The other kids will see that I was crying and laugh at me," I said.

She walked me out to the linoleum hallway of PS 172, put her hands on my shoulders, and squatted down to look me in the eye.

"So what," she said in Spanish. She wiped a thumb across my tearstained cheek. "You've had a bad day. You think all those snot-nosed kids in your class don't have bad days? There's no shame in suffering, the shame is in giving up."

"But I need a break," I whined.

"Me too," she said. "But for now, we're both going back to work. We're a team, right, Sammy? You and me?"

An hour later, I was back in class, head bent over my spelling assignment, two kids snickering in the row behind me. When the tears threatened to come, I pictured my mother, all done up and glossy-smiled, taking down an order at the Cuban diner. I clenched my jaw and, in my neatest handwriting, wrote out the word *kneel*.

In Consuelo's kitchen, I look down at my lap so she can't see my face. I silently count to ten, then I resume taking out knives and laying them on the table, next to a glossy photograph of the matching knife holders and wooden butcher blocks available for order.

"Unlike your standard knife with porous wooden handles, Kutco knives—"

"I'll buy a set," Consuelo says, leaning across the table and putting her hand on mine.

I fight the urge to pull my hand back. "Really?"

"I'll buy the whole kit," she says.

"But that costs over a thousand dollars," I hear myself say. How can I be so bad at this job?

"No problem," she says. She rises and comes back with an expensive-looking leather wallet. She takes out an Amex card and puts it on the table.

"Will selling a kit make your life better?"

"Yes," I say automatically.

"Well," she said. "There's something I've wanted to do for a long time that will make *my* life better." She looks away from me and picks up a napkin. She starts folding it with her bejeweled fingers.

I look at her dumbly, then back over my shoulder at the front door, which is barely visible at the end of the long, dark hallway. My underarms start to sweat.

"It's not dangerous," she says. With steady fingers, she folds the napkin in on itself, over and over, until it's a small fat square. "I want to take your grief out," she says, then says it again when it's clear that I don't understand.

"H-how?"

She unsheathes a butcher knife from its crisp paper sleeve. "In your wrist," she says. "Your grief, I want to cut it out."

I jump up and back, catching my foot in the strap of the messenger bag and knocking over the juice box. Red liquid dribbles onto the table.

"I'll buy two sets of knives, if that will help you decide. What's that, two thousand dollars?" Her voice is low and soft. "And I'll demonstrate on myself first. It won't hurt. I'll show you first and you decide."

Pulling the chair an arm's length from the table, I sit back down, holding my messenger bag in front of my body.

A bird pops out of the cuckoo clock behind Consuelo and we wait while it performs seven pealing, pathetic *coo-koo*s.

Consuelo picks up the knife with her right hand and shows me her left wrist, which already has a thin vertical strip of a scar on it about two inches long. With the tip of the knife, she applies enough pressure to make the scar a wound, a narrow red line. I expect the blood to pour from her wrist like something out of a horror movie, but the cut seems impossibly thin, as if drawn with the tip of a pen.

"I don't have grief," she says. "Someone took it out for me. I can take yours out, too."

I am anchored to the kitchen floor. I look at the inside of my wrist and then I look back at her. "What's the small print?"

"No small print," she says, holding out her wrist for me to see again. "I take the grief out and then it's no longer yours. It's gone."

"What's in it for you?" I say, watching the thin red line begin to darken. Is it already healing?

"Making the world less sad," she says, opening and closing her palm slowly on the table as the line darkens to scab-maroon. "Someone did it for me once, and I want to pass it on. Isn't that what you want?"

I watch as my own arm drapes itself across the small table, my palm turns upward, and my wrist presents itself to her. She cradles my hand and uses the knife to draw a thin, sure line from me to her. I look away from the cut and focus on the vertical lifelines of my palms, the whorled tips of my fingers. I don't feel the knife.

She nudges the cut open with the tip of the blade and shifts the point around until she finds something just beneath the skin. An object the size and shape of a grain of rice sits on the tip of her knife, coated in blood. I feel a sense of release in my belly that I've never felt before. I feel as if I could float up, up, up in Consuelo's kitchen, and touch the ceiling.

"You don't need that anymore," she says brightly. She turns the knife and lets the grain of rice drop to the table with a faint plink, then brushes it to the linoleum floor with the back of her hand, where it bounces and disappears amid the crumbs. Consuelo gets up to rummage around in what appears to be a junk drawer, then returns with a box of medical gauze and a roll of bandage tape. She deftly wraps my wrist in a bandage before wrapping her own.

I take my wrist back and place it on my lap, afraid of reopening the wound. My rib cage blooms.

Consuelo buys $2,000 worth of knives and I swipe her credit card on my Kutco phone attachment. I pack up, unsteady but relishing this new, delicious weightlessness. Everything feels the same, but *easier,* somehow.

When Consuelo walks me to the door, though, I see a small shadow run across the far end of the hallway. A fat, rodent-sized blur.

"Oh, don't worry about the rats," says Consuelo behind me. "They don't hurt anyone."

Reason returns for a split second, a chill thin as thread: I have just allowed a stranger with a rat-infested apartment to perform a bizarre amateur surgical procedure on me in her kitchen. I wrap a hand around the bandage and pray that the wound doesn't get infected.

Then a frisson of pure delight and forgetting washes over me, and all I think is how crisp and cool the air feels in my lungs. I pull my shoulders back to breathe deeper and remember that my rent is now paid for two whole months. My eyes crinkle at the corners when I smile at Consuelo, and my chest feels like it will burst open to release a thousand birds. I thank her and briefly squeeze her hands in mine, then bound toward the door as if my shoes are made of springs.

My pleasant fog practically carries me out of the subway, up the stairs, and down Broadway. In my apartment, I flutter directly to the tower of white garbage bags filled with my dead mother's things.

Possessed by an unfamiliar clarity, I dump one of the bags out on the bedroom floor and pick out the things that might be useful to keep: the angora sweater I loved, her costume jewelry, her makeup, a photo album. I sift through the piles with ruthless fingers, the drugstore pressed powders two shades too light for my skin, the photos of her dancing in Cuba as a girl, a sequined blouse she must have worn before I was born.

Efficiently, I work through all of the Hefty bags and throw away everything except a handful of items, and these I put away among my things, cleaning and humming as I go. I also throw away all of the empty lipstick tubes. As I scrub the remnants of red lipstick from the bathroom sink, I catch my reflection in the mirror and realize that I have not stopped smiling since leaving Consuelo's house.

Out in the kitchen, I open a window and let in the summer night air while I wash the dishes in the sink. The sounds of the city bubble in from the street: car horns, a distant radio, sirens, shouts of kids playing. *Tomorrow*, I think, and for the first time in a long time, the word expands before me like unmarred snow.

When the apartment is clean, I change into pajamas. On my back, I spread my arms and drift, weightless and cradled, on the sea of my bed. I sleep like a baby, my mind blank, pristine.

I wake up with the sun and float around my apartment, getting dressed. I go to two appointments downtown and sell two sets of knives. At the second appointment, the woman says, smiling, "You seem so happy. You must really like your job." On the train home, people smile at me, and it's as if I'm emanating something beautiful and pure, something people want more of.

A memory surfaces, unbidden, of the day after my mother died. How I had gone to the funeral home to choose her casket, and then cried on the subway, my head in my hands, a Hefty bag of her belongings stuffed between my knees. How people had looked in the other direction, and sidled silently away, as if sadness were an airborne disease you could catch.

I let the memory go and focus instead on a cute guy sitting across from me. I catch his eye and smile. He flushes and smiles back. My stop is next and I walk home, awake to the electricity of the city. I turn onto my street and see a rat standing in the middle of the sidewalk, waiting. I give it a wide berth, shivering with disgust as I enter my building, where I spend the evening lounging on the couch, imagining new jobs, boyfriends, and tropical vacations.

The next morning, I raise the blinds of my bedroom window and a rat is perched outside on the air conditioner, watching me. I scream even though the rat can't touch me, even though we are separated by a thick pane of glass. The rat doesn't move. How did it get there?

The rat watches me as I cower behind the bedroom door and peer out at it. After a few tense minutes, I finally do what I do best: I scurry across the room, yank the blinds down, and hope the problem goes away. I spend the morning army-crawling around my bedroom like an idiot, trying to get dressed without—what? Alarming the rat?

I briefly consider dislodging the air conditioning unit and pushing the entire thing out the window, letting it drop three floors into the airshaft below, but then I imagine the rat running up the slope of the air conditioner and onto my arms as I push. I've seen YouTube videos of New York City rats scaling the facades of apartment buildings.

Its stolid, determined rat silhouette is still visible through the blinds when I leave for my first house call. I comfort myself by deciding that I will call an exterminator if the rat is still there when I get home. I put my headphones on and walk toward the subway. It's eight in the morning and the city's already in full swing. I let my attention rove over the street vendors and the schoolteacher walking a caterpillar of toddlers on a giant leash.

I stop to wait for a light and there it is, next to me. A woman standing nearby screams and a man shouts "Rat!" and stomps to scare it away. The rat doesn't run, and the man pulls a leg back and kicks it as hard as he can with a heavy construction boot.

I wince at the thud the boot makes against the rat's body, and then sigh in relief when the rat flies through the air and disappears behind a pile of trash bags waiting for pickup. I run down the steps, onto the subway platform, and jump onto the 1 train right before the doors close. The car is nearly empty. I put my headphones on with shaky fingers as the train pulls out of the station.

A few stops later, a gaggle of teenage girls get on. By the time we start moving again, they're applying lip gloss and tittering and TikTok-ing videos of themselves making faces and doing stupid dances.

My heart rate slows as I watch them and think of all the friends I let drift away. Who would want to hang out with someone who can barely keep it together for a dinner without crying, anyway? I'm ashamed at my old weakness.

For the first time in a long time, I am able to keep my thoughts away from my mother. I think of the friends I might call this weekend instead. I scroll through the contacts on my phone. I can do dinner now; I can feel it.

The girls have gone quiet and they're looking in my direction. Oh, God. What is it? I look for stains on my hideous yellow suit, and the girls start screaming and leap up onto the orange and mustard-colored seats of the moving train. They're clinging to the metal bars and pointing to my left. I follow their eyes and fingers.

There, four seats down from me, its long tail hanging over the edge of the seat like a whip, sits the rat.

I scream, too, and sprint to the door on the other side of the car, where I cower near the girls until the train stops. When it does, I run out onto the platform and, heart pounding, take the stairs three at a time to get out to the street. I run through the first door I come to, a bank. Inside, it's quiet. A line of customers waits for the teller.

"What can we do for you today?" a woman at the information desk asks.

The rat waits outside, watching me through the glass, seemingly indifferent to the throngs of people walking up and down Broadway.

"Um, I'm not sure yet," I say, pulling out my phone. I google "animal control." I google "rat disease." I get a call from Kutco about the house call I am scheduled to make. The client is expecting me, the operator says, and wants to know if I'm running late. I say yes, I am, and apologize. I hang up and book an Uber.

The rat watches me scramble into the car, watches me slam the door hard behind me.

The house call is a bust and the woman seems incredulous that a company has employed someone as untethered as me to sell knives. I pack up my wares and nurse the cup of herbal tea she's given me, just to put off leaving. I do leave, eventually, but I don't see the rat again until I approach my apartment building after two more failed house calls. It's waiting a few feet from the entrance, its fur glimmering in the streetlight.

When I open the door, it doesn't try to dart into the building with me, and for that I mumble a grudging *thank you* as I pull the door shut with trembling hands.

The next morning, the rat is waiting outside my bedroom window again. I finally get up the courage to look at it straight on.

It's ugly, even for a New York City rat: about the size of a squirrel, gray with bald spots and scars. One of its ears is missing. Its tail is as long as a ruler and its eyes are beads of gasoline.

I snap the blinds down again.

The next morning, I take the bandage off and throw it away. Then I scurry to the subway station and take the train back to Hamilton Heights. On the way, I look at the healed line on my wrist.

I march down the musty old hallway and rap-rap-rap on the door like I'm the police, like I'm owed a debt.

A woman I've never seen opens the door just wide enough to release a flood of soapy, Cloroxy air. She is wearing elbow-length dishwashing gloves and an exasperated look. She tells me she doesn't know anything about the previous tenant, this slovenly Consuelo. The new tenant looks me up and down, clearly dismissing me as a grubby acquaintance of Consuelo's.

"She didn't leave a new address," the woman says. Then she dashes back into the apartment and returns with a broom. She pounds it on the tile floor and I realize that the rat has been sitting in the middle of the hallway, behind me. It darts around the corner and out of sight, but I know it hasn't gone far.

"Fucking rats," the woman says, breathless with anger. "They're everywhere."

When I find the rat lingering in the hall outside my apartment the following day, I race past it to buy three packs of rat poison from the deli downstairs. After racing past it again, I mix the poison with mac and cheese. I put this on a plate and set the plate on the floor outside my apartment, where it sits untouched for three days.

It begins to dawn on me that I will not outrun this rat. I google "immortal new york city rat" and get no results. I call an exterminator and they say they'll come next week. I call next week and they say they'll come next week.

I begin to pray that someone else—or something else—will kill the rat. In my prayers, a car flattens the rat. In my prayers, some deadly disease vanquishes the rat. In my prayers, a giant cat descends from above with lethal claws and slaughters the rat.

One night, I drink an entire bottle of wine alone and decide to take care of the problem myself. I unsheathe the large chef's knife from my Kutco kit, pull on a pair of galoshes over my pajama pants, and stalk out into the hallway, bleary-eyed and homicidal.

The rat is there, waiting, and before I can think myself out of it, I raise the knife, close my eyes, and bring the blade down with both arms. The blade passes through something thin and firm, and then connects with the tiled floor. I open my eyes as the rat lets out a keening shriek. It blurs off down the hallway, leaving a thin trail of blood and a tiny piece of its tail behind, no longer than a fingernail.

It is all I can do to throw the knife into the sink, double-lock the doors, and cower in the bathtub for the rest of the night.

The next morning, I don't see the rat outside my apartment door and I don't see it outside my window. I'm too hungover to be elated. Instead, I pull on a pair of jeans and my yellow blazer. I trudge from apartment to apartment, extolling the wonders of the new Kutco steak knives and showcasing the scissors, which can cut straight through a penny.

On the commutes, I google "new york rat life span" (one year). I google "diseases new york rats carry" (all of them). I google "will cutting off a piece of a rat's tail kill it" (no). I blanch at the thought of the knife that's still sitting in the sink, inked in the rat's blood. I google "disinfectant." I google "sterilizing cleaners."

I get home and the rat is waiting inside my house, in the kitchen.

My rat and I look at each other. She is wary and still, as if she is afraid of startling me.

How old is she? She is either an old rat or an extraordinarily war-battered one, with three blooms of mottled skin where her fur no longer grows. The length of my forearm, she must weigh a pound, at least. Her four-fingered paws remind me of human hands. Her front left one is mangled, probably injured in a trap —how she must have fought to free herself. The missing chunk of an ear. The tail, its tip scab-dark, dry, and already healing. She looks up at me, her dark eyes and quivering pink nose track my every breath. I imagine her teeth, sharp and vicious, though I don't see them.

I walk with halting steps toward the kitchen sink. With a shaking hand, I take hold of the knife. I raise it, knowing somehow that this time she will let me bring it down on her body, she will not run or bite me with those jagged teeth. This time, I won't close my eyes as I scythe through her.

The rat watches me.

I take a deep breath. I will kill this rat and put her in the garbage, where she belongs. I will piece my life back together. I will move on. I will move on. I will move on.

Instead, I lay the knife down on the table.

I lean against the wall and let myself slide down to the floor. I trace a finger over the scar on my wrist, a thin, two-inch line, ruler straight. I hug my knees to my chest.

In my memory, my mother picks me up by the underarms and stands me on her dresser. "My big girl," she says. She helps me turn toward the mirror and then holds me against her torso until I am stable on my own two feet, which are clad in black patent leather Mary Janes. Her makeup is littered across the dresser around my feet, her jewelry spread across small, shallow glass saucers. I hold still, proud that she's trusting me not to stumble and kick all these beautiful breakable things.

I look up at us in the mirror. We wear matching dresses: hers a white and red floral sundress with thin straps, mine a cotton shift in the same pattern. It's summer and both our noses are a little red from the sun. She has brushed my damp hair into a neat braid. My lips are the same color as hers, Cherries in the Snow. She has dusted my cheeks with a hint of blush.

"There," she says in Spanish. She hugs me from behind, and her hair curtains over my shoulder in blow-dried auburn waves. Her smell wraps around me, that mix of rose, honey, and tobacco. She taps my chin with a warm hand and the gold bracelets on her wrist tinkle. "I've done it. I've left you my face to remember me by."

On the floor of the kitchen, I let my grief draw closer, let its sour, rotten odor fill my nostrils. I sink my head into my knees and a searing white pain tightens my rib cage: unbearable, necessary, familiar.

As she nears, the rat's body radiates a strange heat. She presses her full weight against my leg and I straighten it out. Cautiously, she climbs onto my shin, and I feel her claws through the thick denim of my jeans. I let her perch herself on my knee.

I let her stay.

Contributors' Notes

Other Notable Science Fiction and
Fantasy Stories of 2020

Contributors' Notes

Senaa Ahmad's short fiction has appeared in *The Paris Review, Lightspeed, Uncanny Magazine, Strange Horizons,* and elsewhere. A Clarion 2018 alum, she's received the generous support of the Octavia Butler Scholarship, the Speculative Literature Foundation, the Canada Council for the Arts, the Ontario Arts Council, and the Toronto Arts Council. She's the recipient of the 2019 Sunburst Award for Short Fiction.

▪ Many years ago, I had this idea for a metafictional, kind of experimental short story collection. I finally wrote the first few stories at the 2018 Clarion Writers' Workshop, mostly in a sweaty, unair-conditioned dorm, mostly in a panicked run against time, still trying to figure out how the collection would feel and work.

"Let's Play Dead" was the first of these stories. I'd been thinking about the ways stories create distance from their readers, ejecting them from the immediacy or emotion of a moment, and where that distance can be useful. For example, how it can dilute or even undercut incidents of violence, so these moments don't become grueling to read. Sometimes, this "useful" distance can come from humor, or surrealism, or breaking the fourth wall, or a particularly slippery narrator.

Other things that fed this story (a very incomplete list): Italo Calvino's mind-bending use of anachronism in "The Dinosaurs," Kate Bernheimer's essay "Fairy Tale Is Form, Form Is Fairy Tale," that Millais painting of Ophelia, how cockroaches can survive decapitation but will die eventually of thirst, all the dazzling stories from my fellow writers at the workshop (a couple weeks after this, Mel Kassel would write the perfect, delightful "Crawfather"). I'm wildly grateful to Hasan Altaf at *The Paris Review* for pulling this story from the slush and for lasering in on things I wanted to improve but didn't know how.

I wrote this story for many of the obvious reasons. I also wrote it as a sort of one-way correspondence to people I have known, mostly women in my life. A profound pleasure of publishing the story was to have some of them read it.

Celeste Rita Baker is a Virgin Islander currently flitting between the beach and the grocery store as she tries to be one of the survivors of de 'rona pandemic. She chronicled COVID-19 in a rudely opinionated timeline from October 2019 through March 2020, after which she just could not "go another further." It's on Amazon as "De Rona Reach." She is also the author of *Back, Belly, and Side,* a short story collection, a mix-up of magical realism, fantasy, and mimetic fiction, some in Caribbean dialect and some in Standard English. Her stories have been included in *The Caribbean Writer, Moko, Strange Horizons, Lightspeed,* and other publications. She used to love doing live performance readings, often in costumes she'd made herself, and hopes to again one day when we can safely gather. A proud 2019 graduate of Clarion West Writers Workshop, she is noticing that her stories are getting more and more silly and absurd and is loving it. Her website is celesteritabaker.com and she is occasionally on Twitter as @tenwest522.

▪ I jumped back and almost fell off the chair several times while doing the research for "Glass Bottle Dancer." Eventually I learned to stand up and reach the keyboard with my arms fully extended. I screamed and cackled and laughed at myself, but I just could not change the roaches to a more socially acceptable creature, like butterflies or grasshoppers. Much as they do in our own homes, they insinuated themselves into the story, which is about a human woman, Mable, and her determination to learn something frivolous just for fun.

I looked at photos of roaches until I learned to appreciate their beauty. I read about roaches until I understood how they contribute to the health of the planet. I knew if I had any hope of readers liking Oswald, Treevia, and their swarm, I had to like them first.

When Mable's ability to dance roaches out of the homes of people and back to their intended environment eliminated the use of pesticides, both of which contribute to asthma and other respiratory conditions, I was delighted with the convergence. I enjoyed being Mable's friend and companion as she stayed dedicated, despite her responsibilities and the opinions of others, to putting time and energy into adding a purely personal joy into her life. It is something I am continually learning to do. I had a great time writing this story and I hope you enjoyed it.

KT Bryski is a Canadian author, playwright, and podcaster. Her short fiction has appeared in *Nightmare, Lightspeed, Apex, Strange Horizons, Augur,* and *PodCastle,* among others, and her audio dramas are available wherever fine podcasts are found. She's won the Parsec and the Toronto Star Short

Story Contest, and she has been a finalist for the Aurora and the Sunburst. KT also cochairs ephemera, a monthly speculative fiction reading series. When she's not writing, KT frolics through Toronto, enjoying choral music and craft beer. Find her on Twitter @ktbryski.

- I suspect that in years to come, saying, "I wrote this story in 2020" will solicit an understanding nod. It was an exceptionally difficult year for most people: global pandemic, long-overdue societal reckoning, trauma, and heartbreak.

For me, there was a lot of anger. As usual, I wrestled it fairly philosophically—and partly through the lens of my own Anglicanism. "What does it *mean,* to forgive? What if the other party doesn't feel remorse? Wait, isn't the point of grace that it's undeserved? Well, maybe for *God,* but I'm only human . . ."

And so it went. Eventually, I thought, "This is interesting. I've never had *rage* as my baseline emotion." But almost immediately, I realized that wasn't true. The last time I'd been so consistently angry, I was in elementary school, getting bullied. (Ironically, I was bullied for liking girls and writing stories. I must admit to a certain amount of satisfaction in growing up to become a queer fantasy author.)

So I took that context, those feelings, and I gave them to Emmy. Maybe I was feeding a tiger of my own. Or maybe I was working through the notion—as Emmy does—that anger isn't inherently bad, a thing to be fought and exorcised. Harnessed correctly, anger is rocket fuel.

Born and raised in New York City, **Yohanca Delgado** is a writer of Cuban and Dominican descent. She is a graduate of American University's MFA program, the Clarion Science Fiction and Fantasy Writers' Workshop, and the Voices of Our Nations workshops. Her fiction appears in *Nightmare, One Story, A Public Space, The Paris Review,* and elsewhere. She is a 2021–2023 Wallace Stegner Fellow at Stanford University.

- "The Rat" was written at the 2019 Clarion Workshop, where the good-but-intense creative pressure helped me bring some seemingly disparate elements together in a single story. I sold Cutco knives for a summer in high school and was atrocious at it, but it was fun to draw on that experience for this story, and to write a character that reminded me so much of myself. As I revised, I found my way to the central question of this story: What if you could bear to look at the full depth of your own grief—and recognize it for what it is, a record of all you have loved and survived in your life?

"Our Language" is tremendously important to me because it allowed me to directly explore my own Dominican lineage. It also taught me a lot about the importance of trust and patience in writing. I let myself write through the wilds of this tale, determined to let it be as strange as it wanted to be, but also knowing, deep down, that I needed the story to resolve in a way that resonated emotionally for me. I didn't know how to balance those two impulses, and so I didn't. Instead, I trusted the story and returned to it, over and over, for three years, until my subconscious told me where to go.

Gene Doucette (genedoucette.me) is a novelist, with over twenty science fiction and fantasy titles to his name, including *The Spaceship Next Door, The Frequency of Aliens,* the Immortal series, and the Tandemstar books. His latest novel is *The Apocalypse Seven.* This story is his first attempt at short-form science fiction. He lives in Cambridge, Massachusetts.

- The title came first.

I was brainstorming possible alternative titles for *The Apocalypse Seven* because at the time—a year after I'd written it—I'd become bored with the working title. (This happens a lot.) I pitched *Schrödinger's Catastrophe* to my editor, only half-seriously, as I thought it was both too clever/obscure and too whimsical. Said editor, who did *not* share my exhaustion with *The Apocalypse Seven* as a title, suggested that while *Schrödinger's Catastrophe* was indeed not a good fit for my apocalypse story, it *would* make for an excellent short story title.

So I wrote a story to go with the title.

I could say that "Schrödinger's Catastrophe" came to me quickly and I wrote it all at once in about ten days, but while this is *true,* it's also incomplete. The more complete version is that a lot of it had taken up permanent residence in my head long before I started writing; I'd explored quantum theory as a story premise before in a stage play I wrote in the early nineties, called *Deus ex Quanta.* (It was a locked-room mystery with two detectives attempting to solve the murder of a professor who was simultaneously alive.) "Schrödinger's Catastrophe," while featuring a very different plot, goes down the same path, but with the added advantage that I don't have to think about how one might stage it before a live audience.

I also apparently had a powerful need to write something a little absurd. That kind of opportunity doesn't come along very often.

Meg Elison is a science fiction author and feminist essayist. Her book series the Road to Nowhere won the 2014 Philip K. Dick award. She was an Otherwise Award Honoree in 2018. In 2020, she published her first short story collection, called *Big Girl,* containing the Hugo- and Nebula-nominated novelette "The Pill." Elison's first young adult novel, *Find Layla,* was published in 2020. Meg has been published in *McSweeney's, Fantasy & Science Fiction, Fangoria, Uncanny, Lightspeed, Nightmare,* and many other places. Elison is a high school dropout and a graduate of UC Berkeley. Learn more at megelison.com and @megelison.

- "The Pill" is a science fiction story that people tell me all the time is not really fiction. It is written from a fat life, about a fat life in a world that would rather we were almost anything than fat. I was inspired to write it by the death of a close friend's mother from complications arising from weight-loss surgery, and by the things people say at a fat person's funeral. I was affirmed in my convictions when the UK government started taking fat children away from their parents as a form of punishment. I wrote it in a white-hot rage after a doctor told me to lose weight to solve an eye infection. It is not really fiction.

Kate Elliott has been publishing for over thirty years with a particular focus in immersive world building and centering women in epic stories of adventure and transformative cultural change. Her most recent novel is *Unconquerable Sun,* gender-spun Alexander the Great in space. She is best known for her Crown of Stars epic fantasy series, the Afro-Celtic post-Roman alt-history fantasy with lawyer dinosaurs *Cold Magic,* and YA fantasy *Court of Fives.* Her work has been nominated for the Nebula, World Fantasy, Norton, and Locus Awards. Her novel *Black Wolves* won the RT Reviewers' Choice Award for Best Epic Fantasy 2015. She lives in Hawaii.
• When Jonathan Strahan invited me to write a story for *The Book of Dragons,* I knew instantly I wanted to tackle the theme of sacrificial women. I've always felt there was something obsessively misogynistic about tales of nubile virgins being sent to appease devouring beasts. Furthermore, in a harsh land ruled by a patriarchal order, it seemed to me that women who could potentially give birth to sons would be deemed too valuable to throw away. Not yet, anyway. Any woman growing older in the USA is all too aware of how often mainstream US culture vanishes older women, how they are seen to "lose value" once they are no longer young, fresh, and fertile. Too many of science fiction and fantasy's modern narratives still elide and erase the presence of these women. So why mightn't a society send worn-out elder women to be sacrificed to the fearsome dragons, who, being beasts, wouldn't realize they were being gifted something the human society found worthless?

Yet having realized that was the story I wanted to tell, I couldn't figure out how to tell it. I set it aside and tried three unrelated ideas, all of which felt flat. Then one day I wrote a paragraph in which an old woman woke to discover her husband had died in his sleep beside her. With each step she took, she would move farther away from the life she'd been told she had to live and the person she'd long ago accepted she had to be. The story became an unfolding scroll into a hidden wilderness that she and I traveled together to find out what the dragons really are.

A. T. Greenblatt is a Nebula Award–winning author and mechanical engineer. Her short stories and novelettes have appeared in *Clarkesworld, Un-*

canny, Tor.com, *Lightspeed, Asimov's,* and other venues. Her work has also been a finalist for the Hugo Award, the Sturgeon Award, and the WSFA Small Press Award. She currently lives in Philadelphia,

▪ This story began as many of my stories do: with an image and an emotion. This time, the image was of a cyclist and a plucky robot going on a journey together, and it felt lighthearted and fun. It made me smile.

But I began writing the first draft of "One Time, a Reluctant Traveler" in the early days of the pandemic lockdown and suddenly, writing something cheerful felt like a farce as the infection rates began to climb, followed closely by the death toll. Everywhere there was a heavy feeling of depression and constant fear. Everyone I talked to felt trapped and powerless.

The feeling spanned across my dissimilar social groups and across generations. So I used those emotions to take this image of a story and grow it into something very different than what I first envisioned. Instead of something lighthearted, this became a story about breaking out of a cycle and persevering in a place where there wasn't much hope. Looking back on it, "One Time, a Reluctant Traveler" was a story I needed to tell myself in that moment.

One day, I'll write that plucky robot story instead.

Daryl Gregory's recent books include the Appalachian horror novel *Revelator* and the novella *The Album of Dr. Moreau,* both out in 2021. His novel *Spoonbenders* was a Nebula, Locus, and World Fantasy Award finalist. The novella *We Are All Completely Fine* won the World Fantasy and the Shirley Jackson Awards. SF novel *Afterparty* was an NPR and Kirkus best book of the year, as well as a finalist for the Campbell and Lambda Literary Awards. His other novels are the Crawford Award–winning *Pandemonium, The Devil's Alphabet, Harrison Squared,* and *Raising Stony Mayhall.* Many of his short stories are collected in *Unpossible and Other Stories,* a *Publishers Weekly* best book of the year. When there's not a pandemic on, he frequently teaches writing seminars and is a regular instructor at the Viable Paradise Writing Workshop. This is Daryl's second appearance in *Best American Science Fiction and Fantasy,* following the Hugo-nominated story "Nine Last Days on Planet Earth" in 2019.

▪ Legendary editor David Hartwell used to call many of my stories "neuro SF" because they were concerned with the hard (and weird) problems of consciousness: the illusion of free will, the nature of the self, the roots of both sociopathy and religious ecstasy, you name it. The idea for "Brother Rifle" was simmering for years after I read about the biological process of decision-making. It turns out that people whose emotion centers are damaged don't become brilliant analysts like Spock; in fact, they find it harder to make even simple decisions. Certainty is an emotion, the signal from our subconscious that an answer has been reached, and that we can stop running in circles now. With the right tech, that signal can be blocked, diverted, or modified.

When Jonathan Strahan told me he was editing a robot anthology called *Made to Order*, I realized that this was an opportunity to write about a kind of human robot whose decisions are shaped by hardware and software. But aren't we all human robots? Even without a chip in our heads, other preexisting conditions—genetics, social institutions, socioeconomic status, the friends and family who surround us, down to the food we ate for lunch and the current chemical states of our neurons—all conspire to narrow our degrees of freedom. Any final decision—red pill or blue pill? —is made inside a black box, beyond our control and outside of conscious awareness. We can only hope that the puppet master living in our brain is a benevolent one.

In other words, my brain decided to write this story, and hopes your brain likes it.

Shingai Njeri Kagunda is an Afrofuturist freedom dreamer, Swahili sea lover, and femme storyteller hailing from Nairobi, Kenya. She holds a Literary Arts MFA from Brown University. Shingai's short story "Holding onto Water" was longlisted for the Nommo Awards 2020 and her flash fiction "Remember Tomorrow in Seasons" was shortlisted for the Fractured Lit Prize 2020. Her work has also been published in *Fantasy Magazine* and *Khōréō Magazine*. She is a Clarion UCSD Class of 2020/2021 candidate and the cofounder of Voodoonauts: A free Afrofuturist workshop for Black writers. Shingai's novella version, *& This Is How to Stay Alive*, is now accessible.

• This story was drawn from grief, both collective and personal. When I think about the ones I've loved and lost and the ones who've remained, I am in awe of a love that lives outside of time, and I think that is the thing that I do not want to be missed. Baraka's life carries a deep sadness (that exists in the lives of so many Kenyan boys who are forced to perform a certain type of masculinity to be considered valid in our society), but it also carries moments of deep hope, love, joy, and faith in family—these moments, for me, are where eternity lives. The in-between moments of dancing and breathless laughter, of swimming and endless stories. I am always incredibly conscious of stating that this is just one version of one story and there are hundreds of thousands of other queer and Kenyan and happy and sad and hopeful and curious Black stories to be told. I'm just grateful that this one gets to sit among them.

Mel Kassel is a writer working on her first story collection and novel. Her work has appeared in *Black Warrior Review*, *The Magazine of Fantasy & Science Fiction*, *Lightspeed*, *The Toast*, and elsewhere. She is a graduate of the

Iowa Writers' Workshop, a Clarion alumna, and a World Fantasy Award winner. Despite being a dog person who loves the ocean, she lives in the Midwest with a big gray cat. Find her on Twitter @MelKassel or online at www.melkassel.com.

▪ "Crawfather" was the third story I wrote at Clarion in 2018. I had spent the previous weeks rigorously attempting to impress my peers, and I was feeling burned out. I decided that my next piece would be a "fun" story that didn't feel weighty or draining to create.

"Crawfather" was indeed the story I had the most fun writing that summer, though it didn't end up being an entirely silly piece. Remembering so many awkward family gatherings in Minnesota gave me the POV—I think there's something innately funny about the self-importance of a conservative family narrating in first-person plural. I wanted to convey how family traditions can become nonsensical and harmful over time, and how they tend to encourage a cultish insularity. So, this family organizes its traditions around the myth that they're being persecuted by a giant crawfish (never mind that it's no smarter than a regular-sized one).

I'm very fond of this story for how it combines some of my favorite elements: a cool creature, the dangers of ritual, and absurdity with a hint of horror. Also, it continues to have the best title of anything I've ever written.

Ted Kosmatka is the author of three novels and numerous short stories. Over the years he's worked as everything from a corn detasseler to a lab tech to a game writer. His short fiction can be found reprinted in more than a dozen year's-best anthologies.

▪ Working on this story was a bit like painting a garage floor. First you have your paint and then your epoxy activator, in its clear little packet, and you stare at them separately for a bit, trying to work out what's what before adding part A to part B, mixing them together, and hoping it'll stick. (And that your dog won't walk across the floor while it's wet.) The part A for this story was an idea about artificial intelligence and consciousness that I'd been kicking around for a while. The part B came months later, and that was the story part, a chase into the darkness; and as I was laying it down, I just hoped I'd gotten the mixture right.

Yoon Ha Lee's debut novel, *Ninefox Gambit,* won the Locus Award for best first novel, and was a finalist for the Hugo, Nebula, and Clarke Awards; its sequels, *Raven Stratagem* and *Revenant Gun,* were also Hugo finalists. His middle grade novel *Dragon Pearl* won the Locus Award for best YA novel and the Mythopoeic Award, and was a *New York Times* best seller. His most recent work, the modern fairy-tale collection *The Fox's Tower and Other Stories,* came out in October 2021. Lee's short fiction has appeared in venues such as Tor.com, *Lightspeed, The Magazine of Fantasy & Science Fiction, Clarkesworld, Beneath Ceaseless Skies,* and *Audubon* magazine. He lives in Louisiana with his family and an extremely lazy cat, and has not yet been eaten by gators.

- "Beyond the Dragon's Gate" came to me because I'm trans. I knew how dysphoria worked in my life, but I wondered how it would affect an AI. I hadn't seen a lot of discussion as to how changing an AI's physical shell would affect it, whether that shell was an android or a starship or anything in between. Surely if an AI was advanced enough to feel emotional attachments and use the capabilities of its current physical body, it might then also have very personal feelings about whether or not that body felt right to it.

At the same time, I wanted to contrast this idea of an AI's dysphoria with the viewpoint of a human character who was fascinated by fluidity of form —who would actively have sought it out, given the opportunity. Even in the space of a short story, I wanted to show that sentient beings could have different visceral reactions to this sort of fluidity of perceived form.

Ken Liu (http://kenliu.name) is an American author of speculative fiction. A winner of the Nebula, Hugo, and World Fantasy Awards, he wrote the Dandelion Dynasty, a silkpunk epic fantasy series in which engineers hold the place of honor reserved for magicians, as well as short story collections *The Paper Menagerie and Other Stories* and *The Hidden Girl and Other Stories.* Prior to becoming a full-time writer, Liu worked as a software engineer, corporate lawyer, and litigation consultant. Liu frequently speaks at conferences and universities on a variety of topics, including futurism, cryptocurrency, history of technology, bookmaking, and the mathematics of origami.

- I wrote "The Cleaners" as part of *Faraway,* an Amazon Original Stories collection of modern retellings of classic fairy tales. But a strict "retelling" didn't appeal to me, so I decided to craft a new fable only loosely inspired by an idea from a classic story—the notion of "extraordinary sensitivity" from Hans Christian Andersen's "The Princess and the Pea." My tale takes a few metaphors that we're all familiar with—our emotions color our memories, our memories are attached to our possessions, psychic pollution and emotional labor—and makes them all literally true in this alternate reality, since the literalization of the metaphorical is our oldest mode of storytelling and my favorite way to approach speculative fiction.

As with everything else written in 2020, the global pandemic hovers over each word in this story like an image filter, leaving a distinctive shift in highlights and hues. I still cannot read it without feeling the isolation, the loneliness, the despair that we all endure, not because we live in a particular time or place or are part of some event, but because we're human.

Barbadian novelist and research consultant **Dr. Karen Lord** is the author of *Redemption in Indigo,* winner of the 2008 Frank Collymore Literary Award, the 2011 William L. Crawford Award, and the 2011 Mythopoeic Fantasy Award for Adult Literature. Her other works include the science fiction duology *The Best of All Possible Worlds* and *The Galaxy Game,* and the crime-fantasy novel *Unraveling.* She edited the anthology *New Worlds, Old Ways: Speculative Tales from the Caribbean,* and has coauthored research on development and on youth employment with the University of the West Indies for the UNDP and the Caribbean Development Bank.

▪ I'm tempted to think that "The Plague Doctors" has had greater impact precisely because less than six months after I handed in the final draft, the world saw the beginnings of COVID-19. But this story is more than accidental zeitgeist. It's the end product of an idea I laid out to my medical adviser for the story, Dr. Adrian Charles: "This is our chance to depict a version of the revolutionary, decentralized approach to health care that we've been discussing for ages."

Dr. Charles knows his sci-fi and did not flinch when I asked him to design a disease that would undermine the global health system by revealing the hubris of the so-called developed world — a disease that looked easy to control until it suddenly (and horribly) was not. The invented pathogen was deadlier and more contagious than the coronavirus, but the resulting massive systemic disruptions were similar. I believe the solutions are also similar: a greater focus on the baseline health of vulnerable communities; decentralized, community-based delivery of free health and well-being services (e.g., clinics and home care) operating in parallel with centralized, specialized medical services (hospitals and specialist centers); and more global interconnectedness, openness, and cooperation, especially among nonstate actors.

These are the survival strategies of small islands, mountain villages, and remote settlements. When you have to plan for disaster or disruption with scarce resources, you learn that system redundancy and access to information are essential, and basic self-sufficiency is fundamental. These lessons are useful for everyone, everywhere, especially those who think they're invincible. Beyond this present pandemic, I hope "The Plague Doctors" will serve as a perennial reminder that whatever the sum of our parts, as a community or a nation, nothing is too big to fail.

Karin Lowachee was born in South America, grew up in Canada, and worked in the Arctic. Her novels have been translated into French, Hebrew, and Japanese, and her short stories have been published in numerous award-winning anthologies and magazines. Many of these stories can be found in her collection *Love & Other Acts of War.*

▪ This is the second story for my contribution to the anthology series the Dystopia Triptych. The premise was to write three connected stories across the anthologies that covered Before, During, and After (or approaching an After) a dystopian society. I chose to tell my stories through the lens of grief and mourning, to capture universal emotions (frustration, anger, depression) through the personal. The first story was from the mother's point of view after the death of a child, the last from the father's. This second story was from the point of view of the best friend of the child. Having worked in the education field in one way or another through the years, I also wanted to tackle the crisis of education and examine some of the issues and mindsets that have failed so many of the world's children and youth. Many factors play into the education crisis, including economic and social, and my reading about the education industrial complex, especially around standardized testing, fed the genesis of this story.

Tochi Onyebuchi is the author of *Riot Baby*, which won the New England Book Award for fiction, an Alex Award, and was a finalist for the Nommo, Hugo, Nebula, Locus, and NAACP Image Awards. His young adult novels include the Beasts Made of Night series and the War Girls series. He holds degrees from Yale University, New York University's Tisch School of the Arts, Columbia Law School, and Sciences Po. His short fiction has appeared in *Asimov's Science Fiction, Omenana, Lightspeed,* and elsewhere. His nonfiction has appeared in Tor.com and the *Harvard Journal of African American Public Policy,* among other places. His most recent book is the nonfiction *(S)kinfolk.*

▪ Readers of "How to Pay Reparations: A Documentary" may recognize the story structure from Ken Liu's "The Man Who Ended History: A Documentary," which itself, arguably, can trace its architectural genealogy to Ted Chiang's "Liking What You See: A Documentary." My original mandate for "Reparations" was large enough that the only way I could pinpoint a story was to write into one of the most challenging and politically/socially taboo subjects I could think of, which is how I alighted on the subject of reparations for African Americans.

I'd tried a few different points of entry, but none of them could capture the totality of what I wanted to cover. Indeed, I might have wound up with an entire novel, but when I thought of those stories that managed the type of panorama I sought, Ken Liu's story stood out to me. (It was also fresh in my mind as I'd taught it in a graduate seminar a few months prior.) I wanted to tell not only the inside story of this effort to accomplish the politically impossible but also its effects on its intended beneficiaries. This format allowed me to do that and then some.

Some readers may find it debatable that this story, set a hop-skip-and-a-jump away from our pandemic present, is science fictional at all, but I think that fantastika shouldn't restrict itself to imaginative expansions of our material reality, but our moral one as well.

Sarah Pinsker is the author of Nebula Award–winning novel *A Song for a New Day* and Philip K. Dick Award–winning collection *Sooner or Later Everything Falls into the Sea.* Her new novel, *We Are Satellites,* came out in 2021. She has over fifty short stories published in magazines, anthologies, and year's bests, translated into almost a dozen languages. She lives in Baltimore, Maryland, with her wife and terrier.

▪ This story had the longest gestation of anything I've ever worked on. My senior year of college, in my fiction independent study, I started a story about Uncle Bob and his weird public access television show. I had trouble finishing stories back then, and this really wasn't anything close to a story; it was at best a character study. I forgot about it for years, until for some reason an old console television in a garage jogged it back to mind. That was when I realized that the story might not be just in the character, but in the act of rediscovering him. I didn't bother looking for the fragment, since Uncle Bob sprung back into my head fully realized.

I needed something to bring to the Sycamore Hill workshop for 2019, so I started fresh with my twenty-years-lost television host and a new character, a woman who didn't remember him until she did. I got to layer in stuff that I wouldn't have been able to write back then either, about memory and possessions and the stories we tell. I'm grateful to everyone at the workshop for their critique, and for helping me mark one of my writer-bingo squares: this is my first story edited by Ellen Datlow. I don't normally write stuff this dark, so I'm strangely proud of having written something that Ellen, the queen of short horror, called creepy.

Amman Sabet is a writer and designer living and working in Los Angeles, California. His stories have appeared in *The New Voices of Science Fiction, The Magazine of Fantasy & Science Fiction, F(r)iction, Metaphorosis,* and other such publications. Amman is a Clarion alumnus and an SFWA member. Between work and writing, he is learning a lot by building an off-grid cabin, deep into COVID year two. Add him on Twitter @AmmanSabet.

▪ Submarine mutinies and Bruce Tuckman's stages of group development are inspirations for "Skipping Stones in the Dark." But this story's mood also comes from working as a designer and witnessing how mistakes get built into products without a mature vision of the future.

Ford Pintos would explode when rear-ended because safety wasn't an objective during manufacturing. Google Glass launched and failed because of neglecting to validate user needs. Pfizer's Bextra was an anti-inflammatory drug that gave heart problems and fatal skin conditions leading to the second largest pharmaceutical settlement in history. Cautionary tales serve as great rallying points for the future of making better things. It's true for cars, computers, drugs, and perhaps also generation ships.

I find that the contest of wills between humans and AI spins out interesting failure modes when you add the pressures of time, space travel, and the mind's instinct to reject unnatural boundaries. For every generation ship to reach its star we could suppose there might be hundreds that don't, right? My thanks to C. C. Finlay and Gordon Van Gelder for taking a chance on this at *F&SF.*

Other Notable Science Fiction and Fantasy Stories of 2020

Selected by John Joseph Adams

RING, LAUREN
   Sunrise, Sunrise, Sunrise. *Apparition Lit,* October

SACHDEVA, ANJALI
   Not Creator, Nor Destroyer. *Fairy Tale Review,* The Coral Issue
SAMATAR, SOFIA
   Fairy Tales for Robots. *Made to Order: Robots and Revolution,* ed. Jonathan Strahan (Solaris)
   The Moon Fairy. *Conjunctions #74*
SANFORD, JASON
   The Eight-Thousanders. *Asimov's,* September/October
SEN, NIBEDITA
   Mandragora. *Fireside,* March
SIDDIQUI, SAMEEM
   AirBody. *Clarkesworld,* April
ST. GEORGE, CARLIE
   Monsters Never Leave You. *Strange Horizons,* June
SWANWICK, MICHAEL
   The Last Days of Old Night. *Clarkesworld,* December

THOMAS, SHEREE RENÉE
   Ancestries. *Nine Bar Blues* (Third Man Books)

TURNBULL, CADWELL
   Shock of Birth. *Asimov's,* September/October

WATTS, PETER
   Test 4 Echo. *Made to Order: Robots and Revolution,* ed. Jonathan Strahan (Solaris)
WELLS, MARTHA
   Obsolescence. *Take Us to a Better Place: Stories,* ed. Robert Wood Johnson Foundation (Melcher Media)
WOLFMOOR, MERC FENN
   The Law Is the Plan, the Plan Is Death. *Or Else the Light,* ed. Hugh Howey, Christie Yant, John Joseph Adams (Broad Reach Publishing + Adamant Press)
WRENWOOD, CLAIRE
   Dead Girls Have No Names. *Nightmare,* August

YOACHIM, CAROLINE M.
   Shadow Prisons. *The Dystopia Triptych,* ed. Hugh Howey, Christie Yant, John Joseph Adams (Broad Reach Publishing + Adamant Press)

THE BEST AMERICAN SERIES®

FIRST, BEST, AND BEST-SELLING

The Best American Essays

The Best American Food Writing

The Best American Mystery and Suspense

The Best American Science and Nature Writing

The Best American Science Fiction and Fantasy

The Best American Short Stories

The Best American Travel Writing

Available in print and e-book wherever books are sold.

Visit our website: MarinerBooks.com/BestAmerican